BETTER DAYS WILL COME

Pregnant Bonnie leaves on a train bound for London, excited to meet boyfriend George, but he never turns up. Somehow she must look after herself and her baby, too ashamed to go home. Her mother is devastated by Bonnie's disappearance and struggles to provide for herself and her other daughter Rita. But when Grace accepts the offer of help from her boss, she has no idea how much he'll want in return... Rita thinks marriage to Italian Emilio is a ticket to a better life. But he is hiding a secret. Can the bond of family love bring them back together in time?

BETTER DAYS WILL COME

by

Pam Weaver

Magna Large Print Books
Long Preston, North Yorkshire,
BD23 4ND, England.

British Library Cataloguing in Publication Data.

Weaver, Pam
Better days will come.

A catalogue record of this book is available from the British Library

ISBN 978-0-7505-3695-0

First published in Great Britain in 2012 by HarperCollins*Publishers*

Published in Large Print 2013 by arrangement with HarperCollins Publishers

Magna Large Print is an imprint of Library Magna Books Ltd.

Printed and bound in Great Britain by
T.J. (International) Ltd., Cornwall, PL28 8RW

Acknowledgements

To Vivien Hawkins who read this first, to my editor Caroline Hogg and my agent Juliet Burton for her unswerving belief in me.

To my two beautiful daughters,
Cathy and Maggie.
I am blessed beyond measure to be their mum.

Prologue

He was fingering the chain, letting it run through his fingers. Was it time to let the locket go? Would he ever need it? After all, nobody suspected a thing. Why should they in a sleepy backwater like Worthing? He might not have the heady power of previous years but that was no bad thing. When you reached the top, there were any number of people wanting to take you out. It had been a stroke of genius living here. The best place to hide was where everyone could see you. Which brought him back to the locket and the little secret inside. Keep it, or ditch it? He held it up to the light and realised that he wasn't ready to burn all his bridges just yet. All he needed was somewhere safe.

One

Worthing 1947

'Looks like they're going to make a start on repairing the pier at last,' Grace Rogers called out as she entered the house but there was no reply. She pulled her wet headscarf from her head and shook it. Water droplets splattered the back of the chair. She ran her fingers through her honey blonde hair which curled neatly at the nape of her neck and then unbuttoned her coat and hung it on a peg behind the front door.

She was a small woman, with a neat figure, pale eyes and long artistic fingers. She'd missed the bus and had to wait for another, so she was soaked. Someone had said that the Littlehampton Road was flooded between Titnore Lane and Limbrick Lane. She wasn't surprised. The rain hadn't let up all week. She kicked off her boots. Her feet were wet too but that was hardly surprising either. There was a hole in the bottom of her left shoe. Grace pulled out a soggy piece of cardboard, the only thing between her foot and the pavement, and threw it into the coalscuttle.

The two reception rooms downstairs had been knocked into one and the kitchen range struggled to heat such a large area. The fire was low. Using an oven glove, Grace opened the door and put the poker in. The fire resettled and flared a little. She added some coal, not a lot, tossed in the soggy cardboard, and closed the door. Coal was still rationed and it was only November 12th. Winter had hardly started yet.

'Bonnie?'

No response. Perhaps she was upstairs in her room. Grace opened the stair door and called up but there was no answer. She glanced up at the clock on the mantelpiece. Almost three thirty. It would be getting dark soon. Where was the girl? It was early closing in Worthing and Bonnie had the afternoon off, but she never went anywhere, not this time of year anyway, and certainly not in this weather. Rita, her youngest, would be coming back from school in less than an hour.

Grace dried her hair with a towel while the kettle boiled. Her bones ached with weariness. She'd jumped at the chance to do an extra shift because even with Bonnie's wages, the money didn't go far. When Michael died in the D-Day landings, she'd never imagined bringing up two girls on her own would be so difficult. Still, she shouldn't grumble. She was a lot better off than some. Even if the rent did keep going up, at least she had a roof over her head, and the knitwear factory, Finley International, where she worked, was doing well. They were producing more than ever, mostly for America and Canada. The war had been over for eighteen months and the country needed all the exports it could get. A year ago they had all hoped that the good times were just around the corner but if anything, things were worse than ever. Even bread was rationed now, and potatoes. Three pounds per person per week, that was all, and that hadn't happened all through the dark days of the war.

Her hair towelled dry, Grace glanced up at the clock again. Where was Bonnie? She said she'd be home to help with the tea. She screwed up some newspaper and stuffed it into the toes of her boots before putting them on the floor by the range. With a bit of luck they'd be dry in the morning.

Grace brushed her hair vigorously. She was lucky that it was naturally curly and she didn't have any grey. The only time she went to the hairdresser was to have it cut.

The kettle boiled and Grace rinsed out the brown teapot before reaching for the caddy. Two scoops of Brooke Bond and she'd be as right as ninepence. She was looking forward to its reviving qualities. She sat at the table and reached for the knitted tea cosy.

The letter was underneath. It must have been propped against the salt and pepper and fallen over when she'd opened the door and created a draught. Grace picked it up. The envelope was unsealed. Was it meant for her or Bonnie? And who had put it there? She took out a single sheet of paper.

A glance at the bottom of the page told her it was from Bonnie. Grace sighed. That meant her daughter was either staying over with her friend from work, or she'd decided to go to the pictures with that new boy she was always going on about. Grace didn't know his name but it was obvious Bonnie was smitten. They'd had words about it last night when Grace had seen her with a neatly wrapped present in striped paper and a red ribbon on the top. Bonnie had sat at the table and pulled out a dark green jewellery box. Grace knew at once that it had come from Whibley's, a quality jeweller at the end of Warwick Street. Although she had never personally had anything from the shop, they advertised in every newspaper in the town and the box was instantly recognisable.

Before Bonnie had even lifted the lid, Grace had stopped her. 'Don't even be tempted,' she cautioned. 'Whatever it is, you can't possibly keep it.'

Bonnie looked up, appalled. 'Why ever not?'

'You're too young to be getting expensive presents from men,' said Grace.

'Oh, Mum,' said Bonnie turning slightly to lift the lid. 'I already know what's inside. I just wanted to show you, that's all.'

Grace caught a glimpse of some kind of locket on a chain before closing the box herself. 'I mean it,' she'd said firmly. 'You hardly know this man and I've never met him. How do you know his intentions are honourable?'

Bonnie smiled mysteriously. 'I know, Mum, and I love him.'

'Don't talk such rot,' Grace had retorted angrily. 'You're far too young…'

Bonnie's eyes blazed. 'I'm the same age as you were when you met Daddy.'

'That's different,' Grace had told her.

They had wrestled over the box with Bonnie eventually gaining the upper hand, and thinking about it now made Grace feel uncomfortable.

She got a cup and saucer down from the dresser and sat down. As she poured her tea Grace began to read,'

Dear Mum,

I am sorry but I am going away. By the time you read this, I shall be on the London train. You are not to worry. I shall be fine. I just need to leave Worthing. I am sorry to let you down but this is for the best. I shall never forget you and Rita and I want you to know I love you both with all my heart. Please don't think too badly of me.

All my love,

Bonnie.

As she reached the end of the page, Grace became aware that she was still pouring tea. Dark brown liquid trickled towards the page because it had filled her cup and saucer and overflowed onto her tablecloth. Her hand trembled as she put the teapot back onto the stand. Her mind struggled to focus. *On the London train.* It had only been a silly tiff. Why go all the way to London? She glanced up at the clock. That train would be leaving the station in less than five minutes. She leapt to her feet and grabbed her boots. It took an age to get all the newspaper out before she could stuff her feet back inside the wet leather. *I just need to leave Worthing.* Why? What did that mean? Surely she wasn't going for good. Her mind struggled to make sense of it. You're only 18, Bonnie. You always seemed happy enough. Grace stumbled out into the hall for her coat. The back of her left boot stubbornly refused to come back up. She had to stop and use her finger to get the heel in properly but there was no time to lace them. As she dashed out of the door she paused only to look at the grandmother clock. Four minutes before the train was due to leave. Without stopping to lock up, she ran blindly down the street, her unbuttoned coat flapping behind her like a cloak and her boots slopping on her feet. Water oozed between the stitches, forming little bubbles as she ran.

There were lights on in the little shop on the corner of Cross Street and Clifton Road and the new owner looked up from whatever he was doing to stare at her as she ran down the middle of the road towards him. The gates were already cranking across the road as she burst into Station Approach. She could feel a painful stitch coming in her side but she refused to ease up. The rain was coming down steadily and by now her hair was plastered to her face. As she raced up the steps of the entrance, the train thundered to a halt on platform 2.

Manny Hart, neat and tidy in his uniform and with his mouth organ tucked into his top pocket, stood at the entrance to the station platform with his hand out. 'Tickets please.' If he was surprised by the state of her, he said nothing.

'I've got to get to the other side before the train leaves,' Grace blurted out.

He glanced over his shoulder, towards a group of men, all in smart suits, walking along the platform. 'Then you'll need a platform ticket.' Manny seemed uncomfortable.

Grace's heart sank. Her purse was sitting on the dresser in the kitchen. 'I'll pay you next time I see you.'

But Manny was in no mood to be placated. 'You need a ticket,' he said stubbornly. The men hovered by the entrance, while on the other side of the track the train shuddered and the steam hissed.

'You don't understand,' Grace cried. 'I've simply got to...' Her hands were searching her empty pockets and she was beginning to panic. She was so angry and frustrated she could have hit him. She looked around wildly and saw a woman who lived just up the road from her. 'Excuse me, Peggy. Could you lend me a penny for a platform ticket, only I must catch someone on the train before it goes.'

'Of course, dear. Hang on a minute, I'm sure I've got a penny in here somewhere.' Peggy Jones opened her bag, found her purse and handed Grace a penny. As it appeared in her hand, Grace almost snatched it and ran to the platform ticket machine, calling, 'Thank you, thank you' over her shoulder. To add to her frustration, the machine was reluctant to yield and she had to thump it a couple of times before the ticket appeared.

The passengers who were getting off at Worthing were already starting to head towards the barrier as she thrust the ticket at Manny Hart. He clipped it and went to hand it back but Grace was already at the top of the stairs leading to the underpass which came up on the other side and platform 2. Now she was hampered by the steady flow of people coming in the opposite direction.

'Close all the doors.'

The porter's cry echoed down the stairs and into the underpass. The train shuddered again and just as she reached the stairwell leading up she heard the powerful shunt of steam and smoke which heralded its departure. She was only half way up the stairs leading to platform 2 when the guard blew his whistle and the lumbering giant was on the move. How she got to the top of the stairs, she never knew but as soon as she emerged onto the platform she knew it was hopeless. Through the smoke and steam, the last two carriages were all that was left. The train was gone.

Someone was walking jauntily towards her, a familiar figure, well dressed, confident and whistling as he came. He flicked his hat with his finger and pushed it back on his head and his coat, open despite the rain, flapped behind him as he walked. Norris Finley, her boss, was a lot heavier and far less attractive than when they were younger but he still behaved like cock of the walk. What was he doing here? Usually, Grace would turn the other way if she saw him coming but her mind was on other things. Throwing aside her usual reserve, she roared out Bonnie's name. As the train gathered speed, she burst into helpless heart-rending tears, and putting her hands on the top of her head, she fell to her knees.

'Are you all right, love?' She heard a woman's voice, kind and concerned. The woman bent over her and touched her arm.

'Grace?' said Norris. 'You seem a bit upset. Anything I can do?'

Grace heard him but didn't respond. She was still staring at the disappearing train, and finally the empty track. She couldn't speak but she felt two arms, one on either side, helping her to her feet. Where was Bonnie going? Who on earth did she know in London?

'Do you know her, dear?' the woman's voice filtered through Grace's befuddled brain.

'Yes.' The man was raising his hat. 'Norris Finley of Finley's International,' he said.

The woman nodded. 'I'll leave you to it then, sir,' and patting Grace's arm she said, 'I'm sure it's not as bad as you think, dear.'

Norris tucked his hand under Grace's elbow and led her back down the stairs into the gloomy underpass.

'She's gone,' Grace said dully when they were alone. 'My Bonnie has left home.'

'Left home?'

She was crying again so they walked on in silence with Grace leaning heavily on his arm. Norris winked as he handed his ticket to Manny Hart and steered Grace onto the concourse.

'Is she all right?' said Manny, suddenly concerned. He took off his hat and scratched his slightly balding head.

'Mrs Rogers has had a bit of an upset, that's all,' said Norris pleasantly.

'If you had let me go,' Grace said, suddenly rounding on Manny, 'I might have been able to stop my daughter making the biggest mistake of her life.'

Manny looked uncomfortable. 'I cannot help that,' he said defensively. 'You know I would do anything for you, Grace. The men on the platform were government inspectors for when the railway goes national next year. Rules are rules and I have to obey.'

'Mrs Rogers ... Grace,' said Norris. 'You're soaked to the skin. Let me take you home. My car is just outside.'

'Your paper, sir,' said Manny.

'Eh?' Norris seemed a little confused.

'You dropped your paper.' He handed him a rolled-up newspaper.

'Oh, right,' grinned Norris, taking it from him.

Manny watched them go.

'Nice man, that Mr Finley,' the woman remarked as she handed Manny her ticket and he nodded.

Outside it was still tipping with rain. 'I'll walk,' said Grace stiffly. 'It's not far and I'm wet through anyway.'

There were still people waiting for taxis or buses. 'Absolutely not, my dear Mrs Rogers,' Finley insisted. 'Hop in.'

As he climbed into the car, he handed her his folded handkerchief before they set off. He drove away like a madman but her mind was so full of Bonnie, Grace hardly noticed. She wiped her eyes and blew her nose. Outside her house, Grace turned to him. 'She left me a note,' she said hopelessly. 'I found it when I got in from work.'

'Where's she gone?'

Grace looked up at him. 'That's just it,' she said. 'I don't know. All she said was she had to leave Worthing.'

'*Had* to leave?' He raised his eyebrows and let

out a short sigh. 'Ah well, you can't keep her tied to your apron strings all her life. She's a sensible girl, isn't she? She'll be fine.'

Grace's eyes grew wide. 'Promise me you didn't have anything to do with this?'

'Of course I didn't! Why should I?'

'Why were you there then? What were you doing on the platform?'

'I've been in Southampton on business,' he said irritably.

'Did you see her get on the train?'

'No, but then I'm hardly likely to, am I?' he said. 'I travel first class. Does Bonnie travel first class? No, I didn't think so, so why would I have seen her? Don't be so melodramatic, Grace.'

Grace fumbled for the door handle but couldn't open the door. 'I didn't expect any sympathy from you but Bonnie leaving like this ... it's breaking my heart.'

'For God's sake, Grace. Nobody died, did they?' Norris said coldly. 'She'll be fine.' He got out of the car and came round to the passenger side. Just as he opened the door Grace's neighbour walked by under a large umbrella.

'There you are, Mrs Rogers,' Norris said loudly and cheerfully as he stepped back. 'Back home safe and sound. Can I help you with your door key?'

Grace shook her head. The door was open anyway. She hadn't stopped to lock it. She turned and he waved cheerfully as he got back into his car. He drove off at speed, leaving Grace standing like a dumb thing on the pavement.

'You'll catch your death of cold,' said a voice.

'You look soaked to the skin.' Their eyes met and she hesitated. 'You all right, Grace?' Her neighbour who lived next-door-but-one, Elsie Dawson, was on her step putting her key into her own door. Dougie, her son, stood behind his mother waiting for her to open it. Elsie, her middle son Dougie and daughter Mo were good friends with Rita and Bonnie, and they had all enjoyed sharing times like Christmas and Easter together. Bob, Elsie's oldest boy, was in the army now and Mo was in the same class as Rita at school but Dougie was what the powers that be called 'retarded', a term which made Grace cross. He might struggle with understanding, but he wasn't stupid. Once he knew what you wanted, Dougie would put his hand to anything.

'I'm fine, thank you,' Grace said with as much dignity as she could muster. But once inside the house, she sat alone on the cold stairs and gave way to her tears once again.

As the train sped towards London, Bonnie stared out of the window. She should have done this earlier in the day while she still had the opportunity. The light was going and by the time she reached Victoria station it would be dark. Never mind, George would be there to meet her. If for some reason they missed each other, he'd told her to wait by the entrance of platform 12.

She had finished work a lot earlier than she'd thought she would. The people in the wages department had worked out that she was owed a half day's holiday so rather than give her the extra in her wage packet, she had been told she could go by ten o'clock. Seeing as how she had arranged to meet George in time for the train, it meant she had a couple of hours to kill. Her case was already in the left luggage department at Worthing and she couldn't go back home, so she went to his digs.

Mrs Kerr, his landlady, was her usual unwelcoming self. 'He's not here,' she'd said curtly, 'and I have no time to entertain his guests.' She had obviously taken her apron off to answer the door and now she was putting it back on again.

'Do you know where he might be?' Bonnie had asked.

'He's going to London.'

'I know that,' Bonnie had said. 'I just wondered if he was still here.'

Mrs Kerr shrugged. 'As far as I know, he's gone to the old factory.'

Bonnie had frowned. 'But why? It's all shut up, isn't it?'

'All I know is he said he'd found something. Now I'm very busy.'

'Do you know what he'd found?' Bonnie persisted.

'Am I my brother's keeper?' Mrs Kerr snapped as she shut the door.

Bonnie had stood on the pavement wondering what to do. There was still plenty of time before the train so she'd decided to walk to the factory. She didn't have to go right into West Worthing. There was a Jacob's ladder in Pavilion Road which was between the stations and came out at the bottom of Heene Road. Although she was wearing her best shoes, which were quite unsuitable for walking, it hadn't taken her long to get to Finley's Knitwear.

She had met George Matthews at a dance in the Assembly Hall. He was a friend of a friend and they'd hit it off straight away. He was so debonair, so handsome and so unlike any of her other friends that it wasn't long before she was hopelessly in love with him. He worked at the knitwear factory in Tarring Road, the same as her mother. He was a machine operator, while her mum worked in the packing room. George was getting good money but he was ambitious so when it was announced that the factory would be moving to new premises, he felt it was time to move on.

'I don't think the boss is a very nice person,' he'd told her. 'Don't let him get too close to you.'

'Whatever do you mean?' she'd asked, thoroughly alarmed.

He'd hesitated for a second then changed the subject. 'There are real opportunities in places like South Africa, and Rhodesia and Australia, the sort of opportunities the likes of you and me will never get in this country. We can get away from all the corruption in high places. It'll be a whole new start, far away from the war and everything to do with it.'

'If Mr Finley is up to something,' she'd asked, 'should I say something to my mother?'

He'd shaken his head. 'Your mother and all the other girls are safe enough if you keep your distance, but he's deep, that one.'

Out of loyalty, he stayed long enough to help clear up the old place, but just lately he'd seemed even more troubled about something. 'I'm glad we're going,' he said one day. 'I really don't want to work for Finley any more.'

Once again she'd asked why but he told her not to worry her pretty little head.

'How will we get to South Africa?' she'd asked.

'Leave all that to me,' he'd said mysteriously, and then he'd filled her imagination with sun-drenched beaches and cocktails before dinner and making their fortune. They'd made love in his digs at Pavilion Road. They had to be very careful for fear of his landlady who was a deeply religious woman, but while she was wrestling with the Devil at the prayer meeting every Tuesday night, Bonnie and George were wrestling between the sheets. And while Mrs Kerr studied the Bible every Thursday, they filled themselves with more carnal delights. Bonnie smiled cosily as she remembered those wonderful nights together.

'Tickets please.' The conductor on the train brought her back to the present day and Bonnie handed him her ticket.

When she'd told him about the baby, George had been wonderful about it. That's when he had bought her the locket. It was so beautiful she'd vowed to wear it all the time. He'd said she should get a job until it was time for the baby to be born and then they would set sail. Having a baby in South Africa wasn't as safe as here in England. He'd promised to get her passport all sorted and she'd saved up the £2 2s 6d she needed. The last thing she'd done as she'd left the house was to remember to take her birth certificate. Bonnie couldn't wait. It was so exciting.

'I shall need references,' she'd told George.

'I'm sure you can get someone to vouch for you,' George said, nibbling her ear in that delicious way of his. 'I think you're a very nice girl.'

She'd giggled. He had a way of making her feel that it would all work out. Right now everything was such a mess but once they were married, it would be all right. She was sure of it.

She had decided to ask her old Sunday school teacher to give her a reference. She didn't really know why, but she trusted Miss Reeves absolutely. She didn't tell her everything, of course, but then how could she? It was easier to be economical with the truth although it did make her feel a bit guilty. Still, it wasn't as if she was lying to the vicar or something. All she did was tell her just enough for Miss Reeves to write a glowing reference addressed *'To whom it may concern.'*

'I know the woman you'll be working for quite well,' George assured her when he gave her the slip of paper. 'Mrs Palmer is a nice woman. You'll like her.'

Bonnie frowned. 'How do you know her?'

He'd pulled her close. 'Don't I know just about everyone who's anyone, silly?'

When she had surprised him at his digs after the row with her mother last night, he had taken her to his room. 'You'll get me thrown out onto the street,' he'd said and she'd laughed. 'Who cares? We're going to live in South Africa,' she'd said, her cornflower-blue eyes dancing with excitement.

George had drawn her down onto the bed with a kiss. Bonnie closed her eyes as she relived the moment. He was so good looking, so strong, so manly... She sighed. She hated doing this to her mother but she had to. If she'd told her mother what she and George were planning, she would have talked her out of it. Grace was a good mother but she still thought of Bonnie as 'her little girl'. Bonnie smiled to herself. If only she knew. She certainly wasn't her little girl any more. Since she'd met George, she had become a fully-grown woman.

When her father had been killed in the D-Day landings, Grace Rogers had been totally lost without him. The day the telegram came, she'd sat on the stairs, hardly even aware that she had two daughters to look after. Rita was the only one able to pacify her and they sat crying together. Without their father, life had become so difficult. They never had much money even though her mother worked all the hours God gave. Bonnie knew her mother would be upset to lose her wage, but it was all swings and roundabouts. There would be one less mouth to feed and Bonnie was determined she'd send a bit of money as soon as she and George were settled in South Africa. Of course, she would write to her mother long before they got there and once they were there, Grace could hardly refuse her consent to their marriage.

Bonnie stared at the name and address on the piece of paper she had been given. Mrs Palmer, 105 Honeypot Lane, Stanmore. Telephone: Stanmore 256. She couldn't wait to see George at the station. Everything was going to be absolutely fine, she just knew it. With a smile of contentment, Bonnie leaned her head against the carriage window and closed her eyes.

Rita was puzzled. When she'd arrived home from school after choir practice, she found her mother sitting in the darkness on the stairs. Rita could tell at once that she had been crying but she didn't seem to be aware that she was wet through and shivering with the cold.

Rita sat down beside her. 'Mum?'

Grace stood up. 'I'm going to get changed.' She knew Rita was wondering what was wrong but she didn't look back as she wearily climbed the steep stairs.

There was little warm water in the tap and the bathroom was very cold, but Grace washed herself slowly. How was she going to tell Rita? She and Bonnie were very close, so close they might almost be twins rather than two years apart. Bonnie had left no note for Rita. The girl would be heartbroken.

As she crossed the landing, a thought struck her. What if Rita already knew Bonnie was going? Maybe they'd planned it this way together. Grace felt a frisson of irritation. How dare they!

By now, she was frozen to the marrow. Pulling out some warmer clothes, Grace dressed quickly; a dry bra, her once pink petticoat, and a blue cable knit jumper over a grey skirt. She sat on the edge of the bed to roll her nylon stockings right down to the toe before putting them on her foot and easing over the heel. Her clothes were shabby, the jumper had darns on one elbow and at the side, her petticoat had odd straps because she'd used one petticoat to repair another, and her skirt, which came from a jumble sale, had been altered to fit. The one luxury she allowed herself was a decent pair of stockings. She rolled them slowly up her leg, careful not to snag them on a jagged nail, and checked her seams for straightness. Fastening the stockings to her suspenders, Grace towel-dried her hair and pulled on her wraparound apron before heading back downstairs to confront Rita.

'Something's happened,' said Rita as she walked back into the kitchen. 'What's wrong, Mum?'

'Your sister has left home,' Grace said, her lips in a tight line, 'but of course you already knew that, didn't you?'

Rita's jaw dropped.

'Left home?' Rita looked so shocked, Grace was thrown. 'Where's she gone?'

'I don't know.'

'What do you mean, you don't know?'

'Precisely what I said, I don't know,' cried her mother, her voice full of anguish. 'I was so sure you'd know all about it.'

Rita seemed bewildered. Grace threw an enamel bowl into the stone sink with a great clatter. All the while that she had believed Rita knew about Bonnie, there was the hope that she could bully her whereabouts out of the girl. 'Mum?'

For a few seconds, Grace stood with her back to her daughter, her hands clenching the sides of the stone sink, as if supporting the weight of her body, then she turned round. Rita was alarmed to see the tears in her eyes. Grace reached out for her but when Rita stood up, scraping her chair on the wooden floor behind her, she ran upstairs. Grace could hear her opening drawers, looking in the wardrobe and searching for the battered suitcase that they kept under the bed. As she listened, she relived every moment of her own fruitless search not half an hour ago. She opened the stair door and sat down. A moment or two later, Rita joined her and laid her head on Grace's shoulder.

Rita chewed her bottom lip. Left home... Bonnie didn't confide in her much these days, but Rita was sure she would have said something if she'd known she was going away. Was she ill or something?

'Has she done something wrong, Mum?'

No answer.

'When is she coming back?'

'Darling, I've told you,' Grace sighed. 'I don't know,'

Rita's stomach fell away. She couldn't bear it if Bonnie was gone. Sometimes Bonnie and her mother had words but neither of them held grudges. It just wasn't their way. A sudden thought struck her. She lifted her head. 'Shall I go and see if she's at Sandra's place?'

'She's not at Sandra's. She's gone to London.'

'London?'

'She told me in a note.'

'What note?'

Grace stood up and they both went back into the kitchen. She showed Rita the single sheet of paper.

'I shall never forget you and Rita ... it all sounds

so final,' said Rita.

Her mother couldn't look her in the eye. She got the saucepan out of the cupboard, put it onto the range and reached for a couple of potatoes. 'Let's clear the table please.'

Rita gathered her schoolbooks into a pile. Tears were already brimming over her eyes. Why go to London? It was fifty miles away. Bonnie didn't know anyone in London, did she? Rita opened her mouth to say something but thought better of it when she saw her mother's expression.

'There's nothing we can do, love,' Grace said firmly but in a more conciliatory tone. 'Your sister has left home. I don't know why she's gone but it's her choice and we'll just have to get on with it.'

The potatoes Grace had cut up went clattering into the pan. She covered them with water before putting them on the range. Their eyes met and a second or two later, unable to contain her grief any more, Rita burst into tears and ran upstairs.

Victoria station was alive with people. Bonnie had arrived in the rush hour. She went straight to platform 12 as agreed with George, but after waiting a long two hours, she was so desperate for the toilet, she had to leave. She wasn't gone for more than ten minutes but he must have come and gone during that time and she'd missed him. Why didn't he wait? Where could he have gone? She didn't know what to do, but she was afraid to move from their agreed meeting place in case she'd got it wrong and he was simply late. As time wore on, it grew colder. The station was getting quieter. She began to feel more conspicuous now that the evening rush hour was drawing to a close, and a lot more anxious. Oh, George, where are you? She scoured the heads of the male passengers, willing George's trilby hat to come bobbing towards her, but it was hopeless. A few passengers who had obviously been to the theatre or some other posh frock do milled around, talking in loud plummy voices. Bonnie bit back her tears and shivered. She wished she and George could have travelled together but she hadn't expected Miss Bridewell to let her go early. She'd worked her notice so that she could get the week's pay owing to her and some of her holiday money. The extra money would come in handy if the job in Stanmore didn't work out for some reason.

'I've got on to a mate who can put us up,' he'd told her. 'Save a bit of money that way. He's not on the telephone so I'll go up and make the arrangements beforehand. I'll meet you at platform 12.'

She saw a party of cleaners emerge from a small storeroom and begin to sweep the concourse and then she noticed a man approaching. Bonnie looked around anxiously. Why was he coming her way? She didn't know him.

'Excuse me, Miss,' he said raising his hat. 'I couldn't help noticing you standing there. Has your friend been delayed?'

Bonnie didn't answer but she felt her face heating up and her heart beat a little faster. Oh, George, she thought, where are you? Please come now...

‘If you’re looking for a place to stay,’ he continued, ‘I know where a respectable girl like you can get a room at a cheap price.’

Bonnie looked at him for the first time. He was smartly dressed in a suit and tie. He looked clean and presentable. He looked like the sort of man she could take home to her mother but she didn’t know him from Adam and she had read of the terrible things that could happen to young girls on their own in London in Uncle Charlie Hanson’s *News of the World*. She turned her head, pretending not to have heard him.

‘Forgive me,’ he smiled pleasantly. ‘I only ask because I can see you look concerned. I don’t normally approach young women like this.’

Bonnie began to tremble. *Oh, where are you, George...*

‘Could I perhaps offer you a cup of tea in the tea bar?’ He was very persistent but that was what the *News of the World* said they were like. Men like him duped girls into going with them and corrupted them into a life of prostitution.

She shook her head. Even though she was tired and sorely tempted, Bonnie didn’t go with him. She had seen the man watching her from behind a pillar for some time and she didn’t like it. She picked up her suitcase and walked towards the newspaper vendor to buy a paper.

Eventually she stopped a passing policeman and after explaining that she had missed her friend, he at first directed her, then, having heard her story about the man who kept pestering her, decided to walk with her to a small hotel just around the corner. Bonnie booked a room for the night. It wasn't until she got undressed that she realised that the locket George had given her was no longer around her neck. Her stomach fell away. Where had she lost it? Had it come off when she was in that horrible factory? What a ghastly day it had been. Everything was going wrong. Bonnie climbed into bed and cried herself to sleep.

Two

Bonnie woke with a start. She heard footsteps outside her door and someone was banging a gong downstairs. It took a couple of seconds to realise where she was. She glanced at the clock on the top of the dresser: 7.30. When she'd arrived here ten days ago, the receptionist had told her breakfast was between 7.30 and 8.15 and she knew she couldn't afford to miss it. Her meagre wage packet and holiday money wouldn't keep her much longer. She had fallen into a pattern of eating as much as she could in the morning and making do with a tuppenny bag of chips and a cup of tea at lunchtime. It was all she could afford.

George had never shown up. Bonnie couldn't understand why. Something must have happened to him. Was he ill? Had he had an accident? He wouldn't have deserted her; he wouldn't. Every night she worried about him and cried herself to sleep. The obvious thing was to go back to Worthing, but what if he'd just been delayed for some reason and she missed him? Bonnie had gone over and over what he'd told her, and their plans together. Everything was crystal clear in her mind – so why wasn't he here?

As soon as the footsteps had gone she nipped across the hallway to the bathroom and gave herself a quick wash. She was dressed and downstairs by eight.

The dining room looked rather tired. It was wallpapered but, probably because it was so hard to find several rolls of the same wallpaper, it was a mish-mash of non-complementary paper, giving the room a rather confused look. The only empty table was next to the kitchen door and Bonnie preferred to keep herself to herself.

'Here we are, dear,' said the waitress as she put a pot of tea and some hot water on the table. 'Did you sleep well?'

'Yes, thank you.' Bonnie poured herself a cup of tea and when she was sure no one was looking, she palmed a couple of slices of bread into her handbag for later. The waitress came back and plonked a plate in front of her. Bonnie stared at the greasy pile and her stomach churned. She tried to force it down but even before she'd left the room she was feeling decidedly unwell. She wasn't used to big fry-ups in the morning and right now it was the last thing she wanted to eat.

Every morning as they left the dining room the guests were told they had to leave their rooms by 10am and that they couldn't return before 2pm in order to facilitate the cleaning. Dinner was at 6pm sharp. Having forced down as much of the greasy breakfast as she could manage, Bonnie booked herself in for one more night. George was bound to turn up at the station tonight. He wouldn't let her down. Would he?

As usual, her first port of call was Victoria station where she enquired if anyone had left a message for her. It didn't sound right for a respectable young woman to be chasing a man so she pretended she was married. 'I was supposed to be meeting my husband,' she told the station master. 'Mr George Matthews.' The station master shook his head. 'Never heard of him.' She was bitterly disappointed. Perhaps it was time to accept the fact that George wasn't coming. She didn't want to think of a reason why he wasn't coming and she really couldn't go back to Worthing, so she'd have to make another plan. She was positive that George wouldn't have let her down if he could help it. He wasn't that sort of man. He loved her. He wanted their baby as much as she did. True, the baby wasn't planned, but George was fine about it. She remembered the moment he'd given her the locket.

'One day we shall put a picture of our baby in it,' he'd smiled.

Tears pricked her eyes but she wouldn't give way to them. What good would that do? The obvious thing was to find Honeypot Lane and the job George had lined up for her; but then another thought crossed her mind. If he *had* let her down, then perhaps the job in Stanmore didn't exist either. She hated herself for thinking like this, but should she risk going all that way and using some of her precious resources for nothing? She had to be practical, didn't she? Her stomach churned. She didn't want to be practical. She wanted George.

Once Bonnie had lost her fight to keep her breakfast down, she decided to set off to find a job of her own. She remembered that when she'd scanned the evening paper she bought on that first night, she'd come across an advertisement for an employment agency. She had left the newspaper on her chest of drawers and whoever cleaned her room had never moved it. Bonnie now made a careful note of the address.

The offices of the London and County Domestic Employment Agency left much to be desired but it was very close to the station. From the roadside, she could hear the trains thundering in and out. The façade of the building was grimy with soot and, walking up the stone steps and wandering through the open door, she noticed that the walls themselves were still pockmarked with bomb damage. The paintwork was badly in need of a new coat and the colour scheme in the hallway, dark brown and cream, was from a bygone era. Clearly Harold Macmillan and his Ministry of Housing and Local Government hadn't got this far yet. When she took her hand from the guardrail even her glove was covered in smut. Should she go in? What if they asked too many questions? How much should she tell them? After twenty minutes of pacing up and down the street, Bonnie climbed the outer steps.

The London and County was three doors along a dingy corridor. As she knocked and walked in, a middle-aged woman with tightly permed hair and wearing some very fashionable glasses looked up from her typewriter. Bonnie introduced herself stiffly and handed over her references.

'Do take a seat, Miss Rogers,' said the woman, indicating some chairs behind her. 'I shall tell Mrs Smythe that you are here.'

Taking Bonnie's references with her, she stepped towards a glass-fronted door to her left and knocked. A distant voice called and the woman walked in and closed the door behind her.

Bonnie looked at herself in the wall mirror, glad that she had stopped crying. If she'd turned up with red eyes and a blotchy face, it wouldn't have helped her cause. She looked smart. Her hat, a new one she'd bought from Hubbard's using the staff discount, suited her. It was a navy, close-fitting baker boy beret, which she wore slightly to the left of her head. Her hair had a side parting with a deep wave on the right side of her face and was curled under on her shoulders. To set off her outfit, Bonnie always carried a navy pencil-slim umbrella. She liked being smart. One of Miss Reeves's little remarks came back to mind. 'Smartness equals efficiency; efficiency equals acceptance; and acceptance means respect.'

She unbuttoned her coat to reveal her dark blue suit with the cameo brooch George had given her pinned on the lapel. It was only from Woolworth's, she knew that, but it looked very pretty, especially next to her crisp white blouse. She absentmindedly smoothed her stomach and pulled down her skirt to get rid of the creases. Thank goodness the baby didn't show yet.

Turning towards the chairs, Bonnie had a choice of three, one with a soft sagging cushion, a high backed leather chair and a wooden chair with a padded seat. Lowering herself carefully onto the wooden chair, Bonnie placed her matching navy handbag on her knees, checked that her black court shoes still looked highly polished, and waited anxiously.

Presently, the secretary came back with a tall languid-looking woman in a tweed skirt and white blouse. She introduced herself as Mrs Smythe and invited Bonnie to step into her office.

Mrs Smythe, as would be expected of the owner of a highly respected agency, had a cut-glass English accent. She had a round face with a downy complexion and wore no make-up apart from a bright red gash of lipstick. The woman examined Bonnie's references carefully. 'These are excellent, Miss Rogers,' she said eventually. 'But shop work is very different from working in the domestic setting.'

'I want to train as a nursery nurse,' said Bonnie, 'but I am not quite experienced enough to be accepted. However, I am a hard worker and I am willing to learn.'

'When did you cease your last employment?'

'Just over a week ago.'

'May I ask, why did you leave Hubbard's?' Mrs Smythe was going back through her papers again.

'Personal reasons.'

Mrs Smythe looked up sharply. Bonnie held her eye with a steady unyielding gaze and didn't elaborate.

'I see,' said Mrs Smythe, clearly not seeing at

all. She waited, obviously hoping that Bonnie might explain, but how could she? Bonnie's heart thumped in her chest. Mrs Smythe wouldn't even consider offering Bonnie employment if she knew the truth.

Bonnie cleared her throat. 'It has absolutely no bearing on my ability to work with children.'

Mrs Smythe stood up and went to the filing cabinet. 'What sort of post were you looking for?'

'I don't mind,' said Bonnie, swallowing hard. 'Anything at all.'

'Here in London,' Mrs Smythe probed, 'or further afield?'

'Really,' Bonnie insisted, 'I have no preference.' Why should she care where she lived? Without George, what did it matter?

Mrs Smythe hesitated for a second before taking a yellow folder from the drawer. 'Tell me, Miss Rogers, would you be willing to travel abroad?'

Bonnie blinked. It took a second or two to let the idea sink in. 'Abroad?'

Could she really go abroad without George to lead the way? Rationing was still being enforced in Britain but in other parts of the world they said people had plenty of everything. She tried to imagine herself as nanny to an Italian prince, or an American film star or perhaps nanny to the child of someone in the diplomatic service. 'Abroad,' she said again, this time with more than a hint of interest in her voice. Yes ... abroad would be exciting. 'Yes, I might consider that.'

Mrs Smythe laid the yellow folder on her desk. 'I have a post here for Africa.'

Africa! Bonnie was startled. This was too much of a coincidence. The very continent where she and George had been planning to set up a new life and here was Mrs Smythe offering Bonnie a post there.

'Kenya,' Mrs Smythe went on.

Bonnie relaxed into her chair. Not South Africa but Kenya. Yet somehow it sounded just as wonderful. Kenya. She'd heard that it was a beautiful place. Didn't they grow tea and coffee for export and exotic things like ginger, and sugar cane, and pineapples? What would it be like to eat food like that every day!

Mrs Smythe was refreshing her memory by reading the papers in the yellow folder. 'I'm instructed to send you by taxi to meet the grand-mother.'

Silently, Bonnie took a deep breath. They must be very rich. She'd never ridden in a taxi before.

'In actual fact,' Mrs Smythe went on, 'the family are already out there. You would be required to escort their son from this country to his father's house in Kenya. Do you think you could undertake that, Miss Rogers?'

Don't be ridiculous, Bonnie told herself. How can you possibly go all that way on your own? You've no experience of being abroad. You've never even been as far as London before. And what about the baby? How on earth would you manage with a baby out in the wilds of Africa? But her mouth said something totally different.

'Oh yes,' said Bonnie, 'I'm sure I could.'

'Any news, dear?'

Elsie Dawson poked her head over the back wall that divided their houses. Grace took the peg out of her mouth and shook her head. Though the sun was weak at this time of year, it was a fine morning and she had decided to peg out some washing. At least hanging it for a while in the fresh air made it smell sweeter. Grace was glad she lived across the road and away from the railway line. Poor old Alice Chamberlain who used to live opposite was always complaining that she could never hang her stuff outside. The trains roaring by every few minutes left sooty deposits on everything.

'Is there anything I can do?'

Grace knew Elsie was fishing for more information but there was nothing to say. Her daughter had upped and left without so much as a by-your-leave. 'Nothing, thank you Elsie, but thanks for the offer. Pop round for a cup of tea, if you've got a minute.' Grace smiled to herself. Elsie wasn't likely to turn down that sort of invitation. She'd be round like a shot.

There was a bang on the front door. Grace threw a tea towel back into the washing basket and hurried indoors. Manny Hart was walking away as she opened it.

He turned around with a sheepish look on his face and raised his hat. 'Oh, I thought you'd be out,' he said carefully.

'Come in, come in,' she said. 'I'll put the kettle on.'

He looked down and, following his gaze, she saw a newspaper parcel on the doorstep. 'Just a couple of eggs I thought you might like,' he said.

'Thanks, Manny,' she said, bending to pick them up, 'it's kind of you.'

'I'm really sorry about the other day, Grace,' said Manny. 'I would have let you through but those men from the government…'

Grace put up her hand to stop him. 'I probably couldn't have stopped her anyway,' she said. 'It's a big train and she wouldn't have been looking out for me, would she? It would have taken me ages to run the length of the train as far as the engine.'

In the long night hours which had passed since Bonnie left, Grace had gone over every last detail of that day. At the time it had felt as if everything and everybody had conspired against her: missing the bus, Manny refusing to let her go without a platform ticket, Peggy being so slow to give her a penny, the machine deciding to hiccup at that very moment... But now, thinking more rationally about it, if her daughter had made up her mind to go, nobody could have stopped her. That was the rational thought, but her heart ached something rotten.

Elsie, her hair still in curlers under her head-scarf, came out of her front door and followed Manny and Grace inside.

Grace Rogers always had an open house. Her neighbours knew that no matter what (and they didn't need to be asked), they could go round to her place and she'd have the kettle on. All through the war, she'd seen them through the dreaded telegrams from the war office, the birth of a baby and the joy of a wedding.

Grace had also set up a couple of small

agencies, one for people caring for their long-term sick relatives and the other for cleaners. For a small joining fee, the women she knew were reliable, could do a couple of hours' sitting with the sick person or a couple of hours' housework. The recipient paid a slightly larger fee to join and got some much needed free time. Elsie had used the service a couple of times.

'How's Harry today?' Grace asked as she busied herself with the tea things.

'So-so,' said Elsie patting her scarf and pulling it forward so that her curlers were hidden. Her husband had survived the war but he wasn't the same man. Once the life and soul of any party, now Harry struggled with depression. In fact, Elsie had a hard job judging his mood swings. When he felt really bad, he would spend more time by the pier staring out to sea. With the onset of winter Elsie was always afraid he'd catch his death of cold.

'I see someone has taken over the corner shop,' said Elsie deliberately changing the subject. Grace vaguely remembered a good-looking man watching her as she flew down the middle of the street the night Bonnie left. 'He's a furniture restorer,' Elsie went on.

'I wouldn't have thought there was much call for that sort of thing around here,' Grace remarked. She pushed two cups of hot dark tea in front of her guests and sat down in the chair opposite.

'I have met him,' said Manny. 'Apparently he works on commissions.' He looked up and noticed the quizzical look the two women were giving him and added, 'He is a nice man. He gets on the train to Aroundel sometimes.'

'It's Arundel,' Grace corrected with a grin.

'Lives on his own?' said Elsie. She was trying to appear nonchalant but it was obvious she was dying to know. Grace suppressed another smile.

'That is correct,' Manny nodded. 'He fought at El Alamein with Field Marshal Monty and came back to find his wife shacked up with a Frenchy.'

Grace and Elsie shook their heads sympathetically. The war had a lot to answer for. It wasn't only the bombs and concentration camps that had changed people's lives. The French Canadians were billeted all over the town. On the whole, they were ordinary young men, three thousand miles away from all that was familiar and, as time went on, frustration set in. They had joined up to fight the Nazis, not to put up barbed wire on the beaches in an English seaside resort. As a result, their behaviour deteriorated and Saturday nights were peppered with drunken brawls in the town. Rumours circulated, although the story always came via a friend who knew a friend of a friend... When the war ended, a lot of ordinary people were left with very complicated lives.

Manny Hart was an attractive man with broad shoulders and a lean body. He had light brown hair, cut short, a strong square jaw and grey-green eyes. Nobody knew much about him except that he came from Coventry and he was a dab hand at playing the mouth organ. He'd apparently lost all his family, and considering the pasting the city had had, nobody liked to pry too much into his grief. He was very methodical, always doing everything exactly the same way, and was obviously a cut above the rest because he spoke public school English.

'Well,' said Manny putting his cup down. 'I must be going. I have got a railway to work for.'

'Thanks for the eggs,' said Grace as she saw him to the door.

'He's sweet on you,' said Elsie as Grace sat back down at the table.

'Don't be daft,' said Grace. 'You read too many romantic novels from that shilling library you belong to.'

'You don't blame me, do you?' Elsie sighed wistfully. 'There's precious little love and happiness around these days.'

Mrs Smythe gave Bonnie some money for a taxi to the address in Aldford Street where she was to meet her prospective employer. It was just off Park Lane and in a very exclusive part of London, near the Dorchester Hotel where Prince Philip, the dashing husband of the Princess Elizabeth, had had his stag night the night before his wedding just a few days ago. She smiled as she recalled the newspaper pictures of the beautiful bride in her wedding dress decorated, they said, with 10,000 white pearls.

Bonnie knew enough about child care to know that most people in this area employed Norlanders, girls from a very exclusive training college in Hungerford. She'd once seen an article in a magazine and when she'd made her career choice, Bonnie had toyed with the idea of applying there herself; but it was totally out of her league. Only rich girls went to places like that. The fees were huge. She wondered why she had been sent to such an exclusive place when there were other girls eminently more qualified than her who could fit the bill, but then she remembered how fat the file on Lady Brayfield was and that Mrs Smythe had mentioned more than once that Richard could be 'a little difficult'.

The house in Aldford Street was up a small flight of steps. Once inside, Bonnie was shown into a large sitting room on the first floor.

'Lady Brayfield will be with you in a minute,' the maid told her as she closed the door, leaving Bonnie alone.

It was a pleasant room with a large stone-built fireplace flanked by a basket on either side, one containing logs and the other a pile of magazines. Bonnie couldn't help admiring the beautiful stone-carved surround. The house was probably seventeenth century, she guessed, maybe even older. It had a large window made up of many small panes of glass which overlooked the street, but the wooden panelling on the walls made the room rather dark. A round table stood under the window with a potted fern in the middle. A snakes and ladders board was positioned between two chairs and it looked as if the players had only just left the room.

The door opened and a middle-aged woman came in. She was elegantly groomed with lightly permed hair. She wore a soft dress of blue-grey material which clung to her stiffly corseted body and a single string pearl necklace. A cocker spaniel followed her in.

'Good afternoon,' she said crisply. 'You must be Miss Rogers. The agency telephoned to say they were sending you.' She lowered herself into one of the two armchairs and indicated with a casual wave of her hand that Bonnie should sit on the settee.

The spaniel sat on the floor next to Bonnie, its haunches on her foot. She moved her toes slightly but she didn't complain. It didn't matter. The animal was quite lightweight.

'I'm not sure how much Mrs Smythe has told you,' Lady Brayfield went on, 'but your charge is a lot older than the children you are probably used to.'

Bonnie's heart constricted. What was she doing here? The whole idea was an idiotic mistake. How could she possibly work for this woman? She was pregnant, for heaven's sake. She started to panic and tried to compose herself as best she could, but already her face was beginning to flame. She cleared her throat noisily and found herself saying, 'I don't envisage that as a problem.' She couldn't bear the embarrassment of having to admit to this woman that she hadn't exactly been honest with Mrs Smythe. No. If she was going to have to go back to the London and County for a more suitable post, she would have to get Lady Brayfield to turn her down for some perfectly logical reason.

'Are you used to travel?'

'No,' Bonnie admitted. She was beginning to feel a bit sick. Instead of coming clean she was getting in deeper and deeper.

'How do you feel about going abroad?' Lady

Brayfield asked.

'It would be a challenge,' said Bonnie. The dog placed his head in her lap. She felt almost comforted by it and smiled faintly as she placed her hand on his head.

'You are between jobs...?' Lady Brayfield ventured.

'Yes,' said Bonnie. There was an awkward moment when Lady Brayfield again waited for her to elaborate but Bonnie's only response was to pat the dog's head. What an idiot she'd been. It was only the lure of riding in a taxi and going to a posh address that had got her here. She had to get herself out of this and quickly. Think, she told her panicking brain, think...

They were interrupted by a footfall and the door swung open. A young boy about ten years old, dark haired and in his school uniform consisting of grey short trousers, a grey blazer with the school emblem on the breast pocket, a white shirt with a yellow and black striped tie, long grey socks and black lace-up shoes came into the room. His hair looked wet, as if someone had made an attempt to tidy him up. Bonnie could see the marks of a comb running through it, although on the crown of his head three spikes of hair stood defiantly up on end. The door closed behind him.

'Ah,' said Lady Brayfield, 'this is Richard, my grandson. Come and say how do you do, Richard.'

Obediently but sullenly, Richard said, 'How do you do.'

'Miss Rogers is going to take you to your

father,' said Lady Brayfield. Bonnie's heart sank. Oh no, she'd got the job.

'I don't want to go,' Richard protested loudly. He stamped his foot and the spaniel began to bark as he kicked the closed door several times.

Lady Brayfield tried to placate the boy. 'Richard, darling, you mustn't get hysterical.'

'I don't want to go and you can't make me!' he cried.

This was Bonnie's chance to extricate herself. She rose to her feet slowly. 'Lady Brayfield...' she began.

The boy threw himself onto the older woman's lap. 'Don't send me, Granny. I'll be good. I promise.'

'But your father wants you out there with him, darling,' said Lady Brayfield helplessly. 'What can I do?'

She patted the boy's back and looked at Bonnie as if seeking advice.

Bonnie chewed her bottom lip. 'I'm sure...' she began, but at the same moment Richard stood up, turned and launched himself at her, causing her to stumble backwards onto the settee.

'No, no,' he shouted. 'You can't make me. I hate it there. I won't go, I tell you.'

Lady Brayfield was horrified.

Bonnie could see at once that he was clearly very spoiled and out of control.

'Richard,' his grandmother demanded, 'stop that at once!'

Bonnie struggled to her feet and righted her hat but as she bent to pick up her fallen handbag, the boy aimed a kick at the settee. The toe of his heavy lace-up shoe made contact with Bonnie. Her hands automatically went to her stomach as she cried out in excruciating pain.

Lady Brayfield gasped. 'Oh Richard, what have you done?'

They both stared in horror as Bonnie screwed up her eyes and fell back onto the settee with a loud cry.

Three

Rita was having a history lesson. Normally the Georgian period fascinated her. Unlike her bored and sleepy classmates, she revelled in the romance of England at the time of Jane Austen, but she would have hated to live back then. It was mainly the treatment of women which horrified Rita. That far-off time was a world of arranged marriages when women had to be submissive, obedient and above all, quiet. Despite her mother's best efforts, Rita wasn't a bit domesticated. She would have failed miserably at weaving, sewing and cooking, and she didn't know the meaning of quiet either!

'For homework,' said Miss Rastrick as she wrote on the blackboard, 'read pages 37–54.'

Rita found the page. *'A wife's duty,'* she read in her textbook, *The History of the Georgians, 'was one of absolute obedience to her husband. It was considered extremely disloyal if she was tempted to be disparaging or critical of him.'*

Rita shook her head. Thank goodness things were different now. The war had meant that when the men were called up, the women had to do their work. She was confident that now that the mould had been broken, it would be impossible to go back. Her future and the future of the girls in her class was a lot more promising than her mother's had been and certainly more than her grandmother's. Rita lived a world away from Regency England. She had no idea what she wanted to be when she left school next Easter, but she was determined to be mistress of her own destiny.

Her thoughts drifted to her sister Bonnie. She still couldn't believe she had gone. Mum didn't want to talk about it but she cried all the time. She tried to pretend everything was all right but every time she stood outside in the scullery, or went outside the back door to get coal or check on the washing, Rita knew she was hiding so that no one saw her tears. It had been almost two weeks and there was still no sign of Bonnie. Mum had been out all day last Saturday, but she wouldn't say where. There were no letters from Bonnie either.

'Rita Rogers, stop daydreaming and get on with your work.' Miss Rastrick's sharp reprimand brought her back to the present day and Rita went back to the text.

The sort of women Rita admired were women like Hannah Penn, wife of William Penn. After the death of her husband, Hannah inherited control over the Pennsylvania colonies he founded. According to her book, Hannah held power and governed them wisely for fourteen years, even though her own son made strenuous efforts to have his father's will nullified. There was no holding Hannah back *and when my time comes, there'll be no holding me back,* Rita thought to herself.

When the bell rang to signify the end of lessons, Rita's excitement mounted. Over the weekend, she had formed a plan. She would follow it through the moment the school day ended. Miss Rastrick tidied the books on her desk and rose to her feet. There was a low rumble as twenty gymslip-clad girls rose to their feet as well.

Tucking her books under her arm, Miss Rastrick said formally, 'Good afternoon girls.'

'Good afternoon, Miss Rastrick,' they chanted in unison. As soon as she'd gone, the class erupted into a wall of sound. Rita's hands trembled as she packed up her desk.

'I forgot to tell you,' said Mo Dawson. 'We had a letter from my brother Bob. He's in Germany now. He asked to be remembered to you.'

'Did he?' Rita wasn't that bothered. Bob, Mo's older brother, was doing his National Service. The last time she'd seen him was at the school concert last year. He had spots.

'Are you coming to athletics practice with us?' Mo smiled.

Mo lived next door but one from Rita. They didn't have much in common but they often walked together to and from school. Mo's dad was a bit funny in the head sometimes but Mo was all right.

Rita shoved the last of her books inside and

shut the lid. 'Can't,' she said mysteriously. 'I've got something on.'

From her school in South Farm Road, Rita took a detour down Pavilion Road. She didn't know exactly where Bonnie's boyfriend lived, but it was down this road somewhere. She had followed them once, but only at a distance for fear that Bonnie would see her. Rita hoped that once she saw the gate, she would remember the house.

Although they were becoming increasingly independent of each other, she and her sister had always been very close. When the news that their father had died came, their mother had retreated into a world of her own, spending hours sitting alone on the stairs, so she and Bonnie comforted each other. The sisters enjoyed the same things – walking on the Downs, experimenting with what little make-up they could lay their hands on and going to the pictures.

Bonnie was what people called a striking woman whereas Rita was regarded as the pretty one. She had long artistic fingers like her mother and dimples on her cheeks like her father. Her dark hair had a hint of bronze in it and it shone. For school she pinned it away from her face but out of school she wore it like the film star Joan Greenwood.

Although she didn't have a boyfriend herself, Rita understood the unwritten rule between women that you shouldn't interfere where a man was concerned. She'd kept her distance when George entered Bonnie's life. She said nothing to her mother because she knew Bonnie was keeping this one under wraps. For some reason, Bonnie didn't want Mum to know about him.

'He's a lot older than me,' she'd confided in Rita one Sunday afternoon. 'Mum will stop us seeing each other if I tell her.'

'What's he like?' Rita wanted to know.

Her sister's expression became dreamy. 'He's the most wonderful man on earth,' she'd sighed. 'He looks like Charles Boyer.' Bonnie's soppy expression changed as she saw her sister's face and she added defensively, 'Well, just a bit...'

'On a dark night, with his hat down and his coat collar up?' Rita quipped.

Bonnie pushed her arm playfully. 'No, really.'

'What's his name?'

'George.'

'George who?'

'You ask too many questions,' Bonnie had frowned. 'We've both got a half day on Wednesday afternoon and we want to go to Brighton. Will you cover for me or not?'

'I suppose,' Rita pouted, 'but what if Mum finds out?'

'The only way she'll find out is if you tell her,' Bonnie insisted. 'Tell Mum because it's half term, you and I are going to see if they've made a start on clearing the barbed wire from the beach at Goring.'

Out of loyalty and love, Rita had lied to her mother with impunity, covering for what Bonnie and George were doing more than once.

She'd reached the bend in Pavilion Road but nothing seemed familiar. George's digs must be around here somewhere. She looked over the hedge of number 131.

'Lost something, love?'

Rita nearly jumped out of her skin as a woman carrying two heavy shopping bags came up behind her. 'I'm looking for a friend's house.'

The woman put one of her bags down and flexed her whitened fingers.

'Can I help you with that?' Rita smiled.

'Thank you, dear,' said the woman. 'I live at number 187. What's your friend's name?'

'George,' said Rita, taking the bag. 'I don't know his last name.'

'What does he look like?'

'He's good looking,' said Rita. 'A bit like Charles Boyer.'

The woman chuckled. 'I think I'd remember if I'd seen him. Has he lived here long?'

Rita shrugged. 'He's got digs on the first floor,' she said, remembering something Bonnie once said.

'If he's in digs, he'll be with Mrs Kerr. She's the only one around here who takes in lodgers. Number 109.' They'd reached the woman's gate and Rita handed her bag back. 'Thank you, dear. Number 109. I hope you find your friend.'

Rita's heart was in her mouth as she walked back and knocked at the door of number 109. The small front garden was very clean and tidy, the path swept, and the name on the wall beside the door said *Maranatha*. Mrs Kerr was a small woman with round black-rimmed glasses. Her hair was completely covered in a dark brown hairnet and she wore a wraparound floral apron.

'Mrs Kerr? I've come about George,' said Rita,

completely forgetting her carefully rehearsed speech.

'About time too,' said Mrs Kerr. She showed her into a small sitting room next to the front door. 'I must say I'm a bit surprised that he's sent a schoolgirl. Why didn't he come back for them himself?'

Rita stared at her with a blank expression. 'Sorry?'

'His things,' Mrs Kerr said. 'That is what you're here about, isn't it? He packed his case and left it in the hall that morning. "I'll be back for it later", he said. You tell him I waited up until half past ten but he never showed up. I'll get it for you now.'

She went back out to the hall and opened the cupboard under the stairs.

'Did George say where he was going?' asked Rita.

'I thought you knew where he was,' said Mrs Kerr, coming back with a suitcase in her hand and a raincoat over her arm. 'I don't know where he is. He never told me. All I know is he paid his rent, gave me back the rent book and that was that. What are you going to do with his things if you don't know where he is?'

Rita chewed her bottom lip and stared at the floor with a frown.

Mrs Kerr looked at her suspiciously. 'Here,' she said. 'There's no hanky panky going on between you and him is there?'

'I've never met George,' Rita confessed. 'He used to go out with my sister.'

'Oh,' said Mrs Kerr. 'Used to go out, did you say? Well, it's best not to interfere, dear. If he doesn't want to go out with her any more, there's bound to be a reason.'

'My sister went to London, very suddenly,' said Rita. 'I was hoping George, Mr ... er...'

'Matthews,' said Mrs Kerr.

'Mr Matthews might know where she is,' Rita went on.

'Well,' said Mrs Kerr. 'This is a mystery, isn't it, but I can't imagine that they'd be together.'

Rita raised a questioning eyebrow.

'Well, he's hardly likely to have gone all the way up to London without taking his things, is he?'

Rita was forced to agree. 'My mother is very worried.'

'I'm sure she is,' said Mrs Kerr, making a big show of putting the case and the raincoat back under the stairs, 'but I can't help you. Now if you'll excuse me...'

Back out on the street, Rita walked with a heavy heart towards South Farm Road and the crossing. Where could she go from here? She had been so sure she would find George and speak to him in person. If Bonnie wasn't with George, where on earth could she be? And why was George missing as well?

It was while she was waiting for the crossing gates to go up that Rita spotted an advertisement on the wall. Hubbard's... Of course, Hubbard's. Why didn't she think of it before? That was where Bonnie worked. She must have confided in one of her work colleagues. Full of resolve, once the gates were wound back in place, Rita quickened her step. She had no money for the bus fare but she was good at running and it wouldn't take long to get to town.

Richard's well-aimed kick at the leg of the settee had, in the split second she had reached for her handbag, landed in Bonnie's nether regions. His shoes were of the outdoor type and very hard. The pain was indescribable. When Bonnie cried out, pandemonium followed. Richard was sent to his room, the sound of his heavy footsteps and wailing tears fading into the distance finally silenced altogether behind a slammed door. Lady Brayfield and her maid did their best for Bonnie who, speechless with pain, could only roll around the settee and wish she was dead. They eventually calmed her and covered her with a blanket.

A doctor summoned from Harley Street arrived shortly afterwards and Lady Brayfield left the room while he examined her. His breath smelled of whisky but he poked and prodded as he asked some very embarrassing questions. When he had finished, he concluded that she was 'fit as a flea' and only needed a period of recovery.

After he'd gone, although the pain had lessened, Bonnie lay on the settee listening to the murmur of voices outside in the corridor. Serves you right, she told herself miserably. You never should have come here in the first place.

She heard the front door slam and a few minutes later, Lady Brayfield returned. Bonnie moved as if to get up but Lady Brayfield held up her hand and sat in the chair opposite. 'How long have you been pregnant?' Her voice was gentle but her mouth was set in a tight line.

Bonnie's face burned with shame and embarrassment. Here it comes, she thought. The lecture ... the moment when she said *think of the shame and disgrace you've brought on your family,* and *what about your reputation,* etc, etc. Bonnie had never had 'the lecture' herself but she remembered the way everybody had treated her neighbour Mary Reed when she got pregnant by a Canadian soldier during the war. 'Keep the baby?' Mary's mother had screamed when Mary told her. 'Don't be stupid. Who is going to marry you with another man's baby?'

In the end, poor Mary had been forced to give her baby up for adoption.

Lady Brayfield looked at her steadily. 'How on earth did you expect to keep it a secret?'

Bonnie swallowed the lump in her throat. It was no use. Obviously the doctor had told Lady Brayfield of her condition. 'I thought that if I worked really hard, by the time you found out, you might let me stay a bit longer.'

A silence trickled between them.

'At least you're honest,' Lady Brayfield said finally.

'I'm not very far gone,' said Bonnie in small voice. 'And the agency said it was a temporary post. I thought if I earned a little money I could...'Embarrassment welled up inside her. It was time to go. She pushed the blanket aside.

'You've been told to rest, Miss Rogers,' Lady Brayfield said firmly. The tone of her voice was authoritative but not unkind. 'Let us discuss the matter.' She paused. 'I take it that you have been deserted?'

Something rose up inside Bonnie to defend

George but how could she? She'd been to the station every day for more than a week and she'd made sure plenty of people saw her looking for him, but of course he hadn't turned up. Time and again she'd asked at the station master's office but he'd left no message either. She had written to Pavilion Road but that was six days ago and as yet she hadn't had a reply. She knew she wasn't the first girl he'd slept with. How could she be? George was older than her and experienced in his lovemaking. She'd been an utter fool. How many other girls had given themselves to men only to find themselves left with the consequences? The story was as old as the hills... But she couldn't possibly say all that, so she just nodded miserably.

'Could you not go back to your mother?'

Bonnie's eyes widened. 'I can't. My mother is a widow...'

Lady Brayfield nodded. 'How many months are you?'

Bonnie's voice was small. 'Four.' Was it really only four months since she and George had lain in bed together dreaming big dreams? He was determined to go abroad. They'd even toyed with the idea of going to the Congo.

'The principal food crops are cassava, bananas, and root crops,' George had told her after he'd read a few books from the library. 'Hot and humid. The central part has rain all year long.'

'Sounds wonderful,' she'd cooed.

'No it doesn't,' he'd laughed, and then he'd kissed her again. Bonnie could feel her eyes smarting.

Lady Brayfield pushed herself deeper into her chair. 'I have a proposal, Miss Rogers. We shall say nothing of this to Dora or to Cook.'

Bonnie frowned. Dora must be the name of the maid who opened the door and presumably it was Cook she could hear singing in the kitchen.

'Richard is very contrite after his outburst,' Lady Brayfield went on. 'He's not a bad boy. It's not the first time he has told me he doesn't want to live with his father, albeit he has never been violent before. My daughter, Richard's mother, is in a nursing home. She's had a nervous breakdown and needs complete rest. I only want to do what is right for the child.'

She rose to her feet and stood facing the window. Whatever she was about to say, Bonnie had already warmed to her.

'My son-in-law is an ambitious man,' Lady Brayfield continued with her back to Bonnie. 'He is very strict, which is probably why Richard does not want to go to Africa. Now I'm beginning to wonder if that's why my daughter...'

Her voice trailed off but she stayed by the window, her back ramrod straight. A couple of times her hand went to her face but she didn't turn around. Eventually, and with a beautifully composed expression, she turned back to Bonnie. 'I was very impressed with the way you conducted yourself when Richard ... er ... did what he did. You didn't retaliate or swear at him.' She paused. 'That took tremendous self-control, Miss Rogers. You have excellent references and Richard needs a young person, someone with drive and energy. His time is mostly taken up with prep school but at the weekends, and with the Christmas holidays coming up, he needs to be amused. Quite frankly, Miss Rogers, I am too old for party games.'

Bonnie sat up. She should say something and say it now. How much energy would she have once the baby started to show?

'After this incident, perhaps it wouldn't be in the boy's best interest to send him to live with his father,' Lady Brayfield went on. 'Not yet, anyway. That being the case, I propose that you come here until after Christmas. I really cannot be without someone right now. Quite frankly, Miss Rogers, I need help. Would you be willing to come for a short period? It would give me time to find another girl for the New Year.'

Bonnie's jaw dropped. 'I won't let you down, Lady Brayfield,' she whispered.

'Clearly your referees had no idea you were pregnant,' she continued, 'so I am taking a gamble that you are not promiscuous.'

Bonnie had never heard the word before but the meaning wasn't lost. 'I made a stupid mistake,' she mumbled.

Lady Brayfield went to her handbag. 'Then we shall leave it there and not talk about it again. Agreed?'

'Agreed,' said Bonnie looking up with a half smile.

'I shall pay you £2 a week, all found. Is that agreeable?'

Bonnie's eyes widened. This was more than she could ever have hoped for. 'Yes, yes thank you.'

Lady Brayfield handed Bonnie a pound note. 'I

have to take Richard to the dentist this afternoon and he is waiting outside to apologise for his disgraceful behaviour. When you are fully recovered, fetch your things and Dora will help you settle in. This should cover your taxi fare. You can start tomorrow.'

With that, she swept out of the room. Bonnie could have kissed her. What an amazing woman. The place where Richard had kicked her was still painful but it was almost worth it to land on her feet in this way. She looked around the room. What a wonderful place to work. It was so warm in this house. No draughty corridors, no sitting huddled around a meagre coal fire for warmth. Of course she knew her newly found comfort wouldn't last, but for the moment, she had been handed a lifeline. A couple or three weeks here and she could put a little more money in the post office. Lady Brayfield had given her more than a job. She had given her hope.

Four

Every day seemed like a week to Grace. She was on 'Packing' in the factory. The sweaters came off the production line and were put into boxes. It was the job of her and her colleagues to steam any creases out and fold the sweaters neatly, three in a box lined with tissue paper. They worked at a table, in pairs, facing each other.

The new factory was a lot more modern than

the old one. In the morning, they played *House-wives' Choice* over the radio and at lunchtime they heard *Workers' Playtime* in the canteen. The people around her hummed and sang as they worked but Grace wasn't really listening. Her thoughts were where they had been for the past ten days – with Bonnie. She had waited a whole week and then she had pawned the brooch she had inherited from Michael's mother. She had always intended to give it to the daughter who got married first. She would have given it to her before they set out for the church on her wedding day but there was no time for sentiment now. She had to find Bonnie.

She'd gone to the pawnbroker along the High Street. It was a dingy little shop, dark and cluttered, and she'd taken the fifteen shillings he'd offered without quibbling. It was probably worth a lot more than that, but there was no time to argue. All she had wanted was to get on the train first thing on Saturday morning.

She'd scoured the concourse at Victoria station and stopped tens of people to ask if they had seen Bonnie. She was met with blank stares, nervous frowns, some hostile reactions and a few sympathetic conversations but nobody remembered seeing her daughter.

'There was one young woman,' the station master had told her, 'but she was looking for her husband.'

'Are you sure about that?' Grace had asked.

The station master had leaned towards her as he made a circular movement with his finger next to his forehead. 'I think she was probably some poor sod who couldn't get over the death of her old man,' he said confidentially. 'We get them all the time. Sometimes a relative will come for them but, worst case scenario, they jump under a train.'

Grace shuddered. 'When did you last see her?'

The station master shrugged. 'Couple of days ago?' They were both together in his office. As he spoke, a bell began to clang behind him. He stood up and put on his jacket. 'Now if you'll excuse me…'

'My daughter is eighteen and she has lovely brown hair,' Grace said quickly. 'She wears it tied at the back, like this. She's very pretty.'

The station master ushered her out of the door and put on his hat. 'This one had a beret,' he said as he hurried away.

'You've got four on that pile.' Grace heard Snowy's voice but she was still deep in thought. Bonnie was a capable girl but Grace worried that she wasn't looking after herself properly in London. Was it possible she was with that man? Who was he anyway? She never talked about him, not properly anyway. What if she'd fallen in with a bad lot? What if some awful man went for her – could Bonnie take care of herself? How was she going to live with no job? Grace realised Bonnie had taken all the money from the green tin; and why not? It was her own money; but she knew Bonnie had been saving it for Christmas. Grace had no real idea how much was in the tin, but it probably wouldn't last long.

'Grace, I said, you've got four sweaters on that pile.'

Grace looked up as Phyllis Snow, Snowy as they all called her, put a hand over hers. At the same time, Snowy jerked her head towards the door.

Grace shook her head. 'Oh sorry.' She quickly rearranged the sweaters before Norah Fox, their supervisor, spotted her mistake. She was coming their way.

The sweaters were lovely colours, one powder blue, one pink and the other an oyster white. Lovely and soft too. Pity they were all going to Canada, Grace thought. After all the hardships of war, everybody looked forward to a bit of luxury in the home markets but it was a long time coming.

'Time for your break, girls,' said Norah.

Snowy linked one arm with Grace and the other with Kaye Wilcox as they headed for the canteen. 'We've been worried about you, Grace,' said Snowy. 'You've not been yourself all week. Anything we can do to help?'

Snowy was a nice woman, about eight or ten years older than Grace, with a matronly figure and steel grey hair arranged in sausage curls around the nape of her neck. Kaye was about thirty with deep-set eyes and raven black hair. She had never married but rumour had it that when she was a young girl she'd had a fling with a married man. Snowy took a packet of Players Navy Cut from the pocket of her wraparound apron and offered one to Grace. Grace shook her head. Kaye put on some more lipstick and rubbed her lips together.

'Oh, sorry, I forgot you don't smoke,' Snowy

smiled as they waited in the queue. 'Now. About your problem, do you want to talk about it?'

Grace could feel her eyes already pricking with tears. She couldn't bear to make a fool of herself but at the same time she desperately needed to talk to someone.

Kaye squeezed her arm encouragingly.

'Come on, love,' said Snowy taking charge.

'You know we can keep a secret,' Kaye encouraged.

They each took their meagre portion of stew and some bread and butter and sat a little way away from the others.

'My Bonnie has left home,' said Grace. It took a few minutes to explain the situation and why she was so concerned but Snowy and Kaye were patient listeners.

'How awful for you,' said Kaye. 'She's not in trouble, is she?'

Grace's eyes widened. 'Both my daughters are good girls,' she said haughtily. She refused to even think about such a thing. The very idea!

'Don't get on your high horse,' said Snowy. 'If she is, she wouldn't be the first now would she?'

Grace's mouth tightened. 'I'll thank you not to cast aspersions.'

'I didn't mean anything by it, Grace,' Kaye protested. She glanced at Snowy for support.

Snowy laid a hand over Grace's. 'I'm sorry. I shouldn't have said that. Take no notice of me. Perhaps I've just seen a bit too much of life.'

But Grace wasn't in the mood for forgiveness. She picked up her tray and went to join the girls on another table. She felt sick. She had refused to let herself think that. Bonnie in trouble. Dear God, that was it. Why else would she up sticks and leave like that? No, she wouldn't believe it. Not Bonnie. Grace recalled what she had said to her when she'd reached sixteen. 'Now don't you go bringing trouble home.' She'd meant it as a caution, but had Bonnie taken it as a threat? Dear Lord, what had she done?

She plonked her tray down next to Poppy Reynolds who interrupted her thoughts. 'What are you doing this Christmas, Grace?' Her bright eyes were dancing with excitement. 'I'm going to the New Year's Eve Ball at the Assembly Rooms.'

'How nice,' Grace smiled. She was happy for her. It was about time the girl had something to look forward to. Poppy had had a difficult war, losing both a brother and her father.

'My auntie's making me a smashing dress. It's got yards and yards in the skirt and it's so tight around the bodice,' she leaned forward confidentially, 'that I won't have to wear a bra.'

'Better watch out for those boys with their wandering hands then, Poppy,' laughed one of the other girls and Poppy's face went pink.

Grace picked at her food. She normally enjoyed listening to their banter, or joining in with the laughter when Gert and Daisy said something funny on *Workers' Playtime* but the ache in her chest got worse and worse with each passing day. Perhaps she shouldn't have been so harsh on the girl. She'd never met her boyfriend, but perhaps he wasn't such a bad lad. It was just that giving a young girl a present so early on in their relationship didn't seem right. If she'd met him, she might have given Bonnie her blessing to go out with him. She might have tried to talk her out of it, but she would have given her blessing in the end. Bonnie was the sort of girl who seized the moment without a thought of the consequences. Grace realised now that she should have sat her down and talked, but she'd been hasty, angry, annoyed. If only she could turn the clock back. What if she had run away with that boy? What if he had left her high and dry? What if Bonnie had come to her senses and wanted to come back home? What if she didn't have enough money? And what if there was a baby? She hated to think of the poor girl going through all that on her own. Added to the worry about her daughter, money was really tight. It had been difficult enough before, but without Bonnie's contribution, Grace would be hard pushed to find the rent each week. Perhaps she shouldn't have spent all that money going up to London to find Bonnie. It was a fruitless exercise anyway. Maybe she should have kept it for more pressing things. Like many in her street, Grace didn't have a proper rent book. The rent kept going up all the time and she wondered sometimes if that was down to the landlord or the rent collector. Without a proper record, there was no way of knowing. She'd toyed with asking Mr Finley for a rent book, and she'd asked the collector countless times, but his promises never came to anything.

When Mr Chard called to collect the rent last Friday, Grace was four bob short. In the end, she'd borrowed the money from the bit she'd put aside for the coalman, but this week she'd still be four bob short and she'd have both of them to pay.

Kaye stopped by another table to have a word with a friend. Grace looked up as Snowy put a cup of tea on the table beside her. 'Grace. I really didn't mean to offend you. Me and my big mouth.'

Grace gave her a thin smile. 'I know, and I'm sorry I was touchy.'

'Touchy?' said Poppy. 'It's not like you to be touchy, Grace. What's up?'

'Never you mind,' said Grace. 'Now tell me a bit more about this ball you're going to.'

Snowy lived in South Farm Road, and as she and Grace walked part of the way home together, Grace talked a bit more about Bonnie.

'Listen, girl,' said Snowy eventually. 'If you need anything, just let me know.'

'Thanks, Snowy.'

'I mean it. I know how hard it can be having your family miles away.'

Snowy's daughter Kate had met and married an Aussie during the war. He was a lovely man but it had broken her mother's heart when Kate announced that she was going to live in Australia. It was 12,000 miles away and took six weeks to go by boat. Snowy knew she would never see them again, but she didn't let that spoil her daughter's plans. Kate had gone away with her mother's blessing, a smile and a cheery wave.

Grace squeezed her elbow. 'I know you do. You're a good pal.'

'Are you doing the Thrift Club again this year?'

Snowy, always slightly embarrassed by compliments, changed the subject quickly.

'Oh, yes and it was so popular last year, I've got even more savers this year.'

The Thrift Club. Grace had quite forgotten about that money. It was meant for Christmas but if push came to shove, she could use the money she had saved to pay back what she owed for the rent and the coalman. Suddenly she felt a whole lot better.

When the end of the war came, money was tight. At the beginning of 1946, Grace had had the idea that if she collected a shilling or two every week from her friends and neighbours and put it into a post office savings account, by the end of the year they would have a nice little bit of interest as well as the money they had put in. It had been so successful, she had repeated it this year.

'Christmas would have been a lean time of it in my house if my family was still living at home,' said Snowy pulling a face. 'I kept meaning to save a few bob but I even had to dip into the bit I put aside for the doctor this year. I wish I'd joined.'

'Do it for next year,' said Grace. 'It's hard enough trying to save but if you put a little bit by each week, it soon mounts up. Perhaps you could have a little holiday.'

'Fat chance,' Snowy laughed. 'With all the shortages, I sometimes wonder who won this bloody war.'

Grace nodded. 'Mind you, according to the newsreels, Germany is having a rough time of it and all.'

'Yes, we're helping them!' said Snowy acidly.

'But who's helping us?'
Grace was forced to agree. It upset her to think of little children going hungry, no matter what the parents had done, but she understood why her friend felt so aggrieved. Snowy's brother had been killed in Burma and her parents who lived in Southampton had been bombed. Fortunately, their house had been repaired, which was more than could be said for the rest of the street. Almost every other house had been obliterated.
'I was going to ask you,' said Grace, changing the subject back again. 'I'm going to draw the club money on Friday 12th and count it out.'
'I'm sure you'll make a good job of it,' said Snowy. 'You're good at sums.'
'It's not that,' said Grace. 'I want to make sure everything is completely above board. I've kept good books throughout the year and I want someone to check my records and sign that it's all legit.'
'Sounds reasonable enough,' said Snowy.
'It protects me more than anything else,' said Grace. 'Could you come and help me with the count?'
They had reached Snowy's gate. 'When do you want me to come over?'
'It's half day,' said Grace. 'About three?'
'Make sure you've got the kettle on,' Snowy grinned.
With a friendly wave, Grace walked on, hardly noticing that just as she passed the Beehive Tea Rooms, a car drew alongside her and the passenger door opened. It was Norris Finley.
'Get in, will you, Grace. I have something I want to tell you.'

'Can't you tell me at work?'
'It's private.'
Grace's heart leapt. Had he found Bonnie? She looked around to make sure nobody was about and jumped into the car quickly. They finished early at the factory on Fridays and sometimes, if Rita was late out of the grammar school, they walked home together. Grace didn't want Rita seeing her getting into someone's car. As she closed the door, Norris turned the car sharply and they headed down St Lawrence Avenue.
'Where are we going?'
'We need to talk,' he said mysteriously. 'Let's find somewhere quiet.'
'You promised me a rent book,' she said running her fingers through her hair nervously.
'Yes, yes, and you'll get one.'
'I can't afford another rent rise.'
He patted her leg in a way that made her feel uncomfortable. 'I'll make sure you get no more rises, Grace. All right?'
'I still want the rent book.'
'All right!' he snapped. He sped up the car.
'Norris, I have to get back home,' she protested. 'You're taking me miles away.'
'Don't worry, I'll get you back.' He drove on until they'd reached Durrington where he turned into the rough track called Pond Lane before he stopped the car.
She waited anxiously. This was beginning to feel unpleasant. 'So? What is it you want to tell me?'
He turned to her. 'We've always been good friends, haven't we, Grace?'
Grace stiffened. 'Hardly,' she snapped. 'You

took advantage of me when I was young and silly and you were old enough to know better. We have nothing in common.'

He smiled. 'Nothing?'

Grace felt her face flame. 'If it hadn't have been for my Michael, my life would have been ruined.'

'There you go again,' he said, 'being melodramatic.'

'Just say what you want to say and then take me back,' she said irritably.

'Grace,' he said, his voice becoming gentle. He touched her sleeve but she snatched her arm away. 'I know you're having a hard time. Look at you. Your coat is practically threadbare, your dress is darned…'

She could feel her face colouring with embarrassment. 'I've just been to work,' she said indignantly. 'I'm hardly going to put on my best togs to go to the factory, am I?'

'You deserve better. I could change all that. You know I've always liked you. I mean, really liked you.'

His words hung between them in the electrically charged atmosphere. She turned her head slowly.

'It's been three years since your Michael died,' he went on quickly. 'You must have needs, Grace.' His hand was on her knee again. 'I have needs too.'

She jerked his hand away. 'You have a wife!'

'She doesn't give me what I want, Grace.' He was giving her that hangdog look of his.

'For God's sake!' she snapped. 'I'm not sixteen any more. If that's all you've got to say, take me back.'

It was obvious he wasn't ready to give up. 'We could come to some arrangement. I really want to be with you, Grace. You've still got your looks and a bit of powder and a new hairdo would do wonders for you.'

'How dare you!' She was furious. Mostly with herself for believing he had anything honourable to say but also for being stupid enough to get into his car. She should have known where this was leading. 'I want to go home.'

'I could make your life so much easier,' he went on. 'How about I set up an account for you in the new Hubbard's? It's a lovely modern store and you could buy any dress you like.'

Grace grabbed the car door handle, but he held her back. 'If you won't do it for yourself, think about that girl of yours. I could get her into secretarial college. If she passes the exam, she could get a really good job, something with prospects. You'd like your girl to get on, wouldn't you, Grace?'

'Now look here, Norris,' she said coldly. 'I'm not going to be anybody's tart. Me and mine are not for sale.'

His hand went up her skirt and groped for her knickers. 'Come on, girl,' he said huskily. 'You know you'd like it. You used to be a little firebrand when you were young. I reckon I could relight that fire again.'

She flung her hand at his face and her finger caught him in the eye. He sprang back into his seat with a howl of pain and lashed out with his arm, hitting her on the side of her head. 'You stupid cow,' he spat. Now Grace wasn't sure what to do. The most sensible thing would be to get out and walk but he had brought her at least three, maybe four miles from home. In the split second before opening the door and getting out, she heard voices. Grace glanced behind them and saw a woman and her three children heading in their direction. Up ahead was a little thatched cottage. There were no other houses in the lane. The woman most likely lived there.

'Norris,' she said as firmly as she could despite the sickening feeling gripping her whole body, 'are you going to turn this car around and take me home or am I going to scream blue bloody murder and let that woman call the police?'

Without another word, he started the car. They drove back in silence but as he dropped her near the crossing, he snatched her arm again. 'Think about it, Grace. I could cut your rent if you prefer. I'll wait to hear from you.'

'Then you'll have a bloody long wait.'

As she slammed the door, he pointed a finger at the glass and shouted, 'I'm warning you, Grace Rogers. You'd be a fool to make an enemy of me.'

Five

When Grace got back home, to her surprise, Rita still wasn't back from school. She wasn't unduly concerned. Rita had probably stayed on in the gym for netball practice or something. Grace set about getting the tea ready. She didn't have many potatoes left in the enamel bin. She had seen some seed potatoes in Potter and Bailey's but if you bought them, you had to sign a paper to say you were going to use them for planting. Grace supposed they would come round to your house and check up on you in the spring so she didn't chance it. She only peeled two. That would be plenty for her and Rita. Bonnie was the one with the big appetite. She sighed and bit back her tears. This was almost as bad as the feeling she'd had when Michael was killed. Almost but not quite.

The loss of her husband was final, she'd known as soon as she'd got the telegram that she would never see him again, but the 'loss' of her daughter was cloaked in hope, the hope that one day she would walk through that door again. She sighed. She didn't want to think of Bonnie ill or, worse still, lying in a ditch somewhere, but sometimes the darker thoughts crept in uninvited. She cleared her throat and swallowed the aching lump that had formed. Be rational, she told herself. There was no reason to think that any harm had befallen her. She had to accept that Bonnie had run away, that was all.

Seeing Norris had unsettled her again. Whatever women saw in the man now she couldn't think, but when they were young, he had been a lot better looking and he could charm the birds from the trees with that silver tongue of his. He'd made no secret of his desire for her when they were youngsters but why now? Why did he still want her when he could have the pick of any girl in Worthing? The years hadn't been kind to him.

These days he was a thickset man with large jowls and a paunch. The richer he became the less attractive he became but he didn't seem all that bothered. He really thought money could buy him anything and he was ruthless. The business with the rent had been going on for years and because people were reluctant to talk about money it had taken ages for them to realise that they were all paying different amounts. There was no doubt that if he cut Grace's rent, it would make life a lot easier, especially now that Bonnie's wage wasn't coming into the house, but she wasn't going to succumb to him – even if she had to wear frayed jumpers and eat half a potato for her dinner for the rest of her life. She still had her pride and her good name, for God's sake.

As well as the potato shortage, there was a paper shortage and the butcher had said there was little hope of poultry being on the menu for Christmas, unless, of course, she wanted to use the black market. Grace had never done that. She didn't want to do it on principle and besides, they charged such high prices.

Rita burst through the door in a state of high excitement and, hardly stopping to draw breath, she blurted out that she'd been to Hubbard's.

'Whatever for?' Grace wanted to know.

'I thought someone might be able to tell me something about Bonnie, Mum.'

Grace stiffened. 'And did they?'

'Not exactly,' said Rita. 'When I got there, the girl in the office thought I had come for an interview.'

Grace lowered herself onto a chair. 'We always

said you would leave school at Easter.'

'I know, Mum, but hear me out, will you? This woman – she had tightly permed hair and a big tummy like you wouldn't believe – she rattled off so many questions, I could hardly think straight. She looked such a sight, Mum.' Rita waved her arms and strutted about, mimicking the woman and making her mother smile, in spite of herself.

'What sort of questions?'

'Was I punctual, did I have a clean bill of health, did I have clean habits, was I teachable and how would I treat a difficult customer. By the time I cottoned on to what was happening, Mum, I felt too embarrassed to say anything. So I ended up being marched up to the ladies' fashion department.'

By this time, Grace was laughing.

'It's so different now,' Rita went on. 'There's no trace of the fire and it looks really classy.'

The whole town had been stunned by the fire which ripped through Hubbard's in the early hours of Wednesday 22nd August. The upper floors had been totally gutted and the damage below was extensive. The fire itself was put out in less than an hour but it took no less than twenty fire crews to do the job, some coming from as far away as Crawley. The family firm reopened the store in time for Christmas, just, and although they had paid their staff since the fire, it was rumoured that they were already short-staffed.

'I was only there five minutes when I was introduced to Miss Bridewell, the manageress,' Rita went on, her eyes dancing with excitement. '"Would you consider being a Saturday girl, Miss

Rogers?"' Rita mimicked her affected accent. '"The run up to Christmas can be hectic and you seem a very capable gel."'

Grace stopped laughing and put her hand to her mouth. Rita was a bright girl. She had passed the eleven-plus and made it to the grammar school and for that reason, Grace had wanted Rita do an extra year, but she would be sixteen in February. Was it time to let her go out to work?

'But what about your weekends at the Railway Café?'

Rita worked there every Saturday morning, clearing tables and helping with the washing up. The owners Salvatore and Liliana Semadini, Italians, had taken over in 1945. Before then it had always been a rather dingy place and not very clean but with Salvatore's cheerfully optimistic outlook, it had completely changed. Liliana was a brilliant cook who could make a little go a very long way.

'I'm sure they'll understand,' said Rita doggedly.

Her mother wasn't about to give up so easily. 'And then there's secretarial college? We had such plans…'

'Mum, they were your plans, not mine. Oh please let me go. This is an opportunity too good to miss. I like being around people. You know me, I like talking. If I was in a typing pool, I wouldn't be allowed to say a word to a soul all day.'

'But being able to type opens up all sorts of possibilities,' Grace insisted.

'Miss Bridewell said if I suit, I can start as a full-time shop assistant in January. January 5th.

It's a Monday.'

Grace couldn't think straight. This was a disappointment because from the moment they were born, she had such plans for her girls. The war had changed everything. There were such good opportunities for women in the jobs market now. She knew Bonnie had wanted to be a nursery nurse, and Grace had been happy with that, but now that the girl had gone, would she get her training? She couldn't do anything about Bonnie but she could do something about Rita. Grace knew that if Rita could get a secretarial post, she would never have the kind of worries about money that she had endured. Shop work was all well and good but it didn't pay very well.

Rita was pressing for an answer. 'So what do you say, Mum?'

There was no doubt that having Rita at work would be a godsend. Her money would make up the shortfall without Bonnie's wage. Grace was already behind on the coal money and if they had another winter like last year and had to cut down any more, they'd both freeze to death long before the spring came.

'Mum?'

'I still want you to learn to type,' Grace insisted.

'I can go to night classes.'

Grace made a big thing of giving in, but in truth she was relieved. She agreed to let Rita become a Saturday girl for the whole of December and to begin in the fashion department on January 5th.

Bonnie was as content as she could be under the

circumstances but she missed her home in Worthing and she missed her mother and Rita terribly. As she walked around the shops in Oxford Street on her afternoon off, she was missing her friend Dinah as well. How they would have loved trying on the dresses and taking tea in Lyons Corner House together.

Up until now, the full extent of bomb damage in the capital had eluded her. There had been several bombing incidents in Worthing but nothing on the scale she saw in London. Large areas were screened off but the obvious gap in the buildings told her straight away where a house or a shop was missing. Although it was strictly forbidden, the bombsites were swarming with boys playing war games and cowboys and Indians. In some areas, whole streets had been reduced to rubble. Shortages of building materials meant that rebuilding the nation's capital was a slow business.

Shortages of other commodities were acute as well. Women still found it necessary to queue for hours outside a butcher's or a grocer's and Bonnie was surprised to see that large areas of public parks were still given over to allotments. There were few cars on the streets either. Petrol rationing kept their numbers down to a bare minimum.

Bonnie was lonely and friendless but the money in her post office account was mounting up. She was careful not to spend a shilling more than she had to. Once her waistline started to expand it wouldn't be long before she'd have to dip into her savings in order to live. Soon she'd have to find a place where she could go to have the baby and then there was the thorny problem of what she would do after that. Where would she live? More importantly how could she take care of the baby and support them both?

When these things weren't swirling around in her head, Bonnie struggled with a terrible ache in her heart. Why, oh why hadn't her romance with George worked out? What had she done wrong? She couldn't ... wouldn't believe he was a rotter. Hadn't he told her time and again how much she meant to him? He'd made plans for his son from the moment she'd told him she was pregnant. She smiled fondly. He'd been so sure the baby was a boy.

'Of course it's a boy,' he'd said with a mixture of indignation and pride when she'd challenged his assumptions. 'That's my boy. In my family, the first one is always a boy.' And when she'd laughed, he'd kissed her until she was breathless.

It was quite ridiculous but the thing she worried about most of all was the locket George had given her. It was her first real present and when he had given it to her, George had declared his undying love. It wasn't new. The catch looked a bit insecure but she was sure that if it did come off it would only fall into her bra. She must have dropped it in the factory because she remembered fingering it just outside the door.

When she'd arrived at the old factory on that last day in Worthing, it was deserted but the door leading to the street was open. She'd heard someone moving about in a room somewhere inside and had gone to see if it was George but she was met by a man in brown overalls she presumed was the caretaker. He had his back to her and didn't know she was there but she'd panicked and made a bolt for the entrance, tripped and dropped her bag.

She was just by the door when he spotted her and shouted. She'd been so anxious to get away she'd just stuffed everything in her bag and run. The locket must have been lost then. If only she had stopped and turned around for a minute, she might have seen it on the ground. She missed it very much. Apart from the baby, it was the only thing she had to remember George by.

To ease her anguish, Bonnie began to write letters to the address in Pavilion Road. She didn't post all of them, but every chance she got she told George about her day. Of the three or four that she did post, she wrote her address at the top of the page and begged him to let her know how he was. Through her tears, she promised not to make any demands on him. She only needed to know that he was alive and well. She did her best to make the letters upbeat. He mustn't know how miserable she was. Once the envelope was sealed, she put her name and address on the back so that Mrs Kerr could get in touch with her and tell her if George was ill or something. Sometimes Bonnie was so miserable she thought she was losing her mind with grief but there was something within her that wanted the whole world to know how much she cared for him.

She did make contact with someone – Miss Reeves. Bonnie had remembered seeing an advertisement in the local paper with a box number for replies. That gave her the idea of going to the post office and asking about it. Bonnie discovered that, for a small rental fee, she could have her own box number with a key in the local branch. It was an ideal way of keeping in touch without anyone knowing where she lived. She reasoned that she had upset her mother enough so she would not worry her again but she was desperate for news of her and her sister. Miss Reeves was the obvious choice. At Sunday school she had made much of honesty and being trustworthy, so Bonnie wrote to her, asking for information about her family. In her letter, she explained that she could not, for very personal reasons, contact them herself, and asked Miss Reeves to send her news of her mother and sister.

Bonnie did her level best to stop thinking about George all the time but the bittersweet memories kept slipping through the crevices of her mind. She was careful not to let Richard or Lady Brayfield see her upset, but night after night her pillow was wet with tears.

Richard turned out to be a boy with a real thirst for knowledge. After a cautious beginning, he and Bonnie quickly became friends. She did her best to keep him occupied whenever he was in the house. After a while, even she could see that Lady Brayfield was less stressed with life. It seemed that if the boy was happy, everyone else was happy. The whole household was more relaxed.

Lady Brayfield visited her daughter two or three times a week.

'She's looking better all the time,' she confided in Bonnie, and nothing more was said about Kenya.

Bonnie was more or less left to her own devices. So long as Richard was happy, Lady Brayfield left them to it. Richard had a fairly full timetable. Bonnie made sure he ate a good breakfast and then they walked to the prep school where he was a dayboy. He was an average student but under Bonnie's tuition, or perhaps it was her encouragement that helped him go that extra mile, his grades began to show a marked improvement. Whenever she could, Bonnie took Richard to see the sights of London. They would walk around Trafalgar Square, or go up to Buckingham Palace. Richard's favourite place in the whole world was the British Museum. He loved looking at the fossils and stuffed animals in cases and gradually his enthusiasm sparked a similar interest in Bonnie.

Back in the town house, she taught him to play whist and patience while he taught her the rudiments of chess. He beat her every time (which he loved) but gradually she got the hang of it. In the evenings, when he'd finished his homework, they would read together, do jigsaws or make Meccano models. Bonnie wasn't so good at the model making, but it gave Richard a real sense of achievement to be able to show an adult what to do. He never talked about his father but at night as he knelt by his bed, he always prayed for his mother.

'God bless Mummy and please help her to get better. I miss her very much but I pray she won't miss me and be unhappy.'

His prayer never failed to bring a tear to Bonnie's eye. What was her own mother doing now? With Christmas only three weeks away, she'd be sorting out the Thrift Club. It was only a small thing but it made such a big difference to her neighbours. Her mother was always thinking of others. Bonnie was proud of her and longed to give her a hug and tell her so. She missed her so much and the small house where they lived had taken on a romantic rose-coloured hue in her memories. Bonnie forgot about the lack of privacy, the freezing cold bedrooms and the fact that she had to wash in the scullery. All she remembered was the fun and laughter she, Rita and Mum shared together.

As she tucked Richard into his bed, she was thinking about the singsongs they'd had around the piano. That piano was her mother's pride and joy, a present from Dad when they were young. Mum was a good pianist and she could pick up a tune in no time. Her father always said she could have been a concert pianist but Mum would push his arm playfully and say, 'Get away with you, you daft 'apeth.'

Bonnie's voice cracked slightly as she said, 'Goodnight, Richard,' but the boy didn't notice. Turning over he snuggled down under his eiderdown with a sleepy, ''Night.'

Bonnie's evenings were her own. If she had no socks to darn (even the wealthy darned their socks it seemed) Bonnie could sit with Dora and Cook in the little parlour and listen to the radio or she could spend time in her own room, knitting bootees and matinee jackets for the baby.

Cook and Dora had worked for Lady Brayfield for years. They didn't talk a lot but it didn't take Bonnie long to realise that life hadn't been kind to them. Dora was roughly the same age as Lady Brayfield. They had played together as children.

'My mother worked in the big 'ouse,' Dora told her with pride. 'She cleaned the master's rooms. Lady Brayfield says she were the best cleaner they ever 'ad.'

When she was sixteen, Dora had fallen for a smooth-talking man and been 'put in the family way' as Cook put it. Her baby was stillborn and Dora was so upset she had been declared mentally unstable and put into an institution. It took Lady Brayfield more than twenty years to get her out. The years of incarceration had left Dora deeply scarred. She was a slave to routine and became upset at any deviation but she was a hard worker. Grey-haired, even though she couldn't be more than forty, Dora was a heavy woman with square hard-working hands.

If Dora was chunky, Cook was dainty. Standing at less than five foot tall, Cook was reluctant to even tell anyone her name. She was an intelligent woman but she found socialising difficult. Bonnie had no idea what had happened to Cook but a chance remark from Lady Brayfield made her wonder if Cook had been the victim of child cruelty. The pair of them were quite content to live together as friends, supporting each other and devoting themselves to the care of the woman who had rescued them and given them their lives back again. They never intruded on Bonnie's privacy but they were welcoming whenever she wanted to share her off duty time with them.

But tonight Bonnie was in no mood for company. As she climbed the stairs to her room, Lady Brayfield called her downstairs into her sitting room. Bonnie's heart began to beat faster as Lady Brayfield closed the door behind them.

'Bonnie, I haven't been disappointed since you came here,' she began. 'But the time has come... You cannot stay here in your condition.'

Bonnie nodded miserably.

'Although you hardly show at the moment, I think you will agree that we must act before Richard has the slightest idea that you may be pregnant. Have you had morning sickness?'

Bonnie shook her head. 'That finished long before I came.'

'Have you said anything to Dora and Cook?'

Bonnie shook her head.

'When you came I proposed that you might stay until the end of January,' Lady Brayfield continued, 'but I overheard Dora mentioning to Cook that she thought you might be in the family way. They had no idea I was there, or I am sure they wouldn't have said it. However, it's left me wondering if you've said anything.'

'No, Madam,' cried Bonnie. 'Honestly I haven't.'

Lady Brayfield looked thoughtful.

'I shall start looking for somewhere to live straight away,' Bonnie said quickly. She was struggling with her emotions. She would be sad to leave this house and her generous employer, but she had no wish to cause any embarrassment.

'Have you any idea what you would like to do?'

Bonnie smiled wistfully. 'I always wanted to look after children,' she said, 'but it's hard to imagine how I could with my own baby to look after.' Her eyes were brimming with tears and she willed them not to fall. 'I would like to try and keep the baby but if I can't, I'll have to let him go for adoption.'

'It's not widely known,' Lady Brayfield said softly, 'but the government has made provision for single women to keep their babies. Would you like me to make some enquiries?'

Bonnie's face lit up. 'Would that mean I could keep my baby?'

'It won't be easy,' said Lady Brayfield. 'You'll have to find somewhere to live and you'll probably have to run the gauntlet when it comes to mean-spirited judgemental moralists.'

'I don't care what people think,' Bonnie said fiercely. 'I made an honest mistake.'

'Perhaps it might be better to pretend you had a husband who was killed.'

Bonnie looked thoughtful. Eventually she said, 'I hate lies. My mother always said a liar had to have a good memory.'

'Your mother sounds like a remarkable woman,' Lady Brayfield remarked. 'Bonnie, are you sure that you couldn't go back home?'

'No,' said Bonnie.

'If it's a question of the train fare...'

'It's not that. It's the shame. I could never go home and shame my mother.' She stood to leave.

'Then I shall make some enquiries.'

'May I ask one thing?' Bonnie asked cautiously.

Lady Brayfield held her gaze.

'May I ask why you are helping me like this?'

'You remind me of someone I once knew,' said

Lady Brayfield turning towards the drinks cabinet. Keeping her back to Bonnie, she reached for the sherry and Bonnie knew she would not be drawn further.

As Bonnie opened the sitting room door she hesitated.

'Is there something else, Bonnie?'

'Thank you,' she said, and the two women smiled.

'By the way,' Bonnie reminded her, 'I'm taking Richard to buy some Christmas presents. We plan to go to Selfridges after school.'

Lady Brayfield nodded. 'Does he have enough money?'

'He's saved almost £5 of his own pocket money,' said Bonnie closing the door softly.

As she walked upstairs, it occurred to her that she would have to use some of her precious savings to buy presents for Lady Brayfield, Richard, Dora and Cook. She groaned inwardly but the moment the thought skittered through her mind, she was eaten up with guilt. How could she resent buying gifts for the very people who had been so kind to her? Wasn't giving to others what Christmas was all about?

When the Christmas cards started to arrive at the house, Bonnie decided that she would at least send a card to her mother and sister. Woolworth's had single cards, and she'd bought one. She didn't have to put her address on it and even if her mother saw the London postmark, London was a very big place.

Alone in her room, Bonnie got the card out again but she couldn't think what to write inside.

Was it wise to rake up all those memories? Her mother would most likely have settled back down to normal life. What right had she to upset her again? How different everything had been last Christmas when she and Rita had put up the decorations together. They hadn't been up to much. The same things had been up and down for all the Christmases Bonnie could remember. 'I'll get you some new ones next year, Mum,' she'd promised.

'Get some pretty ones with plenty of glitter,' Rita had said.

A lump formed in Bonnie's throat. She wouldn't be keeping her promise and she wouldn't see the old ones going up either. Sick at heart, Bonnie wrote a short note inside, addressed the envelope and stuck on a stamp, but she put the Christmas card in a drawer.

Six

As a Saturday girl, it was left to Rita to put the dresses back on hangers in the department once the customers had tried them on. It was also her responsibility to make sure each customer was given a chiffon scarf to put over her face so that she didn't get powder or lipstick on the dresses. Most of Hubbard's clients were happy to comply with the rule but occasionally she would get a complaint. Miss Bridewell usually handled that, and although she was politeness itself, somehow the customer knew not to argue with her if she wanted to try the dress on.

As well as Miss Bridewell, there were three other girls in the department: Sonja, a petite brunette with very high heels; Susan, a rather timid girl with bitten-down nails who seemed terrified of Miss Bridewell; and Dinah Chamberlain. Dinah was a little older than the others. She had been Bonnie's best friend when she worked at Hubbard's. She worked as the mannequin and spent all day modelling the clothes. She only came back into the department when she wanted to change her outfit for something else.

At the first opportunity, Rita was determined to talk to the girls about her sister. It was now December 6th, a whole month since Bonnie had left home. She still hadn't told her mother about George but then what was there to tell? Bonnie had been frugal with the details. Rita hadn't even known his last name and who knows, perhaps they had broken up anyway and Bonnie had left Worthing to get away from him. She told herself not to worry but in truth she was as worried as her mother. If anyone was likely to know Bonnie's plans, it would be one of the girls at work. Rita found her opportunity to talk about her sister when she was called into one of the cubicles.

'I remember her,' said Sonja. 'I was downstairs in the glove department when she worked here. She was going to London, wasn't she?'

They were helping Dinah out of a charcoal grey wrap-over coat with big shoulders which was nipped in at the waist.

The New Look from Paris had swept the country. After years of 'make do and mend', Dior had been extravagant with material. Although expensive, Hubbard's wasn't up to Dior standards but they were a highly fashionable store. Rita loved the flowing lines and small-waisted dresses and jackets. It was obvious that Dinah loved wearing them too.

Dinah would stroll around the store carrying a card with a number on it. She frequented the restaurant where shoppers met their friends for morning coffee or afternoon tea and lingered if she thought a customer was especially interested in what she was wearing. When she got back to the fashion department, the customer would only have to remember the number on the card Dinah was carrying for Miss Bridewell to know exactly which outfit she had admired.

It was Rita's job to put the items back on display as soon as possible in case a customer had followed Dinah back to the dress department and wanted to try it on.

'I can't believe my sister went so far on her own,' said Rita, choosing her words carefully. She folded Dinah's long sage green gloves and put the matching hat back into its hatbox.

'I heard she was going off to be with a man friend,' Susan said, holding up Dinah's next ensemble, a halterneck evening dress in the palest shade of yellow.

As she stuffed the felt hat with tissue paper, Rita's heart leapt. So Bonnie *had* been planning to run away with George.

'Georgie Porgie pudding and pie, kissed the

girls and made them cry...' Susan's chant was cut short when Dinah dug her in the ribs.

Rita hardly noticed. Her thoughts were back with that suitcase under the stairs at Mrs Kerr's house. Why hadn't George come back for it?

'Is Bonnie doing all right then?'

Rita wished she'd persuaded Mrs Kerr to open his suitcase. Should she go back there?

'Rita?'

She looked up sharply. The other girls had been called away to serve two matronly women and she was left alone with Dinah. The older girl was looking intently at her. 'How is Bonnie? I was surprised that she went without a word to anyone. We were pretty good friends when she was here. Did she tell you about me?'

'I think so,' she said absently.

'She promised to write,' said Dinah. 'Can you help me with the buttons at the back?'

Rita wiped her hands on the side of her own dress and walked behind Dinah's back. There were at least ten material-covered buttons. How on earth anyone was expected to get into this dress without help was beyond her. Dinah shuddered slightly as Rita began. 'Sorry,' she said. 'Cold hands.'

'She's very brave going all that way,' said Dinah, patting her hair and pushing in a stray pin. She wore it swept back with a mass of loose curls high on her head.

Rita nodded. She hadn't really thought about it but London was miles away, wasn't it. Fifty at least.

'Just think of all that lovely sunshine,' Dinah

sighed. 'Blue skies and lovely beaches. All white sand, you know.'

All buttoned up, she turned to look at herself in the mirror. Rita gave her a puzzled look. 'In London?'

'No ... South Africa,' Dinah chuckled. 'That's where she was going,' and seeing Rita's horrified expression she added, 'I'm sorry, Rita. Didn't you know?'

As she left the cubicle, the mannequin obviously had no idea of the effect her words had had on Rita. South Africa? Was Bonnie really going all that way with George? Rita felt sick. She couldn't let on to Mum or she'd be frantic with worry. South Africa? It might as well be the far side of the moon. This bit of news had spoiled her first day. It was hard to shake off the deep foreboding and not even collecting her first ever wage packet at the end of the day could make up for it. Her sister had walked out of her life and gone to a rich man's paradise without a backward glance at the family who loved her so much. Rita bristled with anger. How could Bonnie be so selfish? How could she have put them through all this?

The following Friday afternoon, Snowy knocked on the door at three o'clock sharp. When she walked in, Grace was putting the tin bath in front of the range.

'I picked this up on the mat,' said Snowy coming right in. She handed Grace an envelope. Grace tore it open and pulled out a Christmas card. 'It's from my mother,' she said, looking inside.

'How is your mother?' asked Snowy.

'Fine,' said Grace. 'Getting older.' She wiped around the inside of the bath with a damp cloth. A spider scurried away from the cloth but got swept up in it anyway. 'Don't mind me,' Grace went on. 'Rita wants a bath after tea.'

Outside in the scullery, the water in the big boiler was heating up nicely. Grace had cleared the kitchen table but she had left two cups and saucers and one of her legendary 'Cut and Come Again' cakes in the middle.

'Thanks a lot for doing this, Snowy,' she said taking the older woman's coat.

'Gives me something to do,' said Snowy waving her hand dismissively.

'Have you heard from your Kate yet?' Grace was pouring a little hot water into the teapot before swirling it around to warm it. She tipped the water into the sink and reached up for the tea caddy.

Snowy shook her head. 'I don't suppose I will until she reaches Adelaide.'

'It's a long way,' Grace sympathised.

Grace knew that her friend struggled with the fact that her daughter was halfway across the world and now that Bonnie was gone, she had some vague idea how Snowy must feel.

'What are you doing for Christmas?' said Grace passing a cup towards her.

'I asked the King if he could put me up but the miserable old bugger said he was off to Sandringham,' Snowy shrugged.

'Good,' said Grace, 'then you're coming here.'

'No, no,' Snowy protested. 'I couldn't put you out.'

'Don't be daft,' said Grace. 'There'll only be

Rita and me. I was thinking of inviting one or two of the other neighbours in for a bit of a singsong like we did in the war years.'

'If I come,' said Snowy, 'you must allow me to contribute something.'

'There's no need.'

'I insist.'

They gave each other a mutual smile of understanding and carried on sipping their tea. As soon as they'd eaten some cake, Grace brought out the books.

She had been a meticulous bookkeeper, recording the date and amount of money each saver had given her and then the date on which it was banked. Together they counted it out plus the interest accrued since it had been in the post office. Each payout was put into a small envelope with the saver's name on it. It took more than an hour to get everything done properly.

'Aren't you scared with all this money in the house?' said Snowy as they finished.

At that very moment the door opened and a man walked in. He was short and thickset with a boxer's nose and cauliflower ears. Snowy leapt to her feet with a small cry, her chair scraping on the wooden floor.

Grace put up her hand in caution. 'It's all right,' she said with a short laugh. 'You've just been saying I need protection. This is my bodyguard, Charlie Hanson.'

A look of relief flooded Snowy's face and the man in question smiled, flashing a gold tooth. 'Evening.'

'I should have told you he was coming,' Grace

went on. She reached for another cup and saucer and poured Charlie some tea. Charlie pulled up a chair, sat down and began rubbing his hands vigorously to get some warmth back into them.

'Charlie used to be a friend of Michael's,' Grace said by way of explanation. 'We'll be going out with the packets shortly. I've asked him to stay for a bite of tea. Would you like some too?'

Snowy shook her head. 'I'd better be getting back.'

'Why?' Grace persisted. 'You've got nothing to go back for.'

Snowy opened her mouth to say something but Grace was already putting a knife and fork in front of her.

'Oh all right,' Snowy laughed, 'but only a little. You've already given me a piece of cake.'

Rita came in shortly after. As soon as they'd finished their meagre portions of shepherd's pie, Grace got ready to set off on her rounds with the Thrift Club money. Rita was glad her mother was going with Uncle Charlie Hanson, and said so.

'My pleasure,' said Charlie giving her a wink.

Charlie had plainly enjoyed himself being in a room full of women. He flattered and teased them, and they played along with him.

'I'd best be on my way,' said Snowy, fishing in her coat pocket for her torch. 'See you on Monday, Grace.'

'Take care,' said Grace.

'I could do with a big strong man like Charlie to look out for me on the way home,' said Snowy.

'Can't be in two places at once,' said Charlie with a hint of regret in his voice.

As soon as Snowy had gone home, Grace put her coat on and wrapped her scarf around her neck tightly. It was very cold outside. 'Make sure you lock the door after me,' she said to Rita. 'Especially before you get in the bath.'

'Yes, Mum.'

'And mind you don't scald yourself with that water.'

'Yes, Mum. Stop worrying. I'll be fine.'

She waited on the doorstep until she heard Rita turn the key in the lock and then she and Charlie set off. To minimise the possibility of being attacked, the money was in a satchel bag with a strap which went over Grace's shoulder. The bag itself had a sturdy buckle on the front of it. Grace trusted her neighbours but she was walking around with a large sum of money and in these hard times, it might be difficult for some to resist temptation. A lone woman would be an easy target, which was why she had asked Charlie to come along with her. As it was, she tried to make sure she put the money into the hands of the actual women who had entrusted her with their meagre savings. Sometimes their husbands would lie in wait in the front garden or by the gate and demand the money before she reached the house, but Grace knew if she gave it to them, most of it would disappear down the pub long before their wives saw a penny.

'I have to do what the law says,' she would tell them. 'Your wife paid it in and it's her money.'

'What belongs to the wife belongs to me!'

'Her name is on the book, so I have to pay it to her.'

Uncle Charlie was a bodybuilder, as broad as he was tall. He wasn't a relative but the kids called him Uncle when they were young and it had stuck. Grace thought he was a bit lonely so as a woman on her own she had to be very careful not to give him the wrong impression, but there were times, such as now, when he was useful to know. Once Uncle Charlie squared up to a man, any man, there was no argument. Of course, Grace was no fool. She knew as soon as she and Charlie had gone the wife would probably be beaten into submission; but if the woman had any sense, she would manage to squirrel away a fair bit of the money in her apron pocket while the man saw Grace to the door.

The round was uneventful enough but every time someone said, 'How's your Bonnie getting on?' it cut Grace like a knife. The truth was, she hadn't a clue. Every day she looked for a letter to no avail. She'd had a few Christmas cards, but nothing from Bonnie. She had bought one herself in case Bonnie wrote, but with no address to send it to, what could she do?

As she made her way through Station Approach, someone called Charlie's name.

Grace turned in time to see him conversing with a man in the shadows. All at once, the man took a swing at him and Charlie retaliated. At the same moment, someone grabbed her from behind and spun her round. The sudden move took Grace completely by surprise and she stumbled. The man raised his boot to kick her.

'Oi!' Someone near the corner of the street shouted at the top of his voice.

The robber pushed her violently and Grace felt herself falling. The sound of running feet behind him in the silent street obviously focused the robber's mind. He made a grab for the moneybag looped over her head and across her chest, banging her head against the wall. The blow nearly knocked her senseless but even as she hit the ground, Grace knew the moneybag was gone.

Seven

Rita lay on her back with the water touching her shoulders. The tin bath was cramped and the edges a bit cold but it was warm in the kitchen. The fire in the range let out a fairly good heat and her clean clothes were hanging on the clothes horse for when she got out.

She was brooding. Brooding on her sister's disappearance and the unfairness of life. The more she thought about it the less she understood it. Bonnie often talked about George and Rita knew their romance was to be kept a secret but all that stuff about South Africa? Why did that have to be a secret anyway? She should tell Mum really. In fact, now that she thought about it, Rita wished she had told her mother about George in the first place. If she told her now, she would be angry that Rita had kept Bonnie's secret. She soaped the flannel with Lux and then her arm. Mum was reasonable enough. She would have been a bit upset but if Bonnie was a married woman she would never have stopped her going anywhere with her husband.

Mum would never allow any hanky-panky, as Mrs Kerr had called it, but Bonnie was a respectable girl. As they'd lain in their beds at night, she and her sister had talked about their wedding night often enough. Bonnie always said you should save yourself for the man you loved. She said Mum had done it and she would too.

'Anyway,' she told Rita, 'if you give yourself to a boy, he won't respect you and you'll get a reputation for being flighty.'

'I shall save myself for my husband too,' Rita had said stoutly.

She had read a letter on the problems page in *Woman* magazine just the other day. A reader was worried that her fiancé wanted her to go too far. Should she give in to him or wait until her wedding day? In the reply the girl had been advised to remain a virgin. In truth Rita had no real idea what happened on the wedding night but she knew that when a man and a woman got married sooner or later there was a baby. What exactly a man did was a mystery. At school, they had biology lessons but the life cycle of a frog wasn't much help.

Life threw some very unkind things at you. It had come as a shock when her periods started. When Mum explained that this sort of thing was nothing to worry about, and that it happened to every girl, she had talked a lot about the Goodmans' dog.

'Poppet goes into season twice a year,' Mum said. 'Well, it's the same for girls. When girls have their period, it's a bit like going into season.'

'But why?' Rita wondered.

'Your body is getting ready to have a baby.'

Rita had been appalled. 'But I'm only thirteen,' she'd cried. 'I'm not ready to have a baby yet!'

'Of course not, silly,' her mother had laughed. 'You have to get married first.'

Rita was in for another shock a month later. Poppet went into season twice a year but it seemed that girls had their period, now re-named 'country cousins', every month. Not only that, but Mum bought her a regular supply of Velena pads with loops which she had to fix onto a special belt. Twice a day, she had to wrap the used ones in newspaper and Mum burned them in the range. It was horrible. She was very nearly sixteen with three years of preparing her body for a baby behind her and she still didn't know exactly how you got one. Rita swirled the flannel over her flat stomach. Dinah said she had a nice figure but Rita wished her breasts were a bit bigger.

Someone tried the door latch and Rita sat up.

'Who's there?'

Her heart was bumping. Thank goodness Mum had told her to lock the door. She glanced at the clock on the mantelpiece. It was much too early for Mum to come back – she'd only been gone for a half an hour – and besides she had her key.

The door latch went up again. Rita stood up and grabbed a towel. 'Who is it?' she called, willing her voice not to quiver.

'It's me, Rita. Uncle Charlie. Open the door. Your mum's been hurt.'

Rita felt the panic rising in her chest. She

wanted to run and open the door but how could she, covered with only a threadbare towel which barely went round her? 'Just a minute.'

With no time to dry herself let alone get dressed she flew upstairs and pulled Mum's old dressing gown from behind the bedroom door.

When she opened the door, Rita had a shock. Uncle Charlie was doing his best to hold her mother upright but Grace was like a rag doll in his arms. Together they helped her inside and onto a chair.

'What happened?'

'We was robbed,' said Uncle Charlie. 'Some blighter distracted me and his mate snatched the bag.'

Grace moaned and Rita could see a big lump on her forehead. The skin was already going blue and her mother was trembling from head to toe.

'It's the shock,' said Uncle Charlie.

'Shall I get the doctor?' Rita asked anxiously.

'No,' said Grace. 'Yes,' said Uncle Charlie in unison.

'We can't afford it,' said Grace.

Uncle Charlie dampened the end of the tea towel and then he put it over the bruise. Rita was happy to let him do it. He was a second at boxing matches and he knew what to do with a bump. Over the top of her mother's head, he gave Rita the nod to go.

'Will you stay with her?' Rita mouthed.

Uncle Charlie nodded. 'Have you got any butter?'

Rita got the butter dish from inside the drop-down cupboard then, grabbing her clean clothes from the clothes horse in front of the range, she raced back upstairs to dress. A couple of minutes later she was back downstairs. Uncle Charlie was rubbing butter onto the huge egg which had formed on her mother's forehead. Rita grabbed her coat and ran.

When she got back with the doctor, Grace had been sick and Rita was told to fetch Constable Higgins. She ran down to Station Approach and the blue police box. There was a telephone on the side for the use of members of the public. It connected her straight to the police station in the centre of town. Rita explained that her mother had been attacked and robbed and after giving the sergeant her name and address, she was told to go back home and wait for a uniformed officer to attend.

When she got back home, the doctor had just completed a thorough examination of her mother. As soon as she saw her, Grace was angry that Rita had sent for him, but the doctor shook his head. 'You should be proud of her, Mrs Rogers,' he said. 'Head injuries can be very dangerous things. Fortunately, although you will probably have a very bad headache for a while, there is no lasting damage.'

Rita was so relieved she almost kissed him. Inside, she had been panicking. With her father dead and Bonnie gone, what would have happened to her if Mum had been seriously ill? For the first time in her life she'd realised just how fragile life was, how everything could change in an instant. She knew she was being selfish, but she resolved never to take her mother for granted again. Bonnie might have walked out on her but, from now on, Rita was going to be the best daughter in the world.

After telling Grace that an Aspro and bed rest was the best thing, the doctor left with his shilling and soon after a Constable Higgins stopped by and took statements.

'Who knew you were going on the round?' the constable asked. They were all sitting around the kitchen table.

'Everybody,' said Grace. 'They were expecting me.'

'And you started out from here at what time?'

Grace looked at Charlie and shrugged.

'About seven,' said Charlie.

The constable scribbled in his notebook. 'And the attack happened at about eight o'clock by Station Approach?'

'Yes,' said Grace. 'It's a good job Charlie suggested changing the route. If we had gone the usual way, they'd have got a lot more.'

Constable Higgins frowned. 'How d'you mean?'

'I usually go to the end of road and walk up to Station Approach and back by Teville Gate and then I do Tarring Road,' Grace explained. 'Charlie persuaded me to go the other way round.'

'Why did you do that, sir?' asked Constable Higgins accusingly.

'I thought she should vary the route,' Charlie shrugged. 'For safety's sake.'

'Good job you did,' said Grace. 'I heard someone shout just before the robber pushed me down.'

'Mr Warren,' said Constable Higgins. 'He's only

just moved into the shop on the corner. He's already made a statement.'

'I think I owe my life to him,' said Grace. 'I'm sure that man would have kicked me senseless if Mr Warren hadn't come running.'

'How much money are we talking about?' said the constable.

'About £50,' said Grace. 'I only had a few houses to go to. Mrs Oakley, the Parsons, Miss Reeves, Mrs Clements and Mary Minty. Between them they had saved about £7 each through the year. I'd have to look in the books to know exactly how much.'

'That's a lot of money,' said Constable Higgins giving her a disapproving stare.

'I know,' Grace sighed.

The constable pursed his lips. 'You'd be well advised to get everybody to come to you next time, Missus.'

'There won't be a next time,' said Grace bitterly. She leaned forward on the table and laid her head onto her arms.

'I think my mum needs to get to bed,' said Rita.

There was a shuffling of chairs and the men got up to go. By the time Uncle Charlie had left, Grace was crying.

'Does it really hurt that bad, Mum?'

'No, it's not that,' said her mother. 'It's the money. I've let all those poor people down.'

'I'm sure they'll understand, Mum.'

'They need that money, Rita,' said Grace. 'Whether they understand or not isn't the problem. I'll have to pay it all back. Dear Lord above, where am I going to get another £50 to replace it?'

Eight

Grace woke with a sore head. She lay for a while going over the events of the previous night. She should have waited and gone on the rounds in daylight but she hadn't wanted the money in the house overnight. The post office was open on Saturday morning so why hadn't she drawn the money first thing and done the round in the afternoon? And it would have been far more sensible to do what Constable Higgins had suggested and have everyone come to her. She could see now what a fool she had been.

She ran her tongue over her bottom lip. It felt funny. She climbed out of bed. The room was so cold she could see her own breath. She pulled the eiderdown off the bed and around her shoulders and looked at herself in the dressing table mirror. What a sight. Her right eye was as black as the ace of spades. Her forehead was like an artist's paint palette, a mixture of red graze and blue bruise with a hint of green and purple, although the egg-sized swelling had gone down. She had a graze at the corner of her mouth and her bottom lip, the cause of her discomfort, was slightly swollen. She looked as if she'd done ten rounds with Bruce Woodcock, the British and Empire heavyweight boxing champion. When she touched her forehead, it hurt like hell.

Grace lowered herself onto the bed again and

pulled the old eiderdown tight around her shoulders. Boy, was she stiff. She was supposed to go to the police station to make a proper statement but it was the last thing she wanted to do. Constable Higgins had been confident that they would catch the thief but they didn't hold out much hope of getting the money back. 'He'll have put most of it down his neck long before we catch up with him,' Higgins said bleakly.

Grace sighed. She would have to go round and see everyone, explain and apologise. She'd promise that no matter how long it took, they would get their money back ... not this Christmas but maybe in time for next. She shivered with cold but she wasn't ready to face the world just yet so she climbed back into bed and tried to work out how much money she could lay her hands on.

She had saved £6 12s 9d for herself plus the tiny bit of commission she took for running the club. She would use that, but what about the rest? She looked around the room. What could she sell? If only she hadn't used that brooch money on a fruitless trip to London. Still, she hadn't known it would lead to nothing when she'd set out, had she? It was worth a try, but what was left that was of any value now that she needed it? Answer: not much. Most of her furniture was years old. She'd only get pennies for it. The grandmother clock downstairs would have to go. It needed a proper professional clean but she still might get five pounds for that. There was Michael's cup. It would be hard to part with it, because apart from a couple of faded photographs, and his battered leather chair, it was her only link with him. She felt her throat tightening and her eyes pricking. Cyril Harper the rag-and-bone man and that man selling antiques only lived at the other end of the street from each other. Perhaps she could ask him about the chair but she couldn't let Michael's cup go.

But there was her piano. She might get £7 or £8 for that. Grace wiped her eyes with her hand and looked at her wedding ring. She twisted it but it wouldn't come over the knuckle. She suppressed a sob. Oh Michael...

There was a soft knock on the door. 'Cup of tea, Mum?'

'Thanks, love,' said Grace, dabbing her eyes with the sheet and pulling herself up the bed.

Rita put the tea on the bedside table. Her chin was quivering. 'Oh Mum...'

It was obvious from Rita's expression that she was worried about Grace's face. 'It looks worse than it feels,' she said.

'They could have killed you,' said Rita.

'But they didn't,' said Grace softly, 'so let's not worry about something that didn't happen, eh?'

Rita headed for the door. 'Do you want me to come to the station with you, Mum?'

'That would be nice. Are you sure you don't mind?'

'Of course not. You're my mother.'

Grace turned her head away. Rita sniffed loudly. 'I've raked the fire and got it going,' she said in a businesslike way. 'I've put your clothes to warm on the clothes horse.'

Grace managed a smile and Rita closed the door.

Once up and dressed, Grace wasted no time in going to the police station. She kept her headscarf loose around her face and walked with her head down in an effort to hide her bruises. The statement didn't take long.

'And you are certain of the time?' asked the inspector.

'Salvatore Semadini was washing the windows of the Railway Café,' said Grace. 'We passed the time of day.'

The inspector narrowed his eyes. 'You know him well?'

'My daughter does a Saturday morning job there,' said Grace. 'At least she did until a week or two ago.'

Salvatore had asked her when Rita was coming back but Grace had been so anxious to get the round done, she'd told him she couldn't stop. She remembered seeing the time on the big clock inside the café.

'Tell her we miss her,' Salvatore had called after her. 'Tell her to come for her Christmas box.'

'You and Liliana come over to our place on Christmas Day,' she'd called over her shoulder.

'Could he have followed you?' the inspector asked.

'Salvatore?' Grace gasped. 'I don't know what you're suggesting but he is as honest as the day is long. Besides I saw him go back into the shop with his bucket.'

After a rather tetchy interview, Grace and Rita caught the bus back. They were hardly back inside the door before Grace was getting ready to go back out again.

Rita was alarmed. 'The doctor said you should rest, Mum.'

'I've got to tell everyone what's happened,' said Grace.

By the time afternoon came, Grace was exhausted. Despite Rita's offer to tell her savers that their money was gone, Grace insisted that she do it herself. Rita knew how stubborn her mother could be, so rather than pick a fight, she decided to go with her.

'It's better coming from me,' Grace insisted and she was right. Once they saw the state of her, Grace was met by a mixture of alarm, concern and understanding rather than the hostility she'd dreaded. Given time, the bruises would fade, but the humiliation Grace felt as she begged forgiveness and asked for time to repay the money would take a lot longer to heal.

As the day wore on she leaned more heavily on Rita's arm. She was feeling weak but as soon as they got back home and had had a bite to eat, Grace said she was going to the Clifton Arms.

'Whatever do you want to go there for?' Rita's voice was shrill with anxiety. Her mother should be resting. All this rushing about was making her look really pale.

Grace didn't answer. She wanted to conserve what little energy she had for the landlord, Taffy Morgan, rather than wasting it on a futile argument. Her mind was made up. Taffy, it was rumoured, was looking for a piano.

Built around 1863, and named after the Clifton Suspension Bridge, the public house was frequented by the people of New Town, a development of small terraced houses which had been built in Clifton Road, way back in Victorian times. The name still stuck with the old timers in the town.

Grace had fond memories of the Clifton Arms. Before the war, in 1936, the Worthing and District Homing Pigeon Society had held their annual prize night in there and Michael, as winner for three years in a row, had won a silver cup outright.

The piano raised a healthy £6 10s, but it was a solemn pair who returned to the cold house late in the afternoon. Even with the sale of the piano, Grace still had a long way to find an awful lot more money to replace what the thief had taken, and from now on, there was little hope of raising more than pennies. She had nothing else of value.

Apart from Michael's cup. She looked up at the mantelpiece. It was good quality silver and the only engraving was on the plinth, which meant it could be used for something else. The cup had been her rock all through the war. Her security. How many times had she said, 'if things get really bad, we can always sell your father's cup', but they never had. Somehow, they'd pull through and Michael's pride and joy stayed where it was. She sighed. The time had come at last to let it go.

'Rita, go and get Mr Harper and then Mr Warren.'

Cyril Harper lived at the end of the street. He worked as a rag-and-bone man and kept his horse in a stable at the back of his little place and put it out to graze on a piece of waste ground between the houses. The children loved it and many a time, Bonnie and Rita had gone up there to stroke him and give him a carrot or an apple.

People said that beneath Cyril's shabby coat there beat the heart of a very rich man. When it came to buying, he had a reputation as a man who struck a very hard bargain.

'Good God, Missus,' said Cyril as he walked in the door. 'Whatever happened to you?'

Grace didn't elaborate. 'How much will you give me for the grandmother clock?' she said getting straight to the point.

Cyril umm-ed and ah-ed and scratched his head. 'Five pounds.'

'Done,' she said. Cyril looked surprised. He'd obviously expected some haggling.

She took the cup from the mantlepiece and put it into Cyril's hands. He always wore Ebenezer gloves; no one had ever seen him without them, winter or summer. Cyril ran his long fingers over the silver and then took an eyeglass out of his threadbare waistcoat pocket and examined the hallmark.

'Ten bob.'

Grace frowned. 'I want at least thirty.'

Cyril pulled a face. 'Twelve and six?'

'Mum,' Rita protested. They both knew it was worth far more than that.

'Rita, don't,' said Grace firmly. 'I have to. A pound. I can't let it go for less than a pound.'

Cyril turned the cup over in his hands, held it at arm's length as if he was checking to see if it was straight, held it up to the light and then set it down on the table in front of them. The only sound in the room was the ticking of the clock. He continued to stare at the cup in the nerve-racking silence for several minutes before saying, 'Fifteen bob and that's my last offer.'

Grace held out her hand and he shook it. Rita cried silent tears. Her mother picked up the cup one last time and kissed the inscription.

A sharp rap on the front door broke the charged atmosphere and when Rita opened the door Mr Warren came in. While Cyril left with his purchases, Grace thanked the newcomer for his help the previous evening.

'I'm sure I would have been seriously hurt if you hadn't have come along.'

Mr Warren waved away her gratitude. 'It was nothing. Anyone would have done it.' But they both knew he had been the saving of her.

When she finally got down to the business of selling Michael's battered leather chair, she was too choked up to remember to offer Mr Warren a cup of tea.

As he examined the chair, Grace realised she would get next to nothing for it. The stuffing was coming away under the seat. Even with all her thorough cleaning, she hadn't noticed that, and the leather was badly cracked on the arms. It was perfectly understandable. The chair had belonged to Michael, to his father and his father before that.

'I can offer you five pounds,' he said eventually. 'It will need a lot of work on it before I can sell it.'

Grace nodded stiffly and they shook hands. It was a firm shake and she saw the sympathy in his eyes.

‘One other thing,’ she said, her voice thick with emotion, ‘that chair belonged to my husband and I don’t want to see it go. Rita and me will go upstairs and then you can take it.’

Mr Warren’s expression didn’t change. He nodded.

They didn’t get up the stairs. Grace and Rita began to climb but then they sat together on the third stair. The stair door automatically closed slightly and they sat in the gloom with their arms around each other.

Rita cried softly into Grace’s shoulder. ‘Oh, Mum...’

‘It’s just a chair,’ said Grace, her voice tight and wavery. But of course it wasn’t just a chair. It really was their last link with Michael... Michael with his laughing eyes and his cheeky grin; Michael her lover and the father of her girls.

‘Has he gone yet?’

Rita wiped her eyes and listened. They heard the sound of coins rolling on the kitchen table and someone making a neat pile. Grace closed her eyes and leaned her head back in an effort to keep control of her emotions. Then it went very quiet.

‘Is he still there?’ Grace whispered.

Rita peered through the crack in the door and nodded her head.

Grace looked through the crack and he was still standing in the middle of the kitchen stroking his chin. ‘What on earth is he doing?’ she whispered.

All at once, the stair door opened and Mr Warren put his head round. All three of them jumped because he hadn’t expected them to be on the stair and they hadn't expected him to open the door.

Grace blew her nose with her hanky. She put the hanky up her sleeve, tugged at her dress, put her shoulders back and stood up with her head held high.

'I'm afraid I can't take the chair right now, Mrs Rogers,' said Mr Warren. He stepped back into the kitchen and Grace followed him. 'You see, I've been thinking about it and I just don't have enough room in the shop at the moment, so I think it best to leave it here.'

'But you will be collecting it,' said Grace uncertainly.

'Oh yes.' He walked to the front door and with his hand on the latch he paused. 'Something'll go right for you, Mrs Rogers,' he said softly. 'Better days will come. Your five pounds is on the table.'

Nine

The double gates of Holly Acres were shrouded in late afternoon fog. The house was almost invisible, as Lady Brayfield stepped out of the taxi which had brought her from the station. She paid the driver and told him to come back in an hour.

Holly Acres was a two-storey building, with black and white paintwork and a wide portico entrance. In the gathering gloom, she could see the lawns stretching away to the right with a single swing and a climbing frame in the distance. She rang the doorbell and after a few minutes a young girl in a shapeless grey dress opened the door. Lady Brayfield was politely asked to wait in the hallway. The sound of children's voices was coming from all parts of the house. Lady Brayfield played with the hair left exposed by her hat. The mist had made it damp and it clung to her forehead.

Harriet Bennett was surprised to see her visitor. Not many of her friends called at her place of work, especially not on a Sunday and so close to Christmas.

'Marion, how lovely to see you.' The two women embraced lightly. 'Let me take you to my living quarters.'

Lady Brayfield followed her through what seemed like a maze of corridors until at last, just beyond the kitchen and the laundry room, they stepped outside again into a small courtyard. Here the children's shrill voices, dulled by the closing of the back door, finally faded altogether.

'We live in a cottage over what was once the stables,' Harriet called over her shoulder. 'It's such a lovely setting here. Tommy and I are quite settled at last.'

Her friend, a trained nurse, had been imprisoned by the Japanese during the war. She and her husband had been in Singapore when they had overrun the whole area in 1942. Regarded as vital to the protection of the Empire's Commonwealth possessions in the Far East, the British military base had been upgraded in 1938. What no one had expected was that the Japanese high command would push up through the jungle and mangrove swamps of the Malay Peninsula, and with all the British defences pointing out to sea, there had been little chance of gaining the upper hand when they finally appeared.

The RAF had already lost nearly all its aircraft by the time the Japanese air force had attacked the airfields in December 1941. The British planners shifted their confidence to the battleship *Prince of Wales* and the battle cruiser *Repulse* but on December 10th both ships were sunk by repeated attacks from Japanese torpedo bombers. Even with these setbacks, morale was high and so was confidence. After all, the British, Indian and Australian troops led by Lieutenant General Arthur Percival numbered some 90,000 men, whereas the Japanese only had 65,000. In the final showdown, on January 31st 1942, Percival spread his men across the entire coastline of the island, a distance of some 70 miles. This was a disastrous mistake. He had grossly underestimated the strength of the Japanese and the British were soundly defeated.

The Japanese took 100,000 people prisoner in Singapore, including Tommy and Harriet Bennett. The pair spent the next three years interned less than five miles from each other, but never once in all that time did they meet. In fact, neither had any idea if the other was still alive. Harriet seldom spoke of the unspeakable horrors they had endured but the ravages to her body meant that she had lost the ability to have children.

When they returned to the UK, Tommy had been invalided out of the army, but the still relatively young Harriet had taken on the responsibility of this children's home near Kingston Upon Thames.

'Come in, come in.'

The flat itself was warm and cosy; Harriet had a flair for homemaking. She showed Lady Brayfield into a small sitting room with a cheerful fire in the hearth. There was a sofa and two deep armchairs covered in a floral chintz material and hand-embroidered scatter cushions. Lady Brayfield remarked how nice they were.

'I saw them in a magazine,' Harriet smiled.

The middle of the room was carpeted and the surrounds were deep oak-coloured wood. Her sideboard was covered with photographs of family and friends.

'Sit down, sit down,' Harriet said. 'I'll get us some tea.'

Four decades ago the women had been at boarding school together, sharing the same dorm. They had remained friends, a comfortable relationship which had not been altered by the war. Occasionally they met together in London for afternoon tea but this was the first time Lady Brayfield had been to Kingston.

'How's Tommy?'

Harriet was clattering away in the kitchen. 'Doing quite well,' she called. 'He spends a lot of time out of doors in the garden.' She reappeared in the doorway with a tray of cups and saucers. 'He can't bear to be confined, so he's become quite an expert gardener. He's quite content.'

Marion nodded. 'Doesn't he want to return to the diplomatic service?'

Harriet shook her head. 'Actually, he's thinking

of taking holy orders. You know, I think we're the happiest we've ever been. You must let me take you on a tour of the nursery before you leave. Our living companions are a lot smaller than we're used to but I don't think I would swap my life now for the heady existence we had before the war.'

Marion laughed. 'You certainly look well on it.'

Harriet went back into the kitchen and returned a few minutes later with the teapot. They made small talk, catching up with news of old friends, and Harriet sympathised with Marion over her daughter.

'On a more optimistic note,' Marion said, 'she may be allowed out of the nursing home for Christmas.'

'Oh Marion, that's wonderful.' She handed her friend a cup of tea and indicated the sugar bowl.

Lady Brayfield nodded. 'She'll have to go back Boxing Day, but it's a small step, isn't it?'

'It's a bloody big step,' Harriet enthused. 'Excuse my French. I can't imagine how you've coped.'

'Which brings me to the reason why I'm here,' she said. 'It would take me far too long to tell you exactly how it came about but I have found this wonderful Girl Friday.'

Harriet gave Marion her full attention as she told her about Bonnie. 'She's quite turned Richard around. He's polite, enthusiastic about his schoolwork and I sometimes hear him laughing again. He'll never be top drawer of course, but in a very short space of time, the girl has done wonders.'

'She sounds like a real gem,' smiled Harriet.

'You should hang on to her.'

'I wish I could,' said Marion. 'There's only one small problem … she's pregnant.'

'Ah,' said Harriet pausing with a homemade biscuit halfway to her mouth.

'And that's where you come in,' said Marion.

'Surely you're not suggesting I take her in?'

Lady Brayfield nodded. 'Hear me out, darling,' she said. 'You've always said you want to make a difference to those less fortunate than ourselves. This girl is capable and kind. She's made an error of judgement but she's contrite. I honestly believe she should be given a second chance.'

'Then let her give her baby up for adoption.'

'Adoption is all well and good, but I wonder what damage it does to both mother and child being separated. The maternal bond is very strong. If the war taught us anything, it taught us that a mother will go to any length to care for her child and so long as the child has its mother, it can face any deprivation with courage.'

Harriet looked thoughtful. Marion was right. She'd seen it for herself in those terrible camps. She sat back in her chair. 'When is the baby due?'

'April.'

'Tell her to come to me then and I'll see what I can do.'

Lady Brayfield looked pensive. 'Darling, if we're going to do this, I think we need a better commitment than that.'

'I'm not sure the council will allow it,' Harriet frowned. 'Who is going to pay for the upkeep of the child?'

'I've already looked into that,' said Marion undaunted. 'There's a government allowance she can apply for and if you deduct her board and lodging and her child care from her salary, I don't see why she shouldn't live on the premises with her child.'

Harriet opened her mouth but her friend raised her hand and continued. 'Why shouldn't an unmarried mother take full responsibility for her child? Think of it, Harriet. We could be starting a new era of responsible parenting. These girls have their babies and someone else takes the responsibility. If girls had to face up to their responsibility, I'm sure there would be fewer illegitimate births. And besides, what could be more natural than keeping a child with its birth mother?'

Her friend looked thoughtful. 'It won't be easy,' she said. 'How will she find time to care for the baby and work at the same time?'

'I'm sure you could come to some sort of mutual agreement,' said Marion. 'This is a nursery, for heaven's sake.'

Harriet looked thoughtful. 'I can foresee problems further down the line as well,' she said. 'The girl will favour her child above the others. It's only natural.'

'Harriet, I remember some of what you told me about life at the camps,' said Marion. 'I admired the way you set down ground rules and everyone adhered to them. This girl is so desperate to keep her baby, I'm sure she will co-operate with whatever you deem as necessary.'

'Well, you've certainly taken the wind out of my sails,' said Harriet shaking her head. 'I've never heard of such a thing.'

'I can't say I have,' Marion smiled. 'Exciting, isn't it?'

Harriet gave her a slow smile. 'I suppose it is.'

'Good,' said Marion setting down her cup and saucer decisively. 'Then that's settled.'

'Hang on a minute,' Harriet protested. 'I still have to persuade the council yet.'

'I'm sure you'll do an admirable job,' smiled Marion.

'It won't be easy,' Harriet cautioned.

'Talk to them about the cost,' said Marion. 'They love the idea of saving money. Tell them that by the time you've deducted everything, they'll be getting a top-class worker for half the price.'

'You're incorrigible,' Harriet grinned. 'We should have more people like you in government.'

'Whatever for?' said Marion. 'We women already rule the world.'

Ten

The girls at work were horrified when they saw the state of Grace's face on Monday morning. The black eye was beginning to fade and the place where her head had hit the floor was almost back to normal but for some reason her cheek was still quite blue and puffy. They wanted to know what had happened and when she gave them a brief outline of events, they showered her with concern. Snowy was particularly upset.

'I had a bad feeling about you walking around with all that money,' she said. 'I should have said something.'

'I wouldn't have listened,' said Grace honestly. 'I just wanted the money out of the house and into the hands of those who had saved it.'

Once they began their work on the production line, talking was almost impossible over the noise of the machines and Grace certainly didn't want to shout her business to the rooftops. She worked slowly and steadily until their mid-morning break.

'I've got to find a way of getting extra money,' she confided in Snowy. 'Any ideas?'

'None,' Snowy said, 'but if you think of something, let me know. I could do with a bob or two myself.' But no sooner were the words were out of her mouth than she realised Grace was serious. 'You're not thinking of paying them out of your own pocket, are you?'

'I'll have to.'

'No one expects you to,' said Snowy. 'What happened wasn't your fault. That's life.'

'I have to,' Grace repeated.

They sat in silence for a few minutes then Snowy said, 'Can you sell something?'

'The piano's gone and the clock. I had saved a bit of money myself, that can go, and Cyril Harper gave me fifteen bob for Michael's cup.' Grace related the story and Snowy listened wide-eyed with amazement.

'So how much have you got altogether?'

'Twenty-three pounds, seventeen and nine-pence,' said Grace. 'I still need twenty six pounds two shillings and thruppence.'

'Ouch,' said Snowy. 'I've no idea where you could get that kind of money in a hurry.' She thought for a minute. 'Have you asked Taffy Morgan if he needs somebody to play the piano?'

'I think he's already got someone,' said Grace.

'Surely not seven nights a week,' Snowy suggested. 'The fella must have a night off.'

'I'm not sure Taffy would like the idea of a woman playing in a pub but I suppose it's worth a try,' Grace sighed.

'Look here,' said Snowy. 'As you know, I've been making dollies for Christmas.' She had come to the factory last October with a sweet little rag dolly she'd made out of an old pair of stockings and some underwear. She intended to keep it for when her Kate had a child but the girls were so taken with it they pressured her to make dollies for them. She had ended up with a fair-sized order for Christmas. 'I only made them out of scraps. They didn't cost me a penny but everybody paid me. It's not much, but you are welcome to it.'

Grace's eyes pricked with tears. 'Oh Snowy, you are kind but I can't.' She squeezed Snowy's hand. 'You're a real pal.'

Snowy's cheeks flushed. 'Get on with you.'

Norah Fox, the supervisor, blew her whistle and the women went back to the production line. As they stood to go, she said, 'The boss wants to see you in his office, Grace.'

Grace stiffened. 'What for?'

Norah shrugged.

Grace glanced anxiously around at her workmates. He can't do anything here, she thought.

Not with everyone else around. All the same she dreaded the thought of being alone in the same room as him.

Norris Finley's office was up the stairs and along a metal staircase going along the factory wall. As she made her way along, Grace was aware of every eye following her. She knocked on the door and entered.

Norris was sitting behind his desk, on the telephone. He motioned for her to take a seat and finished his call before turning his attention to her.

'Good God, Grace,' he exclaimed as he put the receiver down, 'whatever happened?'

Grace relayed the now familiar story and he regaled her with questions. 'Have you had a doctor look at that face?' She nodded. 'Do you need time off to recover?' She shook her head. 'Have they caught the blighter yet?' Again she shook her head. 'Is there anything I can do for you?'

Grace was poised to shake her head again when a thought crossed her mind. 'Can you give me some overtime? I want to pay the people back.'

'Whatever for?' he said, his voice rising. 'You don't owe them anything. It wasn't your fault.'

'They saved long and hard for that money,' said Grace. 'I've sold some things and I've got nearly twenty-four quid but I still need a lot more.'

'How much?' he said faintly.

'Twenty-six, twenty-seven quid.'

'It would take you months and months to pay them back even with overtime,' he said.

Grace nodded. 'I know, and they've promised they'll wait. I feel badly enough about the miserable Christmas they'll all be having this year.

Don't you see? I have to get their money back.'

Norris was staring so hard she was beginning to feel embarrassed, when all at once he stood up and went to the safe at the back of the office. After turning the dial, he fiddled around inside for several minutes then stood up saying, 'Grace, I want you to have this.'

When he stood up, he had a wad of notes in his hand. Grace rose to her feet. 'Oh no, Mr Finley, I can't. It's very kind but I can't.'

He counted and held out thirty pounds. 'Take it, Grace. For old times' sake. Look, I'm really sorry about the other day. I don't know what got into me. I was way out of line and I'm sorry.'

She hesitated.

'You don't want this to spoil Rita's Christmas, do you?' He waved the notes in her face. 'I'm sure she's upset enough about her sister running off like that. Take this and enjoy the holiday.'

Grace was puzzled. Norris wasn't known for his generosity. If he gave something there was always a catch. What was the real motive behind this? She hated herself for being so churlish but she knew him too well. She shook her head again. 'It's very kind of you but I can't. If you would just give me some overtime...'

'So those people will have to forgo their Christmas this year all because of your pride,' he said sharply.

Grace was cut to the quick. This was the third time someone had offered to help. Each time it came from a totally unexpected source. She turned to face him.

'All right,' she said quietly. 'Thank you, Norris.

I'll take you up on your offer.'

He smiled and reached for an envelope. Stuffing the money inside he pushed the lip inside it and handed it to her.

Grace hesitated before putting out her hand. 'No strings attached?'

'As if,' he grinned.

'I mean it, Norris.'

He looked her straight in the eye. 'No strings attached.'

She turned and left the room, closing the door softly as she left. Norris watched her go, his eyes fixed on her bottom and the gentle sway of her hips under that thick gabardine overall all the factory girls wore. He hadn't really noticed before but it was obvious the woman didn't wear a girdle. A smile played on his mouth and he sighed in anticipation. Let her enjoy her Christmas. Come the New Year and he would claim his prize. Everyone had their price and when the time was right, he'd reel her in. He felt himself harden. It was a long time since he'd wanted a woman so badly.

Eleven

Christmas Eve was a hive of activity in the town house. Bonnie and Richard put up paper chains and she left him putting up the Christmas cards while she went to the kitchen to collect his mid-morning milk and biscuit.

Cook was talking to someone who had just brought some sprigs of holly 'brought up from the country'. He looked suspiciously like a spiv. The government had been talking about cracking down on them but in these austere times they seemed to mushroom on every street corner. Apparently this one had just happened to knock on the back door, but Bonnie wasn't convinced. It seemed to her that he had come by prior arrangement, and Dora had let him in. He was neatly suited and wore highly polished shoes. He and Cook huddled together for a few minutes and then he went outside again.

Bonnie thoroughly disapproved of the black market. Her mother had always refused to be part of it. She couldn't help wondering how much the holly had cost. A tidy penny, she thought. How far away home felt at that moment. It was easy enough to find holly in Titnore Woods or across the fields near Durrington. The spiv came back with a small chicken when Cook turned around and saw Bonnie looking. She put her finger to her lips and shook her head and Bonnie knew to keep quiet.

The spiv was clean-shaven but when she came close up, Bonnie could see that his David Niven-style moustache had been helped along with a black pencil. As he left he bumped her shoulder.

'Want a nice pair of stockings, lady?' he said out of the corner of his mouth. 'Two and a tanner. You won't get better.'

For a second or two Bonnie was sorely tempted. She couldn't remember the last time she had had a nice pair of stockings but she shook her head. She didn't do it out of a noble desire to avoid the black market, nor out of churlishness, but quite simply because she had nowhere to go and no one to wear them for. The door burst open and Lady Brayfield walked in.

'What's he doing here?' she frowned crossly.

Cook blushed a deep red.

'Just on my way, Missus,' said the spiv brightly. He tipped his hat. 'I can see I'll have no joy here. Morning, ladies.'

'And make this the last time,' said Lady Brayfield crisply. 'I'm going to make sure that the side gate is locked so you needn't come back when I'm gone.'

She followed him to the gate and after a few more sharp words, she locked the gate noisily.

'Don't invite that man back in here again,' she said accusingly as she walked through the kitchen.

'Perish the thought, Madam,' said Cook innocently. Lady Brayfield swept out of the room. The doorbell was ringing as she opened the kitchen door. 'Don't worry, Dora,' she called over her shoulder. 'I'll see to it.'

Bonnie took the holly into the sitting room and she and Richard laid it on the mantelpiece and along the picture rails. After that, she helped him wrap his Christmas presents. Richard had bought his grandmother a pretty headscarf and his mother a brooch and some perfume. The child had gone up in Bonnie's estimation when he had happily spent the whole of his £5 on the two women. Thank goodness Lady Brayfield had enough spare coupons although Bonnie suspected most of them had come from Richard's mother. Being incarcerated in the home meant that she had no opportunity to go out or buy new clothes.

After luncheon Bonnie had taken Richard to the pictures, her special Christmas treat for him. She chose *Hue and Cry,* a story about a gang of boys who manage to foil a master crook, and for a couple of hours Bonnie quite forgot her own problems. Richard was on the edge of his seat and thoroughly enjoyed himself.

Back home they had tea and then played card games until bedtime. By the time she had got him settled, Bonnie was tired. Of course, George was never far from her thoughts. She wavered between feeling frantic with worry because she didn't know what had happened to him and angry that he'd left her pregnant and alone. Her heart was heavy and she was very homesick. Did Mum and Rita miss her? She lay staring at the ceiling as she relived some of those precious moments with George and the long walks she'd enjoyed with Rita along Worthing sea front.

She had been to the post office earlier in the day and to her delight there was a letter from Miss Reeves. Bonnie saved it until she was alone in her room.

Dear Bonnie,

I must say I was quite surprised to get your letter and more than a little alarmed that you have left home so abruptly. I have seen your mother in passing but she was reluctant to talk about you, merely saying you were doing well and that you might be coming home shortly. Against my better judgement, but in deference to your wishes, I was very careful not to tell her that you had been in touch with me. Now that I have received your letter, I must ask you to reconsider. It seemed awfully cruel not to inform your mother that you are as well and happy as you indicate.

From what I can gather, from the short conversation I had with your mother, your sister has left school early and is working in Hubbard's. I'm sure this must be a disappointment to your mother because she did so want Rita to go to secretarial college, but times are hard and we must all do our bit.

Bonnie, for whatever reason you have left home, I'm sure you can patch it up. This is the season of goodwill, and Christ came so that we might be reconciled one to another. Won't you reconsider your plans? Let me know if I can help in any way.

Be assured of my prayers, my dear. Come home soon.

Yours sincerely,
Evelyn Reeves.

The pain Bonnie experienced was acute. She felt as if someone had hit her with a ten-foot pole. Because of her, Rita had had to give up her chance of a career. Of course, it was obvious. Mum would have needed her wages to pay the rent. Bonnie felt an absolute heel and there was nothing she could do about it. Even if she went back home, she would only be a burden to them. With a baby on the way, how could she pull her own weight or do her share? There was no way Mum could support her. No, she would have to stay away from home for a long time, perhaps even for good. She threw herself onto the bed and wept bitter tears into her pillow.

The postman came late on Christmas Eve. Grace heard the letterbox rattle and found one envelope on the mat. The card inside was a pretty one with lots of glitter. She opened it, looked at the signature and swayed. *To Mum and Rita, all my love Bonnie.* There were two big 'X's at the bottom. Grace turned it over and looked at the back of the card. No address, only the price, written in pencil in the right-hand corner: 8½d. She sat down at the kitchen table, held it to her chest and rocked herself gently.

When Grace came down on Christmas morning, Rita was sitting on the stairs. Grace gathered her skirt and sat beside her.

'Happy Christmas, love.'

'Happy Christmas, Mum.' Rita's voice was thick with emotion. Grace put her arm around her daughter and Rita laid her head on her mother's shoulder. 'I miss her, Mum.'

'I know,' said Grace.

'We were going to get you some new decorations this year,' said Rita. 'I forgot all about it.'

'There'll be other Christmases,' said Grace. 'I miss her too. I keep wondering where she is, what she's doing, is she warm enough...'

Rita's heart constricted. That was the last thing her mother needed to worry about. Warm enough? What else would she be in South Africa? The funny thing was, although Bonnie's Christmas card bore the message, *Across the miles...*, it had a London postmark. Now was the time to say something, but Rita couldn't. Perhaps her sister had posted it on her way to South Africa? If her mother thought of all those thousands of miles between them, she'd be in a right state. She might not believe her and then she would have to tell her about Dinah and Mrs Kerr. What if her mother went charging round there? She gulped down a sob and Grace tightened her grip around Rita's back.

'I think we ought to make up our minds to have the best Christmas we can,' said Grace. 'I think Bonnie would want that, don't you?'

Rita nodded miserably.

'What about the money, Mum? What are we going to do? It'll take ages to pay it.'

'It's all paid,' Grace smiled.

Rita's eyes widened. 'But how?'

'A friend gave me the money,' said Grace dismissively.

'A friend? What friend?'

'Never you mind,' Grace chuckled. 'Just be thankful that nobody's Christmas, including ours, has been spoiled.'

Rita gave her a tired smile. 'It almost makes me believe in Father Christmas again,' she laughed.

'I still want to pay the money back,' said Grace, 'but you're right. It's good to know there are still a few good people left in this world.'

Rita gave her a hug. 'I'm so glad, Mum.'

'The neighbours will be round later,' Grace went on. 'We don't have the piano but we can still have a high old time. Snowy will be here soon so we've got plenty to do.'

Rita nodded again.

Grace stood up and, taking her hand, said, 'We can only hope your sister's having a good time and we'll make the best of it too.'

When Bonnie woke up on Christmas morning, she could smell bacon cooking and hear Richard's excited cries as he unwrapped his presents. It took several seconds before she realised she wasn't dreaming. She glanced at the clock. It was almost eight. She'd overslept.

By the time she got downstairs, breakfast was almost over. 'I do apologise, Lady Brayfield,' said Bonnie.

'No need,' said Lady Brayfield cheerfully. 'Happy Christmas, Bonnie.'

Bonnie returned the compliment and as soon as they'd finished the meal, Lady Brayfield suddenly announced that she and Richard were going to spend the day with Richard's mother so Bonnie, Cook and Dora could have the house to themselves. It would have been nice to have been given some notice, Bonnie thought crossly, but she didn't say anything.

Until his grandmother was ready, Bonnie helped Richard set up his new clockwork Hornby train set on the dining room floor. He was reluctant to leave the train so she exercised the dog alone. She was glad to be on her own and as she walked around Hyde Park she let her tears fall freely. When she got back to Aldford Street, Bonnie felt a lot better. Lady Brayfield and her charge had already gone.

The house was already filled with an appetising

smell. Bonnie cleared up the sitting room and tidied away the Christmas wrapping paper. She folded it neatly and put it into the laundry room. She would iron it flat before putting it away for next year. The paper shortage was so severe, who knew if they'd be able to buy any Christmas wrapping paper for Christmas 1948? By 12.30 the smell of roast chicken had her drooling and Bonnie realised how hungry she was. Although they had the run of the house, the three of them sat in the kitchen where they felt the most comfortable.

'This chicken looks more like a pigeon,' Cook grumbled as she brought it to the table. She flicked off the radio and the BBC light programme, *Forces Favourites,* died instantly.

'It looks fantastic,' Bonnie insisted. Her voice was thin. She was struggling not to let her feelings of homesickness overwhelm her.

Cook went back to the stove to fetch the gravy. Dora reached over and squeezed Bonnie's hand. It was a move which took Bonnie by surprise.

'I heard you last night,' Dora whispered earnestly, her lined and care-worn face full of concern.

'Sorry?'

'You was crying.'

Embarrassed, Bonnie looked away.

'Don't worry,' Dora went on. 'I'll be your friend.'

Bonnie looked at her and smiled, suddenly very grateful for such sincere and genuine friendships. 'Thank you, Dora,' she said simply. 'I'd like that very much.' And Dora beamed.

After the meal, they exchanged presents. Cook

had given Bonnie a box of three handkerchiefs. They were brand new, very pretty and embroidered in one corner. Dora gave her some talc. Bonnie was delighted with both gifts. She in turn had given them an apron and a tin of toffees. Lady Brayfield had left them each a slim, flat gift. When they opened them, they had all been given the same thing. Stockings.

Bonnie suppressed a smile.

'Oooh,' said Dora. 'Aren't they lovely.'

'Crafty old devil,' murmured Cook.

The day had gone very quickly in Worthing. Snowy had come for dinner just before Grace dished up. She was lavish in her praise of their meagre decorations and Grace showed her Bonnie's card which had pride of place on the mantelpiece.

'I'm so glad you've heard from her,' said Snowy giving Grace an encouraging squeeze of her arm. 'At least you know she's all right.'

Grace had the radio tuned to the Light Programme. She was just about to switch it off when Jean Metcalfe said, 'And now we have a request for Mum and Dad, Dougie and Mo Dawson in Worthing. It comes from Bob to wish you a very happy Christmas. Bob says, "I'll be thinking of you especially when you all gather at Rita's house for tea. Have a wonderful time and I'll see you all at Easter."'

Everybody froze as the strains of Vera Lynn singing, 'We'll meet again' filled the room.

'Well I never!' gasped Snowy as the song finished. 'I had no idea they played records for real people. I thought they made everything up.'

'Wasn't that nice,' smiled Grace. 'I suppose his mum and Mo must have told him we'd invited them for Christmas.'

'He said my name,' Rita murmured. 'I'm famous.'

And they all laughed.

There wasn't a chicken to be had anywhere so they made do with rabbit pie, roast potatoes and a cabbage from Snowy's garden. Grace still had a little sherry left over from some other celebration. The two women had a small glass each and Rita drank homemade ginger beer. For pudding they enjoyed a couple of mince pies and as soon as the washing up was done, they listened to the King's Speech from Sandringham on the Home Service.

The older women drank tea and dozed while Rita wrote her obligatory thank you letters. One to Miss Reeves to thank her for a pretty ornament for her dressing table, and one to Granny who lived in Kirkbymoorside in Yorkshire to thank her for the matching scarf and gloves she had knitted (she did the same every year).

'Anything you want to say to Granny, Mum?'

'Leave the envelope open,' Grace yawned. 'I'll put a letter in tomorrow.'

Finally Rita wrote to Salvatore and Liliana Semadini to thank them for the small purse they had sent her. When she had opened it, Rita found a coin inside.

'Why did they put a tanner in there?'

'To bring good luck,' said Grace. 'So that your purse will never be empty.'

At four they got ready for tea. Rita made some fish paste sandwiches while Snowy put out the plates, cups and saucers. Grace fixed the darts board on the wall.

As the neighbours came, the table began to fill. Sausage rolls from Elsie her next-door-but-one neighbour, and a tin of snoek (some sort of fish from Africa which the government said was as good as salmon). Grace and Snowy weren't convinced by the snoek. They didn't know how to say the name and when they tried to pronounce it, it sounded an awful lot like 'snot' which didn't really help matters, but they mixed it with salad cream and made some more sandwiches. Dougie was happy to help them and he managed to butter some bread very well.

'You've done a good job there, Dougie,' said Snowy, and the lad's eyes lit up.

'Any news of Bob?' Grace asked.

'He gets his demob at Easter,' said his mother. 'He sends his regards to Rita.'

'Oh yes, we heard it on the radio,' said Grace with a grin.

Rita brought some of her old toys downstairs and Grace produced a bag of dressing-up clothes, and a long mirror which had once been the door of a wardrobe. Before long the kids were having a whale of a time. More goodies appeared on the table, including a small trifle, a jelly in the shape of a wobbling red and green tower, and a few sweets. Kaye Wilcox turned up from work. She kissed Grace and gave her a tin of toffees for the party.

'Are you all right, Grace?' she said anxiously.

'I'm fine,' Grace assured her. 'It'll take more than a bump on the head to put me down.'

Kaye sat at the kitchen table talking to Peggy Jones. Grace finally remembered to return the penny she'd lent her for the platform ticket the day Bonnie left.

'Oh you needn't have bothered,' said Peggy 'I was glad to help. Any news of Bonnie?'

Grace shook her head and fortunately Miss Reeves arrived so she was spared having to give an explanation. Soon after, Liliana and Salvatore turned up with some pastries and the little house was full.

'Grace,' said Salvatore gravely. 'I must ask you something.'

'Fire away,' Grace smiled. She liked Salvatore. A rotund man, he was an effervescent character, loud and colourful, but everybody knew he had a heart of gold. Apart from a brief period when he and Liliana had been interned on the Isle of Man during the war, they had lived in Worthing since they were young. When the authorities carted them off, no one in the town could believe that Salvatore and Liliana could be anything other than a very nice couple, totally innocent of the aspersions levelled against them.

Grace looked up from the table where she had been arranging some pickled beetroot and pickled onions on the dish. Liliana let out a little gasp and Grace put her hand up to her face. For a second or two, she had quite forgotten her bruises. When they heard what had happened to Grace just around the corner from them in Station Approach they were shocked.

'I'm fine now,' said Grace. 'Rita looked after me very well. What was it you wanted to tell me?'

'I no wish to take advantage but my nephew, Emilio, he come for to live with us.' Salvatore took the arm of a young man standing behind him and pulled him forward. Emilio smiled and, taking Grace's hand, leaned over to kiss it.

'Pleased to meet you,' said Grace. He was incredibly good looking with dark curly hair and a generous mouth. He was smartly dressed in a suit, a crisp white shirt and a blue tie.

'Emilio, he come from Italy,' said Salvatore. 'His papa, my brother, send him to me. Things very bad in Italy and Emilio, he want the better life.'

'You're very welcome,' Grace nodded. She turned and called, 'Rita.

Her daughter was talking to Kaye. The girl wasn't looking her normal vivacious self and Grace wondered why.

When Liliana saw Rita, she cupped her chin in her hand and kissed both her cheeks. 'You are good girl to your mama,' she gushed.

That was when Rita saw Emilio. Grace saw the colour rising to her daughter's cheeks. It was hardly surprising. There weren't many young men as good looking as Emilio in Worthing. Tall, with large dark eyes and amazingly long eyelashes for a man, he had the physique of a Roman god and all the charm of a film star.

'Offer everyone a drink,' said Grace, giving Rita a nudge in the ribs. She winked at Liliana and the two women shared a knowing smile.

There was another knock at the door and

Dinah walked in. Everyone was transfixed as Rita introduced her. 'Dinah works as the mannequin in Hubbard's.'

'That's never Alice Chamberlain's grand-daughter, is it?' Elsie Dawson asked Grace in a loud whisper.

'Yes, I am,' smiled Dinah. 'I'm surprised you recognised me, Mrs Dawson. It must be more than fifteen years since I was here and I was only a little girl then.'

'Alice missed you something rotten,' Elsie sniffed.

'As I did her,' said Dinah. 'After my parents went their separate ways, my father told me my granny had died.'

'A wicked lie,' Elsie blurted out.

'I tend to agree, Mrs Dawson,' said Dinah, 'but my father had his reasons.'

'Didn't you go to live up north somewhere?' Grace asked.

'Hardly,' Dinah chuckled. 'My father took me to Petworth.'

'Of course, you do know your granny died in November, don't you?' Grace said gently.

'Yes,' said Dinah. 'That's really why I'm here. She left me her house.'

'You mean it wasn't rented?' Elsie gasped. 'I thought Norris Finley had all the houses around here.'

'Not my granny's,' Dinah smiled.

Rita's eyes lit up. 'Does that mean you're going to live just across the street?'

'Probably not,' said Dinah, 'but I shall be popping back to Worthing quite frequently. I've been accepted for a place at RADA.'

Snowy wrinkled her nose. 'RADA?'

'The Royal Academy of Dramatic Art,' said Dinah. 'I'm going to train to be an actress.'

'Oh, will you be in the pictures?' gasped Mo Dawson. 'Maybe you'll star with Margaret Lockwood. I like her. People say I look a bit like her.'

Rita rolled her eyes. Mo was behaving like a silly schoolgirl. Emilio saw her expression and winked at her and Rita's face flamed once more. Everyone was very interested in Dinah's career choice except Kaye. She seemed a little preoccupied; something was clearly worrying her. Grace promised herself she would talk to her before she left.

'You all right, dear?' Snowy asked but she was distracted by one of the children before she had an answer.

Grace felt the lightest touch on her sleeve and turned as Miss Reeves asked to have a word in private. By now the room was heaving with people so the two women stepped outside into the scullery. Miss Reeves drew her cardigan close to her body. It was very cold away from the fire.

'I see you have a card from Bonnie,' she said. 'Rita showed it to me.'

'Yes,' Grace smiled.

'Oh my dear,' Miss Reeves went on. 'You've had such a hard time of late, is there anything I can do to help?'

Grace shook her head. 'You are very kind, but there's nothing.'

'If it's a question of a train fare...'

'Miss Reeves, I went up to London soon after

she first went, but it was hopeless. Where does one begin to look?'

'What if...?' Miss Reeves began and then faltered.

'Bonnie has gone away,' said Grace firmly, 'and we must all get on with our lives and learn to live with it.'

'You don't mean that?'

Grace shook her head. 'Not really but then you wouldn't expect me to,' she smiled. 'I'm her mother.'

They turned sadly towards the kitchen door and rejoined the party.

Just as Grace was thinking she had a full house, Manny Hart turned up with a friend. It was the man from the corner shop. Manny introduced him as Archie Warren and everybody shook hands.

'You told me to bring a friend,' said Manny in his usual perfect accent. 'Archie is new in town. I hope you do not mind?'

Although he'd been to the house when he'd bought Michael's chair, Grace had no idea what Archie's first name was. Manny produced a huge brown paper bag full of broken biscuits and some apples. Archie had a box of Christmas crackers which made him every kid's best friend and half a bottle of whisky which made him every man's pal.

'Are you sure you don't mind me butting in on your party, Mrs Rogers?' Archie asked Grace, his earnest hazel eyes making her heart flutter in a way she hadn't felt for years.

'Of course not,' she smiled affably. 'The more the merrier, and please call me Grace.'

Archie made no comment about the state of her face, but Grace avoided his gaze, suddenly embarrassed. 'Thanks again for trying to help me the other night,' she said quietly.

'You're welcome,' he said. 'I only wish I could have stopped them.'

'When will you be wanting the chair?'

'I'll let you know,' he smiled. 'The shop is still a bit crowded at the moment. You don't mind keeping it here, do you?'

'No, no,' Grace smiled.

Before long, the young ones were playing Monopoly on the small table, Dougie was fixing somebody's broken clockwork toy, the men were playing darts and the women were chatting happily over cups of tea. Emilio sat next to Rita, and Dinah, elegantly sipping a sherry, told them about her future plans to be an actress.

As the evening wore on, Manny got out his harmonica. He was skilled but the tunes he chose were rather mournful.

'Can't you play something a bit more lively, love,' Snowy said eventually and Manny struck up with 'Lili Marleen', sweet, insidious but still melancholy. It wasn't as good as the piano but as their voices blended in harmony, everybody had a good time. Salvatore had a beautiful tenor voice and his rendition of 'Oh my Papa' brought a tear to the eye.

'Do you enjoy walking, Grace?' Picking up a tea towel, Archie joined her at the sink as she did a little washing up. His voice was low so she knew what he was saying was for her ears only.

'As a matter of fact, I do,' she smiled. 'My

husband and I were members of the National Council of Ramblers before the war.'

'A few of us are walking along the sea front on New Year's Day,' he said. 'Would you like to join us?'

Grace hesitated. What would people think? Should she be out enjoying herself when her daughter was missing from home? Then a voice in her head which sounded remarkably like Michael's said, 'Get out and enjoy the countryside. Nature's delights are free.' Nature's delights ... she hadn't thought of that in years. Carefully she placed a cup upside down on the draining board and looked up at Archie.

'You know what?' she smiled. 'I think I would.'

She looked around for Kaye Wilcox.

'She left some time ago,' said Snowy when Grace mentioned it. 'She said she was meeting someone.'

'How odd,' said Grace.

'What, that she was meeting someone?' said Snowy.

'No, that she didn't bother to say goodbye.'

Towards the end of the evening, Grace looked around her kitchen with a sigh of satisfaction. Christmas at the Rogers' place was almost as good as it ever had been. Everybody had enjoyed themselves although Grace still had a Bonnie-shaped ache around her heart.

Twelve

Bonnie left Lady Brayfield's lovely home in the middle of January after an emotional goodbye. Her employer had been amazing and Bonnie's leaving present was more than she could have ever wished for.

'I've arranged for you and the baby, when it comes, to go to Holly Acres,' she told Bonnie. 'You will work in the nursery although not in the same room as your child.'

Bonnie's heart sank until Lady Brayfield explained the thinking behind the plan.

'My friend, Matron Bennett, feels that you might be tempted to favouritism, but more importantly that the other members of staff might not be so inclined to care for your child if you are around,' she said. 'They will be told that you can come any time to see your baby when you are off duty and that you will be treated as an equal.'

'Will they know about my situation?' Bonnie was already beginning to understand just how groundbreaking this was.

'It's up to you what you tell people,' said Lady Brayfield, 'but for the time being, you will be known as a widow.'

Bonnie nodded, her gaze fixed on the floor.

'I suggest you think very carefully about what you want to say,' said Lady Brayfield. 'People can be very cruel and you not only have yourself to consider. There is also the stigma attached to your child as well.'

Bonnie understood.

'You will be paid, of course,' her benefactor went on. 'Your board and lodging will be deducted from your wage and of course something for the care of your child, but you and your baby will be housed and well fed.'

This was worth more than a king's ransom to Bonnie.

'It's the government's best kept secret that they make a small allowance for single mothers,' Lady Brayfield went on. 'The matron of the Mother and Baby Home will give you the paperwork if you ask her.'

Bonnie felt truly humbled. Someone up there must have been looking after her when she came to this house.

'It only goes for me to thank you and to wish you all the best,' said Lady Brayfield.

'No,' insisted Bonnie. 'I owe you an enormous debt of gratitude…' but Lady Brayfield was already waving her away.

Richard was at school but when he had been told Bonnie was leaving for a new position, he'd begged and begged her to stay.

'I'll be good,' he'd promised more than once. 'Please don't go…'

It was so difficult trying to be adamant that she had to go when every part of her wanted to stay. Above all, she wanted him to know that her decision had nothing to do with him. On that last evening, she'd sat on the sofa with her arm around him and told him about the dream she and George had had. It was easy to relive those wonderful memories and they hadn't diminished over time. Everything George had told her came flooding back. Richard listened enraptured as she talked about the ship, and sailing to the Cape, the jobs that were waiting for them and the place where they would live under the shadow of Table Mountain. This was what she would tell everybody. This is what she would tell her baby. The only time she would lie would be when she told people George was dead, and maybe that wasn't a lie anyway. She hated herself for thinking it, but sometimes she reflected that it would be easier if he were dead. At least he wouldn't have deserted her.

As if Lady Brayfield's generosity wasn't enough, Cook and Dora had been busy knitting.

'But how...?' she began when she saw the beautiful layette they had prepared for her.

'We know our mistress,' said Cook. 'We knew you were here for a reason.'

Bonnie had hugged them and promised to write.

'I shouldn't go to all that trouble,' said Cook. 'I can't read and neither can Dora.'

On her half day, Wednesday, Rita found her feet being drawn towards the Railway Café. She had no real reason to go there except to see Salvatore's nephew again. Was he still there?

As usual, Salvatore was behind the counter. He put down the huge brown teapot and flung his arms in the air. 'Little Rita,' he cried. 'Look,

Mama, it is Rita.'

Rita flinched when he said 'little' but she shared his delight. She'd missed Salvatore and Liliana as well but they weren't the reason why she was here.

'Tell us about your new job,' said Liliana, coming round the counter and pulling Rita towards a chair. It was quiet in the café. The four o'clock trade hadn't begun and it was too late for dinner.

Salvatore put a cup and saucer of hot tea in front of them both and sat down with them at the table. 'Emilio,' he shouted, *'occupati del negozio'* ('look after the shop').

The couple stared intently at Rita, eager to hear what she had to tell them. Behind her, Rita heard someone come to the counter and she knew it was *him*. Her whole body tingled with excitement. Every bone in her body wanted to turn to look at him but she daren't.

They shared a brief conversation about English beer and Christmas time when her mother looked after the guests so well, and of course, Dinah, who had captured everybody's attention. Rita had no idea she had once stayed in the street. Mum talked about Dinah playing with her and Bonnie but Rita didn't remember.

'I mostly have to tidy up,' Rita told Salvatore in answer to his question about what she did in Hubbard's. 'Miss Bridewell is very strict, but the girls are really nice. Sometimes, when we've finished at the end of the day we keep watch for each other and take turns to try on the dresses. They are so beautiful, like you wouldn't believe.' She was talking drivel but it was hard concentrating on something else when *he* was around.

'And how is your mama?' Liliana eventually asked.

Rita shrugged. 'She seems all right.'

'Have you heard from your sister yet?'

Rita shook her head. 'I don't suppose we will,' she said and added, 'someone told me she went to South Africa,' when she saw Liliana's puzzled expression.

'South Africa!' cried Salvatore.

'But you mustn't tell my mother,' said Rita, suddenly alarmed that she'd let her mouth run away with her. 'I think it would upset her too much to know Bonnie was so far away.'

The Mother and Baby Home was cold comfort after her stay in Aldford Street. Red Chimneys was a rambling and dilapidated Victorian manor house. The war years, and the austerity which followed, had put a stop to all but the most essential repairs and it hadn't been decorated since the thirties. Winter proved to be very difficult. The coke boiler struggled miserably to heat all the radiators, added to the fact that Matron quite often turned some of them off anyway to save money.

Bonnie lived at the top of the house with all the other mothers-to-be. Each had her own locker and an iron bedstead with a ticking mattress (some heavily stained) and old army issue blankets over the sheets. They were expected to work and work hard. Bonnie helped in the kitchen, lit the fires or cleaned the house and as the girls got nearer their time, they were given lighter jobs such as the mending.

They were expected to go to church on Sunday but they had to sit separately from the rest of the congregation. There were other free times when they could go to the shops or the pictures but it was difficult facing the stares of disapproval from complete strangers.

It was expected that the girls would give their babies up for adoption. Matron continually harangued them about how it would be in baby's best interest to let him or her have a good home.

'I'm sure you want your baby to have a good life,' she said to Bonnie during the routine pep talk each girl had in her office on the day of her arrival. 'What could be better than a loving father and mother who can give your baby the best of everything?'

'I am keeping my baby and I already have a place to go,' Bonnie said. She went on to explain the arrangement Lady Brayfield had made with the matron of Holly Acres. At first Matron puckered her lips in disbelief and then she demanded the telephone numbers. Bonnie was told to return in half an hour. When she went back, Matron scowled in disapproval. She made it plain that Bonnie was going against the system and she didn't like it.

'You are not to talk to the other girls about this,' she commanded. 'It will only upset them.'

Bonnie slept next to Ruth and Gwen at her end of the dormitory. Ruth was a pale-faced girl who was deeply troubled. Gwen was open-faced and from the Welsh valleys.

'Mam sent me away as soon as she knew I was

pregnant,' she grinned. 'I'm supposed to be staying with my Auntie Blodwen in Newport Pagnell to help out in her shop.'

'When's your baby due?' Bonnie asked.

'End of March,' said Gwen. 'Roll on, I say, and then I can get on with the rest of my life.'

'How can you say that?' gasped Ruth. She was sitting on the end of her bed cradling and rocking her bump.

They never talked about the men who had got them into this state. Ruth was broken-hearted at the thought of giving up her baby. Gwen was more philosophical about it. She had already signed the adoption papers but Ruth was holding out.

'Ruthy cries all the time,' Bonnie remarked to Gwen one day when they were both working in the ironing room.

'Matron has been on at her to sign the adoption papers,' said Gwen.

'She doesn't have to, you know,' said Bonnie. 'She has a choice.'

Gwen snorted. 'Little do you know.'

Bonnie looked up from ironing a sheet. 'What do you mean?'

'They never let up,' said Gwen. 'One girl who had her baby soon after I came here refused to sign until the very last minute. She even chucked the fountain pen across the room. We all thought she'd manage to hold them off but then Matron threatened to get her sent to a mental home.'

Bonnie was aghast. 'What?'

'She told her chucking the pen was the first sign of an unstable mind and she'd have her committed, then her kid would be brought up in a children's home.'

'But that's awful,' Bonnie gasped. 'What happened?'

'She signed of course,' said Gwen. 'Broke her heart. She was in such a state when they took the baby, it wouldn't surprise me if she didn't end up in the nut house after all.'

Bonnie was beginning to appreciate just how lucky she had been to find someone like Lady Brayfield. What if she hadn't found that place in Holly Acres? Bonnie shuddered and made an inner vow to keep her baby. In fact she would look after her baby so well she would prove everyone wrong.

As the time for Ruth's baby to be born came nearer, the pressure to sign the adoption papers was stepped up. Matron even made her go to bed without any supper a couple of times and Ruthy cried night after night. Eventually Bonnie could bear it no longer. They were alone in the sitting room, huddled close to the meagre fire trying to get warm. Bonnie had two cardigans and a jumper on and although her front was reasonably comfortable, the draught from the gap under the door meant that her back was perishing cold.

'You know, Ruthy,' she said, 'you don't have to give your baby away. Matron doesn't want you to know this but if you go to the welfare people, you can get help from the government.'

'I'm not good with all that official stuff,' Ruth said dully after Bonnie explained about the single woman's allowance.

'I'll come with you if you like.'

Ruth's eyes lit up. 'Would you? Would you really?'

They collected the paperwork from the welfare office the next day in their free time. On their way back to Red Chimneys Bonnie called in at the post office. She had arranged to have her post office box number address transferred and, to her delight, the clerk handed her a letter. She recognised the handwriting at once. It was from Miss Reeves.

As soon as they got back Matron called Ruth into her office and Bonnie went to find a quiet place to read her letter. She chose the library room. There were no books on the shelves – they had long gone – but the girls knew no one came into this room unless they wanted some time alone or a place to cry.

Bonnie sat on the wide windowsill and looked out onto the barren garden. Winter was losing its grip. Spring was on its way. A few snowdrops nodded in the neglected flowerbeds and a solitary daffodil waved to her from under the window.

She had just torn open the envelope when the door burst open, making Bonnie start. Instinct made her shove her letter into her pocket as she rose to her feet. Matron's face was black with fury.

'How dare you,' she spat. 'How dare you fill this poor girl's mind with your fanciful ideas and ridiculous notions?' She came into the room dragging a sobbing Ruth behind her and holding the allowance application in the air.

'I only told her there was an alternative...'

'Oh, I know what you told her,' Matron said

coldly. 'You gave her false hope.'

'But it's not false hope,' Bonnie protested.

'Oh no?' Matron bellowed before Bonnie could say any more. 'Then tell me, Miss, when she's got this allowance, where is she going to live? Eh? She can't go back to her mother. Her mother is ashamed that her daughter is having an illegitimate child.'

Bonnie felt her face flame. She hadn't thought of that. 'I'm sure the council would house her,' she said lamely.

'Where?' Matron demanded. 'Three-quarters of a million homes have been destroyed and the country is up to its eyes in debt. There are whole families living in two rooms.' She began ripping the form into pieces. 'Where do you think the government's priorities lie? With families needing homes or with one silly girl who went and got herself pregnant with the first pair of trousers she set eyes on?'

Ruth let out a howl and ran from the room. Bonnie blinked, willing herself not to cry too.

'I told you to keep quiet about this, didn't I?' Matron went on. She pointed to the empty doorway. 'I hold you personally responsible for the state that girl is in so from now on, my girl, you are on your own. You will do all your own washing and you can eat your meals when everyone else has finished.' She turned to leave, adding, 'And when your baby comes, don't expect any help from us.'

A chill of fear slid down Bonnie's spine. 'Oh Mum,' she whispered into the cold empty room. 'I wish you were here...'

Thirteen

'Excuse me, young woman...'

Rita was surprised by the sharpness of the customer's tongue until she turned around. It was Mrs Kerr, George's landlady.

'I wish to buy a hat and I don't want to be kept waiting all day.'

'I'm so sorry, Madam,' said Rita glancing around the department. Miss Bridewell was serving one of Hubbard's more wealthy customers and the two assistants were busy in the cubicles.

'Well?' Mrs Kerr demanded, 'are you going to serve me or not?'

Rita wasn't supposed to serve because she wasn't considered 'trained enough'. Mrs Kerr glared at her impatiently.

'Would you like to sit here?' said Rita, indicating a dressing table complete with three mirrors. Miss Bridewell was still deep in conversation. 'May I ask what is the occasion?'

'We're having a very important person come to our church,' said Mrs Kerr, her chest swelling with pride. 'I am to greet him at the door.'

Rita did some quick thinking. She recalled the plainness of Mrs Kerr's home and she noted the rather dour outfit she was wearing today. Mrs Kerr wasn't the sort of woman who would come to a shop like Hubbard's. She was most likely in her best things. 'What colour were you thinking of?' Rita asked.

'Blue,' said Mrs Kerr, 'or maybe brown.' She gave Rita a long hard stare in the mirror. 'Don't I know you?'

Rita smiled. 'I came to your house looking for my sister's gentleman friend,' she said.

'Oh yes,' said Mrs Kerr. 'I remember.'

Rita put a plain blue hat on the table. 'He never came back, you know,' Mrs Kerr said as she tried it on. 'I've still got that suitcase of his.'

'Thank you, Miss Rogers,' Miss Bridewell sniffed. 'I'll deal with Madam. I'm sure there's some dresses over there on the rail you can put back. Now, Madam, what can I do for you?'

Mrs Kerr repeated her story and Rita went back to the rail. She could see that the hats Miss Bridewell was showing Mrs Kerr were quite unsuitable: large brimmed hats, Ascot hats, hats with rosettes and ribbons and even a hat with an ostrich plume. Mrs Kerr was not enjoying the experience.

'Send the other girl back to me,' she barked. 'She knew what I was looking for.'

Miss Bridewell had no alternative but to ask Rita to come over and, ten minutes later, Rita had made her first ever sale, a donkey brown hat with a tan-coloured ribbon on the brim.

'You'd better come round and collect that case,' said Mrs Kerr as they waited for her change and the receipt to come along the wire from the cashier. 'I can't keep it forever. I need the space.'

For the next few weeks Bonnie found herself in Coventry, but surprisingly she didn't mind too much. She did her work and then her own laundry without complaint. Now that the weather was getting more spring-like, she enjoyed going out and looking around the shops although she didn't have the money to buy anything. Queuing was no longer a problem: because of her condition, she had been given a 'Queue Priority' card. That meant she didn't have to stand for hours and hours and she could go to the front of the queue if she wanted something. She got a few dirty looks but it didn't worry her too much.

When she was in her room, Bonnie read and reread Miss Reeves' letter and although it always brought her to the brink of tears, it was a comfort to have news of her family.

Dear Bonnie,

I had been hoping that perhaps you would have returned home by now. I trust that you are well. Your sister is doing well at Hubbard's and I must say I was impressed when I saw the courtesy and care with which she treats her customers. She looks very grown up now. Quite a young lady. The new store is not a patch on the old one which burned down last year, and my dear, it's so expensive!

Your mother has been working very hard as usual. My sister saw her coming out of the police station just days before Christmas with a very nasty bruise on her face and we were shocked to hear that she had been knocked down and robbed of the monies from her savings club.

My sister and I joined in the festivities at your home on Christmas Day as usual and although she still had a bruise, your mother was very well. We all pooled our resources in these desperate times and a good time was had by all. We discovered then that no one lost out because of the theft because your mother had sold the piano to reimburse the money. We had our usual sing-along accompanied by Mr Hart's mouth organ and Mr Semadenny (I don't know how to spell his name) sang beautifully.

As you suggested, I spoke to your mother about you but she seems resigned to the fact that you may not be home for some time. 'We must learn to live without her, if that's what she wants,' those were her very words, but I feel bound to remark that she did look very sad when she told me. My dear, can you not reconsider? Nothing is so terrible that it should separate a family and the three of you always seemed so close. Perhaps you might let me mediate between you, if it would help.

I shall continue to pray for you, my dear.

Yours sincerely,

Evelyn Reeves.

Poor Mother knocked down and robbed? Who could have done such a dreadful thing? And yet it wasn't really that surprising, was it? Everywhere you looked people were being robbed. The papers said shoplifting had reached epidemic proportions. It was the times they were living in. Desperate people did desperate things and her mother must have been an easy target. Now Bonnie worried about her all the time.

Ruth had had her baby, a boy, and at the moment she was spending her time looking after him until the adoption was finalised. That gave her six weeks with her son. She breastfed him and spent every waking moment with him. Whenever Bonnie saw her, she seemed very calm.

As Bonnie came down to the laundry room to do her washing one afternoon, she heard heavy banging on the cupboard door. A face was pressed against the small glass panel in the door. It was Gwen.

'Open the door, Bonnie. Let me out.'

Bonnie frowned. 'What are you doing in there?'

'Open the door, please.' She sounded desperate.

Bonnie looked down. There was no key in the keyhole.

'She put it on the shelf next to the washing powder,' said Gwen.

Bonnie hesitated. 'Who?'

Since Matron's decree, Bonnie had no idea what was going on. Gwen had had a son five and a half weeks ago and had moved to the ground floor with all the other mothers who had recently given birth. Surprisingly, although she had been so blasé about giving him up, Bonnie had seen her in the grounds and she appeared to be a devoted mother.

'Hurry, Bonnie.'

Bonnie found the key and turned the lock. Gwen shot out of the door like a bullet from a gun and raced up the stairs. Bonnie followed as quickly as her bump would allow and as she emerged into the hallway she heard a dreadful commotion. Above the sound of a car being driven away at speed Gwen was howling her head off as she knelt in front of Matron and snatched at the hem of her uniform.

'I want him back,' she sobbed. 'Make them give him back.'

'You signed the papers,' said Matron, pulling her dress away. 'There's nothing you can do about it now. He'll have a good home and you can get on with the rest of your life. You'll soon forget.' She looked up and saw Bonnie. 'Oh, I might have guessed you'd have something to do with this. When will you learn to stop interfering, Miss?'

When she had gone, Bonnie did her best to comfort Gwen but it was hopeless.

'He'll think I didn't want him,' she sobbed. 'But I did, I did.'

'I know,' said Bonnie, her own heart breaking for her friend.

'And I shall never see him again,' Gwen wailed. 'Not this side of the grave, I won't. Oh my poor little boy. I want my little Brian.'

Grace was meeting Archie again. She looked forward to these little Sunday walks together. Sometimes they walked along the sea front noting the changes as the last of the concrete sea defences were removed and a few more planks of wood were added to the store on the pier. Work to repair it was painfully slow because of the shortages; building houses was a priority and everything else had to take second place. During their first excursion, Archie had mentioned that he was making a delivery to Richmond. Grace felt her heartbeat quicken. 'Is that near London?'

'Yes,' said Archie. 'Want to come?'

'It's about my daughter...' she continued.

'I thought it might be,' he smiled. 'You can get the train into central London from there although I doubt you'll bump into her. London is one hell of a place, you know?'

She was so grateful and he'd even agreed to change the day to Friday so she didn't have to ask for time off work.

Today they caught a bus up to High Salvington. The wind was fresh. Grace was glad she had worn her thick knitted cardigan under her coat. Once they'd walked away from the bus stop, it was grand being up there looking across the big meadow towards Highdown Hill in the distance where, during the war years, they had had a radar station. All that was gone now and the countryside was returning to the way it had always been. Trees were coming into bud and everything had a fresh newness about it. As usual, they didn't talk much. They both enjoyed a companionable silence.

Bonnie was never far from her thoughts. What was she doing? Had she met a boy? Was she married? Grace tried to imagine having a married daughter and perhaps one day, a grandchild.

She was worried about Kaye Wilcox as well. The girl had lost a lot of weight and Grace and Snowy wondered if she was ill. She didn't talk much these days, even though they did their best to befriend her. She just got on with her work and walked home alone.

Grace and Archie had been walking together for about five weeks. It started with the New Year's walk with his friends in the Ramblers Association. Although most of the people were retired or well to do, she and Archie hadn't felt out of place at first. Everyone went out of their way to make them feel welcome but after a while, the class divisions began to show. The catalyst came when Mrs Pumfrey asked Grace if she would consider waiting on tables for her at one of her dinner parties. Grace had been happy to do so – after all, the money would come in handy to help get rid of her debt – but once it became known that Grace was a working woman, the rest of the group stuck to their own kind. Far from being offended, Grace didn't really care because by that time Archie had asked her to walk with him.

With no one else able to eavesdrop on their conversations, she and Archie opened up to each other. He told Grace of the shock he had had when he'd come home to find his wife expecting another man's baby.

'I suppose I shouldn't blame her,' he said sadly. 'She was lonely and I was away, but I can't say it didn't hurt. She wrote me such loving letters, I hadn't a clue what was going on.'

'I'm sorry,' Grace said quietly.

'I was willing to try and make a go of it,' he went on, 'but she said she wanted a better life.'

Grace told him about Michael. It felt funny talking about him with another man but Archie was a good listener. 'How is Rita coping without her sister?'

'She pretends to have taken it all in her stride,' Grace said uncertainly, 'and she doesn't talk about her sister much, but she doesn't fool me. They were very close but she's made new friends. She goes around to the café a lot.'

'To Liliana and Salvatore's place?'

'Yes,' said Grace. 'I try not to mind but it is a bit upsetting when she prefers to be with Liliana more than me.'

Archie laughed. 'I think she's more interested in that handsome nephew of hers. All the girls are crazy for him.'

Grace laughed. 'I think Rita is safe from his advances.'

'She does know that he's not interested in women?' said Archie.

'Oh yes,' said Grace, but now that he'd suggested it, she wasn't so sure. She sighed wistfully. 'I wish Bonnie would get in touch. How could she go off like that without even a backward glance?'

'Sometimes people feel awkward about getting in touch again,' said Archie, 'especially when they've left it so long, but I'm sure if you are grieving for her, she'll be grieving for you. Like you say, you're a close knit family.'

Grace wasn't sure how he felt about her, but she liked Archie a lot. He filled her thoughts day and night. She fell asleep thinking about his dark eyes and when she dreamed at night, it was of his kisses. When she woke up, he was her first thought in the morning. She was frustrated that in all this time, he hadn't so much as held her hand. She supposed it was because he had been so badly betrayed. It was hard to trust another person when the one you'd loved had deceived you for so long.

As they walked along Honeysuckle Lane towards Long Furlough, the quietness of the countryside enveloped them. The only sound apart from the occasional bird song was a dog barking in the distance.

'You and I have the same landlord, don't we?' he said, breaking into her thoughts.

Grace nodded. 'Norris Finley. He owns most of the properties around our way.'

Archie looked thoughtful. 'I can't get him to give me a rent book.'

'I'm not surprised,' said Grace. 'That's an old trick of his. He makes a verbal agreement but if he doesn't like you or he wants the property for someone else, he ups the rent until you're forced to move.'

'Is that it,' said Archie. 'I had wondered if the rent collector was adding a bit of commission for himself. My rent has gone up another ten bob since I moved in.'

'It's a real worry for a lot of my neighbours,' said Grace, 'but what can you do? Everybody is scared of eviction.'

'The only way to stop something like that is to band together,' said Archie.

'Easier said than done,' Grace said gloomily.

'Grace,' said Archie changing the subject as quickly as he had brought it up. 'I really enjoy these walks of ours…'

He hesitated. She said nothing but kept walking, willing her face not to flame.

'I don't want to spoil what we already have,' he went on, 'and I don't want to rush you but I should like something more.'

Grace could feel her heart beginning to thud. She felt as giddy as a schoolgirl.

'You're becoming very special to me,' he said,

tugging at her arm and making her stop. 'Grace, could we... I mean is it possible ... perhaps...' She looked up and saw an anguished look flit across his face. 'Oh hell, I'm making a right pig's ear of this, aren't I? What I mean is...'

'Yes,' she said.

He stared at her for a second. 'What?'

'Yes, I'd like to do other things with you,' she smiled. 'I enjoy dancing, and playing whist and the pictures and just being with you.' She laughed softly and all at once she was in his arms and he was holding her so close she could feel his warm breath on her cheek. They stared at each other for a couple of seconds and then slowly, inevitably, he lowered his mouth towards hers and kissed her gently.

They parted and he looked at her again. She could feel the breeze blowing her hair and somewhere above her head a blackbird was singing.

He smiled at her lovingly. 'Oh Gracie,' he murmured and he kissed her again, this time more earnestly.

Rita stared at George's coat and case where it lay on the bed in her room. It felt funny having it there, almost as if she'd stolen it. She had just come back from Mrs Kerr's place and had brought it straight back. She was alone in the house. Mum was out walking with the Ramblers again.

She felt in the pockets of the raincoat first but there were only a couple of sweet wrappers (he liked Murray Mints), some keys and a dirty handkerchief. She tried the case but it was locked.

When she tried one of the keys, it flew open. There were some brochures all about South Africa on the top. So they really were going to South Africa. She sat down beside the case. Hang on a minute, if he'd left the case behind, he couldn't have gone to South Africa, could he? Did that mean that Bonnie had gone all that way on her own? Rita searched through the rest of his things. She didn't take everything out, it didn't feel right, but by sliding her hands inside she could see he had a case full of shirts, socks, underpants, a pair of trousers and some papers. Apart from his passport (he definitely couldn't have gone to South Africa without that) and his birth certificate, the only other thing was an envelope. It was unsealed. Inside she found a letter. She looked at it for a long time before deciding to open it out and read it. A photograph fell out of the folds and Rita's heart almost stopped. She was looking at a man dressed in an SS uniform and if that wasn't shocking enough, the letter itself was in German.

The door banged downstairs and her mother called. 'Hello … Rita?'

'I'm up here,' Rita called back. Her heart was thumping and her mouth felt dry. Her mother mustn't see this. She stuffed the letter and the photograph back into the envelope and shut it in the case. She had to hide it. She looked around wildly. If her mother thought her sister had run away with an ex-Nazi it would kill her.

There was a built-in cupboard underneath the window ledge. Years ago Rita had discovered that one of the boards under the window was loose. She had pulled it up using her finger in the knothole. Nobody knew it was there so she had hidden her childish treasures in there. Rita and Bonnie always kept their shoes neatly lined under the window. She tossed her shoes onto the bed and opened it up. The cavity underneath the window was just big enough to wedge the case inside.

Her mother called out again. 'I've put the kettle on. Want a cup of tea?'

'Thanks, Mum.'

Rita put the board back in place but when she turned around, the coat was still on the bed. She opened it up again and stuffed the coat around the case. Then she heard her mother coming up the stairs.

'Whatever are you doing up here?' Grace was asking.

Rita pushed the board back in place and sat on the bed. As Grace walked into the room, Rita held up a shoe. 'Just look at my shoes, Mum,' she said casually. 'I really need a new pair. Have we got enough coupons?'

Fourteen

Bonnie's waters broke in the middle of the afternoon. An ambulance took her to the hospital where she was left behind a curtained area to 'get on with it'. Occasionally a nurse, complete with mask and gown, would come to tell her how the labour was progressing. It was done with quiet efficiency but the pain was excruciating.

At one point Bonnie murmured, 'I never thought it would hurt this much.'

The sister leaned over the bed. 'You should have thought of that before you opened your legs, shouldn't you,' she hissed unkindly.

A tear sprang to Bonnie's eye but when she had gone another nurse, clearly lower in rank, touched her arm sympathetically. 'Don't take any notice of her, the frustrated dried-up old prune.'

Bonnie smiled gratefully and concentrated on coping with the next pain which was on its way. During the long and protracted labour she thought a lot about George. She had loved him so much. He loved children and she'd thought he'd make a great father. How could he have deceived her so well? She also thought a lot about her mother. How she wished Mum were here. Her soothing voice was all Bonnie needed. How was she? It had been almost six months since she'd seen her. Six long and lonely months. *Oh Mum,* she thought during a short lull, *I miss you. I miss you so much.* And then another pain took away every other thought in her head.

Shirley came into the world at 10.25 the following morning, April 19th. She weighed in at 7lbs 6oz and she had a lusty cry.

'Is she keeping it?' the sister said coldly as she took Shirley from the doctor after her first examination.

'Yes I am,' said Bonnie. She would have dearly loved to get off the bed and smack the old cow but it was important to stay calm. She was afraid that if she antagonised the woman she might take it out on her baby. As soon as the afterbirth came away, the sister left and the nurse cleaned her up. After that, Bonnie was moved to the ward in a wooden wheelchair.

The beds were very close to each other and most were occupied. Each woman had a locker and a chair. At the foot of each bed was a cot but Shirley wasn't in hers. Alarmed, Bonnie spun round.

'She's in the nursery,' said the nurse. 'We always let baby have a rest until the next feed. She'll come to you then. You have a sleep, dear. You've been working very hard.'

Bonnie lay between the crisp white starched sheets and closed her eyes. She was exhausted but she couldn't sleep – not until she'd held her baby, her Shirley.

They brought Shirley for the two o'clock feed. Bonnie put her to the breast and Shirley sucked strongly.

'Ten minutes each side,' said the nurse. 'And sit her up in between to bring up her wind.'

The experience was like nothing she'd ever had before. The intimacy, the wonder of her perfectly formed little fingers, the tug of her mouth on her breast, Bonnie was overawed. She loved this little being more than she had ever loved anyone in her whole life. She would move heaven and earth for her, even die for her.

'Press her chin down with your finger when you want her to come off,' said the woman in the bed next to her when she saw Bonnie watching the clock. 'They never told me that, and I ended up with cracked nipples.'

'Thank you,' Bonnie smiled.

Winded and full, Shirley gave Bonnie a long unfocused stare. She was so like George. She had his nose and his strong jawline. Bonnie sighed. Perhaps it was just as well that he wasn't here. He would have been disappointed not to have a son. She cuddled the baby closer and rubbed her lips on the top of Shirley's downy head, whispering, 'I wonder where your daddy is now, darling.'

The factory had closed in late autumn of the previous year. Already the frontage was covered in weeds and a quantity of household waste, including an old pram with no wheels, had been dumped at the side of the building. Harold White, estate agent, wrinkled his nose with disapproval. Shifting empty buildings was hard enough in these harsh economic times but letting a place go to rack and ruin would make it doubly difficult. No sensible buyer would want to be lumbered with huge clean-up costs as well. He made a mental note that whatever came out of this viewing, he would have some harsh words to say to the vendor.

The door was stiff to open. Clearly no one had been here since the factory closure. He yanked at the handle and the rotting wood splintered.

'You may need to make a few improvements,' he apologised, 'but I'm sure we can come to some sort of arrangement with the seller.'

His buyer seemed unimpressed. He was a stocky man with a rather military bearing who was looking for premises to set up a second-hand repository and shop. The position on the Tarring Broadway was ideal in Harold's opinion. The building had a double frontage and a large storage area around the back. Upstairs there were three rooms, one of which had been used as an office, and two other rooms which could be used either for storage or as another area of shop floor.

As the two men walked in off the street they were hit by a rank, musty smell. The floor was littered with bits and pieces left behind from when the previous occupants had moved. Harold tut-tutted to himself. Really this was too bad. He would never have allowed the tenant to leave the building in such an appalling condition. If only he had been here at the time it was vacated. He would have sent in an army of cleaners and billed the tenant before he'd sanctioned this viewing. It was going to be hard work keeping the prospective buyer interested.

'As you can see,' he began again, 'this is a very good floor space and there's a small kitchen area at the rear.'

A train rumbled by and the ground beneath his feet vibrated. 'The railway line is very close,' he said quickly, 'but I am assured by the other shopkeepers on this parade that it's really no trouble at all and you soon get used to it.'

In fact Harold had no idea how the other shopkeepers felt. This was his first week as area manager of the Worthing branch of Reynard and Sons. The branch wasn't up to scratch as far as the figures went, so Harold had been sent there to shake things up a bit. He'd decided to begin by taking a hands-on approach which was why he was doing this viewing rather than leaving it to one of the more junior staff.

His client walked around upstairs looking into each cluttered room. Harold trailed behind him with a bright smile on his face and acting as if the disgusting state of the building was perfectly normal. Inside he was livid. No wonder this place had remained on the books all this time.

At the client's behest they went outside to examine the small courtyard area between the shop and the beginning of railway property and the line itself. To the left of the building, there was an outside toilet complete with nesting bird on the cistern, and then they came to the courtyard itself. It turned out to be very small – hardly a courtyard at all, more like an alleyway – and it was filled with more rotting rubbish.

A distant hum brought them to a rectangular windowless extension to the building which jutted out into the space. 'What's this?'

Harold studied the brief he'd picked up from the office. 'Oh,' he said, 'this must be the cold storage.'

His client raised an eyebrow.

'This was once a knitwear factory,' Harold explained. 'But I have it on good authority that they also stored fur coats in the summer. Apparently they have to be kept cool to maintain their condition.' He wasn't absolutely sure of his facts, but it sounded feasible. He frowned. 'I can't think why it's still switched on.'

'How do we get in?' asked the client.

'The door must be inside,' said Harold, wishing the minute he'd said it that he'd found a better way of phrasing his comment. Blurting it out like that made him look as if he didn't know what he was doing.

They found the door behind some boxes piled floor to ceiling in front of it. The door itself looked very heavy, more like the door of a bank vault.

'They obviously had some valuable furs in store,' his client remarked as Harold struggled to open it.

With a great deal of effort, they pulled it open together. The cold air and a terrible smell rushed out to meet them. The client cried out, staggered back in horror and pulled his handkerchief over his mouth. He rushed to the front door and only just managed to get outside before he was violently sick.

Harold was paralysed with shock. The room was starkly bare except for the decaying body of a young man curled up in a foetal position.

Fifteen

The first Grace knew of impending trouble was when the police turned up at the factory.

Since Christmas, her life had settled back into a comfortable routine. She and Archie spent at least two or three evenings a week together. Mostly they went to the pictures but there had been the odd concert in the local church hall or the occasional drink in the pub. Usually Snowy and Uncle Charlie Hanson joined them for that.

Output at the factory was good and Norris Finley had just returned from Canada where he had spent four months combining a long holiday with drumming up new business. Grace had taken every minute of overtime on offer and her savings were mounting up. She knew she was being pig-headed and stubborn but there was something in her nature that refused to owe anybody anything. When Michael came across it for the first time soon after they were married, he had laughed and called her 'Independent Annie'. She'd been grateful for Norris's unexpected kindness at Christmas but her one and only New Year's resolution had been to pay the money back as quickly as possible. Even if it took her most of the year, she was determined to do it.

Surprisingly, Rita had settled down quite happily in her job in the fashion department at Hubbard's. She had made new friends and although she was still a helpful girl around the house, she was out most evenings and she went dancing at the Assembly Hall at the weekends. In February, her sixteenth birthday had come and gone and with it, Grace felt, the last of her childhood.

Rita hardly ever spoke of her sister's absence. In one respect, Grace was pleased; after all it wasn't right that her youngest daughter's life should suffer because of Bonnie's inconsiderate behaviour. But on the other hand, it hurt that Rita behaved as if Bonnie was a distant memory. Until Archie filled her life with song, Grace found it much harder to deal with. On really dark days she used to sit on Bonnie's bed, still made up with fresh sheets in case she came home unexpectedly, and fondle her things. Sometimes, after work,

Grace would wait on the platform watching the people getting off the London train. It was quite stupid but there was always that faint hope that Bonnie might be getting off the train to come back home. She would fantasise about how they would meet. Bonnie would run down the platform and into her open arms, or she'd walk towards her with a smile and they'd link arms and go across the road to the Railway Café for a cup of tea and one of those Italian pastry thingies before going home. It was becoming an obsession.

Once, Grace went to the station early in the morning and stopped some of the London-bound passengers.

'Excuse me,' she began. 'My daughter is missing. She's called Bonnie Rogers. If you see a pretty girl, aged 18, oh no, she is 19 now, with long brown hair and cornflower blue eyes, tell her, her mother was asking after her.'

'London is one hell of a place,' one man told her. 'There must be thousands of girls who look like that. Have you got a photograph?'

Grace had shaken her head. That was her one regret, that she didn't have a camera. It wasn't the sort of thing she could afford and her only picture of Bonnie was one taken on a Sunday school outing on the beach at Littlehampton, but that was years ago. Bonnie didn't look remotely like that now. It was very frustrating but Grace wasn't about to give up. Not yet. As soon as she'd paid Norris back, she'd be compelled to take the train to London and look for Bonnie again. Her trip to Richmond with Archie had proved to be fruitless. While he had conducted his business, she had taken the bus into central London and walked about. Ridiculous really. It was like looking for the proverbial needle in a haystack. The captain (she knew his rank by the two stripes in his epaulette) from The Salvation Army had been kind and taken down a few details, but even as she spoke to him, she could see how hopeless it was.

The only new revelation she'd had came when she was spring-cleaning. The range in the kitchen left sooty deposits on the furniture and walls during the winter months, so at the end of March Grace cleaned the house thoroughly from top to bottom.

It was while she was putting new fresh lining paper in the drawers that she'd noticed that her box of official papers had been tampered with. It contained her insurance policies, old letters, her marriage certificate and things like that. She sat on her bed and went through it carefully and realised with horror that two certificates were missing. Bonnie's birth certificate and the letter Mr Finley had written to her when she'd had her son. The only person who could have taken them was Bonnie, and although she could understand that Bonnie might need her own birth certificate for some reason, why on earth had she taken the letter? She'd never told her girls about her first-born. There was no need. It was a part of her life which was over and gone, but why should Bonnie take the one link with him that she had left? The anguish of her discovery brought it all back again. No mother should have to lose two children. 'They're not dead,' she told herself crossly, but it did little to ease her pain. She felt as if her scars were constantly being re-opened – but perhaps that wasn't quite true. They'd never really healed in the first place.

The police car had pulled up right outside the window. Two plainclothes officers got out and when they were actually inside the factory, the driver got out for a cigarette. Cheekily, he winked at the girls, distracted from their work and staring at him from the factory window.

Grace watched the two officers climb the open stairway up to the office. She was beginning to feel anxious. Was this something to do with Kaye Wilcox? Kaye had been accused of stealing a gold watch. She and Snowy could hardly believe it. Kaye had denied it of course, but Norris had dismissed her immediately and without a reference. Grace thought back to Christmas Day and how distant the girl had been. She had most likely been worrying about what was going to happen then. Why did she steal the watch anyway? Grace didn't have Kaye down as a thief.

A new thought crossed her mind. What if the police weren't here to talk about Kaye but about Bonnie's disappearance? Don't be silly, she told herself. There was no reason to think that their coming had anything to do with Bonnie, but as she worked, Grace couldn't resist an occasional glance up at the office window. While the men stood by the door, she could see them clearly but when they went right inside and sat down, they were hidden from view. Grace tried to block out her worries and concentrate on her work.

Eventually, Norah tapped her on the shoulder.

‘Mr Finley wants you in the office.’

Grace stared at her uncomprehending. ‘Me?’

Norah nodded.

Grace felt her blood run cold. ‘What for?’

‘I don’t know, do I?’ her supervisor shrugged. ‘I think somebody died.’

Grace clutched at her chest and looked helplessly at Snowy.

‘Now don’t go jumping to conclusions, love,’ said Snowy as if she had read Grace’s mind.

As Grace ran up the wrought iron steps, the girls looked from one to the other.

‘Her daughter went missing, didn’t she?’

‘Oh God, I’d forgotten all about that.’

‘Here, you don’t think...’

‘Everybody get back to work,’ Norah snapped.

Grace knocked on the office door. Her heart was thumping in her chest.

‘Ah,’ said Norris as she opened the door, ‘this is Mrs Rogers.’ He indicated a chair. ‘Sit down.’

‘Thank you, I’d sooner stand,’ said Grace stiffly.

Finley’s secretary, Miss Samuels, who was working on the other side of the room, turned and looked down her nose at Grace. She was holding a bundle of envelopes. ‘I’ll take this opportunity to go to the post, Mr Finley,’ she sniffed as she left the room.

‘These gentlemen are from the police,’ said Norris rather unnecessarily. ‘They’d like to ask you a few questions. You see, a body...’

‘Thank you, Mr Finley,’ one of the men interrupted. ‘We’ll take it from here.’

Grace swayed. A body? Whose body? It couldn’t possibly be Bonnie. She would have felt it if Bonnie was dead. She'd know. She was her mother.

'I'm Detective Inspector Chester and this is Detective Constable Nyman. Can you tell me your movements on Wednesday 12th November last year?'

How could she forget that day? That was the day Bonnie had left home. Every minute of that day was etched into her memory and would remain there until the day she died. Shakily but clearly, Grace told them her movements ending with, 'When I got to the station, it was too late.'

'Did you see anyone at the station?' asked DI Chester.

'What do you mean?'

'Was there anyone else there? Someone you knew?'

Grace frowned. 'Manny Hart was on the gate,' she said. 'He wouldn't let me go on the platform without a platform ticket even though I begged and begged him.'

'Anyone else?'

Puzzled, Grace looked from one to the other. 'Peggy Jones. She gave me the penny for the machine.'

'I see,' said the DI.

Norris's face became stricken. 'Now hang on a minute...' he began.

'Have you found my Bonnie?' said Grace.

'This isn't about Bonnie,' snapped Norris. 'What they want is...'

'It's plain that this lady saw no one else on the platform that day, Mr Finley,' interrupted the DI again. 'Don't go putting words into her mouth.'

'Don't be bloody ridiculous!' said Norris, rising to his feet as he became heated.

'There was nobody else on that platform!' said Grace loudly.

She hated the raised voices and she was only interested in one thing. 'I don't know what you want me to say. I watched the train leave and I was so upset Mr Finley took me home.'

Norris smiled triumphantly and sat back into his chair. 'See?'

'So Mr Finley was on the platform?' said the inspector.

'Yes!' cried Grace. 'I've just said so. He took me home. Now please, will someone tell me what this is all about?'

'The police have found the body of a young man in the old factory,' said Norris letting out a hollow laugh. 'I think I may have been in the frame for his murder if you hadn't said I was there.'

'Who said anything about murder?' said the inspector tetchily.

Norris looked alarmed and gulped. 'Well, you wouldn't be here if it wasn't something serious, and taking into consideration what you've just told me about the circumstances, what else could it be?' He paused for effect. 'Like I said,' he went on, 'I was returning from Southampton. In fact, I do believe I bought the evening paper while I was down there. Yes, yes, I did. In fact, I used it to line the drawers over there.'

Norris went to the office desk and pulled the drawer open. He emptied it and pulled the newspaper lining onto the table. 'There you are,' he said triumphantly. *'Southampton Evening Standard,* dated 12th November.'

Grace had her mind on other things. She felt terrible but she was glad. Glad the police had come about a young man. Glad it was nothing to do with Bonnie.

The policemen put on their trilby hats and made to leave. 'We may need to ask some of your other employees a few questions,' said the inspector. 'We need to establish the victim's movements on the last day.'

'As far as I'm concerned,' said Norris, rising from his chair to see them to the door, 'I left him to lock up the old factory and I never saw him again.'

'Thank you, sir,' said the inspector.

'Who was he?' said Grace when they'd gone.

'George Matthews,' said Norris.

Grace put her fingers to her lips and gasped. 'George? What George Matthews, the machine operator? But he always seemed nice enough. Why would anyone want to harm him?'

'There were hidden depths to that young man,' said Norris mysteriously.

Grace turned to go.

'In fact,' said Norris. 'I get the feeling he was sweet on your daughter.'

'What?' Grace's head was spinning. Was this the young man Bonnie had a crush on?

'Oh yes,' said Norris. 'I should have warned you but what with the move and everything... He wanted me to invest in some dodgy deal but I was having none of it. I have no time for that sort of thing.' He shuffled some papers on the desk.

'Anyway, you'd better get back to work.'

Grace frowned. 'How do you know he was interested in Bonnie? Where did they find him?'

'He was in the cold room,' said Norris matter of factly. 'There's no handle on the inside so if it slammed shut after him, he wouldn't have been able to get out. The thing was still switched on so if he didn't die of thirst, it must have been the cold.'

'But if he was accidentally shut in,' said Grace, 'why were you talking about murder? And what was all that stuff about the evening paper? I saw Manny give it to you.'

'I'm sorry,' said Norris curtly, 'but I have to get on. I'll talk to you later.'

Reluctantly Grace made no further comment as she left and closed the door quietly. Poor man. What an awful thing to happen. When she got back to her position, she told the girls around the table. They were all as deeply shocked as she was.

'I liked George,' said Snowy. 'Bit of a dreamer but a nice man.'

'Did he have a girlfriend?' Grace tried to make her voice sound casual, but her heart was thumping in her chest. The other girls shook their heads or shrugged. Nobody knew for sure.

As she worked, Grace went over and over what had been said until her head hurt. Had Bonnie been walking out with that man? Did Bonnie know something about George's death? She'd certainly left in a great hurry. Tears pricked at Grace's eyes. Time and again, she shook the terrible thoughts away but they kept coming back. There was no way her Bonnie could be involved, was there? One thing was crystal clear. She had to keep this from Rita.

The day seemed endless. At one point, Norris left the factory in his car.

'Now where's he going?' Grace whispered for Snowy's hearing only. Snowy shrugged but a bit later on the message came back down the assembly line.

'The police wanted him back at the old factory.'

The boss was gone for about an hour and when he came back he glanced over at Grace. That pushed her anxiety back up again.

As they packed up to go home, Norris leaned over the balustrade and called down curtly. 'Mrs Rogers, a word.'

Grace glanced up at him anxiously. What now? And why now? Why hadn't he called her up earlier, as soon as he got back from the old factory? She shot a fear-filled look at Snowy.

'Go on, love,' said Snowy. 'I'll wait for you.' It was an unwritten code. Snowy was telling her: whatever happens I'll be here for you.

The factory was almost empty as Grace climbed the wrought iron staircase once more. She went into the office and Norris made to close the door. 'It's all right, Mrs Snow,' he called down. 'You can go.'

'We always walk together, sir,' said Snowy firmly. 'I'm happy to wait for her.'

Norris closed the door and Grace spotted an almost imperceptible twitch of irritation on his face as he walked around her and sat at his desk. He stared down as if deep in thought.

'Well?' said Grace. 'What is it?' Her tone was

familiar rather than respectful. After his suggestion the day he whisked her off to Durrington in his car, she was wary of him. She didn't want to be alone with him any longer than was necessary.

Norris opened the drawer of his desk and took out a brown envelope. 'I hate doing this to you,' he said, keeping his eyes down, 'but I have to.'

He tipped the contents onto the desk and Grace frowned. A heart-shaped locket spilled onto the inkstand.

'I don't want any presents,' she said tetchily.

'I'm not giving it to you,' he scoffed. 'Don't you recognise it? It's your daughter's.'

Grace gasped in shocked surprise. She made a grab for it but Norris snatched it up again.

'How do you know it's hers? I never saw her wearing it.'

'Of course you didn't. It was a secret present ... from George. He once asked me which was the best jeweller in town and when he'd bought it, he showed it to me.'

Her heart was pounding so hard, Grace thought for a minute it was going to leave her chest altogether. 'Prove it.'

He reached into the drawer and took out a piece of striped paper. Grace's heart nearly stopped. She recognised it at once. It had been the paper wrapped around the Wibley's box, the one Bonnie had had from her admirer.

'Where did you get it?' Now she couldn't take her eyes off the delicate little chain wound around his big sausage fingers. The heart-shaped locket swung against the back of his hand. 'Where did you find it?' she asked again.

That same muscle twitched involuntarily as a slow smile played on his lips. 'In the same place the police found the body.'

Her jaw dropped. 'What? You don't think...'

He nodded slowly. Angry tears sprang into Grace's eyes. 'If you think my daughter had anything to do with that poor man's death...'

Norris shrugged. 'It doesn't matter what I think, Grace,' he said casually. 'But I do think the police might be very interested if I told them about it.'

Grace frowned as she tried to make sense of what he was saying. 'You mean the police don't know you've got it?'

He shook his head.

'How come?'

'Because I picked it up from the floor the day we closed the old factory,' he said. 'I've only just put two and two together. Of course, had I known poor George was still on the premises locked up in the cold room, I might have saved him.'

'I don't understand. You told the police you left *him* to lock up.'

Norris shifted some papers on the table. 'Obviously, someone else went there to meet George.'

Grace covered her mouth with her hand. Was this the reason why Bonnie left in such a hurry? Had she discovered the body too? What was she doing in the factory in the first place?

Grace lowered herself into the chair on the other side of his desk. 'No, it couldn't have been Bonnie. She would have been at work.'

'It was Wednesday, half day closing,' he said. He

put the little locket and chain back into the brown envelope and sealed it down.

'Thank you,' said Grace, expecting him to hand it to her. 'I can't tell you how grateful I am because of this.'

'I'm sure you are.' He stood up and to her horror he turned towards the safe, opened the door, put the envelope inside and slammed it shut.

'What are you doing?' Grace leapt to her feet and rushed to his side, but the click of the combination lock as he turned it was already filling the room.

'I'm sure you'll find a way of showing me just how grateful you are, Grace,' he leered. 'Who knows, you might even find it quite pleasant.'

'You're not suggesting…'

'I'm not suggesting anything.' He smiled again. 'But I'm telling you that locket goes to the police at the end of the month unless you have a change of heart.'

She glared at him in disgust. 'You want me to sell my body for a locket?'

'Perish the thought, my dear,' he purred. 'All I ask is a few hours of your company and as a reward I'll make sure your daughter isn't tried for murder.'

Grace swayed and he caught hold of her arm. Their eyes met and he began to lean his head towards her lips. Gathering every ounce of strength she could muster, Grace pushed him away. 'And I'm telling you,' she spat, 'that hell will freeze over before I let you touch me, Norris Finley.'

He shrugged nonchalantly. 'It's up to you, my dear.'

She made a dash for the door and pulled it open.

'End of the month,' he repeated.

Without a backward glance, Grace swept out and slammed the door.

Alone in the office, Norris listened to her footsteps as they raced down the metal steps and chuckled to himself. He loved the thrill of the chase and he'd waited a long time for this one. She'd flounced off on her high horse now but give her a few days and she'd come crawling back. He wouldn't give her the locket of course. Not until he'd had his fill of her, and who knew how long that might take?

Snowy didn't ask questions but they stood between them as big as houses as the two of them walked home. Grace was so deep in thought she hardly noticed when they'd reached Snowy's place.

'Is that man trying to get into your knickers?'

Grace was jolted back into the here and now by her friend's bluntness. She nodded dully.

'Don't let him, Grace,' said Snowy. 'He's tried that on with a few others, the creepy bastard. I don't know what it is about him but he always leaves them wrecked.'

They walked on and then Snowy said, 'I reckon that's what happened to poor Kaye.'

Grace frowned. 'What do you mean?'

'Sorry, I thought you knew,' Snowy sighed. 'She took the bus to Beachy Head and walked over the top.'

Grace stopped walking. 'What?'

'St George's Day.'

Grace was appalled. She had thought Kaye looked worried about something ever since Christmas. How could she have let so much time go by without even asking her if she could help? 'What made her do it?' she asked faintly.

'I've no idea,' said Snowy, 'but that business with the watch ... there was something very fishy about it.'

'And you think it had something to do with Norris?'

'I'm damned sure of it,' said Snowy. 'I just can't work it out, that's all.' She paused. 'Whatever he's holding over you, Grace, don't get involved with him.'

'Don't worry,' said Grace defiantly. 'This is one woman he's not getting into bed.'

But even as she spoke, her words had a hollow ring.

Sixteen

'Miss Rogers will show you into a cubicle, Madam.' Miss Bridewell's bony fingers dug into Rita's back as she pushed her towards their client, a matronly woman still wearing her winter wardrobe.

At this time of year in the fashion department, they were rushed off their feet. Rita hardly had time to breathe. If she wasn't making a customer comfortable in the cubicles, she was re-hanging the garments or helping the mannequins dress in the outfits Miss Bridewell deemed right for the day. Being the general dogsbody, Rita was also responsible for arranging for a tea tray to be on hand for the wealthier customers. The pettiness of it all got to her sometimes but when they were busy she quite enjoyed herself.

Rita wasn't supposed to talk to the customers but she did. She was careful not to do it when Miss Bridewell was within earshot but there were times when she voiced her opinion. Most customers were grateful but occasionally Rita's honesty got her into trouble.

'What do you think?' asked a particularly difficult-to-please customer.

'Perfect,' gushed Miss Bridewell.

The woman twirled this way and that, unable to make up her mind.

'The dress suits you perfectly, Madam,' Rita smiled conspiratorially when the manageress had moved onto another customer, 'but perhaps you are unsure about the colour? Perhaps the pink is a little too pale for your complexion?'

'I'll thank you to keep your opinions to yourself,' Miss Bridewell hissed when the customer left empty-handed. 'She was on the verge of buying that.'

'But she looked awful,' Rita protested. 'It didn't suit her one bit.'

'Since when did you become such an expert?' Miss Bridewell spat. 'I'll thank you to keep your opinions to yourself, Miss Rogers.' And spotting another customer she slid away with her best smile. 'Can I help you, Madam?'

'Treading on the toes of the Almighty again,' Dinah grinned. 'That was a Rembrandt dress. One of our most expensive.'

'I don't care,' said Rita defiantly. 'It didn't suit her at all.'

'Quite right,' Dinah chuckled.

Rita liked Dinah. She understood why her sister had been such good friends with her. She was older than Rita, more Bonnie's age than her own. Dinah had a wonderful figure that didn't need a foundation garment but she wasn't a bit stuck up about it. Rita was sure if Dinah wore a brown paper bag she'd look good in it.

'I'm going off early today,' Dinah said, 'so only give me a couple of dresses to model. It's the Worthing Musical Comedy show tonight at the Pavilion.' Rita brought her a floral day dress from the rail and helped her with the buttons. 'Are you coming?'

'I've never been to a show,' said Rita shaking her head.

'Then you must,' cried Dinah. 'For the first time since the war, we've got two shows this year. This one's called *No, No, Nanette.*'

Rita smiled. She didn't make any further comment. Tickets would be expensive and she didn't have that much saved. She added a small red belt to Dinah's tiny waist and selected some white gloves to wear with her outfit.

'You simply must come,' Dinah insisted. 'Tell you what, I'll leave a couple of complimentary tickets at the box office for tonight's performance.'

Rita's eyes sparkled. 'Really?'

'The show starts at 7.30pm so be there by 7.15pm. Just say my name and they'll give them to you.' She looked into the mirror and fluffed up her hair. 'You'll love it.'

Miss Bridewell was scowling on the other side of the curtain when they pulled it back. 'Come along, Miss Chamberlain,' Miss Bridewell said tetchily. 'We haven't got all day.'

'I just need a matching hat,' said Dinah cheerfully.

Miss Bridewell spotted another customer and as she scurried off, Dinah pulled a face behind her back. Rita giggled.

The double gates of Holly Acres were a welcome sight as Bonnie struggled along the driveway with her suitcase balanced on the baby's carrycot pram. It seemed a dreary place and she might have been filled with a real sense of foreboding, but she wasn't alone.

As she'd stepped off the train Bonnie had asked a young girl about her own age if she knew how far it was to Holly Acres.

'I'm going there too!' cried the girl. 'Apparently there's a bus stop just around the corner.'

'I shall have to walk,' said Bonnie pointing to the pram.

'Then let me keep you company,' said the girl cheerfully.

'It might be a long way,' Bonnie cautioned, but her new companion wouldn't be deterred.

They finally introduced themselves by the front door as Bonnie offloaded her case. Her new companion, Pat Smith, had three cases in all, all of which were breathtakingly heavy. Bonnie couldn't imagine what she had inside but she had agreed to balance one across the carrycot.

Holly Acres had the faint illusion of grandeur long since gone. The garden was neglected and a dead Christmas tree stood on the wide portico entrance.

'I bet this place was quite something when it was someone's private home,' Pat remarked as she rang the doorbell.

'Looks a bit bleak now,' Bonnie remarked.

A pleasant-faced girl of about their own age opened the door. 'Are you the new girls?'

Bonnie nodded.

'Wait here.'

As they stood in the hallway waiting for someone else to come, Bonnie looked around. So this was to be her home for a while. Hers and Shirley's. After the gruelling day she'd had, she felt in desperate need of a wash but thankfully the baby slept on. Now that they were in the light, Bonnie could see that Pat was an attractive girl. Her long blonde hair was swept up onto the top of her head and she wore it with a kiss curl on the left temple. She still looked fresh and tidy although Bonnie wondered if she should mention that the Cupid's bow on her lips was slightly smudged. Her companion noticed her looking at her and smiled.

Presently, the girl who had opened the door to them came back with another girl. 'Julie will show you to your room,' she told Pat, and turning to Bonnie she said, 'Bring baby upstairs to the nursery.'

Julie said nothing but turning on her heel, she headed back the way she had come. Pat picked up her cases again and trudged wearily behind her. 'See you later,' she smiled.

Bonnie picked Shirley up and followed the other girl up a stone staircase.

The baby room, as it was called, was light and airy. There were six little cots, all painted white, and each cot had a baby in it except the last one by the window.

Bonnie was introduced to a rather strict-looking woman called Nancy. She announced that she was in charge of the baby room and when Bonnie was on duty, she would be taking care of Shirley.

'Has she been fed?'

'She had her last feed at two,' said Bonnie, fingering her 'wedding' ring. It was actually from Woolworth's and it felt strange on her finger.

Nancy looked at the clock. 'We feed everybody at six,' she said tartly. 'You can come back when you've unpacked your things.'

Reluctantly Bonnie handed her little girl to her new carer and went to find her room.

'My name is Doreen,' said her guide. 'We're in together. Our room is in the cottage. You can leave your pram outside in the pram shed. Come on, I'll show you.'

Rita called into the Railway Café on the way home. Salvatore and Liliana were delighted to see her and almost as soon as she was in the door, Rita was sitting at a table with a cup of steaming tea and an Italian pastry in front of her.

'You OK?' Salvatore asked.

Rita nodded.

'The job, it is still good?'

Again Rita nodded.

'He worries,' said Liliana. 'You come many times. He worry you troubled about something.'

'Actually, I came to ask you something,' said Rita.

'Fire away,' said Salvatore mimicking her mother's expression.

'I've been offered two tickets for the WMCS show tonight,' she said all in a rush, 'but I have no one to go with.'

She was distracted because she'd become aware that *he* had come out of the kitchen and was standing behind her, listening. Her heart was beginning to thump in her chest.

'Ah,' said Salvatore.

'They're absolutely free so it won't cost anything,' Rita blundered on, 'and they tell me it's a really good show.'

'Thank you,' smiled Salvatore coyly. 'I come. I would be honoured to be with such a pretty young lady.'

Rita was horrified. That wasn't what she meant at all. She didn't want to go with Salvatore! Much to her relief, Liliana kicked her husband under the table.

'Rita no want to go with an old man like you,' she scowled. 'She like a young man. A handsome young man.' She smiled and looked directly at Emilio.

Salvatore gesticulated with his hands as if he hadn't a clue what his wife was talking about.

Rita chewed her lip anxiously. She hadn't expected it to be so embarrassingly difficult.

'You are right,' said Salvatore. 'I am a very busy man, but,' he stroked his chin thoughtfully, 'who can I send in my place?'

Rita began to feel hot and uncomfortable. She dared not look around. She could feel *his* eyes boring into her back. She never should have started this. Oh flip, what had she done? Girls didn't ask boys out. Perhaps they would think she was 'fast'.

'Stop teasing the girl, Salvatore,' said Liliana.

'I would be pleased to go,' said a voice behind her.

Rita's heart almost stopped. 'Would you?' she said turning around at last and trying to sound casual. 'It might help you with your English.'

'Curatilei. E sola una bambina,' said Salvatore. (Treat her well, she is only a child.)

'Sero un gentiluomo perfetto,' said Emilio. (I am the perfect gentleman.)

The pram shed turned out to be a large rather dilapidated wooden building to the side of the house. When Doreen opened the doors, Bonnie was confronted with two rows of prams lined up against the walls. They were all different shapes and sizes and all coach built. Doreen moved a couple of prams until they were closer together.

'You can put yours here in the corner,' she said. 'When it's too cold to be outside, we leave the babies and tweenies in here.'

'Tweenies?' Bonnie enquired.

Doreen laughed. 'I always forget that it sounds

strange to someone outside of the nursery. We call the children between one and two years old tweenies.'

As soon as Shirley's pram was parked, they went back outside and Doreen closed the door. An empty hollow feeling settled in Bonnie's stomach. Perhaps coming here wasn't going to be so easy after all. The girls seemed friendly enough but the thought of leaving her baby in that dingy shed was not a happy one. She hoped she'd done the right thing, but what choice did she have?

'This is the cottage,' said Doreen as they walked back across the cobbled yard. 'Most of us live here. Matron has a flat over the old stables and the other senior staff live in the main house.'

The stairs were steep and at the top they were faced with another long corridor. Doreen opened a door marked '2'.

'You've got twenty minutes to unpack and then you'll have to go back and feed your baby,' she said looking at her watch. 'Supper is at six thirty. Do you think you can find your way back?'

Bonnie nodded. Her room was predominantly yellow but the walls had holes in them where previous occupants had put up pictures. There were no pictures now but the room was a reasonable size, sparsely furnished and with two beds, one obviously occupied. A small teddy bear leaned against the pillows and the dressing table beside the bed was littered with make-up. She glanced at the people in the photograph on the locker. Standing next to an older man and woman was Doreen, wide eyed and with short bobbed hair, smiling back at her.

Bonnie put her case on the other bed. She felt awkward, as if she was intruding into someone else's privacy. There was an empty locker beside her bed and there was only one wardrobe. Bonnie opened the door. One side was bulging with clothes and on the other side, in only one third of the space, three coat hangers jangled noisily.

She unpacked miserably. She had no photograph of Mum and her sister. She sighed. They would be getting ready to have tea about now. It didn't take long to put her things away and then, because it would soon be time to go and feed Shirley, she went to look for Pat.

Pat's room was blue. The curtains were floral, the pattern made up of big bold flowers, unlike any Bonnie had ever seen, and although they were the same colour, somehow they clashed with the blue splodge pattern wallpaper. To make matters even worse, Pat's candlewick bedspread was purple. There were two beds in the room but it looked as if the other one was unoccupied.

'I wish they had put us in together,' Bonnie observed as Pat unpacked her second case. 'Do you need a hand?'

Pat handed her a floral button-through dress with a small white collar and thin belt. 'Can you hang that for me please?'

'Wow,' said Bonnie. 'This is fantastic.'

'It's brand new,' said Pat obviously pleased. 'Cost me two weeks' wages.'

Bonnie couldn't resist holding the dress next to her as she stood in front of the mirror on the wardrobe door. 'It's lovely.'

'Julie's supposed to be coming back to give me a tour of the nursery,' said Pat. She pushed the last of her cases on top of the wardrobe and they both sat on the edge of the bed until Julie came back.

Their whistle-stop tour of the nursery was totally confusing. 'This is the milk kitchen, here's the Blue Room, that's the sluice room...' – all the details merged into each other. It was obvious that Julie had little interest in the place and Bonnie couldn't help wondering why.

As they swept through the children's bedrooms, Bonnie was aware of several pairs of curious eyes looking at her from under the blankets. She smiled at their little upturned faces. In the baby room she looked at the clock. It was six and Nancy was changing a baby's nappy in the little bathroom.

'This is the last one,' she said. 'You can do your baby now.'

'Oh,' said Bonnie. 'I've left her nappies downstairs in the pram.'

'You're to use ours, Matron said,' said Nancy. 'And if you're breastfeeding, I'm afraid you'll have to put her on the bottle.'

'Why?' Bonnie's voice was small.

'We all think it would interfere too much with your duties,' said Nancy in a no-argument sort of a voice. 'If you're looking after the children downstairs, you can't just leave them to come up here and feed your baby.'

Put like that, it sounded reasonable, but Bonnie loved the intimate moments she and Shirley shared together. Still, she was in no position to argue so she breastfed Shirley for the last time. When she had finished, Nancy brought out some bandages.

'What are they for?'

'You need to bind your breasts,' she said matter of factly. 'To stop the milk coming back in.'

When all the babies had been fed, Nancy put out the big light, leaving a low light in the room. The babies who were awake played by themselves in their cots. Shirley and one other little baby were fast asleep.

'I'm sorry you lost your husband,' said Nancy. 'This must be awful for you.'

'I'm luckier than most,' said Bonnie keeping her back to Nancy for fear she would see her scarlet face. 'I have my baby.'

Trussed up like a chicken, and with two tablets to help dry up the milk, Bonnie headed back downstairs again. As she walked back through the hallway, a gong sounded.

'Supper,' said Nancy. 'I'm off duty now.'

She took Bonnie to the staff room and left. After a few minutes, other girls began congregating.

'This is my new roommate,' said Doreen.

Bonnie smiled. 'My name is Bonnie Rogers.'

'Bonnie!' someone snorted.

'Short for Veronica, isn't it?' said Julie.

It wasn't, but somehow Bonnie didn't like to say anything.

'Come on, girls,' said one of the others. 'Let's get stuck in. I'm starving.'

Supper turned out to be lukewarm tinned

tomatoes on toast.

The Pavilion Theatre was at the entrance to the pier. In 1939, the government had decreed that the pier be blown up in the middle in case of invasion. Because of the acute shortage of raw materials, a large section in the middle was still awaiting reconstruction, but the roadside theatre was back in use.

Rita and Emilio walked in together. Rita felt ten foot tall and a bag of deliriously happy nerves. As instructed, she asked the cashier for tickets in the name of Chamberlain and was handed a brown envelope. It was a good seat, in the centre and fairly near the front. From the moment they sat down, Rita was totally carried away. The show was perfect, as was her company. She had hoped Emilio might hold her hand but he didn't touch her. Still, she told herself, that's fine. He knows I'm a good girl. I'm the sort who wants to wait until I get married to let a boy kiss me. She glanced his way a couple of times during the evening and each time he flashed her one of his wonderful smiles, which made her legs go weak and her heart thump wildly. She was in love. What else could she be? And it was wonderful.

The show was amazing. Dinah was only in the chorus but Rita watched her every move. Everyone at Hubbard's knew she wanted to be an actress and that she'd been waiting to get a place in drama school. She was so tall and elegant that Rita couldn't understand why she hadn't been given the lead role.

In the interval, Emilio insisted on buying her a

cup of tea, but it turned out to be free.

'Are you enjoying the show?'

She hoped her voice sounded sultry and mature but it came out a bit squeaky with excitement. Emilio smiled, making Rita melt all over again. 'It is very kind of you to ask me.'

The silence that grew between them made Rita feel a bit awkward.

'Are you going to work in your uncle's shop?'

Emilio shook his head. 'No, no,' he said with a twinkle in his eye and Rita remembered that the show was called *No, No, Nanette*. 'I am fisherman.'

Rita pulled a face. 'The Worthing fishermen guard their patch very closely,' she said. 'Their rights go back years and years. I doubt you'll get a pitch here.'

He shrugged. 'Then I am lucky guy. I have a boat at East Worthing.'

Rita was surprised.

'I share with a friend,' he explained. 'The waters here are good for mackerel and sea bass. I think I make a good living.'

'So you're staying in Worthing?' Rita said breathlessly and to her utter joy, Emilio nodded.

As the curtain went up for the second half, Rita was trembling with excitement. Salvatore treated her like a silly schoolgirl, but Emilio was treating her like a young woman ... and he was going to live here.

The show was just as good in the second half as it had been in the first. The story was a little confusing but the three couples who found themselves together in a cottage finally got the right man and everybody lived happily ever after. Rita loved the music, especially 'Tea for Two' and 'I Want to be Happy'. Dinah had told Rita to wait for her after the curtain came down. They didn't have to wait long.

'We're all having a party,' she told them. 'You must come.' Rita felt as if she'd died and gone to heaven.

The party was in somebody's house along the sea front. It was rowdy and the gramophone was playing Red Hot Jazz, the sort of music the council had banned from all its public venues. Rita couldn't think why. It was fun. She felt a little out of place because most of the girls were wearing party frocks and she wasn't, but nobody remarked it. In fact, they were all very friendly. Dinah looked so elegant as she smoked her Craven A cigarette in a short holder. 'Enjoying yourself, Rita?'

'Oh yes,' sighed Rita. 'The show was wonderful.'

As everybody squeezed in, the people who wanted to dance stayed in the spacious hallway while the rest of the cast sat around the sitting room drinking and talking. There were no sandwiches or cakes. They ate fiddly bits called *hors d'oeuvres.* Rita tasted her first vol-au-vent and her first olive.

She'd been there for about an hour when a man grabbed her hand. 'Dance, pretty lady,' he cried and, laughing, Rita looked around for Emilio.

'Actually, I came with someone.'

'The tall good-looking chap?' he asked.

She nodded.

'He's gone outside with Jeremy to look at the stars,' said the man. 'He won't mind. Come on.' And he swept her into his arms as somebody changed the record to a waltz.

Seventeen

After supper on that first day in the nursery, Bonnie had gone upstairs to check on Shirley and found her sleeping peacefully.

'I'll come up to give her the ten o'clock feed,' she told the girl in the nursery, and then she went to her room. She supposed she should have stayed in the staff room and made friends, but Bonnie was tired and homesick. She collected her uniform and went back to her room to get ready for duty in the morning.

She had been told her uniform was 'an attractive pink gingham dress'. It turned out to be a shapeless, round-necked garment with a Peter Pan collar, three rubber buttons down the front so that they could be boiled, and from what she could make out, size 20 fitted everybody. She had also been given a list of things she'd need to take with her. At the bottom of the page, alongside a toothbrush and comb it said two pairs of garden knickers. Bonnie had scratched her head. What on earth were garden knickers? Much to her embarrassment, when she had asked around the London stores, she was met by blank stares. The only real suggestion came from an old fossil who had probably been working in the shop since the age of the dinosaurs.

'Could these be what you want?'

She held up a pair of voluminous powder-blue silk drawers with an elasticated waist and long legs which stretched as far as the knee. As soon as Bonnie saw them, she recognised them as the type of garment her granny used to wear.

Bonnie smiled as she recalled the shocked look on the old biddy's face when she'd said, 'If that's what they are, I'd sooner work in the garden with no knickers at all!'

After she'd put her things in the wardrobe, Bonnie got out her small box of private things and tipped them onto the bed. A few old birthday cards, a little round of hair she'd collected from Rita's hairbrush the day she'd left home and Mum's best hanky. It was probably a good idea to keep all her important documents in one place. After all, that's what Mum did. She rounded up her allowance book, her post office book and Shirley's birth certificate, all lurking at the bottom of her handbag, and put them in the box. Then she remembered her own birth certificate. George had told her to bring it with her because she would need it in order to get a passport. She kept that folded up in the lid of her jewellery box. She didn't know why she still kept the box. She'd lost the pretty locket George had given her with it. It had upset her dreadfully when she'd realised it was gone and although she'd racked her brains, she couldn't really remember where she'd last had it. She remembered she'd been fiddling with it when she'd gone into that rundown factory where George used to work. The place was in an awful mess and yet George had told her he was personally in charge of cleaning it up. There were paper and boxes strewn everywhere. It would take ages to clear up. And then the caretaker, wearing a long brown overall and a hat pulled down over his eyes, had come out of that little room at the back and shouted at her.

'What the bloody hell are you doing here?'

He had given her such a shock, she'd dropped her handbag and everything had spilled out. Stuffing it all back inside, she'd just turned on her heel and fled. Luckily, the bus was coming along the road and she was right beside the stop. From the safety of the lower deck of the speeding bus, she saw him come out onto the street, look up and down and then go back inside, slamming the door shut behind him. Her little locket was somewhere in among all that rubbish but she hadn't missed it until she got to London and by then it was far too late.

Bonnie found the certificate and spread it out. She recognised her own certificate, but there was something else folded with it. It was a tissue-thin letter addressed to her mother in her maiden name. Bonnie opened it and read with mounting horror.

It was dated 12th May 1924 and began:

My dear Grace,

I cannot tell you how delighted I was to hear of the birth of your baby yesterday. John is such a nice name. Please keep in touch. My son loved you very much. He should have done the right thing by you,

but we will welcome your son into the family. My dear, I do not have long to live and I would welcome the opportunity to see my grandson before I die.
Yours sincerely,
Edward Finley.

Bonnie took in her breath. The envelope was addressed to Grace Follett. Her mother's maiden name was Follett. What did this mean? Five years before she was born, her mother had had an illegitimate child? Bonnie's hand trembled as she put it to her lips. And that child was called John Finley. She knew a John Finley. Didn't he used to come to the WMCS shows with Dinah? Surely it couldn't be the same person. The only other Finley she knew was the man who had been George's boss ... and come to think of it, her mother's boss too! Was he John Finley's father? Bonnie looked at the certificate again and her blood ran cold. Norris Finley was a horrible man. He'd come to the shop one day with his wife. He'd been so demanding, even shouting at Miss Bridewell, and by the time they left, nearly everyone was in tears, including his poor wife.

The door opened and her roommate came in. 'Sorry. Hope I'm not disturbing you?'

'Not at all.' Bonnie pulled herself together and wiped her face with her thumbs. She glanced at the clock. 'I've got to go and feed the baby in a minute anyway.'

She tumbled everything into the box and shut it in the only drawer with a lock and key. 'What time do we have to be on duty in the morning?'

'Seven,' said Doreen, 'but I think you'll be

earlier, won't you?'

Bonnie nodded. 'The six o'clock feed.'

Doreen groaned in sympathy. 'Sooner you than me.'

It was April 30th. Grace dragged herself to work but she had no appetite for it. She hoped against hope that Norris was away on business but it wasn't to be. His car was in the parking space outside the factory and he was already in his office.

'You look a bit pasty,' Snowy remarked as they had their mid-morning break.

'Me?' said Grace brightly. 'I'm fine. Poor old Elsie is wondering what to do with her Dougie,' Grace went on, desperate to change the subject. 'He's left school and he needs a job.'

'That lad'll never work,' sighed Snowy. 'I know he gets there in the end but who's got the patience with him?'

Grace had to agree.

They were working on another knitwear order, this time for America. They were pretty lacy jumpers with short sleeves in two-ply wool. Grace loved the feel of them. They were so soft, like lambswool or cashmere.

They went back to work but her thoughts were all over the place. Was Norris serious when he said she had to decide by the end of the month? He couldn't make her do it, could he? She worried about it and yet she knew he wouldn't have to. Much as she hated the idea of being alone with him, if he really meant to tell the police about Bonnie's locket, she would walk to hell and back again to stop him. Then there was Archie. He was such a lovely man and she really enjoyed being in his company. They had always loved walking together but now he took her for meals, or to the pictures. Last Friday, her half day and now his, he'd held her hand as they went along that bit of pier that was still open.

He'd opened up a bit about the war. Grace had felt she was privileged at the time. She'd realised quite early on in their relationship that Archie was a private man and that he chose his friends carefully. Every Sunday he visited his grandmother who lived in a nursing home, but he'd lost his parents in the bombing in Cornwall of all places.

'I've been thinking about the Fair Rents panel,' he said. The countrywide panels had been set up by the government after the war to make sure people were not being overcharged by unscrupulous landlords. 'I reckon if we banded together, we could force our landlord to take notice. It's against the law not to have a rent book now.'

Grace looked thoughtful. 'So you think if we draw attention to his wrongdoing he'll be forced to comply?'

'Exactly,' said Archie. 'The thing is, you know the people round here better than I do. You could persuade them to sign the petition.'

Grace had been sceptical. She might be able to persuade her neighbours but in her present predicament how would it leave her? Norris already had the upper hand. He was sure to give the locket to the police if she went ahead with a petition.

'The landlord doesn't need to know about it,' said Archie as if reading her thoughts.

'I'll think about it,' she said. The trouble was, the more she thought about it, the less she liked the idea.

'You coming on the works outing?' Snowy asked as later that morning they made their way back to the canteen.

'Try and stop me,' laughed Grace. 'Exbury Gardens, isn't it?'

Snowy nodded. 'You'd better put your name down. The coach is filling up fast.'

Snowy carried on to the canteen while Grace stopped by the notice board.

'Save me a place,' she called.

Grace picked up the pencil and added her name to the list. 'When is it?'

'It's the end of the month,' said a soft voice behind her. Her blood ran cold. She turned and looked up into Norris's face. He was smiling.

'I can't,' she said helplessly. 'I can't.'

He raised an eyebrow, nodded sagely and walked away. She was immediately seized with panic. If Bonnie had been in there, in that factory the day that boy died, she must have known something. If she were only a witness, why hadn't she come forward? If she had nothing to hide, she would have told the police. Grace stared at Norris's receding back. What was he going to do? If she said no to him, she might as well put a noose around her daughter's neck herself.

'No!' she cried. 'Wait!'

He paused by the iron staircase. 'Mrs Rogers,' he said stiffly and without turning to look at her,

'I wonder if you might come up to my office for a moment?'

Grace turned to look in the direction of the canteen. Snowy had gone; in fact most of the factory girls were either inside already or queuing up to go in. Grace followed Norris up the stairs, her eyes smarting with unshed tears. She was doing this for her daughter – she had to, she had no choice.

'Shut the door,' he said as she came in.

Grace closed the door and stood with her head bowed. 'Why are you making me do this?'

'Let's get one thing clear, Grace,' he said coldly. 'Nobody is making you do anything. You are here because you want to be.'

She looked up but any faint hope that he might not make her go through with it died instantly. He had Bonnie's locket in his hands and was playing with the clasp. As soon as he knew she'd seen it, he put it in his pocket.

'Norris, please...'

He laid a key on the table. 'I am looking for someone to clean one of my properties,' he said matter of factly.

She frowned, puzzled. 'Cleaning?'

'Number 21 North Street,' he went on. 'It's just before Ashdown Road.'

'Cleaning?' she repeated.

'You have to have a reason to be there,' he said. 'Come next Thursday, May 8th. Make it 7.30pm.' He gave her a knowing smile. 'Then I shall have the pleasure of showing you exactly what I want you to do for me.'

Eighteen

Sunday was to be their last time together. Grace had made up her mind that if she had to go to Norris for the sake of her daughter, she couldn't bring herself to cheat on Archie as well. It would hurt him far too much and he had suffered enough already. She had to end their relationship. It was only right.

She also had to go back up to London and try and find Bonnie again. It was imperative to get to the truth, no matter how difficult it might be. Bonnie would never be a party to murder. There had to be another explanation and Grace was all the more determined to find her daughter and get to the bottom of it.

When they met, Archie suggested they go up to Cissbury Ring. The weather couldn't have been more perfect. It was a warm day with a light breeze. She had brought some sandwiches and a flask of tea which he had put into his knapsack when they'd met outside the shop.

'I've got a letter to post to my mother,' she said stealing a glance at him. He looked more handsome than ever. 'Remind me when we go past the letterbox.'

When they got on the bus, Archie told her Cissbury Ring was one of the largest hill forts in Sussex and that it was built two hundred years before Christ. Grace didn't know much about the history of the place but she knew that from the top you could see Chichester Cathedral to the west and as far as Brighton and Beachy Head in the east. During the war, it had been used as a camp for the 2nd Argyll and Sutherland Highlanders. Their manoeuvres damaged a fair bit of the land and some of it had been ploughed up to grow food, none of which went down too well with the locals. Grace listened to every word he said. She wanted to remember every moment of this day.

When they were on the bus, Archie sat so close to her that his thigh and hers were touching. He placed his hand over hers and held it firmly down on his own leg as they sat in companionable silence. The bus went through Broadwater and on to Offington Corner where it turned towards Findon Valley. They got off at the bottom of Nepcote Lane and walked the rest of the way. It was a steep hill and good exercise.

When her girls were small, she and Michael had walked up here. Not very often because Highdown Hill was a lot closer to home, but she remembered the children gathering blackberries on the way.

They walked right to the top and, breathless with exertion, they sat down under a tree with its trunk at their backs. Rumour had it that at night, people practised pagan rites up here but Grace was never sure if that was for real or a yarn. A skylark soared above them and soon the swallows would leave. In the distance a dog was barking and the fields below were dotted with sheep. Being up here in this haven only brought home all the more sharply her own sense of turmoil.

'Have you thought any more about the petition?' he asked.

Grace didn't know what to say. She was caught between the devil and the deep blue sea. She knew Norris wanted Elsie Dawson and her family out, for instance. Harry was becoming more difficult and Dougie had always been a bit odd. Elsie's rent was a good thirty bob more than hers by now and yet the house was identical. The petition was the right thing to do, but what would happen to Bonnie if Grace were a party to it and Norris saw her name on the form?

Archie was waiting for an answer.

'I'll let you know at the end of the day,' she said miserably.

Archie dozed while Grace wrote a letter to Bonnie. There wasn't a day that passed when she didn't think of her daughter, wondering where she was and what she was doing. She still had nowhere to send the letters but the shoebox was half full already. Grace comforted herself that if she didn't see Bonnie this side of the grave, one day her daughter would know she had never forgotten her.

Archie knew that she was writing to Bonnie. He never asked what she said and he never pooh-poohed the idea either and Grace loved him for that. This was her moment: personal, private and tinged with sadness.

Grace leaned back against the tree trunk and read what she had written. She began with the walk and the view. She told Bonnie how Rita had gone to the theatre for the first time. *'Rita spends more and more time with Liliana,'* she wrote. *'She helps in the shop in the evening, clearing up and stuff. Her new friend Dinah has asked her to help her clean up her grandmother's cottage as well.'*

'Finished?' Archie said sitting up. 'I'm starving.'

Grace took the sandwiches out of the knapsack and offered him one. He smiled and took it eagerly. All at once, Grace felt tears spring to her eyes. This would be the last time. She might see him at the shop but this would be their last time together. It wasn't fair. She never thought she would find another good man but she couldn't bring herself to break his heart in the way his wife had done. She comforted herself that it was still early on in their relationship. He'd move on and meet someone else eventually.

'The business is picking up quite well,' he said. 'I had two orders this week, one chair to re-upholster and a three piece suite with a woven cane backing.'

'Is that good?'

'Very,' he smiled. 'The chair will be done in the very best leather I can get and the suite will take me a while.' He lowered his voice confidentially. 'I can tell you now that both of them will be hideously expensive.'

'You need to take my chair,' she reminded him.

'I might not need to if you were my wife.'

The question got lost somewhere. He'd expected some sort of reaction, but Grace pretended she hadn't heard. She was toying with an idea. 'If you're doing so well,' she began, 'is it possible you could offer a job to Dougie?'

'Dougie?'

'Elsie Dawson's boy,' she said. 'You remember him. He was the one fixing the clockwork toy at Christmas.'

'Oh I remember,' said Archie. 'He's a bit simple, isn't he?'

'He's not as thick as they make out,' she said stoutly. 'If you can explain things to him, he'll get it. You just need a little patience that's all.'

'I don't know, Gracie,' he said. 'I'm not sure I'm ready to take on another person. I couldn't pay much either.'

'You wouldn't have to if you took on Dougie,' she insisted. 'All right, he's a bit odd but a more loyal person you could never wish to meet.'

He put his arm around her and pulled her back onto his chest. 'Oh Gracie, you're wonderful,' he said, kissing her hair. 'I'll think about it.'

Grace was tense and on edge. Here she was, sorting out someone else's life, when her own was in such a mess. She had heard him say, *I might not need to if you were my wife...* but she didn't want him to ask her to marry him again. If he did she would have to say no. She didn't want to spoil this last perfect afternoon, she wanted her memories to be completely unsullied. They would soon be all she had left. Coward that she was, she didn't want to tell him up here. She gulped back a sob.

'Are you all right?' he asked anxiously.

'Fine,' she said brightly. 'Just enjoying the view.'

When they got back to Worthing, he stopped outside his shop. 'Coming in while I wash your flask?'

She shook her head. 'Give me the flask here. I

can wash it up when I get home.'

'I don't mind,' he protested mildly.

'No, really,' she said. She held her hand out.

'Aren't you coming in?' He sounded both hurt and puzzled.

She took the flask and the sandwich box and then stood on tiptoe and kissed his cheek. 'No Archie. Thanks for a lovely day but I shan't be coming in.'

He looked stunned. 'What did I say?'

'Nothing,' she said, willing her voice to stay strong. 'I'm afraid you'll have to get someone else to do your petition. I'm sorry, Archie. You've been what you always are, the perfect gent. I shall never forget you, but I'm afraid I can't do this again.'

He snatched at her arm. It was tearing her to shreds saying all this.

'What is this?' he demanded.

Her heart was pounding and her head felt terrible. Don't make me do this, she thought. Don't, Archie, please...

'Look me in the eye and say all that again, Gracie.'

She turned her head and faced him. 'I don't want to see you again,' she said with a strength she didn't know she had. He looked totally shocked. He let go of her and she walked briskly away. 'And I think it would be better if you didn't come to my house any more.'

'Gracie,' he called after her. 'Gracie, wait a minute...'

But she couldn't. She daren't. If she turned back she'd be in his arms and he'd be kissing her.

'Gracie...'

Goodbye dear, dear Archie, she thought. Be happy. Never had she been so glad to reach her own front door.

Rita had spent the day in Alice Chamberlain's house. It was very dark, old fashioned and cluttered. Dinah had persuaded a few of her friends from WMCS and Rita to give her a hand with a big clear out. Rita had been the first to arrive.

Dinah, looking very elegant in an apron and a turban around her head, opened the door. 'I still can't quite believe it,' she told Rita. 'I know it's an awful cliché, but you could have knocked me down with a feather when they told me Granny had left me the house.'

'She owned the house?' Rita gasped.

'Apparently Granddad had the opportunity to buy it in the 1930s,' Dinah went on. 'The owner needed some money pretty darned quick so Granddad took out a loan and bought the house for £78.'

'Will you sell it?' Rita asked.

'Not for the moment,' said Dinah, 'although I must say, I have had an offer. Can you be a darling and help me move this sofa? I'm sure there's loads of things down the back of it.'

They pushed and pulled the heavy furniture away from the wall and Dinah was right. Books, magazines, old newspapers and even a box of old Christmas cards tumbled in disarray to the floor when the sofa was moved.

'Who made you an offer?' Rita asked and she

knelt down and began to pick up everything. She put it on the seat.

'Umm? Norris Finley,' said Dinah, distracted by an old birthday card. 'I gave this to Granny. It must be the last time I sent her a card.'

'Mr Finley owns just about every house in the road,' said Rita.

'Including yours?'

Rita shrugged. 'Our house belongs to my father's family.' She suddenly felt uncomfortable. That implied that she and her family owned their house and yet Rita knew her mother paid rent. She'd never bothered to think of that before. 'Actually, my mother pays some sort of rent to Riverside Properties.'

'I think you'll find that's the name of Mr Finley's companies,' said Dinah.

'Oh,' said Rita.

Someone knocked on the door and Dinah went to answer it. Some friends from the WMCS came in, and Bob Dawson with them.

'Hope you don't mind me gate-crashing,' he said.

'Hey,' cried Dinah. 'You're out of the army at last!'

'Not quite,' he said. 'On leave, but I only have a few months to do.'

Rita smiled and to her surprise was pleased to see him. He looked a lot better for the time he'd been in the army. His spots had gone and apart from his awful army short back and sides haircut, he looked quite handsome. 'I never did write and thank you for that mention in *Forces Favourites* at Christmas,' she said.

'I couldn't get you out of my mind,' he said. 'Did you miss me?'

Emilio sauntered in through the door to another flurry of welcome. Rita's face lit up. 'Emilio came this year.'

Emilio flashed a smile. 'It was good,' he said. 'Good time.'

Rita slipped her arm through Emilio's. 'Come on, let me show you both what Dinah was doing.'

Crestfallen, Bob followed them into the kitchen.

'It's obvious that my granny was a hoarder,' said Dinah once everyone was ready to start. 'I'll have to get rid of most of it but I don't want to throw everything out.'

As they went through the drawers they found everything from bus tickets to old newspapers, magazines, buttons, knitting patterns, old dollies, dresses and photographs.

'It'll take you ages to work through this lot,' someone said.

'There's no hurry,' said Dinah. 'We can take our time.'

Rita was given the job of sorting out the scullery and to her absolute joy, Emilio was sent to join her. They began by turning out the old Rinso packets, half empty used blocks of Drummerboy Blue, bottles with just a dribble of bleach left in them and old milk bottles. They piled everything into the dustbin, put the milk bottles back outside for the milkman and set about cleaning the surfaces.

Being so close to Emilio left Rita feeling quite breathless. She struggled to think of anything to say but she had already worked out that Emilio didn't seem as happy as he had done at Christmas.

How are you enjoying the fishing? Do you have any other brothers and sisters? What did you think of the show? All her questions seemed like an interrogation especially when he didn't elaborate much when he answered.

'I enjoy,' didn't tell her much when it came to the fishing for instance. He was a little more forthcoming when it came to his family but Rita would have liked to be told much, much more.

'My sister, she marry American G.I,' he told her. 'She go to New York. She have good life in America.'

'You didn't want to join her?'

'She say she kill me,' he laughed. 'I come to Uncle Salvatore. He have good business.'

Rita smiled. He sounded almost envious of Salvatore's café and yet he'd made it perfectly clear that he was a fisherman. She had pulled the old copper away from the wall so that she could brush behind it and a couple of mice skittled across the floor. Rita squealed before she could stop herself and Emilio laughed. Dinah poked her head around the corner.

'You've got mice,' Rita blurted out.

Dinah looked horrified. 'Mice! Emilio, do something.'

Bob appeared in the doorway with a long-handled broom.

Jeremy got in on the act as well. 'You need to set a trap, or better still, do you have a cat?'

'Next door does,' said Rita, 'and so does Elsie

Dawson over the road.'

With Emilio and Jeremy's help, she borrowed the cat from next door but after an initial show of vague interest he sauntered off. However, Elsie's cat was a lot leaner and before long she was chasing a mouse out of the back door. Jeremy put his arms around Emilio's and Rita's shoulders and laughed. 'Give pussy a medal, darling.'

By the end of the afternoon, Dinah had three piles in the middle of the sitting room floor, one for a jumble sale, one to keep and one to throw away. The house itself had been virtually gutted.

'All we need now are the decorators,' said Dinah.

'I could do a bit for you,' said Bob. 'I don't have to go back until next week,'

'Oh Bob, could you?' Dinah gushed. 'How much should I give you?'

'No charge,' said Bob firmly and Dinah kissed his cheek.

'When are you moving in?' Rita asked.

'I'm not,' said Dinah. 'I told you, I'm off to RADA next month. Jeremy is going to rent it.'

Rita looked at Jeremy and he did a deep bow.

It seemed a little odd that someone like Jeremy, obviously well educated and talented, should want to live in what was a working-class area. Rita supposed it must be because it was near the station and one of the girls had told her he had a job in London. All the same, why not get a larger house more in keeping with his position in life?

'We're all going back to Emilio's place,' Dinah announced. 'Thank you for your help and I'm buying all of you a meal.' She linked arms with

Bob and walked ahead of them.

As Rita walked back up the road with Emilio on one arm and Jeremy on the other, she couldn't have been happier. After all the dark days since her sister vanished, things were finally on the up.

Nineteen

Grace had had a terrible week. Saying goodbye to Archie had been the worst thing she'd ever had to do. She'd tried to keep her crying private but Rita had noticed.

'Is everything all right between you and Mr Warren, Mum?'

Grace had the ironing board out and was ironing the sheets. Rita was getting ready to go out. 'There's no Mr Warren and me,' said Grace firmly.

'I'm sorry,' said Rita. 'I liked him.'

'I've got a new job,' said Grace.

'You're giving up your job at the factory?'

'No, of course not,' said Grace impatiently. 'This is to earn a little bit of extra money. Mr Finley wants me to do some cleaning.' Grace kept her head down and hoped that Rita would put her flushed cheeks down to the heat of the iron.

'So are you going back to the factory to clean it?' asked Rita anxiously. 'Oh Mum, if you have to walk out and about in the winter, will you be safe? I mean, you know what happened last time.'

'He wants me to clean one of his houses,' said

Grace. 'I'm going there on Thursday night.'

'One of his houses? How many has he got?'

'No idea,' Grace shrugged. 'He rents them out. Anyway, where are you off to tonight?'

'Dinah has invited me to the WMCS auditions.'

'I thought they'd only just finished their show,' Grace frowned.

'They do two shows a year,' said Rita patiently. 'This is for the October show. They're doing Mr Cinders.'

'Very nice,' said Grace.

'I wish you didn't have to work for that Mr Finley, Mum. He's horrible.'

'What makes you say that?'

'He came into the shop the other day and he was really nasty to Miss Bridewell.'

'Oh?' said Grace, suddenly interested. 'What on earth was he doing in Hubbard's dress department?'

'Buying a dress for his fancy woman,' said Rita. 'He chose this lovely midnight blue dress and when Miss Bridewell asked him if he'd like it delivered to his home address, he told her, in front of everybody, to mind her own bloody business and to wrap it up for him to take now.'

Grace stared at her daughter in disbelief.

'And while she was doing that,' said Rita carrying on regardless, 'he told her that if she mentioned the dress to anyone, and I mean anyone,' Rita was beginning to mimic Norris Finley's voice, '"I shall see to it that none of you can get work anywhere between here and Portsmouth."'

Rita pushed her feet into her shoes. 'I mean, I don't like Miss Bridewell very much but there's no need to be nasty, is there? All the girls are talking about it.'

There was a knock at the door. Rita opened it and Elsie Dawson was on the doorstep. 'Is your mother in?'

Grace looked up from her ironing. 'Come in, Else,' she said. 'I've had enough of ironing and you're just the excuse I need to put the kettle on.'

Grace began putting the ironing board back and Rita put her coat on. 'Don't wait up, Mum. We may be late.'

'Don't I get a kiss now?' Grace complained good-naturedly.

Rita blew her one from the doorway.

'I suppose you've heard,' said Elsie when she'd gone.

'Heard what?' said Grace.

'They're burying poor George Matthews tomorrow. Nobody's come forward to claim the body so the council is having to do it.'

Thursday came all too soon. Grace was on time and let herself in with the key. The house was bigger than hers, white fronted with a small front garden protected from the road by a flint wall. It had three floors and back in her mother's day in the thirties, it had been called Montpelier Terrace. Grace remembered old Mrs Pratt who lived there but now it was empty. The house smelled musty and damp.

Grace felt sick with apprehension. She hated the fact that she was even in this position. She should tell Norris to go to hell, but she daren't. What if he did go to the police? Bonnie might be dragged back to town. Even if it were proven in the end that she'd done nothing wrong, Grace knew that the mud would stick. What if she *had* done something to that boy? Grace shuddered. No, not Bonnie. The other puzzle was why she had taken the letter from John's grandfather. Could she be hoping to find him?

A key turned in the lock and Grace jumped as the door opened. It was Norris. Grace tasted the bile in her mouth. She was trembling and her heart had started banging in her chest.

He smiled and took off his coat. 'Hello, Grace,' he purred. 'Make yourself at home. Take off your coat.'

She closed her eyes. The full horror of what was about to happen made her sway. She took off her coat and let it fall to the couch.

'Let's go upstairs,' he said. 'Come on.'

'Norris,' she whispered, 'please don't make me do this.'

'I told you, nobody's making you do anything,' he said again. He took her arm roughly and pushed her towards the hallway and the stairs. She felt like she was being frogmarched. They reached the bedroom door.

'It's nothing you haven't done before, now is it?' he said silkily.

'But I...' She turned towards him and his mouth was over hers. She felt his arm tighten around her waist drawing her towards him while his right hand kneaded her breast. Her heart was pounding, not with desire, but with a plethora of other feelings. Betrayal ... she was falling or perhaps had already fallen in love with Archie.

She had wanted to give herself to him but here she was with this creep. Disgust ... how could she make love, no it would never be like that with Norris, have intercourse with a man she didn't even like? She was nothing more than a tart. Fear ... what if he got her pregnant? She and Michael always joked that he only had to hang his trousers on the bedpost and she'd be pregnant. She wasn't old. She was 41 and would be 42 in June. There was still plenty of time for babies. What if she had yet another Finley out of wedlock?

By now he had her blouse off, her petticoat pulled down and her bra off and was kissing her breasts. She wanted to throw up. He pulled back and looked at her. 'Enjoy it, Grace,' he said. 'You know you want it. It's been a long time since Michael.'

'I'm only here because you've forced me into it,' she said curling her lip. 'I'll never enjoy it with you.'

Norris glared at her with such a terrible expression she honestly thought he was going to hit her. 'I've always wanted you, Grace,' he said in a measured tone. 'And one way or another, I shall have you. You can be nice to me. It won't make any difference what you do but it might be a lot nicer for you if you co-operate.'

She felt her skirt slide to the floor and as he pressed his mouth over hers once again, he was already fully aroused. He pushed her to the bed, spread her legs roughly and mounted her. He was so heavy she could hardly breathe. 'Relax,' he said hoarsely. 'If you think the past was good, you're in for a treat. Now you're in the hands of a real man.'

When it was finally over Grace waited until he fell asleep. It didn't take long. She slipped out of bed and reached for her things. Fully dressed she stared down at him. Where was the locket? His trousers lay in a heap on the floor. She picked them up and felt the pockets. Some loose change made a clinking sound and she froze. She didn't see him open his eyes because as she slowly turned, he snapped them shut. To her way of thinking, he hadn't moved. She laid the trousers on the chair at the end of the bed and picked up his jacket. It had three pockets, two on the outside and an inside breast pocket. One of the outside pockets had a soiled handkerchief but the other was empty. The inside pocket contained his wallet, a style which only took notes. She put it back and hung the coat neatly around the back of the chair and put her hand to her mouth. What an idiot she'd been. He had no intention of giving her the locket, had he? She stared at him, hatred and loathing welling up in her chest like a fiery rod and then he opened his eyes.

'Going somewhere, Grace?'

She couldn't speak. Her heart was racing and her voice died in her throat. She wanted to hit him. He smiled but it was more than a smile. It was a look of triumph, a look of superiority. She'd seen that look before. The first time was when they were kids. She and a whole crowd of other children played with him during the long summer holidays when he'd bullied Eric Millam to climb a tree over by Northbrook Farm. It was far too big of course, and Eric fell. He'd broken his leg and walked with a pronounced limp ever since. The second time was the day his brother died and he'd come all the way over to Mum's house to tell her.

She raised her hand at him but he caught her by the wrist and pulled her down towards him.

'Where is it?' she hissed.

He pulled her hand onto his member. 'Here.'

She tried to snatch her hand away, refusing to touch him. 'You know what I mean,' she said coldly. 'The locket.'

'Oh, the locket,' he mocked. 'Sorry, I forgot to bring it.'

'Then we're finished here, Norris,' she said, tugging at her arm.

'Were you going to hit me, Grace?' He tightened his grip and she couldn't break free. 'You could get into serious trouble if you hit your boss, you know. It might even cost you your job.'

She stared at him in horror. Still keeping hold of her wrist, he began to unbutton her blouse again. She tried to jerk away but he was too strong for her. 'And if you upset your landlord as well...'

Their eyes met and they both knew she was defeated. She closed her eyes and threw her head back with an anguished moan.

He carried on undoing her blouse, and then slipped his hand into her bra. 'But let's not waste time talking about all that, Grace. It's far too early to go home just yet. You still have some more cleaning to do.'

He let her go at around 9.30pm. She slunk out of the house, terrified that someone, a neighbour or a passing policeman, might see her. She had never before felt such utter shame. It scalded her whole body. She wanted to die but even that wasn't an option. There was still Rita to consider. She shuddered. Dear Lord, what if Rita found out? She was crying silent tears when she reached the house. Wiping her eyes with the heel of her hand, she braced herself and unlocked the door.

For a second she thought the house was in darkness but then she saw the light coming from the open stair door. 'Is that you, Mum?'

'Yes, love.'

'I didn't expect you to be this late,' Rita called. 'You must be shattered. Want me to come down and make you a cup of tea?'

'No!' Grace spoke far too quickly but she knew she couldn't look her daughter in the eye, not tonight. She pulled herself together and spoke in a more conciliatory tone. 'I'm fine, love. Really. I just need a wash and then I'll be up.'

'OK,' said Rita. 'Night, Mum.'

'Goodnight, love.'

Wearily, Grace boiled the kettle and went into the scullery. She washed herself all over, paying special attention to 'down below', but no matter how many times she soaped the flannel, she still didn't feel clean. What upset her most was that her body was still ready for him. That was the real betrayal. She wanted to shut down and be so small he could never get inside her again. He filled her thoughts as well. As she relived some of the moments she would feel her body responding. She hated this. She was trapped and helpless. He had threatened her job and her home. If he wanted her to do it again, she would have to go.

What terrified her the most was the thought that in the end she wouldn't mind. Perish the thought ... perish the thought!

Washed and clean on the outside, she sat at the kitchen table with a cup of tea. He had given her a brown paper bag as she'd headed for the door. 'Don't forget your wages,' he'd said. She'd snatched it from him, anxious to get away. He'd laughed softly. 'I've bought you a pinny to wear next time you come.'

She'd thrown it into Michael's chair as she made her way to the scullery. It lay there, accusing and mysterious.

She opened the bag and pulled out a dress, perhaps the most beautiful dress she'd ever seen. She could tell without even holding it up to look at it that it was very expensive. Grace gagged involuntarily. She stood up quickly and, stuffing it back into the bag, she looked around desperately for somewhere to hide it. But where? It would have to be in her bedroom. Rita respected her privacy as she did hers but she couldn't bear to have this ... thing in the same room while she slept. It would be like being with him again. Not here. Not in her own bedroom.

Her breathing had become very fast. Her head was spinning and her chest was so tight, it felt like a lead weight was pressing down on it. Where could she put it?

The coalhole. She could bury it. One thing was absolutely sure: she'd never wear it, so what did it matter? She went back into the scullery and opened the coalhole door. Throwing the dress right to the back, she shovelled half a dozen shovels full of coal on the top of it until it was completely buried. Mr Hudson was bringing her a half hundredweight next week. Once it was buried under that lot, nobody would find it.

She shut the coalhole door and gulped back a sob. Did he really think he could pay her with a dress? What good would a dress do? It wouldn't pay the bills, would it? Not that she would ever touch a shilling of that man's money, ever again. What was it Rita had said only this week? 'He was buying a dress for his fancy woman ... midnight blue...'

That's what she was, wasn't it? Norris Finley's fancy woman. Of course she was. The dress she had just buried in the coalhole had a Hubbard's label tied to the zip and it was a beautiful midnight blue.

Twenty

Bonnie had been at the nursery for six months already. She had settled in quite quickly and she and Shirley were very happy. On her days off (she had one a week), Bonnie would take Shirley out and about. Sometimes they would walk in Richmond Park, sometimes she would make the trek down the hill into Kingston itself. On summer days she would stroll along the riverbanks or look around the shops. There was a Bentalls in Kingston and Bonnie would wander around, remembering the Bentalls in Worthing. She seldom bought anything because she tried to save every penny she had. One day, Shirley would need things like school uniforms or new shoes and books and pencils. Bonnie also harboured the faint hope that one day she might find a little flat of their own. She had to carry on working and so for the moment it was better to stay where she was, but she longed for the freedom of being able to do what she wanted to do when she wanted to do it.

The only thing she didn't like was having to lie about George. Because it was still fresh in everybody's mind, she'd told them he'd been killed in the awful train crash at South Croydon in October last year. Thirty-two people had lost their lives and she was sure no one would remember all their names nearly a year on. The papers had made much of the fact that the accident happened in the rush hour and with 800 people on one train and 1,000 on the other, George's death could easily be swallowed up by the enormity of the event. When Shirley was two months old, it was her mother's birthday. Bonnie sent a card but of course she made no mention of her first grandchild.

The nursery had a very strict routine. Bonnie worked a twelve-hour stretch with two hours off during the day. Off duty was either 9.30 till 11.30, 2 till 4 or, best of all, 5 till 7. Because tea was at 4.30, when she had a 5 to 7 off duty that gave her an extra half hour and a lovely long evening to herself. Having that afternoon break was a definite advantage in the summer, because she could spend more time with Shirley, but the girls preferred the evening too especially if they were going out. They were only allowed to stay out until 10pm, or if they had a 'Late Pass' they could stay out until 10.45pm. By the time they'd come off duty at 7 and got ready, they were lucky to have two hours away from the home. Everybody knew that if they rang the doorbell after 10.45pm to get in, they would forfeit some of their precious off duty another time.

Anyone out after 10.45pm, was, according to Matron, 'up to one thing and one thing only.' Bonnie mused that she was probably right. They would be running like mad up Kingston Hill because they'd missed the bus!

Everyone did 'lates' two evenings a week and everybody had to take turns to do ten nights of night duty, which lasted from 9pm until 7am. In between her rounds of the nursery, Bonnie would sit in the nursery watching her child sleep. After the ten nights on duty, the bonus was that she got two days off together. Normally they had one day off a week but they could never guarantee when it would be. She might get Monday off one week and then Saturday the following week which meant she'd work eleven days on the trot.

The nursery was kept scrupulously clean. The floors were like mirrors. Every day it was part of the routine to sweep, wash and polish them. The sweeping and washing was done by hand as was the application of the polish. Then Bonnie used the polisher to get a decent shine, a back-breaking and thankless task because the next day you had to do it all over again.

Another of her jobs was nappy washing. The

laundry itself was outside the main building and cold. When she'd arrived the others told her it was the worst job in the world in the winter. They taught Bonnie how to make an art form out of washing nappies. First they were sluiced, and then rinsed in the huge sinks. After they had been boiled for what seemed like forever in huge boiler-like vats, they were pulled scalding hot over to the sinks with a pair of wooden tongs. There they were rinsed by hand and finally spun in an industrial spin-dryer. Soap powder was strictly rationed and Matron watched the girls in the laundry like a hawk. She constantly suspected everyone of thieving but, poor as they were, nobody wanted to wash their personal clothes in council soapsuds. They smelled like Jeyes Fluid and stale lavender all rolled into one.

The handknitted baby cardigans and other delicates were washed in soap flakes which were the devil to get to melt in the water. If the weather was too damp or wet to dry the clothes Bonnie had to hang them in industrial driers which were lit by gas. The one blessing of being on laundry duty was that it gave a homesick nineteen-year-old single mum a few moments to cry alone without being castigated or ridiculed.

Bonnie's best friend turned out to be Nancy, the girl in charge of the baby room, and she loved Shirley as if she were her own.

A month ago, Matron had called Bonnie into her office. Bonnie liked Harriet and Tommy Bennett. She never called them that – Matron and Mr Bennett were the correct forms of address to use – but she had plenty of reasons to be grateful for their pioneering spirits.

'You seem to have settled in really well, Bonnie,' said Matron. 'Even the members of the council are impressed by your progress.'

Bonnie blushed. Matron rarely went out of her way to give a compliment so this was high praise indeed.

'I wonder if you are up for another challenge?'

'It depends on what it is,' Bonnie said cautiously.

'Do you think you could get your NNEB?' The NNEB stood for the National Nursery Examination Board. It was a relatively new course the government offered which led to a recognised qualification in childcare. 'It takes two years,' Matron went on. 'You will have to study at college, but Kingston County Council will fund it for you with a grant.'

Bonnie took in her breath. 'Oh, Matron…'

'It won't be easy, Bonnie. You'll have to do everything you do now, look after Shirley *and* do the course.'

'I would love the chance,' Bonnie cried.

Matron smiled. 'And I'm sure you can rise to the challenge,' she said. 'That being the case, you're to go to County Hall next Thursday to talk to the nursery supervisor, a Miss Brown, about what's entailed in it.' She rose to her feet and extended her hand. 'Good luck.'

'Thank you, Matron,' said Bonnie shaking her hand politely.

Outside in the corridor, Bonnie punched the air with both fists and said a loud 'Yes!'

'You all right, Mum?' Rita was sitting at the kitchen table writing a letter.

Grace had seemed preoccupied for weeks. Rita had noticed how quiet she had become and was worried. Was she ill? Had she found out about Bonnie and George? The inquest on George had recorded an open verdict. Rita had asked Dinah what that meant.

'It means that there is not enough evidence to say how he died,' she said. 'Apparently there wasn't a mark on him and nobody can work out why he was in there in the first place.'

It was obvious to Rita that someone must have locked the door behind him. He was supposed to be tidying the place up, but according to what the estate agent said in the papers, the factory was a tip. Rita had never discussed the matter with her mother, but something was clearly troubling her.

'Mum?'

Grace was miles away. She still hadn't answered her but she had put her knitting in her lap and was staring into space. Archie had come round with a big bunch of flowers and the petition earlier in the week but she hadn't signed it. Grace couldn't help noticing there were few names on the list. She had taken the opportunity to remind Archie not to keep writing notes and she made him take back his flowers. It cut her to ribbons to do it but she had to make him understand that it was over.

'I wish you would explain why, Gracie,' he'd said. 'Was it something I said?' Rita got up from the table where she was writing a letter and touched her mother's shoulder. 'Mum, I've been talking to you and you're crying. Are you all right?'

Grace jumped and smiled. 'Yes, I'm fine, love. Shall I put the kettle on?'

Rita wasn't in the mood to be fobbed off tonight. They'd had this conversation, or lack of conversation, before. 'Something is worrying you, Mum. What is it? Can I help?'

Grace looked at her as if seeing her for the first time. Rita was growing up fast. That job at Hubbard's had been a good idea after all. Dinah was a good friend to her and Emilio was harmless enough. She patted her daughter's hand. 'Who are you writing to?'

'Mum, don't change the subject,' said Rita. 'Tell me.'

Grace got up to make the tea. How could she tell her? Where could she find the words to say that she'd been cleaning Norris's houses for weeks? That every time she went out she felt no better than a prostitute. How could she explain that it was only the fear that Bonnie might be in serious trouble if she refused to go that made her do it? She should never have got herself in this mess in the first place, and now that she had, her only hope of getting out of it was when he got tired of her. Yet, if anything, he wanted her more and more. She'd buried the dress but he gave her other things, sometimes money, sometimes luxuries. Her drawers were lined with perfume, delicate soaps, pretty handkerchiefs and silk stockings. How could she tell her sweet innocent daughter that her mother was no better than a tramp?

As Grace struggled to control herself, Rita put her arms around her mother's shoulders. 'Oh, Mum,' she whispered. 'I miss her too.'

Her words had an amazing effect on them both. For the first time since Bonnie left home, they wept together, hard gut-wrenching sobs that engulfed them both. It was simpler to let Rita believe she was only crying for her lost daughter, but for Grace it was much, much more. Grace grieved for her lost chance of happiness with Archie, for the loss of her good name and her self-respect ... all gone. She wept for every lie she'd told, every deceit, and for the false impression she had to maintain if she was to get away with it.

Their emotions spent, the two of them sat red-eyed at the table and drank tasteless tea.

'Who's the letter for?' Grace asked again.

'Emilio.'

Grace looked puzzled. 'Has he gone back to Italy then?'

Rita shook her head. 'His friend Jeremy has been called up to do his National Service. He's doing his basic training first. Oswestry. Emilio has gone up there for the weekend to keep him company.'

'I bet he has,' said Grace with a smile and her daughter grinned.

'He's ever so fond of Jeremy.'

So Rita did understand about that boy. That was a relief. It was one less thing to worry about. But then the thought of Rita finding out about Norris came swirling back into her mind. She was being very careful, but the pessimistic streak in her told her it was only a matter of time...

'I should have listened to you, Mum,' said Rita flexing her fingers. 'If I had learned to type, I could write this letter a whole lot quicker.'

Grace looked up sharply. 'You could still do it, love.' Little did she know but Rita had just thrown her a lifeline. If she could get the girl away from Worthing, it would make dealing with Norris a lot easier. The dread of being found out was clouding her judgement. Without Rita to worry about, she could concentrate on getting that locket ... break into the safe if necessary.

'Do what?'

'The secretarial course we talked about,' said Grace. She willed herself to keep the suggestion low key. If she came over as too keen, Rita would dig her heels in and refuse to go, or worse still, know she wanted her out of the way.

'I'm quite happy at Hubbard's, Mum.'

'I was thinking of writing to Aunt Rene,' Grace ploughed on. 'They have some good courses over in Brighton. The sort of courses the London people like girls to have. Aunt Rene could put you up I'm sure.'

Rita hesitated. Emilio had said he might try the fishing further along the coast in Rye or Hastings. Both places were half a world away from Worthing. Brighton was a lot closer. Aunt Rene wasn't a real aunt but she had been a close friend of her mother's and children were never allowed to call adults by their first name. She looked at her mother and saw for the first time in ages how tired she looked. She never had anything nice. Her clothes were threadbare and she even cut her own hair rather than go to the hairdresser.

'Mum, these places cost money,' she said. 'Where are we going to find enough for the college fees? And I'd have to have my own typewriter for practice.'

'I've got a bit saved up,' said Grace.

Rita gave her a sceptical look.

'You know I've been saving money to repay the person who helped me out with the Christmas club money,' said Grace. 'You said yourself I didn't need to pay it back. It's only stubbornness on my part. You can use that.'

'Oh Mum...'

'I can send Aunt Rene something out of my wages each week for your board and lodging.' Grace was on a roll now. 'We can work something out.'

'I don't like the idea of leaving you on your own, Mum.'

'Don't be silly, darling,' said Grace. 'You'll be leaving me to get married one day, won't you? It's not like Bonnie. I shall know where you are and we can write.'

Rita nodded. The more she thought about it the more she liked the idea. She'd aim high. She wouldn't end up in the typing pool. She'd be a secretary and if she got a good job, she'd soon pay her mother back.

'All right, Mum. Write to Aunt Rene and if she says yes, I'll apply to the college.'

When Rita went to bed, Grace sat at the table and composed a letter to Rene. They had been very close friends when they'd left school, but even though they only lived thirteen miles apart from each other, they didn't see each other very often. Grace made the war an excuse but now that it was over, they still didn't get together much. However, she was fairly confident that Rene would be glad of the company. She had two sons, both of whom were married and living away from home. Her husband, Bill, spent most of his time in the pub. He wasn't a drunk or anything bad like that, but he preferred to play darts with the boys rather than sit at home with Rene. Rita was a good girl and she'd be no trouble, and Grace said as much in her letter.

Alone in her room, Rita allowed herself a secret smile. There was no telling where Jeremy might be posted next but if she was living away from home, it would be a lot easier to join them for a weekend away. She and Emilio could keep each other company on the train journey, and who knew where that might lead?

Grace's thoughts returned to the issue of Michael's chair. After she'd been with Norris, it was the first thing she saw the minute she opened the door. It was ridiculous but she felt as if the chair had taken on a persona of its own. Everything else in the room faded into the background and the chair loomed large, like a reproachful preacher in the pulpit. *What have you done, Grace? Dirty cow. Who are you kidding? You enjoy it, don't you? All those presents, all that attention. What did he give you tonight, Grace? A silk petticoat eh?*

There was no doubt about it, the chair had to go.

She had pushed a note through Archie's letterbox a week ago asking him to take it, but he hadn't responded. She was aware that every now and again he was watching her as she walked over the crossing or down her street when she got home from the factory. Since that note he had been standing in the window every evening but she didn't acknowledge him. She held her head high and pretended she hadn't seen him. If she had looked at him, she would have broken down, but even though she ignored him, his eyes bored into her back until she reached her door. Yet he still made no attempt to come for the chair.

On Saturday morning, as soon as Rita had left for work, she manoeuvred it towards the front door. It had casters but one of them was damaged and the chair was heavy. It took a mammoth effort to get it over the doorstep and her short path leading to the road wasn't as wide as the chair. It kept sinking into the flowerbeds on either side. It was difficult to steer and at one point she heard the bus coming. The chair was determined to veer into the road but somehow she managed to keep it on the pavement before the bus ran them both down.

The blinds were still down in the shop when she got there. She didn't want to see Archie or to speak to him – how could she when she knew what she'd done – so she pushed it into the recess of the door and left it. She left no note. He would know where it had come from. All she wanted was to get on with her life.

Twenty-One

Bonnie had a long weekend off. She had nowhere to go but she'd made up her mind to try and make it special for Shirley. She was eight months old now and as bright as a button. In fact she would soon be moving from the Baby room into Tweenies. Sometimes Bonnie took Shirley down into the playroom to be with them. Shirley was crawling and standing about but she had to get used to being with bigger children. The Baby room was an oasis of calm compared with being with the boisterous one to two year olds and life was a lot more robust in the Tweenies room.

Bonnie decided to go up to Oxford Street and see the Christmas lights. Someone had told her the windows at Selfridges were a wonder to behold and she wanted Shirley to see them. She knew the baby would never remember them, but she would and she would write it all down in the scrapbook she kept for Shirley. Called 'My Life', the scrapbook contained details of every event in her baby's life. 'When I had my first meal,' Bonnie wrote, 'my mummy gave me baby rice. I didn't like it and I shuddered and spat it out.' Another time she wrote, 'I took my first step today. Auntie Norah said I was very clever. Some babies don't walk until they are much older.' And on another page she had written, 'Today is my Granny's birthday. I've never seen her but Mummy says if she knew about me she would love me very much.' There was a birthday card stuck on the opposite page. It was inscribed, 'To my Granny. Happy birthday. Lots of love Shirley x.'

Bonnie caught the train from Kingston and arrived at London Waterloo. The last time she had travelled to the capital was when she had arranged to meet George. That all seemed a long time ago now and Waterloo was quite different from Victoria.

It was only as she caught the bus to Selfridges that Bonnie decided to look up Dora and Cook. It was a bit awkward getting on the bus with the pushchair but the conductor was very helpful, putting it under the stairwell himself. Shirley was as good as gold. She loved sitting on Bonnie's lap and looking out of the window.

The streets were packed with shoppers. Bonnie had to be careful that people with heavy bulging bags didn't bash Shirley as they pushed past her. Selfridges was every bit as amazing as she'd been told. This year's theme was Toyland and every window was decorated in a totally different way.

Bonnie had been warned about pickpockets so she kept her purse on the inside of her buttoned-up coat as she lifted Shirley up to see the moving figures on display. A little toy train ran around a village snow scene in one window and a huge smiley Father Christmas laughed as he packed his toys into a sack in the next one. All around her, children pressed their faces to the glass, no doubt wishing that they could have a quarter of the toys on display for themselves. Shirley stared, her eyes wide with wonder.

By the time they had seen all the windows, Shirley was tired. She'd missed her usual mid-morning nap. Bonnie changed her nappy (fortunately only wet) on her lap in the ladies then, tucking her up warmly, Bonnie walked to a bus shelter to give her a bottle. She'd wrapped it in two clean nappies and it was still fairly warm.

Lady Brayfield had expressed the wish that Richard should not be told about Bonnie's baby and she respected that, but Richard still kept in touch with her via her post office box number. Because of that, Bonnie knew Lady Brayfield was taking him and his mother to a Bournemouth hotel for a pre-Christmas break. In his letter, Richard had grumbled that it was going to be boring, boring, boring... She would be sorry not to see him but, with luck, only Dora and Cook would be at home.

Bonnie walked around the back and knocked lightly on the door. A few minutes later, Cook opened it. Bonnie felt sure she would be welcomed, but she had no idea just how much. The two women were absolutely thrilled to see her and ten minutes later Bonnie was sitting at the kitchen table while a rather bemused and still sleepy Shirley was being cuddled and spoiled by them both. There was a lot to catch up on.

'I took a chance that you'd both be here,' Bonnie explained. 'Richard told me the family were off to Bournemouth. Is his mother well?'

'Back to normal,' said Cook giving Shirley a biscuit.

'She's divorced him,' Dora added. 'Missus says he's already married someone else.'

'Poor fish,' Cook muttered. 'Now,' she said looking at Bonnie and settling back in her chair with Shirley on her lap, 'tell us what you've been doing and where you live.'

Bonnie skipped the Mother and Baby Home and told her all about her training and the nursery.

'Sounds like you've fallen on your feet, dear,' said Cook.

Dora had put the tea things on the table. 'Have we got any cake, Cook?'

'You know very well there's a fruit cake in the larder,' said Cook putting Shirley down and helping her to walk to the next chair. 'You've had your eye on it ever since it came out of the oven.'

Bonnie smiled. They always seemed to be bickering but she knew they were totally devoted to each other.

The time went all too quickly and it was important to get Shirley home for bedtime. Bonnie kissed her dear friends and they stood by the rear entrance and waved to her until she'd left the mews. She turned into the next street and a young woman came rushing out of a side street and they collided.

'Sorry,' they both said and Bonnie froze.

'Bonnie! What on earth are you doing here?' It was Dinah. There wasn't time to stop. She quickly explained that she had to get the baby back to the nursery where she worked and that her bus would be along at any minute.

'What a pretty child,' Dinah remarked. 'How could a mother bear to put her in a nursery?'

Bonnie couldn't look at her.

'I can't believe it's really you,' cried Dinah.

'When is your next day off?'

'Not until after Christmas,' said Bonnie.

'Let's meet then,' said Dinah. A young man wandered back to where they were standing. Bonnie was aware of him but didn't really look. 'Do you know Lyons Corner House at Marble Arch?'

Bonnie nodded.

'Then meet me on January 5th for lunch,' said Dinah, looking in her pocket diary. 'It's a Wednesday. I'll be there at 12.30.'

'All right,' said Bonnie. It shouldn't be too difficult to request a weekday off, especially a Wednesday. It was half day closing and most of the girls preferred a day when they could go shopping, so Wednesday was not a popular choice. 'Oh, my bus!'

The three of them ran to the stop, the man with his hand out, and the bus pulled up.

'Your mother will be so pleased to hear that I've found you,' said Dinah.

'Please don't tell her,' Bonnie panicked. 'I'll explain everything when we meet, but please don't tell her now.'

The man began collapsing the pushchair as Bonnie snatched Shirley from it.

'Sorry, darling,' said Dinah. 'Bonnie, this is my friend, John Finley.'

It was only then that Bonnie looked at him.

'We've already met.' He winked at Bonnie as he leaned past her and pushed the pushchair under the stairs. 'I saw you once at one of the WMCS shows.'

Bonnie stared at his back, the shock of seeing

him making her legs wobble.

'Thanks,' she said weakly.

'Hurry up and sit down, if you please, Miss,' said the conductor. He had his hand on the bell. 'I don't want you and baby to fall down when we move off.'

John got off the platform and Bonnie stepped onto the bus with Shirley in her arms. As she sat in the first available seat, Dinah knocked on the window. 'Wednesday the 5th. Promise me you'll come.'

'I promise,' said Bonnie and as the bus pulled into the Christmas traffic, she took a long look at John Finley.

Later that day, Bonnie sat alone in her bedroom, completely stunned. She had bathed and fed Shirley as soon as she'd got back to the nursery and now her little girl was fast asleep after her big adventure. Nancy wanted to hear all about her day and Bonnie told her about the beautiful windows at Selfridges and her meeting with Dora and Cook. She had smiled as she talked, not wanting Nancy to guess the turmoil that was going on inside. Fancy bumping into Dinah like that. It was the last thing she'd expected to happen, and it had been even more shocking to meet her friend.

The stare she had given him from the window of the bus was chewed up with emotion. Blind panic, because it was so unexpected; fear that he might know who she was, or suspect something from her behaviour; curiosity; and the need to make sure everything appeared normal in front of Dinah. Coupled with all that was the fear that, despite her promise, Dinah might talk to her mother about Shirley.

As she thought about it more carefully, she realised that Dinah might not actually connect her and Shirley as being together. Hadn't she said, 'what a pretty child. How could a mother bear to put her in a nursery?'

A wave of relief washed over Bonnie, but there was still the vexed question of John's birth. How would her mother feel if Dinah took John across the road to her house? Oh God, it was all such a mess.

Her roommate, Doreen, was on lates. She glanced at the clock. It was 8.15pm. Doreen wouldn't be back upstairs for at least another three-quarters of an hour. Bonnie got her box out and opened it for the first time since she'd arrived at the nursery eight months before. She rummaged through the old birthday cards, fondled her mother's best hanky and kissed Shirley's birth certificate. It was the letter she was looking for. She spread it out and read the bare bones again. A boy, John Finley, mother's name Grace Follett, father's name Maxwell. If the letter was dated the 12th, he must have been born on 11th May 1924. There was no doubt about it, John Finley was her half brother.

She tried to recall the stories her mother had told her about her courting days. Not a lot. As far as Bonnie could remember, her mother had met her father when she was 19. They had married three years later when she was still 22. Her eldest child, Bonnie, had come along on September 4th 1929 ... but according to this letter, she wasn't

Grace's first child. John had been born the year her mother turned 17.

She folded the letter carefully. When Dinah had been making arrangements to see her again, Bonnie had had no intention of meeting her, but now she wanted to go. She had to find out about John without Dinah wondering about her interest. As she packed the box back into the little drawer with a key, a realisation was growing in Bonnie's mind. If her mother had given birth to a child out of wedlock, she would have no real reason to reject Shirley. Perhaps John Finley was the one person who could bring the family back together again.

Grace had been 'cleaning' again but this time as she walked home she was feeling a whole heap better. Norris had told her he was going away. His wife needed a break, apparently, so he was taking her to America. They were due to sail in February on the *Queen Mary*. Because of the Christmas celebrations and the amount of organising it would take to get away for such a long period of time, he wouldn't be requiring her until after his trip. Grace couldn't have had a better Christmas present.

Three months without his lecherous hands all over her body. What bliss. And if she was lucky, they might never touch her again. This was her golden opportunity to get that locket. Somehow she had to get into the office without anyone seeing.

'I hope you have a wonderful holiday, Mrs Finley,' she said aloud. 'In fact, why not take two?

Take the whole bloomin' year if you like.'

The lights were on in Archie's shop as she went past and Michael's chair was in the window. There was a notice across the seat. 'To be restored...'

One part had been stripped away to the bare wood. The stuffing lay all around. Grace felt somehow at one with the chair. Her insides had been pulled out the day she'd walked away from Archie. A beautiful piece of red leather lay across the arm and a piece of green leather hung over the back of the chair. One day the chair would be beautiful again, its past torn away and forgotten. If only it was that easy for her.

She could see him at the back of the shop, bent over his work, and her heart lurched. He was working late. He'd be tired and then he'd have to go into the little flat and get his own tea. How she longed to offer him a meal, to sit by the fire and talk over the day. She thought back to that last day they'd had together, and his kisses. She closed her eyes for a second and sighed. If only, if only... She opened her eyes and saw a woman coming from the back of the shop with a cup of tea in her hands. She put it down next to where Archie was working. He stood up and held out a necklace of some sort. The woman clapped her hands and kissed his cheek. It was an awful shock. She didn't know why but she had never expected Archie to find someone else. But why shouldn't he? He was an attractive man, warm and friendly, the sort of man any woman would be proud to have. Grace turned her back and walked with hurried steps towards her home. Her heart was aching. Even if she were free to love him, he wouldn't want her anyway, she told herself fiercely. She'd been in Finley's bed. She was nothing more than a tramp and she hated herself.

Back home she washed herself in the scullery, but even when she'd finished, she still didn't feel clean; and besides she couldn't wash away the terrible ache in her heart. Life was so unfair.

With the onset of another Christmas without Bonnie, Grace struggled to pretend that everything was all right. More than a year had passed since she'd seen her daughter. What was she doing? Where was she living now? Was she happy? It was hard to believe that Bonnie could go a whole twelve months without a thought for the mother and sister she'd left behind. On dark days, Grace was convinced that Bonnie was ill, had perhaps contracted some God-awful disease like polio and was too ill to tell the authorities who she was. On really dark days, Grace imagined her daughter lying in a ditch somewhere, her poor body exposed to the elements, but then she remembered the birthday card. Bonnie couldn't be dead if she'd sent her a card, and then it upset her that she couldn't send one to her. She had no idea what Rita was thinking but after the night they had sobbed together in each other's arms, it seemed that the girl was getting on with her life. They'd been shopping for a new suitcase – 'part of your Christmas present', Grace told her – and using her staff discount, Rita had bought a few more affordable things from Hubbard's.

When Christmas came, fewer of their old friends came round. Uncle Charlie Hanson had taken Snowy to Dorset to meet his relations. It looked as if things were getting quite serious between them and Grace was glad. Snowy wasn't meant to be alone. They still had a good time, but she missed Manny Hart. He had a heavy cold. Of course, Archie didn't come, but then she hadn't expected him to.

January 2nd 1949 found Grace on platform 2 of Worthing station to wave goodbye to Rita. Now that it was really happening, Rita was excited about the course but Grace had very mixed feelings.

'Don't forget to write,' Grace told her for the umpteenth time. 'And if there's an emergency, ring Salvatore and he'll come and get me.'

'Mum,' said Rita patiently. 'Everything will be fine.' The train pulled into the station and Rita gathered her things. 'Try not to miss me too much.'

They gave each other a knowing look and hugged each other tight. 'I promise, I *will* keep in touch,' said Rita emphatically and Grace nodded.

Rita climbed aboard and leaned out of the window.

'You've got Aunt Rene's money safe?' said Grace unnecessarily.

Rita nodded and kissed her cheek. 'Take care, Mum.'

Grace was dry-eyed as the train pulled out of the station but down in the underpass a tear trickled down her cheek. Bonnie was gone, and now Rita. She sniffed. If it hadn't have been for that damned war, she would still have Michael to go home to. If it hadn't have been for Norris

Finley, she'd still have a son ... and she might have been going home to Archie. Just the thought of him made her heart constrict. She forced herself to pull herself together. It was no use hankering after something that would never be. There were plenty of people far worse off. She walked out of the station with a newfound determination. She still had a life to live and she could see things a lot clearer now. She had to stop kowtowing to Norris. All she had to do was get her hands on that locket.

Twenty-Two

The steel grey sky threatened snow. Bonnie had two jumpers on under her winter coat, a scarf and thick woollen gloves, yet the chilly January air still found a way to rob her body of warmth. London was as busy as ever. The Christmas lights were gone but the January sales were in full swing. Bonnie willed herself not to be tempted as she walked along Oxford Street. She needed every penny she could get if she was going to find a proper home for Shirley one day.

Her training was going well but it was surprisingly hard work. She had to make notes during her lectures and write them up in two folders, one called 'Child Education' and the other called 'Child Care'. She was expected to illustrate the folders with pictures from magazines and the newspapers, all of which took time.

The course included visits to day nurseries and nursery schools in the area and she had to produce a written report on each of them. Bonnie was becoming competent in everything from mixing infant feeds to understanding the benefits of dressing-up play for the toddler, the use of rhyme and poetry in the nursery and planning a nutritious meal for a faddy eater. The course was exacting for all the girls but slightly more so for a single mother flying the flag for other single mothers who someday might be allowed to follow in her footsteps. For that reason, from day one, Bonnie had knuckled down and given 100 per cent.

She arrived at Lyons Corner House at Marble Arch in good time. She was alone. Nancy had agreed to look after Shirley. It was her day off too. 'She's no trouble,' Nancy smiled. 'She's a little treasure.'

One of the waitresses, Nippies as they were called, took her order and Bonnie relaxed. Would Dinah turn up? More to the point, would John be with her? Bonnie felt sick with apprehension.

She had rehearsed what she would say a million times. She would tell Dinah about Shirley. It disturbed her that Dinah's remark, 'What a pretty child, how could a mother bear to put her in a nursery?' made it obvious that she thought Shirley belonged to someone else. She would have to put that right. It felt too much a betrayal of the little girl she loved so passionately.

She'd also find out about her mother and Rita, although she still wasn't sure what she would do with the information. She kept swinging from one idea to another. On the one hand, she thought it would be better to stay away. After all this time, her mother would have settled down to life without her. If only she had known about John before she left Worthing she could have come back when she realised that George had walked out on her. Her mother had been unmarried when she had John. She would have understood what Bonnie was going through. On the other hand, the shame of what she'd done overwhelmed Bonnie and she decided she couldn't possibly go back. If she brought her child back home, how would Mum and Rita hold their heads up in Worthing again? Everybody would be talking about it.

'Of course you know little Shirley Rogers is illegitimate … who was her father? I heard he walked out on her...' Could she really put her mother and Rita through all that? Shirley would have to know the truth about her father one day, but for now everyone thought she was a widow and that Shirley's father had been killed in that awful train crash.

Bonnie looked down at her tea. The cup was almost empty and the teapot was getting cold. She glanced up at the big clock. Dinah was three-quarters of an hour late. It was obvious she wasn't coming. She rose to her feet just as Dinah burst through the door.

'Sorry, sorry,' she blurted out. She was totally out of breath. 'Rehearsals went on far longer than I anticipated, and I had to race for the bus.' She was taking her coat off as she spoke but all at once she stopped. 'Darling, I've treated you very badly and I am most desperately sorry. Please forgive me and let me buy you lunch?'

Bonnie was already laughing. She embraced Dinah warmly. It was so good to see her friend again, and best of all, she was quite alone.

His father's sitting room had a very masculine ambience. The walls were oak-panelled and the few pictures which hung from the picture rail were of Scottish highland cattle grazing in purple and yellow grasslands. Apart from the old chesterfield, there were two armchairs next to the fireplace and a leatherbound desk next to the window. A red patterned carpet covered most of the floor area and a cheerful fire in the grate made the room very cosy.

'Sit down, son,' said Norris. 'Whisky?'

John Finley nodded. Perhaps the drink would give him a bit of Dutch courage.

He'd tried broaching the subject at the meal table but somehow it didn't quite work out. His mother wanted to know what he'd been doing with himself and he found himself talking about Dinah and the weekend he'd enjoyed with friends.

'Anyone I know there?' his mother asked.

John shook his head. 'Funnily enough, I did meet a Worthing girl there though,' he said. 'Bonnie Rogers.'

He would have told them more but his father dropped a tablespoon of peas all over the tablecloth and the chaos distracted them for several minutes. When they got back to normality, his father dominated the conversation by talking about his forthcoming trip on the *Queen Mary*. Norris called it a business trip but it seemed like he was taking in the whole of New York and half of the east coast of America before setting off in a plane to South America for another week. John couldn't for the life of him think what sort of business his father was doing in Argentina, but his knitwear factory had certainly taken off in the past few years. It must be doing brilliantly well for Norris to be able to afford such lavish cruising.

As he sipped his whisky, John wasn't looking forward to this one bit. He wished Dinah was with him. She could charm the birds out of the trees, and buttering up the old man would be as easy as anything to her.

He and his father didn't get on. There had been too many thrashings when John was a boy for that. Norris was still a powerfully built man but he hadn't touched John since he was fourteen. That was the day John stood up to his father for the first time. He'd grabbed a garden rake as Norris had cornered him in the summerhouse, the belt of his trousers wrapped around his hand, and told him in no uncertain terms that if he ever laid a finger on him again, when he grew up and was a man, he would exact his revenge. Norris no longer hit his son, but his tongue was just as powerful.

Norris handed John another whisky. 'As soon as I get back,' he said, 'I plan to branch out a bit. I may open another factory. There's plenty of scope around here and the council welcomes employment.'

'Good for you, sir,' said John.

'I might have a go at running for office. You know, make a name for myself.'

John smiled. They were like chalk and cheese. Wealth and power held no interest for John. At almost twenty-four he still had to embark on a career – which was precisely why he was here.

'It would be marvellous if you would take over the factory for me while your mother and I are away,' Norris went on. 'Miss Samuels will show you the ropes, and without me there, you can be your own man.'

'That's very generous of you, sir,' said John, 'but I have other plans.'

Norris's lips set in a hard line. 'Other plans? What plans?'

John took a deep breath, probably the last one he would take before the explosion that was sure to follow. 'I've already enrolled in a college in London,' he began. 'RADA. I finish the course at the end of the year. Apparently, I have a talent and everyone seems quietly confident that I could make a go of it.'

His father stared at him with a blank expression. 'What the deuce is RADA?'

'The Royal Academy of Dramatic Arts.'

John took a swig of the whisky. Norris froze in his seat. He continued to stare. 'You mean to tell me that you've been mixing with a load of nancy boys and poofters?' he bellowed.

'I didn't say that at all,' said John calmly. 'It's a perfectly legitimate occupation. People like John Gielgud and Laurence Olivier got their training there.'

'Bloody pansies,' sneered his father. 'Oh well, I

must say, that should suit you down to the bloody ground but if you think I'm wasting my hard earned money…'

'You don't need to,' said John staring into the bottom of the empty glass. 'I have money of my own.'

'Where from?' his father demanded to know.

'From the country,' said John. 'I spent few of my wages while I was flying during the war. I didn't have the appetite for it with all my friends dying around me, and I never touched a penny of what my grandfather left me, so I'm using it now.'

'Oh no you're not, you ungrateful little sod,' Norris bellowed.

'I'm old enough to make my own decisions now, Father,' said John. 'In fact I don't have to listen to this any more.' He rose to his feet and put the whisky glass on the table.

Norris was purple with rage. 'When I think of all that I've done for you…'

But by now he was speaking to the closing door.

Bonnie and Dinah slipped back into their friendship easily. It felt like they'd never been apart but even so, Bonnie searched for the right words to tell Dinah about Shirley. In the end, she just came out with it.

'Remember the baby in the pushchair when we last met?' Bonnie began.

Dinah nodded. 'Such a sweet little thing. Who is she?'

'She's mine,' said Bonnie, watching Dinah's face carefully.

Dinah smiled. 'I'm not surprised,' she said.

'She looked exactly like you. I would have been astonished if you had said any different.'

Bonnie's jaw dropped. She hadn't expected that at all. She'd been so sure Dinah would have been shocked, or called her a tart, or maybe walked out of the restaurant. 'You knew...'

'Not until I saw her,' said Dinah. 'I had no idea why you ran off like that. When your mother came to the store…'

'My mother came to Hubbard's?' Bonnie interrupted.

'She was really worried about you,' said Dinah. 'She asked all of us about you. Of course we didn't know anything. You're a bit of a dark horse, aren't you?' She laughed. 'What did you call her?'

'Shirley.'

'Shirley. I like that name. After Shirley Temple, is it?'

Bonnie shook her head. 'To be honest I never thought of that. I just like the name.'

'She's George's child, I take it.'

It was then that Bonnie decided to tell Dinah everything. She began with Lady Brayfield, that awful Mother and Baby Home, the nursery and the fact that she was now working towards her NNEB. She explained that it was such a new innovation, having only come about because wartime experiences had forced the government to realise that they needed a recognised qualification for those who cared for children.

Dinah was impressed. 'I'm so glad you were able to piece your life together so well after what happened to George.'

Bonnie froze. 'What happened to George?' she

repeated. 'What are you talking about?'

The waitress interrupted them by taking away their dirty plates. 'Would you like desserts?'

Dinah shook her head. 'Not for me, how about you?'

Bonnie shook her head as well. She wished the waitress away, to the far side of the moon if necessary. Something had happened to George. Had he married someone else, had a car accident, broken his leg, or what? Perhaps he hadn't deserted her after all. Was Dinah going to tell her he'd got TB or some other dreadful illness and was languishing in some hospital somewhere?

'More tea?' said the waitress. 'Or can I get you a coffee?'

'Coffee,' said Dinah. She glanced at Bonnie who just stared back at her with a blank expression. 'Make that two coffees,' she called as the waitress hurried away.

'What happened to George?' said Bonnie. Her voice was urgent.

'My dear,' said Dinah. 'Of course, you can't possibly know, can you? I think you'd better brace yourself for some bad news.' She leaned forward and held Bonnie's hand. 'There's no easy way to say this, but George is dead.'

Bonnie felt the room sway. Her dinner churned uncomfortably in her stomach and she felt cold and clammy. She was going to be sick. She rose from the table looking around desperately for the cloakroom sign and then ran between the tables towards it like a woman possessed.

John Finley went to the sitting room where his

mother sat with her sewing. It was a much cosier room than his father's, with a stone fireplace and deep chairs drowning in chintz-covered cushions. There was a roaring fire in the hearth.

'Hello, dear.' She glanced up from her embroidery as he came into the room. 'Finished your talk with your father?'

He marvelled that she was always so calm. His altercations with his father always left him angry and frustrated. It was totally ridiculous. He was a man now. He'd fought the bloody Germans and yet Norris had this ... power over him. He had no desire to follow in the old man's footsteps, but he just couldn't make him see that. To John's way of thinking, his mother had a bit of a dog's life, always having to fall in with the old man's plans, and yet she was never flustered. These days she seemed to be a very contented person, although he couldn't understand for the life of him why.

He flopped into a chair and stretched out his legs. 'I've just told the old man I'm an actor.'

His mother looked at him over the rim of her glasses. 'Good for you,' she said, 'but I'd much rather hear about the girl who has put that twinkle in your eye.'

How Bonnie got from Lyons Corner House to Dinah's flat in Primrose Hill she hardly knew. She allowed herself to be bundled into a taxi but she remembered little of the journey. The flat was on the first floor, or was it the second? She could only remember a lot of stairs.

Dinah was apologising that it was so small, but Bonnie couldn't focus her mind on anything except what she had told her in the restaurant.

George is dead. George is dead. It banged around her head like a dinner gong. *George is dead, dead, dead.* She kept asking stupid questions. 'How can you be so sure it was him?' 'Did the police actually see his body?' 'How can they be sure he's dead?' Every time she asked, Dinah answered her but the words didn't go in.

She had developed a terrible gnawing emptiness in her chest and the pain around her heart was so unbearable she honestly wanted to die herself.

Once she reached the flat, Bonnie allowed herself to give way to her tears. She cried solidly for half an hour. It left her with a terrible headache and feeling cold and clammy. After a while, someone came into the room and gave her an injection and everything went still.

When she woke up, the room was getting dark. She sat up suddenly and realised that although she was fully dressed apart from her shoes, she was under a pink satin bedcover. It took a few minutes to understand where she was and why and then the terrible grief came flooding back in, crushing her spirit and driving the breath from her body. He was dead. Her lovely, fun-loving George was dead. Shirley would never know her father, never call him Daddy. She closed her eyes and imagined her daughter, their daughter, just a little bit older, maybe three or four, in a meadow with the sun streaming down. She was chasing butterflies among the flowers, running along in that endearing way small children do and giggling as she went. Then George came up behind her and swept her into his arms, twirling her around as she gasped, 'Put me down, Daddy, put me down...'

Bonnie swung her feet over the edge of the bed and back into the here and now. That would never happen, would it? George was dead. She sighed. She had to get back to Shirley. She had told Nancy she would be back in time to put her to bed.

The door opened very slowly and the light from another room flooded in.

'Oh, you're awake.'

'What time is it?'

There was a pause and then Dinah said, 'Five thirty.'

Bonnie shot to her feet. 'I have to get back to the nursery.' She swayed and her head began to spin.

Dinah rushed to her side. 'You're in no fit state to go anywhere. You've had a massive shock. I had to call my doctor and he gave you something to calm you down.'

'But I have to bath Shirley and put her to bed. I'm her mummy. She's expecting me.'

'Give me the telephone number,' said Dinah, pushing Bonnie gently into a sitting position. 'I'll explain everything.'

'I need to know about George,' said Bonnie, her eyes filling with tears again.

'I know, darling. I know.'

As soon as she'd told Matron, Dinah made some tea and telephoned John. They had planned to meet later that evening. Dinah quickly explained what had happened.

'John, please don't rush back to London,' she

said. 'I can't leave Bonnie. She's in such a state. She had no idea her boyfriend was dead.'

'Her boyfriend?' said John.

'Shirley's father,' Dinah explained. 'The man they found in your father's cold storage room.'

'Good God!' exclaimed John. 'How absolutely bloody.'

'I know,' said Dinah. 'You do understand, don't you, darling?'

'Of course,' said John. 'Give her my love.'

Dinah put the phone down and went back to Bonnie. Clasping her hand gently, she began to tell her all that she knew.

'But I went to the factory,' Bonnie protested. 'I finished work early. I went to his digs and he wasn't there so I went on to the factory.'

'He was found in the cold room at the back,' said Dinah.

'I didn't go right inside,' Bonnie admitted. 'There was some horrible chap there throwing stuff around. He shouted at me and I fled.' She frowned. 'What's a cold room?'

'They used to store valuable fur coats there in the summer.'

Bonnie was hardly listening. 'Was there an inquest?'

Dinah stared at Bonnie's hands in hers. 'It was an open verdict.'

'So they don't really know how he died.'

There was a pause and then Dinah said, 'Did you get a good look at this man?'

Bonnie shook her head. 'He was wearing a sort of brown coat overall. I didn't see his face. He had a funny cap pulled down over his eyes.'

'What sort of cap?'

'I don't know,' said Bonnie. 'It wasn't the usual sort of cap men wear. It looked ... odd. Like a train driver or something.' She put her hand on her forehead. 'Oh I don't know. I can't think.'

'It's all right,' said Dinah softly. 'He may not…'

'He may not have been dead then,' said Bonnie bitterly. 'And if I'd stayed I might have saved him.'

'I wasn't going to say that,' Dinah said. 'He may not have even been in the factory. He could have been put there or even gone there, later. It seems to be the general consensus of opinion that the door closed on him and nobody knew he was there.'

Bonnie blew her nose again. 'I can't believe he's dead.'

'You must concentrate on Shirley,' said Dinah. 'You've managed without him this far. Nothing's changed.'

'Everything has changed,' Bonnie protested.

'No it hasn't,' Dinah insisted. 'He was dead back then, darling. The only thing that's altered is that now you know it.'

Bonnie nodded. She was right.

'Have an early night,' said Dinah, 'and then I'll get you back to the nursery tomorrow. It's all a bit bloody to start with, but you will get through it, I promise. Just thank God you've got Shirley.'

Bonnie knew then that Dinah was thinking about her own poor husband who had died in the war. After a whirlwind courtship, they had had only five weeks of marriage before he was blown up in a convoy bringing much needed food supplies from Spain and Portugal on the Lisbon Run. He'd gone before Dinah had got pregnant and, as miserable as she felt, Bonnie knew she was right.

'Yes,' she said, smiling at her friend. 'Thank God for Shirley.'

Twenty-Three

It wasn't going to be easy getting into the office. Grace had no real reason to be there. Factory floor workers only went upstairs if they were summoned for some reason.

She'd thought about confiding in Snowy but she couldn't bring herself to say the words. Somehow, while her fears and suspicions were constantly on her mind, they were manageable so long as they stayed in her head. Once she'd voiced them, her greatest fear was that they would take on a life of their own. Thinking bad thoughts was not nearly as terrible as speaking them. Much as she would welcome Snowy's clear thinking and wise advice, Grace couldn't bring herself to confide in her.

Apparently the petition had gone to the Fair Rents panel and everybody who had signed had their fingers crossed. There weren't as many names as Archie had hoped for but together they made a bigger voice than one lone complaint. Grace wished now that she'd been a part of it.

By the time Easter was on the horizon, Grace

was getting desperate. Norris would be back any time now and she still hadn't got the locket. The thought of doing more 'cleaning' with him quite frankly made her feel ill.

As it turned out, it was Snowy who enabled her, albeit unwittingly, to get into the office. Norah Fox was away. She'd had a bereavement in the family and had taken the day off for the funeral. Her absence led to a much more relaxed atmosphere on the factory floor. Too relaxed as it turned out, because Polly Reynolds got her fingers caught up in the machine. Her terrified screams brought everybody running and the production line was halted. Grace was sent upstairs to get help.

As she burst through the office door, Miss Samuels was leaning over the open safe.

'Polly's got herself trapped in the machine,' Grace blurted out.

Miss Samuels stood up. 'Where's Norah?'

'She's got a day off, remember?'

Another wail from downstairs made Miss Samuels's face go pale and she rushed past Grace and headed for the stairs. Grace made as if to follow but stopped by the door. There was pandemonium downstairs. Polly was screaming, more out of fear than pain, and people were beginning to argue about what to do. Snowy was barking orders. They didn't need another person down there and the safe door was still wide open. Grace darted back. It was now or never. She wouldn't get another chance like this.

There was a box of money at the front. Grace put it onto the floor and began to rummage through the papers underneath. Where was the little brown envelope? Her hands were trembling so much she could hardly make them work. If Miss Samuels came back, she'd get the sack immediately. She'd be caught red-handed with her hand in the safe. She might even get arrested and end up with her name in the paper.

She could hear Miss Samuels's voice above the others now. 'Go and get the first aid box.'

Careful not to disturb the piles too much, Grace carried on. Right at the back of the safe, her fingers touched something quite large. She pulled it towards the light and gasped. It was her Thrift Club moneybag, the one that had been stolen. What on earth was it doing in Norris's safe? She opened up the flap and looked inside. The little envelopes were still there, all torn open, but the money was all gone. Puzzled, she frowned but her brain refused to function. Why did Norris have it? Had he found it? If so, why didn't he tell her?

Downstairs she heard Miss Samuels say, 'You stay there. I'll go and ring for an ambulance.'

Grace threw the bag to the back of the safe and frantically searched for the locket again. She couldn't go without it.

Just as the woman's hurried footfall mounted the staircase, she found a small brown envelope identical to the one she'd seen Norris put the locket into, but it was far too heavy. It wasn't sealed so she looked inside – and there was the locket. Stuffing it into the pocket of her overall, she glanced at the other item in the envelope but there wasn't time to take it out and look at it properly. Miss Samuels was almost at the door. Grace flung the envelope back and shoved the box of money onto the top of the papers.

When Miss Samuels came back into the room, Grace had her back to the safe and was standing with the telephone receiver in her hand.

The voice at the other end was saying, 'Emergency, which service do you require?'

'You want me to run through it again?' said Grace. She looked at Miss Samuels and rolled her eyes. 'Right. We need an ambulance immediately at Finley's International. One of our employees has trapped her hand in a machine.'

'It's out now,' said Miss Samuels dully.

'Oh,' said Grace, covering the mouthpiece with her hand, 'so does she need an ambulance or not?' The slightly confused operator on the other end of the line was asking for the address.

'Better to be safe than sorry,' said Miss Samuels and coming around the desk she noticed the safe was still open. Uttering a small cry, she rushed to it, slammed the door and looked directly at Grace. Grace, who was still giving the emergency services directions, looked nonchalantly down as the door banged.

'I was halfway downstairs,' said Grace, when she'd finished the call and an ambulance was on its way, 'then I thought it might be a good idea to ring for the ambulance.' As she left the office, she was aware of Miss Samuels bending down again, obviously about to check the contents of the safe.

Much to Polly's disappointment, there was no need for a trip to hospital and she was treated on the spot. Now that treatment was free under the health service, she had been looking forward to the ride, especially if the ambulance man rang the bell all the way.

Every now and then throughout the day, Grace squeezed her pocket with a contented smile. The locket was still there. She was free. Norris couldn't hurt Bonnie any more and Grace didn't have to put up with his podgy hands all over her body any more. The one thing that puzzled her ... why was her moneybag in the safe? She thought back to the day when Norris had given her the £30, and then the full horror dawned on her. Norris must have arranged for those men to jump her with the Thrift Club money. Could Uncle Charlie have been sucked in too? No, she decided. He and Michael had been good pals and Uncle Charlie and Snowy had been seeing each other for some time. Both people were good judges of character. Uncle Charlie was as honest as the day was long. But that pig Norris had her eating out of his hand with her own money! Never mind, she told herself. Don't dwell on what you haven't got, think of what you have got. And she'd got the locket.

Her contentment was short-lived. When she got home that evening, the telegram boy had left a card through the letterbox. Grace ran all the way back to the post office at the end of the road. It was only five minutes before closing time, but she just made it.

The telegram was from her mother's neighbour. *'Mother ill STOP Rushed to hospital STOP Serious STOP Molly Hare.'*

Molly Hare was her mother's close friend and

neighbour. She would never have sent a telegram unless it was absolutely necessary. Back home, Grace sat with her head in her hands. She'd have to go of course, first thing in the morning. It was far too late to go tonight. Besides, there was so much to see to first. She'd probably lose her job but she had to go. Whatever their differences, she was still her mother, and Grace was an only child. Her hand went to her overall pocket once more and she pulled out the locket. At least one good thing had happened today. She wondered what was inside. A picture of Bonnie perhaps? She tried to open the catch but it was too stubborn. After a few minutes of trying, Grace gave up and shoved it to the back of a drawer.

There was a lot to do before she could set out for Yorkshire in the morning. For once, money wasn't a problem. Since the Thrift Club incident, Grace had been a good saver so she would be able to draw money out of her post office savings account first thing in the morning. The rent was up to date but she would have to make sure somebody was on hand to pay it when the rent man called. If she had to be up there any length of time, she would get a job, anything, shop work, scrubbing floors if necessary, in order to pay the rent. Her little courtyard garden would go to pot but Elsie Dawson could eat whatever was ready if she came round to pick it. It would help her out, if nothing else.

As soon as she'd swallowed a bit of tea, Grace went to see Snowy. Uncle Charlie Hanson was sitting at the table in his vest. So they've finally got together, thought Grace. Good.

'How long are you going to be in Yorkshire?' Snowy asked when Grace told her about her mother.

'That's just it,' said Grace as they sat in Snowy's little lean-to at the back. They were able to enjoy the last of the evening light without getting cold. Charlie had gone to the pub. 'I have no idea, but I reckon with Rita away and no sign of Bonnie, it'll be more sensible for me to stay up there until she's either well again or...' Grace looked away.

'You're right,' said Snowy. 'Train fares aren't cheap. I'll tell them at work. You're bound to get good references if they decide to let you go, but you never know your luck, Finley may even keep you on.'

'I doubt it,' said Grace. She had no illusions about Norris. He used people and threw them away. 'D'you know what,' she added defiantly, 'I'm not even sure I want to go back. With both my girls off my hands, maybe this is my chance to do something for myself for a change.'

'Oh my,' laughed Snowy. 'That sounds like fighting talk.'

'And you?' Grace waved her hands rather than ask outright.

Snowy nodded. 'I quite like having a man around the place again,' she smiled. 'He's pretty solid – in more ways than one.'

They both laughed.

Grace would have liked to ask Uncle Charlie about the attack before he'd gone to the pub. What would he think when she told him Norris was the instigator?

'You came here for a reason,' said Snowy.

'I'm here to ask you, if I send you a postal order each week, would you make sure my rent is paid?' said Grace.

'Of course, dear.'

'And keep an eye on the house?'

'Consider it done.'

On the way back home, Grace couldn't resist peeking into Archie's shop. The light was on in the workroom at the back but the shop itself was in darkness. She cupped her eyes and pressed her face to the glass to get a better look at Michael's chair. The horsehair padding on one of the arms was in place now.

'Want to take a closer look?' said a voice behind her.

She spun around. Archie stood beside her with a newspaper parcel under his arm. The delicious smell of fish and chips wafted towards her as he stepped up and unlocked the door.

'You can come in,' he smiled. 'Have a cup of tea. Share my supper, if you like.'

She was staring at him. He looked tired. He was working too hard. There was a hole in his jumper, right at the front. It needed darning. She had some wool that colour in her workbox. She looked up at his twinkling eyes, and stared at his mouth, his oh so kissable mouth... 'I have to go,' she blurted out. 'My mother, she's ill. I have to pack.'

His face clouded. 'Oh Gracie,' he said gently. 'I'm so sorry. Is there anything I can do?'

Gracie. He called her Gracie. He was the only person to call her that and it was nice. She shook her head.

'Please come in,' he coaxed. 'Just for a minute.'

She felt her feet turning towards the shop. Inside, it smelled of leather and linseed oil. He switched on the light and the door clicked shut behind her.

'Come into the back room,' he said. 'I'll put the kettle on, or maybe, in view of the circumstances, you'd like something stronger?'

She shook her head and followed him into the cluttered workshop. He pushed a pile of papers, some twine and a protesting cat from a chair. 'Sit down, Gracie.'

She lowered herself onto the chair, never taking her eyes from his face. Putting his supper to one side, he busied himself with the kettle and the teapot.

'Don't let your supper get cold,' she said eventually.

He smiled. 'Want some?'

She shook her head.

'How are you, Gracie? I've missed you.'

She looked away. 'Fine,' she said dully. She wanted to ask him about that woman kissing him but what was the point?

'Any news of Bonnie?'

She looked up again. Nobody asked her that any more. People acted as if Bonnie didn't exist. She supposed it was because they didn't want to upset her, but in truth, it upset her more that nobody wanted to talk about her daughter. She wanted to tell Archie how much she appreciated his asking.

'No.'

'I'm sorry,' he said. 'I suppose you've tried just about everything by now, haven't you?'

She nodded. What hadn't she tried? In the early days she'd stopped people getting off the trains and people getting on them. Bonnie's friends, their neighbours, the people in the place where Bonnie worked, even the girls going into the dances at the Assembly Hall, she'd stopped them all and asked the same question: 'Do you have any idea where Bonnie might be?' As soon as she'd got the money together, she'd been up to London more than half a dozen times and walked the streets but it was hopeless. Lately she'd taken to writing letters to the magazines Bonnie used to love in the hopes that they'd publish them, and she'd placed advertisements in the personal columns of the newspapers. What more could she do?

Archie leaned towards her and placed a cup of tea in front of her. The closeness of his body, the smell of him, made her heart beat quicken.

'What's wrong with your mother?'

'Cancer. I had a telegram asking me to go up to York. I think it may be the beginning of the end.'

'I'm sorry,' he said again. 'Do you need any money?'

She took a gulp of the hot tea and shook her head. 'I've just been round to Snowy's to ask her to keep an eye on my place while I'm away. What with Rita going to secretarial college, there'll be no one there most of the time.'

'I'll keep an eye on it if you like,' he said. 'I often look up the road when I'm working in the shop.'

'I know,' she said. They stared at each other. A vision of Norris, all hot and sweaty, lying on top of her, floated in front of her eyes. 'I have to go,' she said quickly.

'You wanted to see the chair,' he said. He went ahead of her and switched on a light which flooded the chair. The side facing her was the side which was broken and worn. The cracks in the leather resembled the undernourished skin on a dried-up heel. It was flaky, white, lumpy and unattractive. Norris made her feel like that. Thank God she didn't have to face him any more. But though she might be free of him, Archie deserved better.

'Which colour do you think would look best?' he was saying. 'Green, burgundy or midnight blue?'

At the mention of midnight blue, she shuddered involuntarily. That dress Norris had given her. After all this time, she'd quite forgotten it. 'Definitely not midnight blue,' she said.

'Green or burgundy it is then,' he smiled. He laid the midnight blue down onto the chair and moved closer to her with the other two strips of leather in his hand.

Grace felt her heart do a flip. His head was down and she stared at his hair as it flopped over his forehead. Everything in her wanted to touch it ... to touch him. He looked up and their eyes met.

'Gracie...'

'I have to go,' she said turning towards the door. She tugged at the handle but it didn't move. She could feel him coming up behind her, standing close, too close.

He put his hand over hers and she snatched it away. She was breathing quickly and her heart was pounding but she didn't move. She dared not move or she would surrender herself to him. He turned the lock with his left hand and pulled the door open with his right. He was still holding the two strips of leather and they fell to the floor. As he let go of the handle to pick them up, she yanked the door open and walked out into the night.

'Don't worry about anything, Gracie,' he called after her. 'I'll keep an eye out. Good luck with your mother.'

Grace strode on, her back stiff and her face set like a flint towards her own front door. By the time she reached it, the scalding tears were streaming down her face.

For the past couple of months, Bonnie had thrown herself into her work. Every test she had, she came top of the class. Her folder work was second to none and she had high marks for her practical work as well. The girls were puzzled by her paleness when she'd returned from London, but they had been told she'd suffered a sudden bereavement in the family. Only Matron and Dinah knew it was Shirley's father. Because of the depth of Bonnie's grief, everyone else was content to second-guess it was her mother. After all Bonnie was already a widow.

Everyone was very kind, though Shirley looked a little bewildered at times, especially when her mother let a tear or two escape while she was with her. The little girl would point at her tears and then pull her mother's hair and open her mouth wide as if to 'eat' her. Young as she was, she understood her mother was upset. Their bond grew stronger and stronger.

Every time Bonnie spoke to Dinah on the telephone, Dinah begged Bonnie to let her talk to her mother but Bonnie couldn't face the possible rejection. Not yet.

Bonnie took Shirley to Dinah's flat in time for her first birthday. Dinah put on a tea and some of her theatrical friends came to the party. Bonnie was dreading seeing John again but in the end it was all right. It was plainly obvious he knew nothing about his roots, or that they were connected, and she certainly wasn't going to tell him.

Shirley was dressed in a pretty pink dress with pink and white smocking. She loved being the centre of attention and everybody thought she was adorable. John was a gifted pianist and singer. When his fingers danced over the keyboard, her heart fluttered a little for her mother. John's way of playing was so like hers and when Shirley heard him playing she laughed and clapped her podgy little hands.

'Why won't you go back to Worthing?' Dinah said as they cleared up the aftermath of the party. Shirley was playing with building blocks with John. 'Your mother would love her to bits.'

Bonnie shook her head. 'How can I after all this time? I don't want to hurt her again.'

'You do know she spent days on end at the station looking for you?'

Bonnie looked away. 'I didn't know,' she said brokenly. 'I must have hurt her deeply. I can't do it again.'

'Tell me,' said Dinah. 'If Shirley went away for a couple of years and then you could have her back, no questions asked, would you refuse to have her?'

'That's a bit below the belt,' said Bonnie.

'Is it?' said Dinah. 'You were your mother's little baby once.'

Bonnie put the glass she was drying back into the cupboard. 'I'll think about it.'

Twenty-Four

Emilio hadn't answered Rita's letters so she had come home for the weekend. She wanted to ask Salvatore where he was. Her mother was still at Granny's and not likely to be home for a while. It was strange being in the house all alone. Snowy had popped by to check up on her on Saturday morning. Rita was still in bed.

'Your mother wrote to me this week,' said Snowy. 'I'm afraid it's not good news. You know your grandmother has cancer, don't you? I'm afraid it's only a matter of time and your mother wants to stay up there until the end.'

Rita nodded her head sleepily and did her best to stifle the yawn that was coming. She wasn't very fond of her grandmother. She hadn't seen her very often as a child. The distance between them hadn't helped, but she'd sent a knitted scarf every Christmas and she'd written the occasional letter. Rita's mother worked hard to please the old lady, sending her parcels and letters very regularly, but there was clearly something between them, something unspoken but large enough to affect their relationship.

Rita had thanked Snowy and promised to come for a meal later in the day. She would head over that way once she'd seen Salvatore.

Rita had been surprised that she'd enjoyed doing the shorthand and typing course as much as she did. The course itself wasn't exactly scintillating, but the girls training with her were brilliant. They all had so many laughs together. Most weekday evenings were taken up with practice homework but at the weekends she was able to go dancing. Brighton was such a lively place compared to Worthing and now that the war was well and truly over, the bright lights beckoned every young girl to the sea front and the dance halls where she could dance the night away with the best-looking boys in town.

Rita's favourite places were the two piers, which had both reopened the year before. As with Worthing's pier, in 1940 the council had removed large chunks to hamper enemy invasion, but as soon as hostilities were at an end, the piers were repaired in time for the holiday season. The West Pier was a little more grand than the Palace Pier but both had their charms. If she and her friends fancied kiss-me-quick hats and candyfloss, the Palace Pier was the place to be, while the theatre on the West Pier had some really good shows. She wrote to Dinah, now studying at RADA, and told her all about them, adding that they weren't a patch on the Worthing Musical Comedy Shows.

Rita was never short of offers from good-looking young men, to her great surprise. She'd had several letters from Bob. He was kind and he was funny, so she enjoyed reading them again and again, but her heart was already given to Emilio. He was her first thought in the morning and her last at night, which was why she was so anxious that she hadn't heard from him.

The Railway Café was buzzing when she walked in, but even though they were rushed off their feet, Salvatore threw his arms out in his usual exuberant way and kissed Rita on both cheeks.

'Sit, sit,' he begged. 'I just serve and then we talk.' He went to the hatch and called, 'Mama, Rita is here.'

Liliana, all pink and flustered, came out of the kitchen a few minutes later, a pastry in one hand and a coffee in the other. She put them in front of Rita and shook her head as Rita reached for her purse. 'Sit,' she said repeating Salvatore's instruction. 'Eat. Enjoy. We talk later.'

It was more than an hour before they could take a quick break to talk to Rita. First they wanted to know how her grandmother was, and when Grace would be coming home and then they bombarded her with questions. What was the course like? Had she made new friends? What were the lodgings like? Rita answered everything with as much attention to detail as she could and eventually there came the lull in conversation she'd been looking for.

'I've been writing to Emilio,' she ventured as Salvatore and Liliana sat opposite her beaming as proudly as any parent, 'but he doesn't reply to my letters.'

She saw the colour drain from Liliana's face as she stood up and excused herself. 'I needed in the kitchen.'

Salvatore picked at a loose thread on his apron. 'Emilio, he stay with friend.'

'Is he all right?'

'He fine,' said Salvatore.

'It's just that Liliana...' Rita began anxiously.

'She angry that he not say he was going,' said Salvatore quickly.

Rita breathed a sigh of relief. 'Any news of Jeremy?' Rita continued. 'We wrote all the time when he was doing his basic training but he forgot to tell me where his next posting would be.'

Salvatore shot out his lip and shook his head. 'Emilio, he back after Christmas,' he said giving her a long hard stare. 'You come back then, Rita. All Emilio needs is the love of a good woman.'

Rita blushed. Christmas was a long way away. 'Can you give me his address?'

'He travel around,' said Salvatore avoiding her eye. 'You send here. I post for you.'

The customers were beginning to build again and the new help behind the counter was struggling to cope. 'I go,' Salvatore apologised.

'Of course,' said Rita finishing the last of her coffee. 'I'm on my way to Mum's friend's for tea anyway.'

By the time July came, Bonnie and Dinah had been meeting on a regular basis.

Bonnie usually arranged to see Cook and Dora first and then to meet Dinah to have tea or a stroll in Hyde Park. It came as a pleasant surprise when Dinah suggested that she and Shirley join her for a weekend break.

'I have a friend who has a cottage in the country,' she said. 'I can't tell you how much I'm looking forward to a real holiday.'

'I'm not sure it would be much of a holiday with Shirley around,' Bonnie laughed. 'She's such a live wire these days.'

'Remind me again?' said Dinah. 'How old is she?'

'Fifteen months,' said Bonnie. 'She's got four teeth and she's toddling, so she's in to everything.'

'Oh do come,' said Dinah. 'She's such a poppet and the place is huge. The garden goes on for ever.'

In the end Bonnie relented. They made arrangements to pick her up by car early Friday evening and said they would be back late Sunday afternoon. 'I would stay longer,' Dinah apologised, 'but I have rehearsals first thing Monday morning and I'll never get up in time if I don't have a good night's sleep.'

'That's fine,' said Bonnie. 'I have to start work at seven in the morning myself.'

Dinah shuddered. 'Ghastly hour. Whoever invented it wants shooting.'

The cottage was more like a house. It was set deep in the heart of the unspoiled Kent countryside. Although the nursery backed onto Richmond Park and had its own private gate, somehow Bonnie never lost the feeling that she was in an enclosed space. Here, in Kent, she was able to stand in the back garden and look across the county for miles.

Shirley loved toddling around the garden. She picked up stones, pointed out the flowers saying, ‘’ook, ’ook…’ and ate dirt. Bonnie kept a very close eye on her, but she even managed the three little steps that led to a lower garden by herself. Shirley soon had the adults playing ‘boo!’ by the dustbins and her little giggle was highly infectious.

There were three others in the party. Mick and Clare spent most of the weekend in their bedroom, only emerging for meals or the occasional walk. They were passionately in love and to start with they hardly seemed to notice anyone else, certainly not Shirley. The other person was John Finley.

On Saturday, Bonnie walked into the village with Shirley in the pushchair. Mick and Clare hadn’t yet emerged from the night before while Dinah and John were sitting in the garden learning their lines.

Bonnie was enjoying herself. She and Shirley stopped in a tea room for drinks and watched the world go by.

‘She’s such a good little girl,’ the waitress remarked as Bonnie paid the bill. Shirley was already winning hearts as she waved, ‘Bye, bye,’ and smiled at the remaining customers.

When she got back to the cottage, Shirley was asleep. Bonnie left the pushchair round the back and tiptoed away. They had decided at breakfast that they would have bread, cheese and pickles for lunch, so she set about preparing it. Dinah had dozed off in her chair and she could hear laughter from upstairs.

'Did you enjoy your walk?' The sound of John's voice made her jump.

'Yes, thank you,' she smiled.

'I'll get the wine,' he said.

She found a lettuce and a few tomatoes in the refrigerator and washed them.

'We make a great team,' he said coming back with a bottle of wine.

'Do you have a family?' She did her best to sound casual and willed her cheeks not to go red.

'Just me and my parents. And you?'

'I have a mother and a sister. My father was killed in the D-Day landings.'

'I'm sorry,' he said.

'What does your father do?'

'He owns a knitwear factory, among other things,' said John. 'He wants me to take over from him, but it's really not for me, I'm afraid.'

'He must be upset.'

'Very.'

She smiled. She'd wanted to ask more pertinent questions including, *Are you adopted?*, but she had backed herself into a corner. There was no way she could say that without raising suspicion and she didn't want to do that. Not yet.

'I hear you're a bit of a pioneer in the nursery,' he said putting wine glasses onto the tray she had already prepared.

'I wouldn't put it quite like that,' she chuckled. 'It feels more like darned hard work.'

There was a small silence and then he said, 'I was sorry to hear about your man.' She looked up sharply. 'Dinah told me. Sorry, but we made up our minds from the word go not to keep secrets from each other.'

'I like that,' said Bonnie, thinking about her own mother. 'We should all be open and honest.'

'He was found in my father's old factory, you know,' said John. 'Odd, isn't it?'

A distant memory nudged her mind. What was it George had said about John's father? She couldn't quite put her finger on it but it felt important. John picked up the tray and they went outside.

'Oh darling, how marvellous,' Dinah cried as John put the tray onto the all weathers table.

'I can't take all the credit,' said John stooping to give her a kiss. 'Bonnie helped me a bit.'

Behind his back Bonnie grinned and Dinah winked at her. 'I'm so glad you both get on,' she said. 'You're my two most favourite people in the world.'

'Of course we do,' said John, putting his hand to his forehead in a dramatic gesture. 'We are such a comfort to each other in this time of trial.'

Dinah hit his arm playfully. 'Don't tease me. I mean it.'

Shirley woke up and Bonnie left them to see to her child. She felt a bit of a gooseberry but she didn't mind too much. It was good to see Dinah so happy after all the heartbreak of losing her husband so young.

As Bonnie changed Shirley's nappy inside, she began to think about George again. She wished she had a photograph of him. Sometimes she struggled to remember what he looked like, but then she tickled Shirley's bare tummy and in her giggly face, she saw him there.

'Don't let him get too close to you...' That's what George had said about Finley, but what did it mean?

The whole day was wonderfully relaxing. Dinah and John took it in turns to amuse Shirley and of course she lapped up the extra attention.

'I've never had Shirley christened,' she said. 'If I do, will you two be her godparents?'

'We'd love to, wouldn't we, John?' cried Dinah enthusiastically.

'Rather,' said John. Shirley was sitting on his lap. He kissed her blonde curls and when she looked up at him he said, 'You'd like to have an Uncle John, wouldn't you, sweetheart?'

Shirley stared at him for a few seconds and then reached up and tweaked his nose, making everybody laugh. Bonnie watched them with pleasure. Uncle John in more ways than one, she thought.

Twenty-Five

The train pulled into the station four minutes late. Even before it came to a halt, several passengers had leaned out of their carriage windows and turned the outside handle to open the door. The train was made up of individual carriages and most had two or three passengers, with the exception of first class.

Oswald Matthews gathered his things with a heavy heart. As the train came to a stop, a deep sense of foreboding descended upon him. As he alighted from the carriage, the chilly English weather hit him once again. Manny Hart was calling, 'Worthing, this is Worthing.'

A porter came up to him. 'Carry your bags, sir?'

Oswald nodded and the man lifted his heavy leather suitcase with ease. 'Taxi is it, sir?'

Oswald nodded again and followed him to the exit. The bleak windswept platform matched his mood. How he longed to be back under the warmth of the South African sun. Ensconced in the taxi, Oswald gave the porter a sixpenny bit once the case was safely stowed inside.

'Where to, guv?'

'The Chatsworth Hotel,' said Oswald, 'and then I want you to wait for me. I want to go on to Worthing police station.'

The drive wasn't far and he liked what little he saw of the town. There weren't many people about, probably because of the weather. Most were hunched under umbrellas or keeping under the large blue blinds pulled down in front of almost every shop which sheltered shoppers from the rain. The taxi turned by the pier where the Christmas panto was in full swing and then along the sea front for a short while. His attention was caught by the fishing boats on the beach, their bright triangular flags tugging at the long poles which secured them. He spotted a blackboard with 'Fresh fish for sale', but the rain had made the chalk run and there was no sign of customers. As his taxi turned the corner, he passed a few people, huddled under a shelter, looking anxiously up the street as they waited for the bus. The taxi drew up and the doorman called for a young boy who ran down the steps to take his bags.

'Will you be staying long, sir?' the receptionist enquired as he checked in.

Oswald shrugged. 'Not sure.'

At the police station he was met by the newly promoted Detective Sergeant Nyman, who, immediately after he had introduced himself, took him into an interview room. The room was windowless and smelled stale. Oswald was trembling as he lit a cigarette and sat down. The DS had followed him in and put a brown folder onto the table between them.

'I'll get straight to the point, sir,' said Nyman. 'I don't suppose you want me to keep you in suspense.'

He laid a photograph on the table and turned it around so that the subject was facing Oswald. Oswald took a deep breath and looked down but he could not prevent a sound of anguish escaping his lips. He screwed up his eyes and began to rock slightly. Then he took a long drag of the cigarette and looked up at the ceiling. He could feel the tears filling his eyes and his nose. He swallowed hard. When he looked back at Nyman, out of respect for him the detective sergeant had turned the picture over and was looking away. Oswald fished in his pocket for a handkerchief and blew his nose noisily. He cleared his throat and said the words he wished with all his heart he didn't have to say. 'Yes, that's my son. That's George.'

As if on cue, the door opened and a fresh-faced constable came in with two cups of tea. He put them silently onto the table and Oswald watched the cup in front of him wobble slightly, spilling some tea in the saucer. His mind was in a fog. He would never see his son again. How was he going to tell Mildred? What the devil was the boy doing here in the first place?

As the constable left the room, Oswald cleared his throat again. 'When did it happen?'

'Coming up for two years ago, sir.'

Oswald looked up sharply. 'Two years? Two bloody years. My boy has been dead all that time and you didn't tell me?'

For the first time, Nyman heard the soft South African lilt in his voice.

'I'm sorry,' he said. 'It took us some time to locate you and I'm afraid the South African police were more than a little slow in replying. We wanted to make completely sure of the facts before we asked you to come all this way.'

Oswald nodded sagely.

'Do you want me to tell you everything, sir?' Nyman began again. 'It's not exactly pleasant.'

Oswald nodded. 'I'd appreciate your candour.'

'It took some while to find out who he was,' Nyman explained. 'The body was in an advanced state of decomposition so he had to be formally identified by dental records. That photograph comes from the local paper. They did a feature on the new factory and your son was pictured working the machine.' He paused, anxious that the man in front of him had no colour in his face. 'Do you want me to go on, sir?'

Oswald took a gulp of the scalding tea and nodded. 'I want to know everything, Detective, er...'

'Detective Sergeant Nyman. I was the DC on the case when we found the body. Detective Inspector Chester was in charge.'

The name was meaningless to Oswald. 'Tell me everything.'

'Your son was working in a knitwear factory,' said Nyman.

'Not very exciting.' Oswald sucked his bottom lip. 'What happened?'

'He was found in the cold room of a disused factory. There was an inquest but because of lack of evidence...' he opened his hands as a gesture of incomprehension, 'as to how he got locked in there and why, and the state of the body ... the coroner returned an open verdict.'

Silence drifted between them as Oswald picked up the photograph again. It was definitely his son. He was side on to the camera and concentrating on the machine he was working. Oswald rubbed his thumb over the boy's face and his chest grew tight. He was only twenty-six, he thought. That's no life, no life at all.

'Do you want me to carry on, sir?'

Oswald cleared his throat again. He liked this man. He was kind, sensitive, and respectful. 'Yes.'

'We carried out extensive enquiries. Your son was seeing a local girl but no one is sure who she is. She's never come forward and anyway we have no reason to believe she is in any way implicated in your son's death.'

'What about the other people in the factory?'

Nyman consulted his notes. He had been part of the investigation for the first two days, that was all. Inspector Chester had bumped him off the case for some reason he couldn't quite remember now, but they didn't get on anyway. 'We interviewed the owner,' he said, 'but he was unable to shed any light on the subject.' Smarmy-looking bastard, he remembered.

'I should like to talk to him myself,' said Oswald.

'I don't think there's anything to be gained,' said Nyman, but seeing Oswald's determined face, added, 'Having said that, I'm sure Mr Finley would be happy to help in any way he could.'

'What sort of chap is he?'

Nyman shrugged. 'He's a well-respected employer and property owner in the town. What you might call the very model of an Englishman.'

Oswald stubbed out his cigarette. 'I'm staying at the Chatsworth Hotel for a few days. Now that I am certain that it really is George, I must go back and fetch my wife from South Africa. She's an invalid. She can't travel alone.' He paused. 'You said my son was buried. Where?'

'Offington cemetery,' said Nyman. 'I'm afraid he has an unmarked grave.'

'I intend to alter that as soon as my wife gets here. Where was he living?'

'109 Pavilion Road. He was lodging with a Mrs Kerr.'

'And what happened to his things?'

Nyman consulted his notes again. After much flicking through papers, he was none the wiser. 'I'll check on that for you, sir.' He hoped Mr Matthews hadn't noticed that his face was flushed with embarrassment.

The two men stood up and shook hands. 'Can

I keep this photograph?'

'I'm afraid this one is police property, sir, but I am sure the *Worthing Herald* would be pleased to accommodate you with a copy.'

Oswald looked at it for one last time. The boy looked more at peace with himself after his dreadful experiences during the war. His hair was pushed back and tidy. Oswald longed to make it flop in the same way as it had when he was a lad. He sighed. The last time he'd seen his son was in 1945, soon after the war ended, when he'd travelled with them to Southampton to see them off. Mildred needed to be in a warmer climate and they had seized the opportunity to go to South Africa. They had begged their son to go with them but he'd said he had some unfinished business to attend to, something to do with that damned war, Oswald supposed. But it wasn't that memory which filled his mind. All he could see was a tousle-haired little boy with a dirty face and a runny nose. He was holding up a jam jar full of tiddlers by a piece of string. 'Look, Dad. Look what I've got.'

Oswald swayed and Nyman grabbed his arm.

'I'm all right,' Oswald said huskily as he steadied himself.

'Tell you what, sir,' said Nyman. 'I'll see if I can get you a copy.'

Oswald nodded and walked out of the room. After a year of fruitless searching, he'd found his only son. What irony. George had made it all through that damned war only to end up on the floor of a cold room in this god-forsaken seaside town. And for what? Nyman had been kind enough but Oswald needed to know what had happened. Until he did, he could never rest. They had rung for a taxi and as soon as it arrived, he thanked the police officers and went outside. As soon as he felt able to, he would find as many people as possible who knew George. But there was no need to rush for now. He didn't want to start something he couldn't finish before his wife came over. He felt in no fit state to ask questions and besides, he couldn't trust his emotions. For the sake of George's memory, he didn't want to make a fool of himself in front of strangers. First of all, he'd have to tell Mildred. She'd be devastated. God, what a bloody thing to happen. He'd have to travel back to South Africa and fetch her of course. Then they'd come back and bury their dear boy with dignity.

Twenty-Six

Norris was bored. What he wanted was a bit of excitement. He picked up a letter left on his drinks table. It had a Worthing postmark and the address was typed. He tore it open but then the two phone calls came one after the other and right out of the blue. The first was from Major Freeman, chairman of the cricket club.

'Been thinking, Finley,' he told Norris. 'Your family has been in Worthing for donkey's years. Fine, upstanding, useful members of the community. Remember your father. Bloody fine officer. Could have done with more of his ilk in the last bloody show. Damned shame he died so young. Anyway, got to thinking. Have you ever thought of running for office?'

Norris stared blankly out of his office window.

'Thing is, old boy,' the major went on, 'the council could do with some new blood. Someone to get things done. Popular man like you could rustle up a few votes quite easily. Anyway, think about it and get back to me, will you? I'm sure I could drum up some support to get you on the borough council. Who knows where that might lead in a few years, eh, what?'

By the time he had put the receiver down, Norris's imagination was already working overtime. He'd been thinking about running for office for some time. Just never got around to it, that was all. He could just picture himself in mayoral robes. He'd have his portrait painted and hung in the town hall. Of course he'd have no problem in getting votes. He was still young. Women liked him and he could call in a few favours when the time came. He wished his father were still alive. How he would have loved to say, 'Look at me, Pa. You never thought I'd amount to much but I'm a really important man in this town now. How wrong can you be? You always favoured my brother over me. You never gave *me* a sports car for my twenty-first.' Norris gripped the arms of his chair until his knuckles went white. Bloody unfair, that's what it was. But perhaps it was just as well after all. He might have gone and got himself killed too. Right now, he was very much alive and on his way at last. Mayor of Worthing...

It had a nice ring to it. Cllr Norris Finley, Mayor of Worthing. Yes, the more he thought about it, the more he liked the idea. His only problem was that public office inevitably led to public scrutiny.

He'd successfully buried much of his past. In the thirties, when Mosley came to the Pavilion for his meetings, he'd spent many an evening writing Fascist slogans all over Worthing. He'd signed them 'P.J' and there had been speculation for years as to who P.J. was. Nobody guessed it was him. It was the one time all those gruelling Latin lessons had come in useful. *Perficio justicia* – perfect justice, that's what it meant.

He'd never actually joined the Blackshirts because he found crowds of people intimidating, but he had attended the rallies, usually slipping in at the back and moving on at the first sign of trouble.

The only thorn in his flesh at the moment was this blasted Fair Rents panel. They had insisted that all of his tenants have a proper rent book and he had to agree to a much reduced rate for some properties. He'd been furious, vowing to fight them all the way. He would have done too, but this changed everything. Now he needed to impress people with his generosity. Damn and blast it. He'd have to get onto his collectors and tell them to issue the books. The panel hadn't offered to buy the books, so that would be another expense.

Of course, he'd have to get rid of Grace once and for all. He hadn't bothered to use her lately; he had another dainty little morsel on the go, but he had planned to get back to her later on when the new girl began to bore him. Pity he had to let Grace go. He hadn't meant for it to happen but he liked being with her. She'd been unwilling at first but he'd soon sorted that. Now she wanted it as much as he did, gagging for it, he was sure of that.

He stood in front of his desk and admired his reflection in the office door. He was still an attractive man and women flocked to men in power. They said Il Duce used to wave to the crowds on the balcony, step back into his office and take one of his secretaries on the floor, and then go back out and enjoy the adulation of the crowds again. There were three little balconies on the front of Worthing Town Hall, but he'd never seen them in use, more's the pity. Perhaps he could get them opened up when he was mayor. *When he was mayor* – he liked the sound of that.

The second telephone call came as the most appalling shock. It was from Detective Sergeant Nyman.

'You'll be relieved to hear that we have had a relative come forward to claim the body of George Matthews.'

Norris hardly dared to breathe.

'It's his father,' the DS went on.

'Why on earth didn't he come forward before?' demanded Norris. He cleared his throat. His voice was high with panic.

'It's taken us all this time to trace him,' said the DS. 'It turns out that he lives in South Africa.'

Norris lowered himself into a chair. 'So what happens now?'

'Apparently the boy's mother is an invalid,' Nyman continued. 'Mr Matthews has gone back to South Africa so that he can accompany his wife back here. They must have more money than sense if you ask me.'

'Why would they want to come back again?' said Norris. 'Matthews is dead and buried.'

'They want him re-interred after a Christian funeral,' said Nyman. 'Give him a proper send off, if you like. I just thought I'd inform you because the father may want to come and ask you a few questions about his son. And perhaps you might like to be there when the time comes to re-inter the body?'

Norris hesitated. The man must be joking! This was the last thing he wanted.

'Unfortunately,' said Norris, 'I'm about to leave the country on business. I would have been there but my hands are tied.'

'Well, it'll take a while to organise anyway,' said Nyman. 'I told him he'll have to jump through a few official hoops, so to speak. You may be back home again by that time.'

'Probably,' Norris conceded, although he was thinking, *not bloody likely*.

'Shall I set up a meeting then, sir?'

'Yes, you do that,' said Norris. 'Contact my secretary. She has my diary.' As he replaced the receiver, he became aware of the letter still in his hand. It came from his father's solicitors. Norris read it twice before he fully digested the contents. Everything had just gone from bad to worse.

The solicitor was reminding him that John was

about to come into his inheritance from his grandfather. The letter concluded by saying:

As a result of the agreement, the accumulated funds will pass into the Finley estate when John reaches his twenty-fifth birthday. I cannot help wonder why, even though she was in communication with your late father (the late Mr Edward Finley wrote a letter dictated and sent from this firm), Grace Follett has never contacted this office.

Norris lowered himself into his chair. His father had written to Grace? Good God, what on earth did he say to her? And why the hell hadn't Grace ever told him?

His dreams of a balcony conquest suddenly evaporated. 'Damn,' he said. 'Damn, damn, damn!'

The soles of her shoes squeaked noisily as Grace walked along the hospital corridors and every step seemed a mile long. She met a few people coming in the opposite direction, but she made no eye contact. She was beginning to feel slightly ridiculous with a wilting bunch of flowers in her hand. They were from her mother's garden. The last couple of roses and some Michaelmas daisies. She had thought her mother would enjoy them but now the garden posy seemed inadequate. Her mother deserved better.

These past few months had been cathartic for both of them. They started a little awkwardly but as time went on and Freda became more dependent, they found a friendship together that they both enjoyed.

She reached Room 6 and pushed the door open slowly. Her mother was lying flat in the bed with her eyes closed. Her hair was down. It lay like silver clouds all over the pillow. Grace had never seen it like that before. Her mother always wore it scraped back in a tight bun, but it was beautiful. If it wasn't for the colour, it could have been the hair of a young woman. She looked so small, so fragile. Her skin was like parchment, her hands limp by her side.

'Mum,' Grace said quietly. 'Mum, it's me.'

Freda Follett opened her eyes and her face lit up. 'I knew you would come one last time. I just knew it...' Her voice trailed and Grace saw her eyes filling with tears.

'It's all right, Mum,' she said quietly. She sat in the chair beside the bed and reached for her hand. Her mother tried to pull herself up but the effort was too much.

'Rest, Mum. Don't get up.'

'I've never been much for talking,' Freda said, 'but I've enjoyed our time together.'

Grace was cut to the quick. She had never heard her mother say anything even remotely like that before. Her whole life, Grace had always felt as if she could never please her mother.

Freda reached up and touched her daughter's face then let her hand drop to the bed. Grace reached for it and held it firmly. 'Are you in pain?'

Freda shook her head. 'I think I don't have much time,' she said, squeezing Grace's fingers lightly. 'Our secret is still safe?'

Grace nodded. 'It's still safe, Mum.' Grace

fumbled for a handkerchief and blew her nose.

'He left you some money, you know.'

Grace was puzzled, but she let her go on talking. She's rambling, she thought. Old people do that.

'The solicitor told me.'

'Who left me some money?'

'Old man Finley.'

Grace stared at her mother in shocked surprise. John's grandfather had died just days after he was born.

'He left you money so that you could keep your baby.'

The shock made Grace rise to her feet. 'Why didn't you tell me?'

Her mother closed her eyes and pursed her lips together in anguish. 'Now you're angry with me.'

Too right she was angry, but Grace realised that her mother had something important to say and if she didn't listen now, she would never hear it. The hospital was very strict with visiting hours. They had told her to come even though it was way past eight o'clock, so Freda's life must be coming to an end. Before the morning came, she would probably be meeting her maker. This was no time for playing games. Grace sat back down and took the old lady's hand again. 'I'm sorry, Mum,' she said gently. 'It was a surprise, that's all. Tell me. Whatever you want to tell me I won't be angry. I promise.'

'The solicitor wrote to you, Grace, but I thought when John went to Mr Finley it was better to let things lie. The boy needed a mother and a father.' Freda became agitated. 'They said if you asked for the money, he would have you declared unfit and the baby would be sent to an orphanage.'

Grace was appalled. 'Who said that?'

'Mr Norris.' Freda's voice became a whisper. 'I was scared, Grace, and you were so full of grief, that if I let them take you, I might never have seen you again.'

'Oh Mum...' Grace began.

Freda put her bony finger to her lips and shook her head. 'Shhh,' she whispered. 'Don't be upset. It's all right. It was for the best, wasn't it? The baby went to a good home, didn't he? No one knows. Our secret is safe.'

There was a sound outside in the corridor and her mother came to life. 'Quick, my bag, my bag.' She leaned towards the cupboard beside her bed and tried to open the door.

Grace rushed around to help her. 'It's OK, Mum. I'll get it.'

The old familiar bag was right at the back behind her cardigan and a book. Grace placed it reverently on the bed beside her. Freda worked the clasp eagerly until it opened and then she fell exhausted against the pillows. Grace couldn't bear it.

'What is it, Mum? What are you looking for?'

'The letter,' she gasped.

Grace tipped the contents of the bag onto the bed. Lipstick, a comb, a battered purse, some pictures of her father as a young man, some till receipts, assorted pens and miscellaneous items tumbled onto the counterpane. Her mother pushed her hand through them quickly and picked up a small, tired-looking envelope. She handed it to Grace with a conspiratorial look.

'Take it back now,' she said, her voice coming in ragged gasps. 'Go and see them. Waiting for you.'

Grace glanced at the envelope but still didn't fully understand. All she knew was her mother's sense of urgency. She pushed it into her pocket. Together they put everything back in the bag and Grace placed it back in the bedside locker.

It was then that Freda noticed the garden posy. 'Oh they're lovely!' she cried.

'Mum...' Grace began again, but instinctively she knew the time for conversation was over. Her mother's eyes closed and she relaxed on the pillow.

The letter burned in Grace's pocket. Eventually she took it out.

The envelope was limp with age and dog-eared from much handling. Grace stared at her own name and address written in a beautiful copper-plate hand. She fingered the old-fashioned stamp, King George V, as she squinted to see the postmark: 1924, the year John was born.

Silently she let the letter slide out of its envelope and glanced back at her mother. She still had her eyes closed. Grace looked back at the piece of paper in her hand but she could only bear to read the heading. Clifton and Sons Solicitors.

She sat there for a full fifteen minutes. Fifteen minutes with a piece of paper which could have changed her life forever had she known of its existence. As she slid it back into the envelope her mother let out a long sigh and Grace knew she was gone.

How long she sat there looking at her mother's face, she never knew, but when Grace came to herself, her cheeks were wet with tears. She had never felt quite like this before. Not even when Michael died. Her mother, the one who had brought her into the world, was gone. As old as she was, Grace felt like an orphan and it wasn't a pleasant experience. She began to shake and before long her body was racked by silent sobs. She had pressed her handkerchief to her mouth in a vain attempt to keep all the sound in. Thank God that she and Freda had made their peace. Grace blew her nose. 'Oh Mum, I love you. I'm going to miss you.' Something made her look up and she noticed something quite remarkable. All the lines and wrinkles in her mother's face had gone. She looked as if she was sleeping and, more importantly, she was young again.

Grace stood up, leaned over and kissed her mother's forehead. 'Good night Mum,' she said, her throat still tight with emotion. 'See you in the morning.' She paused for a moment to wipe her eyes and blow her nose and then, with head held high, she left the room to find one of the nursing staff.

When Rita came home, she was overjoyed to see Emilio was back. He looked pale and he'd lost weight, but he was as handsome as ever dressed in a white shirt, open at the neck and with a red and white spotted kerchief around his neck. Liliana was away visiting her sister so Salvatore let them use his sitting room.

'I've missed you,' Rita said shyly. 'Are you all right?'

Emilio had made some tea and they sat at the small table by the window. Rita would have far rather been sitting with him on the sofa.

'Fine.'

You don't look it my darling, she thought. You look as if you could do with looking after. 'Where did you go?'

He didn't answer but instead stared out of the window. Rita was suddenly concerned. 'Emilio, what is it?'

'I have to go back.'

'Back, where?'

'To Italy.' He hung his head and his hair flopped onto his forehead.

Rita was horrified. If he went back to Italy, she would never see him again. Her eyes filled with tears. How could she bear it?

'Surely there must be a way of staying here. I don't understand. Who says you must go back?'

'The government,' he said, his voice breaking with emotion. She placed her trembling hand over his. Rita had never heard of such a thing. The British always seemed so welcoming to foreigners. Hadn't the *Empire Windrush* docked in Tilbury with nearly 500 passengers from Jamaica just last June? Nobody made a fuss about them and the passengers had even been offered cheap fares.

'I have no ties, no family. They say I must go, Rita.'

'There's no restriction on members of the British Empire,' she said stoutly.

'Italy doesn't belong to the British Empire,' he pointed out with a shrug of his shoulders. 'And we lost the war.'

'But you have Salvatore,' said Rita. 'Can't you tell them he's your uncle?'

Emilio shrugged again. 'Is not enough.'

Rita caught her breath. 'But what if you had a wife?' she began cautiously, not wanting to appear too fast. Her heart was beginning to thump. 'What if you were married? Would you be allowed to stay then?'

He looked up with a puzzled expression. 'I have no time to find a wife,' he smiled.

Oh Emilio, Emilio, she thought, look at me! But he resumed his stare out of the window. Rita chewed her bottom lip anxiously. 'I'll do it for you if you like?'

'What?'

'Marry you so that you can stay.' Her heart was pounding in her chest and she hardly dared breathe.

His hand covered hers. 'You would really do this for me?' Her eyes danced with excitement but she still had the presence of mind to nod modestly.

'But you are too young, Rita,' he said. 'Your mama, she say no.'

'There is a way,' said Rita, suddenly feeling the wonderful romance of it all. 'We could always go to Gretna Green.'

Salvatore was overjoyed when they told him. Later, much later when Rita had gone back home, the two men shared a bottle of wine and a plate of spaghetti together.

'Hai dovuto persuaderla? (Did you have to

persuade her?)

'È stato facile.' (It was easy.)

Salvatore gripped his nephew's arm. *'Ti prendi cura di lei. È una buona ragazza.'* (You do right by her. She's a good girl.)

Back at her mother's place, Rita found some letters on the mat. One was from Bob. 'On my way home at last,' he wrote. 'I hope you will come dancing with me.'

Rita stuffed the letter back into the envelope. 'I'm afraid I can't,' she said aloud. 'By the time you come through that door, I shall be a married woman.'

Bonnie was happy. She'd spent the afternoon wrapping Christmas presents for the children in the nursery as well as some for Shirley. The girls had decorated the nursery the night before and now paper chains hung across the rooms and all the Disney cartoons festooned the windows: Dumbo, Bambi, Pinocchio, Snow White and Mickey Mouse. She wasn't very good at cartooning, but with a picture in front of her, Bonnie found that she could make a reasonable stab at a likeness.

Shirley enjoyed painting too. Bonnie had several of her splodge paintings hanging in her bedroom. Most of them were on a corkboard she had bought from Woolworth's but the others were Sellotaped directly onto the walls. They looked a lot better than the holes where previous pictures had been and one effort in particular covered a fairly large place where the plaster had fallen away.

Tonight Bonnie had been invited to go out with some people from the local church when they went carol singing in the streets. She was looking forward to that and for the first time since she'd left home, Bonnie felt she was going to enjoy the festive season.

The car door opened and a figure dressed all in black got in.

'Is it safe to stay here?' Norris asked.

'Nobody saw me,' said his passenger. He reached into his coat pocket and pulled out some papers. 'There is another shipment on the way.'

Norris kept his hands on the steering wheel. His passenger flapped the envelope impatiently.

'I can't do this any more,' said Norris. 'It's too dangerous and I have too much to lose.'

'That has never stopped you before. In the beginning you liked the danger.'

'I did, but things change. Since that George Matthews business, I don't have the stomach for it any more.'

'It's all blown over, hasn't it?' snapped his passenger. 'His father has gone back to South Africa.'

'What if Grace Follett tells him her daughter was there?'

'Don't be daft! If she does that, she implicates the girl, doesn't she?'

Norris stared at his fingernails. 'The locket has gone.'

'*Gone?* What do you mean, gone?'

'She must have taken it from the safe.'

His passenger stared at him and then lashed out, raining blows over Norris's head. 'You bloody idiot,' he shouted. 'That was my way out of here.'

Norris didn't retaliate, rather he curled himself up and tried to take the blows on his arms. When it was all over, they sat in shocked silence, the only sound in the car being heavy breathing.

A man rounded the corner of the street and walked briskly towards them. His passenger pulled his coat collar up and his hat a little further down. 'If you were worried about being seen with me, you were a bit daft parking so close to the street lamp,' he grumbled.

'What if the boy's father makes waves?' said Norris. 'What if he and Grace put two and two together?'

The man beside him didn't answer but Norris felt his body stiffen.

'The police may want to reopen the case,' he pressed.

'Then put the frighteners on her,' said the man. He put the papers onto Norris's lap. 'You've done it before. Do it again.'

'You're not listening,' said Norris. 'The locket has gone. I've got nothing to bargain with. I'm telling you. I want out!'

'Now listen to me, matey,' snapped his passenger. 'You're in this up to your neck. When it gets this far, it can't be turned back. I'll pass on your concerns to headquarters but for now it's business as usual.'

The pedestrian had crossed the street and it was empty again.

'I never thought it would go on for so long,' said Norris.

'Yeah,' said the man, getting out of the car, 'and Hitler never thought he'd lose the bloody war, did he?'

Twenty-Seven

Grace threw her bag onto the table and put her suitcase by the stair door. It was good to be home again. She felt as if she had been away forever. Her mother had passed away three weeks ago and she had travelled back from Yorkshire for the last time.

She had stayed long enough to bury her mother and to clean and clear out her house. It was all very quick and very final. Her mother had died on a Monday, been buried on the following Monday (Rita couldn't come because she had her final exam) and Grace had posted the keys through the landlord's door the Monday after that.

In the lonely days before her mother's funeral, Grace had done a lot of thinking. She couldn't understand why she never stopped to work things out long before now. Life had dealt her some difficult cards but instead of asking why, she'd just got on with it.

Since reading her mother's letter she'd realised that so many of her problems were down to Norris Finley. He'd taken her baby, when she'd been given provision to keep him. He'd pressured her mother into silence and that guilt had blighted their relationship for more than twenty-four years. Her children had been denied a real relationship with their grandmother because Freda had felt compelled to move up to Yorkshire rather than betray her promise to Norris.

Ever since she could remember, Grace had lived in one of the many properties Norris had scattered around the town, with no rent book and the fear of rising rents looming over her head every week. And then there was the blackmail. Keeping Bonnie's locket in exchange for favours was revolting but now that she was thinking straight, Grace was sure she wasn't the only victim. When she'd picked up the little envelope, it felt heavy. She'd tipped the contents into her hand, and found Bonnie's locket but she'd also glimpsed a gold watch. She'd thought and thought about it. Could it have been the gold watch Kaye had been accused of stealing? She would probably never know because the poor girl had been so upset, she'd taken a bus to Beachy Head and never come back. Did she do that rather than sleep with Norris? Had she chosen death rather than dishonour?

Snowy wasn't much for writing but she had mentioned once again that Polly was looking increasingly thin and that she was a bag of nerves. It wouldn't surprise Grace if Norris hadn't forced the girl to do something she was ashamed of. Every time Grace thought about Polly, she grew angry. She was only a kid. Somebody had to stop Norris before yet another young girl in the first bloom of her life went over the cliff. There were more ways than one of being a monster.

As she chewed things over, other people came to mind. People she hadn't thought of for years. What really happened to that girl whose husband had accused her of going with another man? She had worked in the factory and when her husband ... Desmond, that was his name, Desmond Peterson came home on leave, Dolly had ended up in hosptial. She was never the same again. The beating he gave her did something to her brain. Everybody hated Des for what he'd done and he'd been sent to prison. Quite right, everyone said, but now Grace remembered how he'd protested his innocence all along. Did Norris have a part in that too? Who had knocked her down when the Thrift Club money was taken, if not one of Norris's thugs? Or ... could it have been Norris himself? How else could she explain the torn and empty envelopes and her bag in his safe?

Whatever happened when she got home, Grace was determined to expose Norris somehow. He mustn't be allowed to ruin anyone else's life.

There was little to bring back. Most of her mother's things were too far gone to be much use to anyone, but her furniture still had a bit of life in it. She had shared the big things around the neighbours, and been content to give them as gifts.

'Surely you want summat for it, lass?' one of them said but Grace shook her head. 'Mother would have wanted you to have it.'

She had boxed a few things up and brought them with her on the train. Right now they were in the porter's room at Worthing station because

Manny Hart had promised to bring the box with him on his way home.

'You heard from that girl of yours yet?' he'd asked.

Grace shook her head. The question coming so soon after she'd arrived back home cut her to the quick but she was grateful as well. At least Bonnie wasn't totally forgotten.

It was late. Grace was shattered; she'd been travelling all day. She looked around. Everything was neat and tidy, and sparkling clean. Snowy had been working very hard. It was only then that she noticed the Christmas decorations. Snowy wouldn't have bothered with them. Her heart skipped a beat. Hadn't Bonnie always said how much she hated the old decorations? She'd promised to put up new ones two Christmases ago. Could it be...? She heard a footfall upstairs and her heart leapt.

'Bonnie? Is that you?'

'No, Mum,' came a voice. 'It's me. Rita.'

Grace stood for a second, her hand on the rail while she steadied herself and swallowed her disappointment, then she bounded up the stairs as quickly as her tired legs would allow.

'I wasn't expecting you home until tomorrow,' she said, her face wreathed in smiles. She wished she hadn't called Bonnie's name. Poor Rita. She must have been hurt. Mother and daughter hugged and kissed each other.

'I'm sorry about Granny. How was the funeral?'

Grace was surprised to find her eyes immediately filling with tears. 'All right. All the neighbours came.'

'I'm sorry,' said Rita, hugging her again.

As they separated, Grace fumbled for a handkerchief and blew her nose. 'What's that you've got in your hand?'

Rita held up her diploma. 'Da-daaa.'

'Oh Rita,' Grace beamed. 'Let me look.'

The piece of paper was impressive. *This is to certify that Rita Elizabeth Rogers has successfully completed a shorthand and typing course.*

'And before you ask,' she went on, 'I already have a job.'

Grace took in her breath.

'I went for a job in the office at Southdown buses but then I saw Bob Dawson. He drives one of the buses and he told me they're desperate for conductresses. Mum, it was £2 3s 11d rising to £2 15/- after a three-month trial.'

'But all that hard work with your shorthand and typing,' Grace protested.

'Please don't let's fight about it, Mum.'

Grace hesitated and then cupped her daughter's face in her hands. Grace didn't want to fight either. She felt the past year had been a waste, but what could she do? She could tell by Rita's face that she was utterly determined and it was, after all, her life. 'When do you start?'

'In the New Year,' said Rita, 'which means we can enjoy Christmas and the New Year together.'

'Oh darling,' said Grace. 'I'm so glad for you. It's time things started to go right for you.'

'They are, Mum,' said Rita sitting back down on the bed. 'Emilio is coming back after Christmas.'

Grace looked away. 'Perhaps you shouldn't

spend so much time with him,' she said carefully. 'Find yourself a nice boy and settle down.'

'I don't want another boy,' said Rita. Her voice had an edge to it.

'Rita...'

'I don't want to talk about it, Mum,' Rita interjected. 'You always try to put a dampener on me and Emilio. I can never understand why. He's kind and gentle and he treats me very well.'

Grace felt uncomfortable. Could it be that Rita *still* didn't understand about Emilio? 'Did you ask him where he was, while he was away?'

'No,' said Rita defensively. 'Why should I? I trust him. Besides, he's already told me he's learning all about the fishing around here. He wants to be the best fisherman along this part of the coast.'

Grace felt her stomach fall away. Dear Lord, Rita *really* didn't know. She should have been more explicit with her. 'Darling,' Grace began again, 'you don't understand...'

'No, Mum, it's you that doesn't understand,' said Rita. 'Look, it's our first night together for ages. I really don't want an argument.'

Grace nodded sadly. 'You're right. I'm sorry.' She'd have to make sure they had time together and then she would explain. Of course her daughter didn't know Emilio's preferences. She was an innocent.

Rita stood up and went into her mother's arms. 'Was it awful with Granny?'

'No,' said Grace softly. 'She was old and tired and she was ready to go. In the end, it was very peaceful.'

‘She was a funny old thing,’ said Rita. ‘I’m not sure she liked us very much.’

‘That’s where you’re wrong,’ said Grace. ‘She loved us more than we could have ever known. One day I shall tell you about the sacrifice she made.’

There was a sharp knock at the door and they heard it open. Manny’s voice called out, ‘I’ve brought your box, Grace.’

‘I’d better go,’ said Grace, squeezing her daughter one more time. ‘Shall I get fish ’n’ chips for tea?’

‘Rather,’ Rita enthused. ‘It’ll certainly make a change from Aunt Rene’s boiled cabbage.’

‘Grace?’ Manny sounded impatient.

‘Coming, Manny,’ and laughing, Grace ran downstairs.

There were only four and a half shopping days to Christmas and so much still to do.

Rita was home and Snowy presented her with a brand new rent book. What was even more wonderful, thanks to the Fair Rents panel, she was paying 5/- a week less than she had been.

Grace set about everything with a purpose. She left a list of things at the counter of Potter and Bailey’s and asked for the boy to bring them round in the afternoon, then she walked to the bus stop to catch the bus into town. She passed Archie’s shop on the way. Michael’s chair was still in the window. It was still in one piece but it had been neatly divided into two sections. One side was still exactly the same as when she had sold it to him but the other arm had been completely restored in the burgundy leather. It looked wonderful.

She slowed her footsteps as she caught sight of it and her heart lurched. She was filled with a mixture of emotions, chief of which was the poignancy of Michael not being here any more. She'd never ever forget him but it didn't hurt as much as it had done. Like her mother, he was gone forever. She remembered curling up on the chair with the girls when they were younger and telling them stories of princes and princesses and happily ever after.

When she pushed a thank you note for the rent book through the letterbox, she looked up and Archie was watching her. Her whole body still yearned for him and she found herself making as if to go into the shop. All at once she stopped herself. Archie had a customer. A man, who had been bending over a chesterfield couch and running his hands along the refurbished leather, stood up and opened his wallet. He began counting a lot of notes on the counter, until he noticed Archie's attention was elsewhere. The man turned to look, a slow smile touching his lips. He glanced back at Archie then back at Grace. It was Norris. As Grace turned away in disgust, she was aware of Archie's puzzled expression as he saw Norris blow her a kiss.

It was a shock later that day when Grace opened the door and Norris stood on the doorstep. 'Anyone here with you?'

She stepped back, her clenched fist pressed over her mouth as he walked in uninvited. She'd never seen him like this before. He looked like a man possessed.

'I suppose you've heard that the boy's father is here, in Worthing,' he blurted out.

Grace didn't know what he was talking about but she was too terrified to speak.

'If you want me to keep quiet about your daughter,' he growled, 'you'd better tell me where you've put the letter my father wrote to you before he died.'

Grace tried bluffing. 'Letter, what letter?'

He hit her across her ear with such force it sent her crashing into the small table which stood against the wall. The vase in the centre wobbled precariously for a few seconds before it went crashing to the floor.

'You know what I'm talking about, woman. Where is it?'

'I don't know,' she wailed. 'I haven't got it. Bonnie took it with her.'

'Coo-ee,' Elsie called over the back wall. 'Is that you, Grace? Everything all right?'

They stared at each other in shocked surprise.

'If I find out you've been lying,' he hissed.

'I haven't,' she protested.

'I'm here to warn you, Grace Follett,' said Norris, using her maiden name and jabbing at her arm with his finger, 'you keep your big fat trap shut. D'you hear me?'

She stepped back as he poked her because it hurt so much and stumbled against the chair.

'You tell them anything,' he said, 'and I'll tell them you were caught rifling through my safe. Got it?'

'Grace?' Elsie's voice came again. 'Are you there?'

'I'll be out in a minute, Else,' she called.

Norris grabbed her wrist and pulling her arm back painfully, he repeated, 'Keep quiet. Do you understand?'

'Yes,' she whimpered. 'I understand.' And then he was gone.

Grace stared at the closing door and something dawned on her. He was just as scared of the police being involved as she had been. The bigger question was, why?

Rubbing her wrist, she hurried to the back to see what Elsie wanted.

Bob stopped by with a small present for Rita on Christmas Eve and she surprised herself by being pleased to see him. He was more good looking than ever since he'd come out of the army, more confident. Her mother made some excuse about getting some wrapping for presents and went upstairs. Rita didn't ask him in or to sit down so they stood awkwardly near the open front door.

'You look lovelier than ever, Rita,' Bob smiled shyly.

Rita felt her cheeks glow. 'And you look so ... so different.'

'I came to ask you out,' he said, suddenly emboldened. 'There's a dance at the Assembly Hall this Saturday. It's a good band and they tell me the singer is pretty good too.'

Rita's eyes sparkled. How she would love to put on a pretty dress and dance the night away in the arms of a handsome man. She'd never asked

Emilio if he could dance...

'Rita?' Bob's voice brought her back to the here and now. His face was so eager she knew she'd have to let him down gently.

'I'm sorry, Bob,' she said, 'I would have loved to have come but I can't.'

He turned with a pained expression and instinctively Rita reached out to touch him. Her hand froze in mid-air. She mustn't. She shouldn't do anything to encourage him.

'Another time perhaps?' he said looking right into her eyes.

She shook her head. 'I'm sorry.' Her voice was thick and she swallowed hard. Why was she feeling like this? It was stupid. Emilio was the man for her.

'There's someone else, isn't there?' said Bob quietly.

Rita held his gaze but couldn't speak. She nodded her head and he turned away.

'Then I wish you every happiness,' he said stepping towards the small front gate.

He didn't look back. Rita watched him walk down the street, his back straight and his arms still swinging as if he were marching. For the time being, the army still had a hold over him.

As she watched him go, Rita felt strangely uneasy until her mother called, 'Are you going to keep that door open all night? You're letting all the heat out, Rita. Bring Bob in.'

Rita returned alone and by the look on her face, it was obvious that her mother was disappointed.

They were determined to enjoy their Christmas

as much as they had done in the previous years. As usual, friends and neighbours stopped by on Christmas night and Boxing Day and Grace had the kettle on as soon as they walked through the door. It was so good to see all her old friends again. Uncle Charlie Hanson had more muscles than ever. His arms were so pumped up he had a job putting them close to his sides. He came with Snowy so Grace was sure they were still together.

Miss Reeves had passed away, quite peacefully, so she was told, earlier in the year. She soon caught up with all the news. Hubbard's was being enlarged. Soon it would be part of 14, 16, 18 and 20 South Street. The fight to save Beach House, a lovely old Victorian building on the East Worthing border had intensified, and the Christmas tree outside the Town Hall sported no less than three hundred Christmas tree lights this year. She thought of the song they'd sung through the war: *When the lights go on again all over the world.* It was happening at last.

'I think I enjoy Christmas lights more than ever since the war,' Grace smiled.

'Bloody waste of money if you ask me,' mumbled Elsie Dawson.

Snowy had done well keeping an eye on the place. She'd used the postal order Grace sent each week to pay the rent. Grace's gratitude knew no bounds. By helping her out in this way, Snowy had kept a roof over their heads. Snowy was her usual dismissive self. 'Go on with you. It was nothing.' She hesitated. 'Funny thing though. I had the feeling someone had been round here once. Nothing was taken as far as I could see but the kitchen range was quite warm.'

Grace pulled a face. 'How odd. Perhaps the sun came in through the curtains.'

'Perhaps,' said Snowy but neither of them was convinced.

'Maybe it was when Rita came back,' said Elsie.

'Rita came back?' said Grace.

'About a month ago,' said Elsie. 'She stayed a couple of days and went off again.'

Grace would have taken it further but she was distracted by Manny Hart wanting a Mackeson Stout for old Mrs Oakley. They were all lined up on the floor in the scullery to keep them a bit cool. She took him out there and showed him where they were.

Grace had splashed out on a lovely handbag for Snowy. After she'd unwrapped it and protested half a dozen times that she shouldn't have done it, Grace caught her several times just looking at it with a smile.

'Tell me about the factory,' Grace asked cautiously as they washed up a few cups for another round of tea. She was really fishing to find out about Norris. Was he expecting to carry on using her or had he found some other woman to take her place? She wouldn't wish him on her worst enemy but she hoped he wouldn't want her to resume her 'cleaning' job. Anyway, there was no need to do it any more, not since she'd got the locket, but she didn't fancy the argument and he'd become violent, something she'd never experienced before.

'It's ticking over nicely,' said Snowy. 'Oh, one thing you might like to know. He's thinking of running for office.'

So that was why Norris had come here to warn her off. What did he think she was going to say? She didn't know anything about poor George's death and she would certainly never voice her own fears. Grace's heart went out to George's father. How dreadful to find your missing son had been dead all this time. Her thoughts sprang to Bonnie and her stomach fell away.

Snowy carried on regardless. 'Mind if I have one of them sausage rolls? Did you make them, Grace?'

Grace nodded.

'They say the police are going to reopen the case,' said Snowy.

Rita dropped a glass and it shattered on the kitchen tiles. Everybody's attention was directed to the glass as the women galvanised themselves into action to sweep it all up before one of the children cut themselves. The fact that her daughter's face was bright red was not lost on Grace.

'How about a game of musical statues?' cried Rita, catching a glimpse of her mother's wondering stare. The children cheered with excitement and Rita put a record on the old gramophone.

Later, at midnight, when everyone had gone home, Grace decided to tackle the subject of George Matthews. Rita was filling her hot-water bottle.

'Do you know something about Bonnie that I don't?' said Grace, coming straight to the point.

'I don't know what you mean,' Rita said indignantly but her face was colouring again.

'You were quite upset when Snowy talked about George's father turning up,' said Grace. 'Was Bonnie stepping out with him?'

Rita laughed. 'Oh, Mum, that's so old fashioned. Nobody steps out these days.'

'You know what I mean,' said Grace irritably.

Rita sighed. 'I did hear that she was seeing him.'

'Who told you?'

Rita hesitated. 'Dinah.'

Their eyes met. 'I should have told you sooner but that's all I know, Mum,' said Rita quickly. 'Honest.'

Grace nodded. It wasn't enough but she'd have to be satisfied.

'There's something I have to tell you, Mum,' said Rita cautiously. 'It's about me and Emilio.'

'I do wish you wouldn't hang around that boy so much, Rita,' Grace began.

'You can wish all you want, Mum,' Rita said sharply, 'but from now on I'm going to be hanging around him all the time.'

'You're wasting your time with him,' Grace frowned. 'You're just a young girl. You don't know the world like I do and I'm telling you, he's not the marrying kind.'

'Well, that's just where you're wrong, Mum,' Rita said. Her voice was raised and she had developed two bright pink spots on her cheeks. Her eyes were flaming with indignation. 'He *is* the marrying kind. In fact, Emilio and I got married just last week, so there.'

For a split second, Grace couldn't grasp what she'd just said.

'Don't be so ridiculous,' she snapped. 'You're too young. You have to have my permission to get married.'

'Not if you go to Gretna Green!' Rita shouted.

They stared at each other for several seconds and then Grace said, 'Oh Rita, please tell me you didn't do that.'

'I did,' Rita said defiantly. She went to the cutlery drawer and pulled it open. Her wedding certificate was under the inner tray.

Grace lowered herself into a chair as she took it with a trembling hand. 'Oh, darling…'

'College exams finished in November. You only stayed on for interviews,' she said. 'Emilio and I went straight to Gretna Green. We had to stay there for three weeks before we could do it.'

Grace shook her head. 'No, no…'

'I don't understand why you hate him so much,' said Rita petulantly. 'When he comes to live with us, he can help around the house. You wanted to redecorate in here, well, Emilio can do it for you. If you try and like him I'm sure we'll all get along famously, Mum.'

'He's not coming here,' Grace blurted out and seeing her daughter's shocked look added in a more conciliatory tone, 'Look, I don't hate him, but where is he now? Why isn't he spending his first Christmas with his wife?'

'He went to see his friend Jeremy,' said Rita innocently. 'Ever since he was called up, he's been ill, poor man. They've even chucked him out of the army now, so Emilio went to help out.'

Grace put her head onto her hand. 'Look,' she said, looking at Rita and pulling herself together again. 'I'm sure if we ask someone we can do something about it. You don't have to stay married to him.'

'Mum!' cried Rita.

'He won't make you a good husband. You see…'

'Since when have you been such a bloody expert on men?' Rita shrieked.

Grace was both horrified and furious. Neither of her children had ever spoken to her like that, and she certainly had never heard either of them swear.

'How dare you!' she cried as she jumped to her feet and slapped Rita across the face.

They glared at each other and then Rita flounced off into the scullery. A couple of seconds later she threw something across the kitchen table. 'At least I had the decency to get married before I jumped into his bed.'

Grace turned to see what it was and her heart nearly stopped. Filthy dirty, and torn, it was the midnight blue dress Norris had given her that first time.

'Rita,' she began, her face flaming with embarrassment. 'Listen to me. I can explain…'

'D'you know what, Mum,' said Rita, her eyes bright with unshed tears. 'I don't think I can be bothered to listen. Why should I? You never listen to me.'

'This is not the same thing,' said Grace, desperately trying to find some middle ground. 'I was put in an awkward position.'

'Lucky you,' Rita said. 'I hope you enjoyed it.'

'Don't be so crude,' Grace snapped. 'How can

you talk like that? I'm your mother…'

'Right now, I wish that you weren't my mother,' said Rita, going to the stair door. '*He* gave you that dress, didn't he? I remember the day he came into the shop to buy it, and how rude he was to Miss Bridewell. Does it look nice on? I bet it does. It cost a pretty penny too. I can't quite remember how much but it was something in the region of forty guineas. You must have done something pretty amazing to get that, Mum. Most girls around here only get a quid a time, but I guess you'd get a lot more being Norris Finley's tart!'

She slammed the door so hard behind her, it flew straight back open again. Grace listened to the sound of her angry footsteps going up the stairs and then her bedroom door slammed shut too.

Left alone downstairs, Grace sat at the table and put her head in her hands. What was happening in her life? What more could go wrong? Bonnie had been gone more than two years now and the pain of her loss was as keen as it had ever been. As she tried to piece together what surrounded her disappearance, she was gathering a shed-load of fear along the way. The fear that Bonnie had been in that factory the day George had died. Had she been the one who'd shut the door on him and left him in the cold? Did she kill that boy, unintentionally or – worse still – deliberately?

And now all this stuff with Rita. The silly girl just didn't understand. She honestly thought Emilio loved her. How could he? What sort of a life would Rita have with him as a husband? Grace refused to cry; besides, she had no more tears left. Dear God, she prayed, please ... please help me sort out this mess.

A couple of minutes later, Rita came downstairs with a suitcase.

Grace leapt to her feet. 'Where are you going?'

'Anywhere but here,' said Rita. 'I shall go to Liliana and Salvatore. They'll take me in. After all, I'm family now that I'm married to their nephew.' She paused, her hand on the door latch. 'Oh and before you ask, Mum,' she said, she voice shrill with anger, 'yes, I did have a wonderful wedding. I didn't invite my mother because I knew she would object. You see, she hates me being happy. By the way, I saved you a piece of cake. It's in the larder.' She walked out into the darkness, only leaning back in the doorway to add, 'Oh, and don't bother to try and persuade me to come back. I shan't be coming here again. Not ever.'

Twenty-Eight

It took Grace about two weeks to realise that nobody was speaking to her. The night Rita left, she didn't sleep. Everything was whirling around her head and even when she did drop off somewhere around four thirty, she was troubled by dreams.

She had gone around to the café the next day

and it was as much as she could do to be civil to Salvatore. Their conversation began in hushed tones over the counter.

'Salvatore, I want to see my daughter.'

Salvatore shrugged. 'She no here.'

'Then where is she?'

'She is with her 'usband.' He grinned. 'It is her 'oneymoon.'

Grace took a deep breath. 'How could you let this happen, Salvatore?'

He came around the counter and took her arm. Despite the cold, they stood in the alleyway at the side of the building. 'It no my fault,' he said waving his hands expansively. 'Rita say she love him. What can I do?'

'But he doesn't love her, does he?' Grace challenged.

'Emilio is a good boy,' Salvatore insisted.

'Why didn't you talk to me about it?' Grace said bitterly but he had no answer. 'I'll tell you why, Salvatore. You tricked her, didn't you? You took advantage of a young and innocent girl. I thought we were friends. I don't think I can ever forgive you for this. Now, where is my daughter?'

Salvatore's face clouded. 'She gone away,' he insisted. 'Now you go.'

'I give you fair warning, Salvatore. I shall move heaven and earth to get this marriage annulled.'

She saw the alarm in his face. 'Rita say the Gretna Green no need permission of the mummy.'

'That's as maybe,' said Grace, 'but when the authorities hear what you've done...'

Salvatore's face grew dark. 'You leave,' he

interrupted loudly. 'You leave now or I tell the 'hole world of Mr Finley!' Grace stared at him in horror. 'Now go, you go.'

As he propelled her along the alleyway she was suddenly seized with the idea that Rita might even be within earshot. 'Rita,' she screamed. 'If you're in there, whenever you want to, you can come home. I love you, Rita. I love you.'

Liliana had stayed in the kitchen the whole time, but as Grace stood in the road outside the café where Salvatore had left her, she could hear furious shouting and the sound of breaking china.

Grace went home and cried angry frustrated tears. When she was all cried out, she washed her face. Crying does no good at all, she told herself. Now pull yourself together and work out what you're going to do about all this. Brave words, but half an hour later she still couldn't think of a single thing.

There was something else troubling her. She had mice. She could hear them quite clearly, their hurried squeaking breaking into the silent night watches with an urgency that had to be stopped. But she didn't know what to do. If they heard her they ran away and she was never really sure where they were nesting. In the end, she got up early, and moved stealthily around the house. She finally decided that the noise was coming from Rita's bedroom. She was beginning to hate that room. The two unused beds silently accused her of being a bad mother. She knew a good mother shouldn't keep her children tied to her apron strings but both of her daughters had left her for good. Where had she gone wrong?

Perhaps she'd been too hard on them both. She'd all but driven them away. If only she could go back in time.

She sat quietly on Rita's bed for some time and then the scurrying began again. It seemed to be coming from under the window. She ran her fingers along the wood and found a knothole. When she put her finger inside the whole thing moved slightly and the mice went quiet.

It was no good just opening up and diving inside. The mice would simply scatter all over the house and that would be ten times worse. She would have to ask some of her neighbours for help. If a crowd of them got together, they'd soon rid her of the mice.

Over the next few days, Grace tried to ask for help but everybody seemed too busy to stop. It was then that she noticed a change in the atmosphere. Friends and neighbours didn't return her friendly wave and when she called out, 'Good morning', their response was muted. She'd been sent to Coventry. She had been so wrapped up in her own thoughts and humiliation she hadn't even noticed. If she had any doubts they came to an end the morning she walked into Potter and Bailey's. A little huddle of women parted as they caught sight of her and she knew they'd been talking about her. Something rose up inside her. She wasn't just put out or cross, she was angry. These people were supposed to be her friends. When had she ever turned her back on them? For years, three of them, Elsie Dawson, Mary Minty and old Mrs Oakley had spent Christmas Day at her house. Until her mother took ill, she'd given them stuff from her little courtyard garden, done their shopping when they were ill, got them good cleaning jobs to help ends meet. She'd washed their heavy blackout curtains and made draught excluders for their doors. And here they were turning their backs on her and whispering behind patched woollen gloves.

'If anyone has something to say,' she began in ringing tones, 'you can say it to my face.'

A few noses went a little higher in the air but nobody moved.

'Why are you doing this?' Grace challenged. 'What have I ever done to you? Come on, what's this all about?'

It was Elsie who turned around first. 'Oh if it isn't Mrs High and Mighty,' she sneered. 'Stand back, girls, let the *lady* through.'

Grace felt her face go scarlet. Behind the counter, Mr Seagrove looked increasingly uncomfortable. 'Come, come, ladies, let's keep calm, shall we? Now, who's next?'

Elsie was standing, feet akimbo and her arms folded under her bust. 'We wondered how you managed to keep the rent man happy all the time you were at your mother's, and now we know. I would have thought better of you, Grace Rogers, letting your fancy man pay the rent.'

'I paid my rent out of my own money,' Grace retorted. 'Not that it's any of your business.'

'Ladies, ladies,' Mr Seagrove pleaded.

'I can't stand here gossiping all day,' said Elsie. 'Didn't I tell you, girls? I'm off to Hubbard's this afternoon to see if I can pick up a nice little blue dress.'

So, Rita had told them everything. Grace stood her ground and even though her heart was pounding in her chest, she wouldn't give them the satisfaction of walking out of the shop. It was an uncomfortable few minutes until the other two assistants had finished serving her neighbours but then it was Grace's turn.

They were waiting for her when she came out of the shop.

'Finley's whore,' said Mary Minty.

'Off for a ride in his car, are we?' Elsie sneered. 'My, my, I wouldn't mind looking for a fancy man for myself.'

'I shouldn't bother,' Grace said as she walked by, 'men don't like tarts who have a face like the back of a bus.'

As she rounded the corner, Archie came out of his shop. 'You look upset, Gracie.'

Her chin began to wobble. Not you and all, she thought. 'All right, out with it,' she said defiantly. 'You may as well get it off your chest now.'

'We looked out of the window,' he said gently, 'and saw you walking down the middle of the road. You look as if you mean business.'

'I'm angry.'

'I can see that. Do you want to talk about it?'

'No!'

He shrugged his shoulders. 'Just trying to be a friend, Gracie.'

'You didn't bother to come for Christmas,' she challenged.

'Oh, was I invited? I'm sorry. I seem to remember you telling me you would rather I didn't come to your house any more.'

She shifted her weight from one foot to the other. 'We?'

'Sorry?'

'You said *we* looked out of the window.'

'Oh, Snowy and me.'

She was stunned.

'Do you need a friend, Gracie?'

She nodded miserably and he stepped aside. 'Better come in then. Snowy has put the kettle on.'

Archie poured a little brandy into her tea as he sat down. 'This is about more than Bonnie going away, isn't it, Gracie?' he said gently. He reached out and rubbed the side of her arm comfortingly. She gave him a helpless look. 'What is it you're not telling us, Gracie?'

And it all came out. How Bonnie was seeing George Matthews, that Grace was afraid that Bonnie might know something about George's death and how Norris Finley had said she was in the old factory the day George died.

'I knew it!' cried Snowy. 'I had a feeling that Finley was up to something bad.'

'What do you mean, something bad?' said Archie.

'That man is a womaniser,' said Snowy. 'He's ruined many a life here in Worthing and the minute he set his cap for Grace, I knew she'd only go to him if he had some kind of hold over her.' There was an ominous silence and then she said, 'Oh God, Grace, I'm sorry.'

'Did you go to him?' said Archie. His voice was barely more than a whisper.

'I saw some woman kissing you in the shop a little while back,' she accused.

Archie looked puzzled and then relaxed. 'She'd lost a necklace inside the chair,' he said. 'I pulled it out.'

Grace felt her stomach churn. She'd been a complete idiot, hadn't she? Why hold back now? It was all over anyway. She'd sent him away and now he'd know why. 'I'm sorry.' She looked up at him, her eyes filling with tears.

'I didn't want to go with him,' Grace said, her voice racked by huge sobs. 'I hated it but he had Bonnie's locket, you see. He said he would take it to the police and tell them she was there. I couldn't let them do that, could I? She's my own flesh and blood. I couldn't let him put the hangman's noose around my own daughter's neck.'

He nodded, stood up and turned his back on her.

'Don't you see? I had to send you away,' she said. 'I didn't want to spoil your good name. I didn't want anyone to say you were friends with Finley's tart.'

Grace began to cry softly and Snowy put her hand over the top of her hands.

Archie turned and stared at her back and Snowy saw the tears in his eyes as well. She got up from the table and jerked her head. 'Excuse me. I need to go to the lavvy,' she said in a loud voice, and left the room.

As the door closed, Archie put his arms around Grace and pulled her to her feet. 'Why didn't you tell me?' he said. 'Why did you suffer all alone?' She looked up at him in disbelief. 'Gracie, you don't have to do everything on your own any more. I'm here and I want to help you.'

He hugged her close and she relaxed in his warm embrace. 'So does Snowy,' he went on and she stiffened. Snowy as well? So friendship, that's all he was offering ... just friendship.

'Thank you,' she said stiffly, pulling herself from his embrace. 'It's good to have such wonderful friends.'

They sat back down and Snowy came back indoors.

'What's it with you and Rita?' said Snowy.

Grace told them about Emilio and Rita's escapade to Gretna Green. 'It's her birthday next week but she's cut herself off from me. I've written to her but all her letters have been returned to sender. If I see her in the street, she crosses over the road. I'm at my wits' end.'

Snowy leaned back in her chair and blew out her lips. 'It's all a bit of a mess, isn't it?'

Grace nodded. 'And that's not all,' she said, her eyes filling up again. 'Now I've got mice. Not just one or two, but a serious infestation I shouldn't wonder. I can hear them running about all night.'

'Well that's one problem we can help with,' said Snowy.

'We can?' said Archie faintly.

'Of course we can,' said Snowy. 'With my cat and your brawn, we'll soon get rid of the little blighters.'

'Pity we couldn't do the same with Norris Finley,' sighed Archie.

Twenty-Nine

Bonnie was on tenterhooks. Over the past few months, she, Dinah and John had become really close friends. It would be no exaggeration to say she really loved them but it was difficult to find time to be together. She only had one day off a week and the two actors were very busy with rehearsals and auditions, but now they had invited her for another weekend away. She wanted to go, and she could request the days off, the Saturday for one week and the Sunday for the following week, but she knew that if she showed John the letter it could be a difficult two days.

It had surprised Bonnie to realise just what their course entailed. She had the mistaken idea that actors simply learned the lines and then performed them on stage, but Dinah and John had to spend hours and hours honing their craft. They studied movement, voice coaching, breath control and how to project their voices for the stage, but they had to develop a much more intimate style of acting for the silver screen. They must have been good because, little by little, the parts were coming in.

When they did get together, they had a wonderful time. Dinah adored Shirley and was always giving her little presents. John spent every moment teaching her how to do things and playing 'Boo'. Shirley adored it when John threw her into the air and caught her or when he and Dinah held her hands as they ran along the road and swung her up. Dinah did her best, every time they met, to persuade Bonnie to write to her mother but somehow, although she promised faithfully that she would, Bonnie could never actually put the letters she wrote into the post. It seemed that the more time passed, the harder it became.

Her letters from Miss Reeves had dried up. Perhaps Miss Reeves had given up trying to make her go home too? She wished she had news of her mother and Rita. No news, far from being a good thing, only created a greater hunger for them, but pride stopped her every time.

Dinah still collected rent from her property in the same road as Bonnie's house, but all that was done through an agent now. Her first tenant had apparently moved out after only a few short weeks. She never went back to Worthing – there was always something else to do.

Bonnie was happy in the nursery. Her training course was coming to an end and, without being cocky about it, she was sure she would pass the exam. Matron Bennett had invited her to stay on as a staff nursery nurse once she got her badge and of course she would get a pay rise.

To stay in the nursery seemed expedient for the time being. It provided twenty-four-hour care for Shirley when Bonnie was on duty and, best of all, she was being looked after by people Bonnie trusted.

Christmas in the nursery was wonderful. Each room was decorated with paper chains and balloons, and the routine, normally so strict, was relaxed for the two days of the holiday. In fairness to everyone, nobody had either Christmas or Boxing Day off. Father Christmas turned up in the afternoon (thanks to Mr Bennett) and the children each had a special gift. Shirley had a rag doll called Leggy Peggy. She loved it from the minute she saw it.

With the onset of a new year, Bonnie began to think more and more about showing John the letter. The secret was becoming a burden to her. She couldn't think of anything else when she was with him, but it left her on the horns of a dilemma. What if he was angry, or rejected her? He and Dinah were the closest she'd got to family now. She hated the thought of being alone again.

'Can you get a weekend off from the third to the fifth of February?' Dinah wrote in her letter. 'We've got something to tell you.'

Bonnie smiled to herself. They were getting married, weren't they? She was thrilled to bits. It couldn't have happened to nicer people; but her excitement was short-lived. John still didn't know he was adopted. She would have to tell him now. The thought of some toffee-nosed, unfeeling official letting it slip was awful. John would be devastated. Although he didn't say much about his father, he adored his mother and they often met in London for lunch or tea in Dickins & Jones in Regent Street. She wondered why his mother hadn't told him. It was really her place, not Bonnie's, but all the same, she couldn't put it off any longer.

Rita Semadini's arms felt as if they were coming away from their sockets. Her shopping bags weighed a ton. She must have been mad to spend the rest of the afternoon in the Plaza and then to buy all these groceries from Potter and Bailey's on the way home, but it seemed like a good idea at the time.

She almost ran to her house. She and Emilio had managed to find rented rooms at the other end of Station Approach. They weren't wonderful but it meant that she could stay in the area where she had grown up while still being far enough away from her old home not to have to face her mother every day.

Rita had to get rid of her bags before she went to the Railway Café to help out in the kitchen and if she didn't hurry she'd be late. Fumbling with the key, Rita opened the door and threw her bags onto the chair as the clock Salvatore and Liliana had given them as a wedding present chimed seven.

'Emilio?' She didn't really expect anyone to answer because the house was in darkness but she called all the same. Most likely her husband had already gone fishing.

There was a loud thud in the bedroom, as if a boot had fallen onto the floor.

'Emilio?'

'Hullo,' came the reply. She thought she could hear him scrambling out of bed. What was he doing?

'Aren't you going fishing tonight?'

As she walked towards the door Emilio called,

'I must have dozed off. I'll be up in a minute.'

'Are you all right? You're not ill, are you?'

'No, darling. I just 'aving a kip, that's all.'

Rita frowned. It wasn't like Emilio to be in bed at this time. There must be something wrong. As she put her hand on the door handle, it flew open. Emilio, still pulling on his trousers, came out.

'No worry, darling,' he shrugged. 'I'm fine.'

She stared at him wide-eyed. He was so handsome. His thick dark hair flopped over his forehead and his dark brown eyes twinkled. She still couldn't quite believe he'd actually married her. What a pity that ... but she wasn't going to think about that. Not today. Not on her birthday, and not when she'd had such a lovely time looking around the shops, and buying a dress with the money he'd given her and then going to the pictures. She kissed his cheek.

'Can I show you what I bought?'

He kissed the end of her nose and chuckled. 'You'd better go, you'll be late.'

'Yes, but...'

'Later, darling. Salvatore, he get worked up.' He laughed as he held her away from him. 'But you no work there much longer, eh? Soon you conducting on the bus.'

Rita chuckled. 'I'll be a bus conductress,' she corrected as she reluctantly turned to go.

Back out in the street, Rita carried on down the road and turned the corner. Pointless in hurrying now. She was already late.

Her marriage hadn't turned out to be as wonderful as she had expected. It was all very upsetting and frustrating, yet what could she do? Emilio was older than her, but it was obvious that he wasn't as experienced as some. Give him time, that's what she must do.

The café was in darkness when she got there, so she went around the back. As she walked into the kitchen she was surprised to find it empty. Salvatore had been so insistent that he'd needed help for some big do he was having tomorrow, which was why she had come. So where were they?

Rita made her way cautiously into the café and turned on the lights. All at once a great cry went up and it seemed as if half the street was crowded in the café. All around she heard cries of 'Happy birthday', and 'All the best, Rita.' Then Manny Hart started up 'Happy birthday' on his mouth organ and Liliana came out of the kitchen with a cake. Totally overwhelmed, Rita waved and smiled. Although she still missed her mother and Bonnie, she was the luckiest person in the world to have such good friends and neighbours.

Some gave her presents. Mrs Oakley gave her some Coty L'Aimant from the chemist, Manny Hart gave her a block of Cadbury's Milk Tray with coffee cream, almond whirl and her favourite, marzipan diamond. Elsie Dawson gave her a box of hankies.

'What film did you see?' her daughter Mo wanted to know.

Rita clasped her hands in front of her in a theatrical fashion. *'C'est grand, c'est magnifique,'* she said, quoting the cinema trailer. 'Doris Day in *April in Paris.*'

'Good?' Mo asked.

'Wonderful,' sighed Rita. 'And her dresses were out of this world.'

Elsie looked a little more serious. 'Why didn't you wait for the evening performance and go with your husband?'

'I couldn't have made eyes at Claude Dauphin if I had,' Rita quipped.

No one understood how impossible it was to go out with Emilio, even on her birthday. He was always fishing. He was quite easygoing about what she did with her life, but he rarely took her anywhere. She thought back wistfully to the invitation to the dance Bob had given her. She would have loved that.

For the next few moments, Salvatore Semadini's booming voice filled the room as he gathered his nephew's wife into his arms and kissed her cheek noisily. ''Appy birthday.'

Liliana came up behind him and slapped his arm heartily. 'Move over, Salvatore, and let Mama kiss the birthday girl.' She had been cutting the huge chocolate cake and now everyone was helping themselves. Liliana kissed Rita on both cheeks.

'You two spoil me,' said Rita, eyeing the cake.

Salvatore laughed heartily. 'And where is Emilio? Where is my nephew?'

As if on cue, Emilio walked into the room accompanied by much backslapping and handshaking from the other neighbours and friends. Rita smiled at his handsome face. Yes, she was a lucky, lucky girl. She was aware that just about every woman in the room was staring at him.

They all wanted Emilio but he was hers. He was so good looking. Under his thick winter coat he was wearing a crisp white shirt open at the neck. The top of his vest was showing, the hairs on his muscular chest curling attractively around the crucifix he always wore. He came over to her and, slipping his arm around her waist, nuzzled her neck. Rita arched her back and closed her eyes, her heart pounding so loudly she feared everyone in the room would hear it.

'Happy birthday, darling.'

She didn't want him to stop but he stepped back and held out a long box with a tiny gold clasp. Inside was a double row of pearls. There was a collective gasp from the onlookers as he turned her around and put them on her neck.

'They're beautiful,' she whispered.

'And so are you...'

All other activity in the café had come to a halt as everyone applauded the happy couple. Rita fingered the pearls and smiled up at her husband, her eyes saying *kiss me, kiss me*.

'I love you,' she whispered into Emilio's shirt.

She felt him stiffen. 'I have to go.'

'So soon?' she pleaded. 'It is my birthday.'

He caught hold of the tops of her arms and gently pulled away from her. 'Sorry, darling. The fish ... you understand.'

'OK,' she said, her voice small. 'But we will talk tomorrow, won't we?'

He shrugged in the same exaggerated way Salvatore did. 'Of course.' And then he was gone. Rita stared at the closing door, tears biting the backs of her eyes.

Thirty

When Grace opened her front door a couple of days later, all the awkwardness she felt about Archie fell away and she burst out laughing. He stood there in his leather apron, motorcycle gauntlets and a beekeeper's hat complete with a black net over his face. He was carrying a bucket in one hand and a mousetrap in the other. 'I was a Boy Scout,' he announced. 'And they taught me to be prepared.'

It was the first bit of light relief Grace had had in a long time. She hauled him inside before the neighbours reached for their net curtains.

Grace had tried to get a card to Rita for her birthday but it had just come back in the post the next day with 'Return to sender, not known here' on the envelope. She was dreadfully hurt, but what more could she do? And dear Archie had made her smile again.

As soon as Snowy arrived with her cat in a cat basket, they went upstairs. They blocked the door and shut the windows before opening the cavity under the window ledge. It was alive with mice and the next few minutes were a frenzy of jumping, shrieking, banging the floor with the motorcycle gauntlet and shouting instructions at the bemused cat. When it was all over, all the mice had gone ... somewhere, but not one had been trapped, caught or killed. The three of them sat on Bonnie's bed and laughed. The cat stretched itself and began washing its paws furiously.

'Some mice catchers we are,' laughed Grace.

'What do you mean?' said Snowy, pretending to be indignant. 'We could set ourselves up in business. They've all gone, haven't they?'

'Yes, but where?' said Grace, wiping her eyes with the corner of her apron.

'Some of them will be back, no doubt,' said Archie. 'I'll put down some mouse traps and try and block off this cavity.' He was leaning over and peering inside. 'There's something in here.' He gave it a yank and pulled out what had once been a man's mackintosh. It was half eaten and stank to high heaven. 'Who does that belong to?'

Grace shrugged. 'Search me. Anything in the pockets?'

Archie put his hand inside gingerly but where the pockets remained intact there were only mouse droppings.

'There's a case in there too,' said Grace. 'Look.'

The case was stained but seemed undamaged. The mice had made an attempt to get inside but fortunately they had chosen to chew the re-inforced corner. Grace tried to open it but it was locked.

'Who does it belong to?' asked Snowy.

Grace shrugged. 'I've never seen it before.'

While Archie attempted to prise it open using a screwdriver, Grace ran downstairs and got some newspaper. They laid it on the bed. Archie hesitated. 'Are you sure we should be doing this?'

Grace looked at Snowy. 'I think we should,' Snowy said. 'If not for anything else but to put your mind at rest.' Then Archie threw back the lid and they all looked inside.

There were men's clothes on the top. And papers.

'Good Lord,' said Snowy eventually. 'I recognise that shirt. I think this case belongs to George Matthews.'

'How can you possibly know that?' cried Grace.

'I sewed that button on for him,' said Snowy. 'I did it one day at the factory in the lunch hour. I only had brown cotton.'

'Who is George Matthews?' asked Archie.

'He was the chap who was found dead in the old factory,' said Snowy. 'You remember, it was in all the papers.'

Archie nodded. 'So what's his suitcase doing here?'

They looked at Grace. Her face was white. Snowy squeezed her hand. 'Don't go jumping to conclusions,' she said softly. 'There's probably a perfectly logical explanation.'

'Any chance of a cuppa?' said Archie. Gratefully, Grace left them to it and went downstairs. If she had been alone, she would have taken the case to the allotments at West Tarring and got someone to set fire to the lot. She wouldn't have bothered to look any further. She was numb with fear as she prepared the tea.

When she got back upstairs, Archie had sorted everything into two piles on the bed. George's clothes and personal effects, such as his shaving things, a jar of Brylcreem, his toothbrush and hairbrush were on one side. On the second pile, he'd put things like his passport, a couple of letters, a photograph and some papers.

Grace handed them their teas and sat down at the other end of the bed.

'It looks as if he was about to go to South Africa,' said Archie. 'There are quite a lot of pamphlets here. This is his passport,' he went on, handing it to Grace, 'but I've no idea who this is.' He was holding a picture of a man in SS uniform. There was also a letter.

'That's written in German, isn't it?' whispered Grace.

Archie nodded.

'Can you read it?'

He shook his head.

Snowy had been reading some of the papers stuffed into a long brown envelope. 'I can't make head nor tail of this either but it looks like some sort of job offer.'

They fell silent for a minute, each lost to his or her own thoughts.

'We should hand this in to the police,' said Snowy.

'I don't want to go to the police,' said Grace. 'I can't. What if Bonnie was involved in some way?'

'I think you have to take it to the police,' said Archie. 'If Bonnie was involved, she wouldn't have left all this stuff here. She would have burnt it.'

Grace nodded. What they said sounded logical but she still wasn't keen. 'Isn't his father in town?'

'That's right,' said Snowy. 'I saw it in the papers. He wants his son re-interred. He was upset that he's been put in a pauper's grave.'

'I think I'll take it to him,' said Grace. They put

everything back into the case and it was agreed that Grace should look through everything carefully to familiarise herself with the papers and then go to see George's father. Archie offered to come with her but Grace felt this was something she had to do on her own. He seemed a little put out, but she couldn't help that. It was time she took control of her life instead of just letting things happen.

Snowy accepted Grace's invitation to stay for some cheese on toast for lunch, but Archie said he had to get back to the shop.

'How's Dougie doing?' Grace asked as he was going. She remembered how excited Dougie had been to get a job, something which no one in the street would ever have predicted.

'Actually, he does very well,' said Archie. 'He keeps everything in the shop clean and tidy and I've been teaching him how to re-cane chair seats. He can prepare the canes, and he knows how to whittle down the ends. He's slow but he's very thorough especially when it comes to cleaning up the chair properly. He's even had a couple of goes at weaving. He's not up to my standard yet, but he'll get there.'

'He's lucky you've got the patience,' Snowy observed.

'And that Gracie saw his potential,' said Archie, squeezing Grace's fingers.

Grace saw him to the door and then went back upstairs to the bedroom where Snowy was still tidying everything away. 'Had any more trouble with His Nibs?' she asked as she and Grace closed the lid and pressed down hard to lock it.

'If you mean Norris, no,' said Grace.

'I'm pretty sure he's after Polly now,' said Snowy. 'Bloody lecher. She's young enough to be his daughter.'

As the two women went downstairs, the cat jumped onto the bed. After all the activity of the morning, she seemed glad of the little bit of peace and quiet.

With Dinah's birthday coming up, Bonnie agreed to meet John to help him choose a present. Having missed Rita's birthday yet again, Bonnie was only too pleased to help him. They spent an afternoon looking around Kingston and eventually settled on a butterfly necklace on a silver chain. They bought it in H. Samuels, John joking that his father would be pleased because he had recently bought some shares when the company was successfully floated on the stock exchange.

'Fancy some tea in Bentalls?'

'Why not,' said Bonnie. This would be the ideal opportunity to talk to John about their mother.

They sat at a table near the window and enjoyed the view. The waitress brought them tea and a tray of sandwiches with the promise of cake to follow. Bonnie loved the daintiness of it all. John was obviously feeling a bit hungry and complained that the sandwiches were 'far too titchy for a man'.

'John,' she began cautiously. 'Can I ask you something about your family?'

'My family?' He sounded surprised. 'Nothing much to say really. Like I told you, there's only me and my parents left now. I had an uncle but he died before I was born and my grandfather died soon after. Apparently my grandmother was never the same after that but I don't remember much about her. Why?'

'Just curious,' Bonnie smiled. 'Do you and your parents get on well together?'

'As a matter of fact, I don't get on too well with my father but my mother is a sweetie. No matter what's going on around her, she's always so calm. She paints and she does this incredible embroidery. I suppose she's what you might call creative. It must be in the blood. Are we shaped by nature or nurture?'

Bonnie must have looked uncomfortable because he frowned. 'Why do I get the feeling you're about to say something awful?'

'Not awful,' she said, 'but I think it may be a bit of a shock.'

'Go on…'

Bonnie decided that the best thing was to be direct. 'John, I've found out that you're adopted.'

He laughed but she didn't return his laughter. 'You're serious.'

She nodded and he looked away. Bonnie could feel the tension between them. 'No one ever told you?'

He shook his head. 'If this is true then my whole bloody life has been a lie.'

Bonnie was appalled. She'd never expected this kind of reaction. 'Please don't say that, John,' she began again. 'If they didn't tell you, they must have had their reasons.'

'What bloody reasons!' His expression was a

mixture of anger, hurt and bewilderment. She felt terrible. She never should have started this. She should have waited until Dinah was around.

'How the devil do you know so much about me and my family?' His voice had an edge to it. 'Have you been snooping into my private affairs?'

Embarrassed, Bonnie looked around. 'This is difficult for me too,' said Bonnie. 'Apparently your private affairs are mine as well.'

A couple of women were watching them, but everyone else seemed to be making a deliberate attempt not to notice them at all. The dead give-away was the fact that all other conversation in the restaurant had died.

'Perhaps this isn't the best place to deal with this,' she apologised. 'I'm sorry I brought it up.'

'You can't stop now,' he challenged. 'What exactly are we talking about, Bonnie?'

Bonnie put her hand to her mouth. 'I've upset you...' she began.

'Too right you have,' said John. 'But I want to know why we're having this conversation. What has my adoption got to do with you?'

The waitress came back with the cake tier. 'Leave it,' John snapped at her as she tried to find a space on the table. The girl hurried away, taking the plate with her.

Bonnie reached into her bag and handed him his grandfather's letter. John read it carefully. Bonnie's heart was thumping and as she looked around she wanted to say to the people on the adjoining tables, *Stop earwigging and get on with your tea!* She looked at John. He was still staring at the letter. What was he going to do? What if he made a scene? Or stormed out of Bentalls and refused to speak to her again? Shirley would be devastated not to have him in her life but she was still young enough for him to be a person she would never recall. As she watched him, she saw the tension leave his body.

He was looking at her now. 'Is this for real?' he said quietly.

She nodded. The whole restaurant held its breath.

'Who is Grace Follett?'

'My mother.'

He looked her straight in the eye and although he said nothing, she could almost read his thoughts. 'So, according to this,' he said sitting back in his chair and flicking the end of the paper, 'you and I are brother and sister.'

'Half brother and sister,' she corrected. 'We have the same mother but different fathers.'

His expression remained unchanged as he continued to stare. Bonnie shifted in her seat. How did he feel about that? Did he hate the idea?

'Am I older than you?'

She nodded again.

'Ha!' he said, his face suddenly wreathed in smiles. 'This will take some getting used to but I always wanted a sibling.'

'You don't mind?'

'Mind? Of course not. And I'm not surprised either.' He paused, adding after a moment's thought, 'You know how sometimes you get the feeling that there's a secret nobody's telling you? I think I may have already guessed.'

It seemed to Bonnie as if the whole restaurant

heaved a collective sigh of relief.

Later, when they told Dinah, her one thought was that John was now Shirley's genuine uncle and when they married, she would be her aunt. John was obviously still trying to come to terms with what he'd been told. He insisted that Bonnie tell him all about their mother and as she did so, she was struck by the similarities in their personalities. Her mother loved playing the piano, her pride and joy. She enjoyed telling a good story and entertaining, just as John did. Bonnie told him about her happy childhood, of days spent on Highdown Hill, or High Salvington where before the war, they could have tea in the Windmill Tea Rooms. She told him about lazy days on the beach, or pond-dipping in the rough ground between Sea Lane and George V Avenue when her mother would take them out for the day on the bus. As she told him, Bonnie's heart began to constrict again. How she missed her mother and Rita. How she longed to see them playing with Shirley. Every grandmother enjoyed spoiling her grandchild but by staying away she had denied Shirley that pleasure. Was it possible, after all this time, to start again? She had totally underestimated John's reaction. Could it be possible she was wrong about her mother as well?

'Weird,' he said. 'And even more of a surprise finding out about you.'

'It must have been very hard for your mother,' said Bonnie, thinking how gracious she must have been to adopt someone else's child. 'To bring up your husband's child by somebody else is such a totally unselfish act.' Just as difficult, she thought to herself, as her own mother giving up her baby son.

'I think it makes me admire my mother all the more,' said John gravely.

Me too, thought Bonnie, but she didn't voice it.

They parted friends although she could tell John was still very much in shock at the revelation she'd dropped in his lap. Talking at such great length about Worthing had had a profound effect on Bonnie. She was homesick. She hadn't felt like this since she was at Lady Brayfield's place. It gnawed into her bones and she couldn't get it out of her mind. It became almost an obsession. There were times in the days that followed when she'd be walking past the kitchen in the nursery and she could almost smell her mother's cooking. The lavender polish on the floors began to remind her of the lavender bags her mother put upstairs in her chest of drawers, and the smell of the laundry room reminded her of the damp washing on the clothes horse in front of the fire. She longed to see how Mum was getting on with her little garden. She'd always hated being out there when she was young, but now she wanted Shirley to have the chance to pick peas, or carry a cabbage indoors, just as she had done when she was a child. She remembered silly things too. The scribbled drawing on the stairs that Rita had got into big trouble for doing when she was six. The bedside lampshade in their bedroom which was burned on one side because they'd put it too close to the bulb. When Matron Bennett came into the Tweenies nursery to play some nursery rhymes on Sunday afternoon,

Bonnie thought about her mother playing the piano while she and Rita sang together. For too long she had told herself she didn't want to upset her mother again, that she was too ashamed to go back, but now something was tugging at her heart. A call she was finding hard to ignore.

'Worthing... I want to go back to Worthing.'

Thirty-One

'Does this bus stop at the pier?'

'I should hope so, darlin'. We'll all get flipping wet if it doesn't.' To the sound of laughter, Rita took three florins from her passenger's hand and searched her leather pouch for change. She issued the two tickets from the machine around her neck, giving him a bob and a tanner change. Rita moved along the bus. 'Any more fares? Any more fares?'

She was more than happy to be a conductress on the Southdown buses. It felt so right, so Rita. The uniform was more attractive than most. In summer the drivers wore a cream linen jacket and the conductors had a lovely shade of evergreen. Everyone wore a peaked cap with the Southdown logo. The men wore white shirt, black ties, black trousers and black shoes. Rita had a black tie, a crisp white shirt and black knee-length skirt. She wore flesh-coloured stockings and black lace-up shoes. The company was quite strict about uniform. Anyone turning up for work 'inappropriately dressed' was likely to be sent home and lose a day's pay. That would never happen to Rita. She was always on time and always smartly turned out, but just like every other raw recruit, she'd been caught out on her first day.

'If you're on the last run up Salvington Hill,' one of the older drivers had said, 'don't forget to bring the litter bin back.'

Rita never thought to question the order and when she got back to the depot with the bin safely stashed in the luggage compartment, everybody fell about with laughter. She knew at once that she'd been had, and although she could feel her cheeks warming with embarrassment, Rita laughed along with the rest of them and they loved her for it.

The passengers loved her too. If she wasn't too busy, she'd listen to their tales of woe, or she'd enjoy their excitement if someone was getting married or had won a bob or two on the football pools. They treated her as if she were a personal friend. Rita let them into her private life too, although she did hold back on some things. They knew she was married to Emilio but few of them knew she had a sister.

It had come as a bit of a surprise when she'd been partnered with Bob. She thought about making a fuss but she didn't want to risk being labelled a troublemaker on her first day. It was all right though. It had obviously come as a shock to him that she was married, but now he treated her as a friend and work colleague.

She loved his little jokes.

'I wanted to get a dog for my granny but the pet shop don't do swaps.'

'Here, old Taffy was walking down the street when he saw a runaway bus. I said to him, what steps did you take? And he said, long ones.' If Rita repeated them they weren't half as funny, but when Bob did it, meal times in the bus canteen were filled with laughter.

As the bus pulled up at the next stop, Rita walked back to the platform. 'Hurry along now. Two in the upper circle and three in the basement,' she quipped as more passengers climbed aboard. It was turning out to be a busy day.

As the bus made its way through East Worthing, she stood on the platform and leaned out to catch a glimpse of Emilio. His boat was on the shingle but there was no sign of him. Disappointed, Rita climbed the stairs to collect more fares. Two of her female passengers were talking confidentially; Rita couldn't help overhearing.

'What you want to do,' said a middle-aged woman in a brown felt hat, 'is make him a nice meal. Save up a few coupons and buy a chicken if you can, or a nice leg of lamb. Make sure everybody else is out and then you can talk.'

Her companion put her head up as Rita went to the front of the bus. Their eyes met.

'Any more fares?' Rita said quickly.

The younger woman looked at her but without seeing. She turned back to her friend. 'I suppose you're right,' she said. 'But he'll go loopy when I tell him.'

'Just remind him it takes two to make a baby,' said her confidante, patting her hand. 'And besides, with his belly nice and full, he'll have his mind on other appetites, won't he…'

Rita was pondering this as she went back down the stairs. Time alone, that's what she and Emilio needed too. She'd plan a romantic evening for two. She thought about what the woman had said, 'with his belly nice and full, he'll have his mind on other appetites...' and smiled to herself. Next Tuesday was St Valentine's Day. Emilio was in for a lovely surprise.

A passenger just inside the door looked at his watch. 'Is this bus on time?'

'It is,' said Rita climbing the stairs. 'Any more fares?'

In fact, Bob was an excellent timekeeper. If the bus was late he risked the wrath of the ticket inspector ('jumpers', as the other drivers called them) but if the bus was early ... well, that was almost a hanging offence. Missing a customer was just about the worst thing a Southdown bus driver could do and the conductor risked losing his or her good conduct bonus.

There was little time to think when she was working and for this Rita was grateful. She still had a gnawing in the pit of her stomach whenever she thought about Bonnie, although it wasn't as sharp as it had been the day she'd left, and now she'd fallen out with her mother. If only Mum would accept Emilio. She didn't want to have to choose between the two of them, but what could she do?

The bus slowed and Rita returned to the platform. 'Pool Valley,' she called.

Pool Valley was the end of the line and Rita was

dying for the ladies'. Bob rounded the Old Steine and in a second or two he would pull into the middle of the road because he had to have room to swing the bus down the narrow slope and into the bay. This bus was going straight back in service so Rita had little time. She leaned out of the platform as Bob lined up and began a slow reverse between two parked buses. Her finger was poised over the bell and as the rear of the bus reached the edge of the pavement, she gave it three sharp pushes. The few passengers still left began to stand and move down the aisle. As they got off they called their goodbyes and thanked her.

Rita left the empty bus and hurried to the loo while Bob got out of his cab for a stretch. The queue snaked around the corner and the waiting passengers climbed aboard for the trip back to Worthing. As Bob went round the corner for a fag, an inspector sauntered by.

A woman with a small child came up to him. 'Is this bus going to Worthing?'

'In about two minutes,' he said. 'You'd better hurry, lady. It looks like it's a full house.'

A woman loaded down with bags of shopping hurried up to the bus, brushing his arm as she jumped onto the platform. She didn't seem to notice the young woman and her child were in front of her. 'Just in time,' she said as she pushed her way down the aisle. The inspector heard the young woman catch her breath.

'There's a seat there,' he said trying to reassure her. She was a pleasant-looking girl and the old duck with the bags had no right to push in front like that.

The young woman hesitated and the little girl looked up at her. 'Play sand, Mummy.'

'Yes.' The woman smiled as if it was just the excuse she needed. 'Let's go to the beach instead.'

'The bus will be going straight away,' the inspector encouraged. 'As soon as the conductress comes back from the toilets.'

But the woman and her child turned towards the pier. 'It would be a daft idea to spend another hour and a half on the bus going to Worthing,' she said, 'when we've already been cooped up that long on the train.'

'Down from London then?' said the inspector making an educated guess.

The woman nodded and the little girl waved, 'Bye, bye, bus.'

Bob came back round the corner and still tugging at her skirt, Rita hopped onto the platform. The inspector looked at his watch. 'Right on time,' he smiled.

As the bus pulled back out into the traffic, Rita was aware of a little girl with a mass of blonde curls walking across the road, obviously on her way to the beach. She smiled. The child, trailing her bucket and spade, was soon swallowed up by the crowd. Rita turned and began to walk down the aisle, calling, 'Fares please.'

Bonnie watched the bus swing across the traffic and head for Worthing. Seeing Miss Bridewell push past her on the bus like that had quite put her off going. And when she saw that the only available seat was right next to her, Bonnie knew that the whole bus would know all her business before they got to Hove. It would have been nice to go and see Mum and Rita, but they'd probably be at work anyway.

Thirty-Two

Rita was eager to get home. By the time she had finished her shift, she had just enough time to dash to the shops to buy some Yardley's lavender talc from Woolworth's and some lipstick. It was the middle of the week so she didn't have much money or spare coupons but the butcher had some nice sausage meat and she found a few half decent cooking apples in the greengrocers. During the war, her mother used to make a lovely meal she called piggy-pie, in which she layered everything on a baking tray with a bit of onion and some herbs. Rita was no great cook but it looked easy enough and she knew it was tasty. What was it her passenger had said? 'With his belly nice and full, he'll have his mind on other appetites...' This was the answer she'd been looking for. You brazen hussy, she smiled to herself. You are going to seduce your husband.

Everything was quiet when she let herself in. Emilio would either be sorting out his nets down on the beach or still asleep after a night's fishing. Let him sleep on. He was going to need all the strength he could muster by the time she was ready for him. She would wear her best dress and tidy her hair, but first she had to get the piggy-pie in the oven. What a lovely surprise he was going to have tonight.

She laid the enamel board on the table and got the flour down from the cupboard. Rita rolled out the sausage meat and placed it on the baking tray but as she layered the chopped apple over the top, she became aware of a strange noise coming from the bedroom.

At first she was scared. Was there a burglar in the house? She picked up the rolling pin and listened. The bedsprings were squeaking with a rhythmical sound and someone was moaning. No ... no. It couldn't be ... could it? The moans became more intense and she knew instinctively that whoever was making the sound wasn't in pain, they were in the throes of ecstasy.

Her heart was beating very fast but, mustering every ounce of self-control she had, she crept towards the bedroom door. The grunting became more and more urgent and now she realised it wasn't one but two voices, and one of them was Emilio's. How could he? They had only been married five minutes and here he was being unfaithful, in broad daylight and in their own bed. Tears started in her eyes.

The bedroom door was firmly closed. She waited for a second or two, conscious of her own breathing, then Rita turned the doorknob slowly and let it swing open.

Emilio had his back to her. His trousers were on the floor and she was looking at his bare bottom but she couldn't see who was with him. As soon as he felt the cold draught from the open door, he raised himself up. Her eye went up to the mirror on the other side of the wall and Emilio's eyes met hers. The other person rose up too, and three startled faces were caught in the frame. Rita gasped in horror as the other person lifted a hairy arm. It was Jeremy.

Heaving and retching, Rita tripped, stumbling into furniture in her haste to get out of the house.

'No, Rita. Wait!'

But she couldn't wait. She couldn't breathe. She didn't want to be there.

Pulling on his trousers, Emilio raced after her. He caught her by the wrist as she reached out for the front door handle and pulled her back into their rooms. 'Please...'

It was then that she was sick. Her vomit splashed up her legs as it hit the wooden floor and her head began to spin. She heard Jeremy say his name. 'Emilio?' and her husband said, 'You'd better go.' And it struck her that there was a love and a gentle passion in his voice she'd never heard before. He couldn't have hurt her more if he had stabbed her through the heart.

As he left the room, Jeremy, shamefaced and embarrassed, reached out to touch her. 'I'm sorry, Rita.'

'Don't touch me.' She had enough presence of mind to jerk herself away from him. 'Leave me alone.'

'What can I do?' Jeremy sounded genuinely sorry. He finished dressing.

'Go,' said Emilio. 'I will sort it.'

She wiped her mouth with her handkerchief and rounded on him. 'Sort it? And just how do you think you can sort it, Emilio? I've just caught you in bed with...' she could hardly bear to say the words '...another man!'

Behind her, she heard the front door click and they were alone. Emilio got a bowl of water to mop up the mess.

'I never meant for this to happen.' He squeezed out the floor cloth and threw it over her vomit. 'I'm sorry. We never should have come, but there was nowhere else to go.'

'I've been a complete idiot, haven't I?' she said. 'You've never loved me. I can't think why on earth you would want to marry me.'

'I no want to go back to Italy,' he said miserably. 'My uncle, he persuaded me. I no want to hurt you, Rita. And you're wrong when you say I don't love you. You are good woman. Good friend. I cannot help what I do.'

'Can't help it?' she shrieked. 'Can't help it? You knew what you wanted and it wasn't me, was it, Emilio? So why involve me in the first place? I'm only 18 years old.' She was wailing now. 'I wanted love and marriage and babies. What have you done to me?' Her colour was high and her eyes blazed.

'I'm sorry,' he said feebly. 'I never...'

'Don't keep saying that,' she shouted. 'You must have known you could never love me right from the start.'

He sat down and stared at the floor.

'Get out,' she said quietly.

'What are you going to do?' he said.

She didn't answer. In truth she didn't know what to do. She kept thinking about his bare bottom and the noises he'd been making seconds before she'd opened the door. Her stomach churned. She was going to be sick again. At least there was a bowl there now.

'Just go,' she said when she had recovered.

'Please don't go to the police,' he said rising to his feet. 'If you do they'll send me back to that place.'

'What place?'

'Prison,' he said quietly.

She frowned. 'You were in prison?' And then it finally dawned on her. All those weeks he was away and she wrote to him nearly every day, he wasn't checking up on the fishing. He was in Lewis prison! What an idiot she had been. How could she ever lift her head in public again?

'Get out,' she hissed. 'I don't want to see you again as long as I live.'

He pulled his braces up over his shoulders and did up his flies. 'I need my things.' He came by her cautiously but she didn't object as he went into the bedroom and pushed a few of his clothes into a bag. When he emerged a few minutes later, Rita was still standing exactly as he'd left her.

'For what it's worth,' he said. 'I am very fond of you, Rita.'

She remained ramrod stiff and said nothing. As soon as she heard his footsteps on the pavement outside, Rita threw herself into a chair and wept.

Major Freeman, chairman of the cricket club, walked into Norris's den with his hand extended. 'Sorry to barge in on you like this, Finley, but I need to know if you've given the matter of being on the council any more thought.'

'As a matter of fact...' Norris began.

'Good, good,' said the major. 'Now what I propose is this.' He threw himself into a chair and looked around for the drinks trolley. 'Is that Scotch malt? Make mine a double, there's a good man.'

Norris obliged. 'Most of us are in the Freemasons,' the major continued. 'I'll introduce you and once you've been vetted...'

'Vetted?' said Norris faintly.

'Got to check up on you, old boy,' said the major taking a gulp from his glass. 'Just as you'll be wanting to check up on us.' He downed the rest of his drink and held out the glass for more. 'If all is well, and I'm sure it will be ... got no skeletons in your cupboard, eh, what? Then you'll be invited to meet the committee members. We hold a secret ballot to admit new members.'

'What sort of things do they want to know?' said Norris, reluctantly handing over another glass of his best malt.

'Family, business, any other organisations you belong to, that sort of thing,' said the major. 'Don't want any strong political opinions, or any naughties going on that might bring the Lodge into disrepute.' He snorted. 'You know the sort of thing. Anyway, once you've joined, getting elected should be a peach. Cllr Norris Finley. Got a good ring to it, eh, what?'

He stood up again and downed the rest of his whisky. 'I'll get the bloodhounds onto you and once they've done their checks, I'll be in touch. Goodnight, Finley. My regards to your wife.'

As soon as he'd swept out, Norris lowered himself into a chair. He'd have to tidy a few things up, and do it quickly. When he'd come down for the weekend, John had talked about spending time with friends, including the Rogers girl. It had to be the same one. Nobody else would have a daft name like Bonnie. He'd arranged for John to be followed in the hope it would lead him to Bonnie Rogers and that damned letter she'd taken from her mother. His only dread was that she might have already shown it to John. That would really put the cat among the pigeons.

And then there were all the little 'perks' he'd collected in the safe, like that gold watch he'd used to lever that Wilcox girl into bed and the bag Grace Follett was using when his men had taken the Thrift Club money. If anyone stumbled onto them it would be a disaster. Thank goodness there was nothing to connect him to Dolly Peterson. Her husband was still in prison for the beating Norris had given her but there was little likelihood of him getting out, and Dolly was incurable now. Norris had surprised even himself with the violence he'd used, but he'd learned from the experience. He'd turned over a new leaf. He'd controlled his temper ever since. Look at the restraint he'd used the last time he saw Grace Follett. He was sure Grace had taken the locket and he hoped to God she never found out who it really belonged to. It was a good thing the clasp was damaged. If she ever opened that... Well, she would never guess what the little pill inside was, but what if somebody swallowed it? He shuddered.

He reached for the telephone. Everything else would have to wait. If he was going to run for high office, now was the time to clean up his whole life and it wasn't going to be easy.

Thirty-Three

It was decided that the older children from the nursery would have an outing once a year. After a lot of discussion, the staff picked Chessington Zoo and the date happened to coincide with Shirley's birthday.

Bonnie was assigned two children, four-year-old Peter Churchill and five-year-old Vera Porter. They weren't related in any way but they got on fairly well. The outing was the first experience of its kind that they had ever had. Peter had come to the nursery three years before in the dead of night. He had been brought by the police who'd had a tip-off that a child was alone in a flat. When they broke in, Peter was in his cot, covered in faeces, distressed and very hungry. The neighbour was in tears when she saw him.

'I should have done something before,' she wept, 'but you don't like to interfere, do you.'

There was a court case which took months to get underway and Peter's mother was sent to prison for child neglect. Peter had been in care ever since.

Vera's mother had been too ill to look after her and her father couldn't deal with a young child.

He remarried soon after Vera's mother died but his new wife wasn't keen to have Vera. The child was up for adoption but her chances of a new family were practically nil. Vera had a condition they called mongolism. Both children loved the idea of 'helping' Bonnie with Shirley and a trip on the Green Line bus was more excitement than they'd had in a long time.

There were ten in the party, seven children and three adults. As Bonnie crossed the road, a black Lanchester Eleven slowed to let her and the children pass. They were at the bus stop in good time and Bonnie was in charge of the fares.

The zoo was quite large. For safety's sake the girls stuck together. The children loved it. They saw lions and monkeys and even a camel. The highlight of the day was a ride on the back of an elephant. After climbing some steps, they were perched on a long bench-type seat which was strapped either side of the animal. There were no straps for the children but they could push their feet against a footrest to keep their balance. Bonnie held Shirley on her lap while Peter and Vera sat either side. It was a bit precarious as they set off but that only added to their sense of adventure.

The two girls with Bonnie were Doreen her roommate and a new girl called Monica. Monica had a Box Brownie camera and she took some pictures. They ate their sandwiches for lunch and drank hot tea from a flask. The children had orange juice in Bakelite mugs brought for the purpose.

After a while Monica said, 'You keep looking

round. What's wrong?'

'It's probably nothing,' said Bonnie, 'but I get the feeling we're being watched.'

'I bet we are,' laughed Doreen. 'Look at us. We've got the whole United Nations here.'

Bonnie hadn't really thought about it before but she was right. They had white children, mixed race children and one full-blooded African child. Peter was the only one with flaming red hair and of course, there was little Vera.

The council had allocated five shillings for each child for the day. That meant everyone could have one ice cream and a few sweets. Peter and Vera chose an identical bar of Cadbury's chocolate. As Bonnie held them out, she said, 'Which one would you like?'

As quick as a flash, Peter said, 'Vera's.'

'Tell you what,' said Bonnie as Vera's lip trembled, and the other girls giggled and walked on, 'You have this one and I'll give Vera that one.'

Peter was content with that and so was Vera.

By three thirty, everyone had had enough. The children were tired and Shirley was already sucking her thumb as they went through the exit and headed for the bus stop.

There weren't many cars about but Bonnie noticed a black Lanchester Eleven parked near the exit. It looked awfully like the one she had seen at the start of the day, but it couldn't be, could it? She kept her eye on it as they waited for the bus but she never saw the driver.

'It occurs to me,' she said to Doreen and Monica as the children dozed around them, 'nobody keeps a record of what happens to these children. One day they will be all grown up with no real memories of their childhood.'

Monica pulled a face. 'You're probably right,' she said, 'but who is going to do it?'

'Who's got the time?' laughed Doreen. 'By the time we get this lot into bed, I shall be knackered.'

Bonnie knew she'd be very tired as well but it didn't seem fair. These children had already had a rough start in life. Perhaps she should volunteer to do it herself? Good idea – but that meant she would have to write it out seven times. Doreen was right. Who had the time?

As she stood to help Peter down from his seat when they reached their destination, Bonnie glanced up. They had all been sitting on the long seat at the back of the bus. A black Lanchester Eleven had just pulled into the side of the road behind them. She still couldn't see the occupants but her blood chilled. There was no doubt in her mind now. It was exactly the same car. One of them was being followed.

When they got off the bus Bonnie grabbed Doreen's arm. 'Look after my children for a minute.'

'Where are you going?'

Bonnie didn't answer. They watched her go up to the car.

'That's the car she said was following us,' said Doreen faintly.

The driver pretended not to see her coming. Bonnie rapped sharply on the window. He feigned surprise and wound it down.

'You've been following us all day,' she challenged.

He was a man with a swarthy complexion and small deep-set eyes. 'I've got no idea what you are talking about,' he said in a rasping voice.

'Oh yes you have,' Bonnie said stoutly, 'and if you know what's good for you...'

His eyes had narrowed and Bonnie's sense of outrage evaporated as she saw his lip curl. 'You've got something that belongs to Mr Finley and he wants it back. If you value your daughter's life, you'll see that he gets it.'

With that, the car drove off at speed. When Bonnie got back to the others, her face was white.

'What did he want?' asked Doreen.

'Nothing,' said Bonnie. 'Just some stupid crank trying to scare us.'

Later, alone in her room, Bonnie opened her locked drawer and took out her treasured things. She examined them one by one.

What was so important that John should send someone to follow her all the way to Chessington? And why threaten Shirley? He could have asked her for whatever he wanted. Then it dawned on her. John loved Shirley. There was no way he would threaten her. He had also told her that he and his father didn't get on. So it wasn't *John* Finley who had sent someone to threaten her today. It must have been his father. That was scary. How did Norris Finley find out where she was and what did he want? She had pretended not to be upset when the driver gave her his message but she could still hear his rasping voice when she put the light out later that night.

'If you value your daughter's life, you'll see that he gets it.'

If Mr and Mrs Matthews told Grace once, they told her a hundred times how much they appreciated her kindness. Now that their son George was decently buried in his own plot of ground, they said they could begin to plan a headstone as a memorial. Grace had taken the case to them the previous week, soon after Mrs Matthews had arrived in the country. Introductions had been slightly awkward but the Matthews had been polite. When they'd told her they were burying their son, she had asked if she could attend the funeral. The offer had touched them both deeply. Archie had promised to go with her.

Archie and Grace had walked to the church but they had gone in the funeral car with the Matthews to the churchyard at Offington Corner.

'Could you come back here next week?' said Oswald as they all shook hands back at their rented house in Goring. 'I've tried to read the papers George left, but I'm afraid I can't concentrate at the moment and Mrs Matthews is all done in. I've asked an old mate of mine, an ex-police officer, to take a look at everything, especially that photograph.'

'Of course,' said Grace.

They decided to walk back home in spite of Oswald's offer of a taxi. It was a fair distance but it was a nice afternoon and Grace welcomed the opportunity to be alone with Archie again. They kept to the beach road until they reached Heene Road. Along Marine Parade, dog owners were striding along the empty beach below the high bank of stone and shingle. Gulls wheeled and turned overhead and at the water's edge, little sandpipers ran in and out of the water looking for food.

Grace smiled. How she loved this place. Worthing had none of the brashness of Brighton but it did have a special quality of its own. How many times had she heard newcomers saying, 'I never wanted to like this place but it has grown on me.'

Worthing did just that. It crept in uninvited and wrapped itself around your heart, until you became fond of it. The council had some fantastic plans for the future of the town. They wanted to do away with the old and create a brand new modern seaside town. Plenty of people were up in arms about it, especially the plan to bulldoze most of the lovely old houses in Station Approach, but Grace had the feeling that even if the powers that be mutilated the town, it would always remain dearly loved by its residents.

On the last stretch before home she was tired and looking forward to a rest and a cup of tea. They parted at the end of the road because Archie was anxious to get back to the shop. It was warm inside the cottage and Grace put the kettle on. Poor George, and poor Oswald and Mrs Matthews. What a dark deed had been done that day in the factory, but at least by putting George into his final resting place, they had gone some way to putting things right.

She heard a rustling sound on the stairs and spun round. 'Who's there?'

Her mouth went dry. Burglars? And then she relaxed. Who would steal from her? She had nothing left. Grace picked up the poker and moved cautiously towards the stair door. Yanking it open, she gasped as the light from the kitchen flooded the staircase.

Rita was sitting on the third step, her hair dishevelled and her face wet with tears.

'Mum,' she choked. 'I'm sorry. Can I come home?'

Dropping the poker, Grace bounded up to meet her. Putting her arms around Rita's shaking shoulders, she kissed her daughter's lovely chestnut hair again and again as she held her tightly against her chest.

While the telegram boy waited for an answer, the maid took the yellow envelope to Norris. He was sitting in his den, with the radio on. She coughed and he turned to look at her. Pretty girl, he thought. A conquest for a future date perhaps?

'Telegram, sir.'

He took it and tore it open. 'No reply,' he said gruffly and the girl left the room.

Norris smiled to himself and read the message one more time before striking a match and watching it burn. Two words, but they meant that he would be able to apply for the Lodge and a place on the council.

Girl found.

Thirty-Four

Bonnie was tired as she started work the next morning but it was worth it. Yesterday had been a lovely day. Today she was working from 7am until 7pm but she had 2pm until 4pm off duty so perhaps she could catch up with a little sleep then.

At the bottom of the stairs, she bumped into a man dressed in paint-splashed overalls.

'Morning,' Bonnie smiled.

'Morning.' The man was lining up his tins of paint by the door.

Oh good, she thought as she crossed the courtyard and went into the nursery, it's about time the council had the place done up. A fresh coat of paint would brighten things up no end.

Grace and Rita had talked long into the night. It was wonderful to have her daughter back but Grace wished with all her heart that Rita hadn't had to suffer this indignity. She couldn't help feeling that she should shoulder some of the blame. She was careful not to say anything which might smack of 'I told you so…' but as they talked, Grace could see that much of this could have been avoided if she had done some plain speaking.

Emilio had been Rita's first and only love and her daughter had based much of her knowledge of romance on Hollywood films. Considering that in the pictures men and women only kissed with their lips closed, and marriages on the silver screen were kept firmly behind the bedroom door, it had given Rita an unrealistic view of life.

'I never really knew what a man does, Mum,' she'd said tearfully. 'I still don't but I know enough to know something was very wrong with Emilio and me.'

'He should never have put you in this position,' said Grace. 'But what's done is done.'

'I don't want to stay married to him all my life,' Rita wept.

'I don't think you have to,' said Grace. 'Would you mind if I talk to someone about this?'

Rita's eyes had grown wide. 'Who? Whatever for? Mum, I don't want the whole street knowing my business.'

'They won't,' said Grace. 'Solicitors are bound by the law not to talk about their clients. I think a solicitor would tell us that a judge in a divorce court would annul a marriage that wasn't consummated and...'

'Consummated?' Rita had interrupted. 'What's that?'

Grace was moved with compassion. What sort of a mother had she been? She should have done some plain talking but instead she'd allowed her daughter to remain ignorant of the facts of life. Poor Rita. So innocent, so naive.

'That you and Emilio never made love together.'

'I'd have to tell a judge that!'

'Darling, if you do, you'll be rid of him forever.'

Rita stared at her mother as if unable to speak. Grace had patted her hand. She needed time to think, Grace could see that. 'Let's sleep on it,' she'd said brightly. 'Things will look a whole lot better in the morning.'

They parted on the stair with a hug. Grace lay awake for some time thinking. Uppermost in her mind was this business with Emilio, but gradually her thoughts moved in another direction. Norris Finley had been panic-stricken when he'd turned up here just before Christmas. Why? He'd never come back to the house, nor had he asked her why she wasn't returning to work. He'd mentioned the locket and as abruptly as he'd barged into her life, he'd disappeared from it. Once more her thoughts turned to the other things he'd got in that safe. The gold watch and her moneybag. She should have thought of this before but what with her mother dying and all of Rita's troubles, she'd had no time to dwell on other things. Had Norris really arranged for her to be attacked and then given her back her own money? The answer was probably yes, because he wanted a hold over her. Now that Snowy had told her he'd got his hands on poor little Polly, the man had to be stopped, but the question was, how? Exposure was the only answer but with his exposure came the exposure of others. Innocent people could be ruined.

When Rita came down the next morning, although her eyes still looked puffy, she was a lot calmer. 'I thought you'd be at work.'

'I never went back to the factory,' said Grace. 'I've started another arm to the agency. Babysitting this time. I can work when I like.'

'Babysitting?' Rita smiled.

'Simple enough,' said Grace. 'I saw the idea in *Woman* magazine and I got to thinking about some of the girls round here stuck at home all the time because there's no one to look after their babies. I charge five bob to join which will cover my costs and the babysitters get about a bob an hour.'

'Never short on ideas, are you, Mum,' Rita grinned.

'Well, if ever you've got a spare evening and you want some cash...' Grace teased and Rita laughed.

A few minutes later, Rita sat down at the table with some toast and a cup of tea.

'Rita,' Grace began cautiously. 'We found a suitcase in your bedroom.'

'I'd forgotten all about that.' Rita's face had coloured.

'It belongs to George Matthews,' Grace went on. 'Have you any idea why Bonnie was keeping it?'

'It wasn't Bonnie,' said Rita. 'It was me.'

Now Grace was puzzled. Was Rita going out with George too? 'What?'

Rita told her about meeting Mrs Kerr, and going to George's digs. 'A few months later, when she came into Hubbard's,' Rita continued, 'she told me to come and get it.'

Grace frowned. 'But why didn't you take it to the police? Or tell me about it?'

'Have you looked inside, Mum? There's stuff about the Nazis in it. I didn't tell you because I was scared Bonnie was mixed up in something.' Rita cut herself another slice of bread. 'Will you come back to the flat tonight and help me collect my things? Emilio will be out fishing.'

'Of course, darling.' Grace avoided her eye. She would dearly love to thump Emilio, and Salvatore and Liliana for that matter. She blamed herself for not being more forthright when talking about Emilio's preferences, but Salvatore and Liliana had played their part in this sorry state of affairs as well. They had known all along what the boy was like, and yet they had encouraged the marriage. How could they have let it happen?

'Have you thought any more about asking a solicitor what to do?'

Rita put her bread under the grill. 'I suppose we'd better get it over and done with.'

Clara Cooper wasn't looking forward to clearing out her aunt's house and she had put it off for far too long. Miss Reeves had been a meticulous person with a place for everything and everything in its place, but it was painful packing up a person's life like this. The furniture was positively ancient and most of her clothes were hopelessly old fashioned, but Clara had a mind to take them to the church anyway. Sometimes the church gave furniture to people starting out in life. Auntie would have approved of her things helping some poor soul in need. Her dresses could be cut up and the material used for more modern dresses or children's clothes, and there were plenty of women skilled enough to do it. The country had moved on from make do and mend to alter and re-create.

It was when she had almost finished that she came across the box of letters. Her aunt had been corresponding with Bonnie Rogers. Clara could hardly believe it. Her daughter had gone to school with Bonnie and they had been quite good friends at one time. She had been as shocked as anybody when Bonnie left Worthing. They said that her poor mother spent days and days at the station asking people if they had seen her. She looked distraught.

Rumour and gossip had been rife. They said Bonnie had stolen something and run away, or that she'd got herself in the family way and when George Matthews was found in the old factory, there were plenty who said they'd seen her in his company. A couple of times she had seen Mrs Rogers in the street but she had crossed over the road rather than speak to her. It was all too embarrassing.

Clara spent some time reading the letters but there was nothing in them. Bonnie was doing her nursery nurse training, but all she talked about was her mother and sister. Clara thought about throwing the letters in the bin. After all, Bonnie had written them to her aunt and her aunt was dead. Whatever passed between them was their business... But then her conscience got the better of her. It wouldn't be fair to deny her the letters. They wouldn't do much good. There was no address at the top of the page but at least knowing that her daughter was doing well would give her a crumb of comfort. She put the letters into a large envelope. She would drop them in sometime when she was passing.

Lunch in the nursery was over. Shirley was asleep in her cot in the Tweenies room when Bonnie went in to see her. She ran her fingers gently through her blonde curls and smiled. 'You would have loved our little girl, George,' she whispered, swallowing the lump that was forming in her throat.

She lingered a while to talk to Monica who was cleaning the paint pots and painting aprons the children had been using during the morning then, yawning, she made her way back to her room in the staff cottage. That's funny, she thought, there's no sign of the painters and they hadn't done any work. Perhaps they were only measuring up or something.

She knew something was wrong as soon as she walked along the corridor towards her room. Her door was ajar and there was a petticoat in the doorway. Bonnie's heart began to quicken.

'Who's there?' she called but there was no answer. Bonnie pushed the door gingerly and looked inside. The room was completely ransacked. Her clothes and bedding were on the floor, her mattress on the top. Doreen's part of the room was the same. The wardrobe was empty. Of the chest of drawers, every drawer had been emptied and tipped on top of the already mountainous pile in the middle of the room. Even the corkboard with Shirley's paintings had been taken off the wall. Bonnie stood in the doorway with her mouth open. Who could have done this? And why? She glanced around nervously.

Her mind went back to the day before and the man with the rasping voice and she turned and ran back to the main house.

Matron and Mr Bennett called the police. Bonnie went to find Doreen and to arrange cover for her to come back to their room. When she saw the mess, she was beside herself with fear.

'It was that bloke,' she said. 'You never should have gone back and spoken to him.'

The same thought had crossed Bonnie's mind too.

'Oh Lord,' Doreen went on, 'if I'd been in here, he would have had his evil way with me and all.'

'He wasn't a rapist,' said Bonnie. 'He was a thief.'

'So, what was he looking for?' Doreen wailed.

Bonnie had a shrewd idea but said nothing. They waited until the police came before beginning the mammoth task of clearing up. In the end, a bobby on a bicycle turned up and a Detective Constable Elliot, who was dropped off by car, quickly followed him.

Their interest was really aroused when Bonnie told them about the painter.

'Who was he?' asked Elliot.

Doreen was already giving him the glad eye. 'I never saw him,' she sighed.

'I've never seen him before either,' said Bonnie.

'Did he threaten you?'

Doreen gasped and burst into tears.

'No,' said Bonnie, putting her arm around Doreen's shoulders. 'We just said good morning.'

'So you weren't in the least bit suspicious?'

'No,' said Bonnie. 'I thought how good it was

that the place was going to get a lick of paint.'

'That's not very likely to happen,' Matron interrupted. 'The council is strapped for cash. Even if we were able to decorate, the only colours available are deadly dull. Who wants battleship grey everywhere?'

Bonnie was asked to describe the man which she did as best she could. 'I didn't take that much notice of him. After all, it was only seven in the morning.'

'He must have been looking for something,' the DC said accusingly.

Doreen blew her nose noisily.

'Can't you see you're upsetting her?' said Bonnie.

'If either of you has got herself involved with some lowlife, you'd be sensible to tell us before this gets any worse,' said the DC. He waited for an answer but Bonnie comforted the sobbing Doreen who probably hadn't even heard the question.

'Is anything missing?'

'How do we know?' Bonnie retorted. 'We can't possibly tell until we've put everything back.'

'I bet it was that man from yesterday,' said Doreen.

Bonnie glanced at Shirley's picture on the wall and remembered the driver's rasping voice. 'You've got something that belongs to Mr Finley…'

Doreen began to tell the police about the black Lanchester which had followed them to Chessington. 'Bonnie confronted the driver when we got off the Green Line bus.'

For the first time, Bonnie felt afraid. She was in danger. Worse than that, Shirley was in danger. 'If you value your daughter's life...' the man had said. She had to get away from here. They knew she lived here, they'd be back. She wished she had pursued her plan to visit her mother. She would have had somewhere to go if she had done, but she couldn't turn up on her mother's doorstep unannounced, not with all this trouble in her wake and with a baby in tow. It would be too much to bear. And besides, her mother worked for Mr Finley.

'Miss Rogers,' the policeman was saying. 'Could the driver and the painter have been the same person?'

Bonnie shook her head. 'I don't think so ... no.'

The questioning went on for some time. 'If you find something is missing,' the DC said as they got ready to leave, 'let us know.'

As soon as the police had gone, Matron told Bonnie she needn't come back on duty until six and she gave Doreen the rest of the day off. 'That,' she told them, 'should give you both time to clear this mess up.'

Doreen was so upset, it took a while to get everything straight. She was too scared to walk to the bus stop on her own, so Bonnie went with her. On her way back to the nursery, Bonnie went to the telephone box.

Dinah gasped when Bonnie told her what had happened.

'What were they looking for?'

'I'll tell you when I see you. I need to get away from here,' said Bonnie. 'I have the feeling that if they haven't found what they're looking for, they'll be back, and I must protect Shirley.'

'Of course, darling,' said Dinah. 'Leave it with me. John and I have friends we can call on. Be ready at seven and someone will be there to fetch you.'

Quick-thinking, Bonnie said, 'How will I know they've come from you?'

'Don't worry, I'll be with them,' said Dinah.

As Bonnie hurried back, she couldn't help looking over her shoulder a couple of times. Dear Lord, she was getting as jumpy as Doreen. It was plainly obvious that the man had been looking for that letter, but why? *You've got something that belongs to Mr Finley...* Why would he want his son's letter? It didn't say anything important.

When she got back to her room and she was alone, Bonnie lifted the corner of Shirley's painting on the wall and relaxed. Thank God they hadn't found it. After the confrontation with the driver of the car, she had folded it carefully and pushed it into one of the holes on the wall. She'd picked a little more plaster away so that it fitted snugly and then she'd Sellotaped it in. The little painting covered it perfectly. She would leave it there until she had finished her duty for today and then she'd take it with her. She'd lose her job of course, as well as the chance to take her exams. She'd have to let Matron and Lady Brayfield down badly, but it couldn't be helped. Her only thought was to protect Shirley.

Dinah took her to a friend's flat.

'It's all right,' she said as Bonnie was looking

around. 'She's in the States. She told me I could use it any time I wanted. As soon as I can get a transatlantic line, I'll telephone her to say you and Shirley are here.'

They had to put Shirley in a single bed. She was dry at night, so Bonnie wasn't worried about spoiling the mattress, but there was a danger she would fall out of bed. They pushed it against the wall and managed to get a chair wedged on the other side so that the back of the chair made a guard.

'I hope we'll be safe,' said Bonnie.

'Of course you will, darling,' said Dinah. 'Even if we were followed, which we weren't, you can only get in with the permission of the concierge on the door. You have a double lock on the front door to the flat as well. Now what's this all about?'

'I don't want to sound mysterious,' she said, 'but I really need to speak to John.'

'Curiouser and curiouser,' smiled Dinah, and Bonnie couldn't resist giving her a hug.

'You are such a wonderful friend,' she said. 'Anyone else would be upset and think I was keeping them in the dark, but you don't seem to mind.'

'I am absolutely furious,' Dinah joked. 'But I trust you, and I know you will tell me when you can.'

'Thanks Dinah.'

As soon as Bonnie was settled, Dinah turned to go. 'I'll bring John here the day after tomorrow,' she said. 'He's in Bournemouth. He'll be back by then.'

'Would you do me one more favour?' Bonnie asked. She handed Dinah Shirley's doll, the one Dinah had given her.

'Didn't she like it?'

'She loves it. Would you give it to her again? I don't want her to have all her toys at once. She'll get bored with them and besides she's still got Leggy Peggy.'

'Good idea,' smiled Dinah. 'See you the day after tomorrow with John.'

'It's really coming together with you two, isn't it?' said Bonnie. 'You both deserve it. Will you live in the house in Worthing?'

'Didn't I tell you?' said Dinah. 'I sold Granny's house.'

Bonnie gasped.

'I had an offer I couldn't refuse,' Dinah went on. 'Most of our lives are in London now. What do I want with a little house in Worthing?'

'What indeed,' Bonnie sighed wistfully.

Thirty-Five

Bonnie and Shirley spent a pleasant day together in the flat. It was a beautiful home and after Bonnie had spent some time moving ornaments and precious things out of the reach of inquisitive little hands, they played chase and made dens under the table and behind the dressing table curtain. Dinah had brought a little food with her, only the basic stuff, eggs, cheese and a little bread, but it was enough for a couple of days, so Bonnie decided to lie low for a while. She missed her friends in the nursery and there was a serious risk that she would not be able to complete her course, but Shirley's safety was paramount.

She had just put Shirley to bed when the telephone rang. Bonnie picked it up cautiously. 'Hello?'

'This is your concierge, Madam. There is a Mr Finley here. Shall I give him admittance?'

'Oh yes, yes,' Bonnie cried. 'Send him up.'

In the few minutes before John arrived, she rushed around the flat, plumping up cushions and picking up Shirley's few toys. She only had time to glance in the mirror to tidy her hair before the doorbell rang, but her beaming smile died as she opened it and Norris Finley barged his way inside.

When she opened the front door, Bonnie nearly died of shock. She tried to close it quickly but Norris Finley pushed his way past her.

'What do you want?' Bonnie willed her voice to be steady. 'How did you find me?'

'It was easy enough to have you followed, and you know perfectly well what I want,' he said, walking into the flat and looking around.

'I haven't the faintest idea,' said Bonnie, 'and if you don't get out of here, I shall call security.'

Norris rounded on her and grabbed her cardigan, pulling her towards him. 'Now listen to me, you stupid cow, I've no time to mess around. I want that letter you took from your mother's place.'

Bonnie hit his hand away from her and backed away. 'I don't have it.'

His expression grew dark. 'If you value that little brat of yours, you'll give me what's mine.'

Before she could stop herself Bonnie involuntarily glanced towards the bedroom where Shirley was hiding. Norris smiled. 'I'll just take a little look around, shall I?'

'She's not here,' said Bonnie rushing to put herself between him and the door. He brushed her aside with one swipe of his hand and opened the door. 'No, Mr Finley, please…'

The room was in chaos. The bed was empty and the covers were on the floor. Bonnie's practised eye searched the room and she saw Leggy Peggy's foot beneath the dressing table curtain. She willed her daughter to stay where she was. For God's sake, don't come out and shout 'Boo'. Stay where you are for just a little longer, darling...

'See? I've already told you,' said Bonnie in a cold voice. 'Now get out.'

'You interfering little slut!' Norris snarled. 'If I find out you've shown it to anyone, *anyone,* do you hear, I swear I'll come back and I'll kill you.'

Norris grabbed Bonnie's hair and began pulling her out of the room. Bonnie screamed in pain. Under the dressing table, the terrified little girl pressed Leggy Peggy's long legs over her ears but it was impossible to shut the sounds out.

'I know your little game, you witch,' Norris said, pushing Bonnie to the ground, 'but you're not getting a penny out of me.'

As the door swung to a close behind them, Shirley noticed a loose thread on the carpet, and picked at it with her fingers. What game? Was Mummy playing a game with the nasty man? If he was, she didn't like it. Shirley screwed up her face really tight and wiped her eyes with Leggy Peggy's plait. Then she heard a slap, like the one Monica gave Jimmy on his leg when he tried to poke the guinea pig's eye out with a pencil. Jimmy cried but Shirley didn't hear Mummy cry. Mummy must be very brave.

'I don't want your money!' Mummy shouted. 'I've made a new life for my daughter and myself. I don't give a fig about you or what you're up to.'

Now Shirley was dying to do a wee-wee. She jigged her legs up and down and squeezed her bottom tight but she was just busting. She wanted Mummy, but she didn't want to see the nasty man. So Shirley hugged Leggy Peggy and waited.

Back in the sitting room, Norris had finally let go of Bonnie's hair. He smiled sardonically. 'You know your mother spent weeks looking for you,' he said. 'I wonder what she would think about having a bastard for a grandchild.' There was a pause and then he said, 'I thought that might change your tune. You'd have to explain what you're doing here, wouldn't you? What sort of a life are you living? I bet you're on the bloody game.'

'How dare you!' Bonnie scrambled to her feet. Her head hurt like hell but at least she'd got him away from Shirley.

'Like mother, like daughter,' he sneered. 'Both of you are bloody tarts.'

'You have no right...' she began.

'Well, the likes of you could never afford a place like this, could you?' He paused. 'On second thoughts, maybe I've got a better idea. *I'll* phone the police and they'll send for the Welfare and they'll take that little maggot away from you.'

Bonnie was horrified. 'No!'

'Something wrong, Bonnie? You've gone a bit pale.'

'All right,' she cried. 'I haven't got the letter here but I'll get it back and I'll give it to you.'

'That's more like it,' he said. 'But no funny business.' He tore a piece of paper out of his diary and scribbled something before handing it to her. 'Ring me and I'll tell you where to come.'

Bonnie snatched the paper, and said through her teeth, 'Now get out, get out.'

The door closed and the silence grew louder. Hidden behind the curtain, Shirley listened and trembled. The silence wasn't empty, like when you're lying all tucked up and cosy in bed in the middle of the night. It was scary. Shirley felt her legs grow warm. Oh no, now she'd wet herself. It didn't feel very safe but she crept out from behind the curtain. Shirley's knees were wobbly and there was a tight feeling in her chest.

'Mummy,' she whimpered.

Bonnie came into the bedroom with a big smile. 'There you are,' she cried and she put her arms around Shirley, lifting her up.

'I was frighted,' said Shirley. 'I wet myself.'

'There's no need to be frightened,' said Bonnie. 'Mummy's here darling.'

Ashamed, Shirley repeated, 'I wet myself.' Tears rolled down her cheeks but Bonnie just hugged

Shirley tight and kissed her.

There was a sharp knock at the door, and they both nearly jumped out of their skins.

'Go to blazes,' Bonnie snapped.

'Are you all right, Madam?' said a man's voice, and she recognised it as the concierge's.

'Oh yes, yes I'm fine,' said Bonnie. 'I'm sorry to be rude, I thought you were somebody else.'

'We've had a complaint about raised voices,' he said. 'Can you open the door please, Madam.'

Bonnie hoiked her daughter onto her hip and opened the front door. 'I'm sorry about the noise,' she said. 'If that man comes back again, please don't let him in.'

'Of course, Madam, but you said...'

'I know and I made a terrible mistake. Thank you for your concern, but I ... we are fine now.'

Grace enlisted Snowy's help when she went back to see Oswald and his wife. Archie had a rush order on and had to stay in the shop in order to finish it. When he told her, Grace felt her heart sink. Perhaps friendship was really all he wanted. Grace wanted someone with her because she was afraid of what Oswald might say and she wanted some moral support.

'Mrs Matthews is lying down,' said Oswald as he opened the door. 'She's not feeling too good at the moment.'

'I'm sorry to hear that,' said Grace. She handed him a bunch of lilies of the valley picked fresh that morning from her small courtyard garden.

Oswald was visibly moved. 'Her favourite flowers,' he said hoarsely as he laid them on the hall table. 'I'll put them in water later.'

Grace introduced Snowy and the three of them went into the spacious sitting room where a white-haired man sat in an armchair. As they came in, he rose and they all shook hands.

'Walter Stanyon,' said the stranger. 'I'm a retired detective inspector.'

George's suitcase was open and the contents spread on a low table in between the settees and the armchairs. Walter Stanyon got straight to the point.

'How did you get this?'

'My daughter had it in her room,' said Grace.

'Who gave it to her?'

'George's landlady,' said Grace. Seeing Walter's thunderous expression she added, 'Apparently the police didn't bother to collect it.'

'The burning question for me,' Oswald began, 'is why was there no post-mortem on my son?'

Walter Stanyon shook his head. 'There seems to have been a presumption that the door simply slammed, trapping him in the room.'

'And I am at a loss to understand why no one went around to George's lodgings after his body was found,' said Oswald.

'It's really no excuse, sir,' said Walter. 'But we have to remember the times. In the run up to D-Day even the Met was 6,000 police officers short. Provincial police forces had their numbers depleted to make up the numbers elsewhere. I imagine this looked like an open and shut case, so nobody dug very deeply.'

Nobody spoke but the atmosphere was charged with anger and disgust.

'I know it doesn't look good,' Walter went on, 'but in 1947 even paper was being rationed as well. It takes four sheets of foolscap to write a crime report.'

'What are you saying?' said Oswald tetchily. 'To save the cost of four sheets of paper, my son's killer got off scot-free?'

'I know it's completely unacceptable,' Walter agreed, 'but I can only apologise.'

There was a pregnant silence then Snowy said, 'Perhaps if we could all calm down and talk about the suitcase...'

'I've no wish to cast aspersions,' Grace began, 'but I seem to remember that Mr Finley went to great lengths to explain where he was on the day in question.' She told them about the day the police came to the factory to tell them about George and they were a bit puzzled as to why he made such a song and dance about the Southampton newspaper he was carrying.

'There are more than a few anomalies surrounding this case,' Walter observed. 'I get the feeling that George believed he had uncovered some sort of Nazi ratrun,' he went on. 'As you know, we have a bit of history of it in these parts. Mosley was a frequent visitor to Worthing between the wars and a couple of years before your son was found dead, seven members of the Imperial Fascist League were arrested for harbouring two members of the German SS. They were attempting to get the men to Argentina but a few days before they were to be shipped out, they were found in a loft.'

'I remember that,' said Snowy. 'It was in a

house on the Littlehampton Road, wasn't it?'

'That's right,' said Walter.

Oswald leaned back in his chair.

'We now know that your son was the man who tipped the authorities off, but it wasn't until you began making your enquiries that we finally put two and two together.'

'My son wasn't asked to testify in the case?'

'No, sir. MI5 kept his identity a secret.'

'Are you saying my son was in the British secret service?'

'No, sir, but he was helping them.'

Oswald stubbed out his cigarette and reached for another one. 'It's a lot to take in.'

'It sounds like he was a brave man,' said Grace. 'What about the letter? It's all in German.'

Walter nodded. 'The papers you found in the suitcase related to some people MI5 already had on their radar, so that part has become classified information. But we do know George had already arranged to meet someone from MI5 in London. Unfortunately he never showed up.'

'There was always some question about his death,' said Snowy. 'None of us could work out why he was in the factory.'

'I made enquiries but the police believe there's no case to answer,' said Walter.

Grace picked up the photograph of the man in SS uniform. 'So, who is this man?'

'Oh,' said Walter, handing her another much larger photograph. 'I had the picture blown up and we were able to identify him. That's Josef Mengele.'

Snowy took in her breath. 'The Angel of Death?'

Mengele was standing in front of a group of fellow officers.

Walter nodded. 'The picture was taken in January 1942 when he was awarded the Iron Cross First Class for pulling a couple of soldiers out of a burning tank before it exploded.'

'And yet he went on to murder thousands of people in the concentration camps,' said Oswald bitterly.

'A true monster,' Walter agreed.

'There has to be something about this picture...' Grace muttered as she took it back and looked more carefully.

'My son helped to liberate those places,' said Oswald. 'It affected him deeply.'

'Is that how he got hold of the picture?' said Snowy.

'Possibly,' said Walter. 'He could have got it from one of the victims.'

Grace was still staring at the picture. She exhaled her breath slowly, 'Oh my God...'

'Do we know where Mengele is now?' Snowy asked.

Walter shook his head. 'In hiding somewhere I guess, but not in Worthing.' He chuckled sardonically. 'He's more likely to be somewhere a lot closer to home.'

Grace passed the picture to Snowy. 'Look.'

'I just did,' said Snowy irritably.

'Look again,' said Grace. 'Who's that man standing in the background?'

Snowy looked at the group of SS men gathered in a small group behind the proud Mengele holding up his Iron Cross for the camera. She glanced up with a look of horror on her face. 'No...'

'That's what George recognised, isn't it,' said Grace. 'That German officer standing behind him is either his double or it's Manny Hart.'

Thirty-Six

John Finley threaded his way through the tables in the restaurant at Dickens & Jones. His mother enjoyed watching the Regent Street shoppers so she liked to sit near the window. He admired his mother a great deal. Unlike the mothers his friends had, who always left everything to Nanny, she had been the one cooling his fevered brow with a damp flannel when he was sick as a boy. She'd taught him to play the piano, although it wasn't long before he'd outstripped her abilities. She'd got him through prep school, which he hated, and boarding school, which he'd loved. She was proud of his wartime achievements and never let it show how much she worried. He knew she did worry about him, but whenever he turned up on leave, although she was delighted to see him, she carried on as usual. He appreciated that. It gave him time to unwind with what was familiar and sane in a mad, mad world.

She didn't mind his indecision after the war either, and when he'd told her he wanted to work in the theatre, she'd been a stalwart supporter.

Only one thing had changed. All his life, he'd

had an unspoken feeling that she wasn't a happy woman, but now, at last, all that had changed. As she rose to meet him, and they kissed, he gave her a tender hug.

'Darling,' she said as she sat back down and moved a pile of glossy magazines onto the empty chair beside her, 'I've ordered tea and cakes. How are you?'

'Fine,' said John. He didn't need to ask how she was. She was positively glowing. 'The play didn't make the summer season at Bournemouth. That went to Jimmy Jewel and Ben Warris.'

'Oh dear,' said his mother, 'but I shouldn't worry. As Mr Micawber says, "Something will turn up."'

'I rather think it has.'

'Oh John,' she said, her eyes dancing with excitement. 'The girl?'

He laughed softly. 'Not much gets past you, Mother, and yes, I've asked her to marry me.'

The waitress had arrived with the tea and the next few minutes were taken up with rearranging the table. When she'd gone, his mother was wiping a tear from her eye. 'I'm so happy for you. Now tell me all about her.'

'Actually, she'll be here shortly. I hope you don't mind but I've invited her to meet you.'

His mother gasped. 'Oh John, you should have said. We could have waited.'

'Perhaps we can order another pot of tea when she comes,' said John. 'I rather wanted you all to myself for a bit.'

'Darling…' She handed him a cup and saucer. 'Now tell me all about her.'

John spent the next ten minutes waxing lyrical about Dinah. He told his mother he'd been seeing her for some time, that she was the love of his life and that she positively shone on the stage. He explained how she lit up a room when she walked in and was not only talented but also clever and lovely to look at.

'I can see that you are very much in love with her,' his mother said at last. 'I'm glad to see you looking so happy, John dear.'

'Which brings me on to something else,' said John. 'I can't think why on earth you never told me but I've found out that I'm adopted.'

'Oh good.'

He was taken aback. That was the one reaction he never expected. '*Good?* Is that all you can say, Mother? How could you keep such a big thing a secret? Don't you think I have a right to know?'

'I always wanted you to know,' she said. 'But your father wouldn't allow it. I'm so sorry it's taken all this time. Do you mind awfully?'

'It takes a bit of getting used to,' he said. 'It never once occurred to me. I was very angry at first. It felt like a betrayal.'

'I loved you from the moment they put you in my arms,' she said gravely.

They talked in hushed tones about what had happened until finally John said, 'I don't care much about Father. He and I have never got on, but I want you to know that you'll always be my mother.'

'Thank you, John dear,' she said brightly. 'You've just given me the best moment of my whole life ... and my freedom.'

He frowned again. 'I don't understand.'

'There's still a lot you don't know, John,' she said. 'Perhaps you're the one who is going to have a shock.'

'Go on,' he said cautiously.

'Your father is a vain man,' she said. 'We found out soon after we married that he couldn't have children. It was a bitter blow for him. At the time, I was a little relieved. I'm sure now that he only married me for my father's money.'

John went to say something but she lifted her hand to stop him. 'Let me tell you everything, dear. I'm all right about it. It really doesn't hurt any more.'

He smiled and took the second scone she offered.

'When you came up for adoption, he did something incredibly stupid. He went to another district to get your birth registered and falsified the documents. He had you registered as our child. I was so besotted by my beautiful little baby boy, the seriousness of the matter didn't really register.'

John shook his head in disbelief. 'Isn't that a criminal offence?'

She nodded. 'When I found out what he'd done, I wanted to put it right, but he told me they would take you from me and that I would go to prison as an accessory. By that time, I loved you so much, it was a risk I couldn't bear to take.'

'I always knew you weren't a happy woman,' said John slowly, 'but you stuck it out all this time because of me?'

'Oh, don't be sad, dear,' she protested. 'It's fine.

From that moment Norris and I lived very separate lives and to have you as my son was more than worth it. You brightened every dark day and made me so proud of you. I would do it all over again, and gladly.'

John felt his throat constrict.

'I'm sorry that you've been hurt,' she went on, 'but there wasn't a moment in your whole life when you weren't truly loved.'

He felt so emotional he could hardly speak and he could barely believe the level of self-sacrifice meted out on his behalf.

'Let's talk of happier things,' she said changing the subject. 'Tell me what you've found out about your mother.'

'I haven't met her yet,' he said, 'but I have found my half sister.'

'How wonderful,' she cried. 'It wasn't right that you were an only child. Tell me about her.'

'She's training to be a nursery nurse,' he said. 'I am to be godfather to her child.'

'So you're an uncle too.' She gave him a quizzical look. 'You're keeping something back. I want you to tell me everything. The time for keeping secrets is over between us.'

It was relief to tell her about Bonnie and Shirley and the incident in the London flat. 'We weren't sure why, but Father threatened her and her daughter. Now that you've told me what he did, it's obvious to me why he wants the letter my grandfather wrote to Grace Follett. I've seen it and it clearly states that my grandfather acknowledges me as part of his family.'

'Bring it all out into the open,' his mother said.

'But what about you? I don't want you to be in trouble with the law.'

'I wasn't the one to falsify the record,' she said. 'I can always plead ignorance and with a good lawyer, I can stand up for myself. That man doesn't scare me any more.'

'I've never heard you sound so confident before,' he remarked.

She smiled mysteriously. 'There are going to be a lot of changes around here. I've had your father trailed and I have plenty of grounds for a divorce.'

John reached for his wallet. It was very flat but hopefully he would find a few quid in there to help her out.

'No, no,' she cried. 'I don't need any money, really I don't.' She looked at him with an expression he'd never seen before. 'Your father would be furious, but I've made myself a very wealthy woman.' She lifted the pile of glossy magazines from the chair and handed them to him. 'Look at the middle page on that one, and page nine in that one.'

He turned to the middle page and found himself looking at a sweet little house. On page nine there was a two up two down cottage which had been completely transformed and modernised. The before and after pictures were stunning.

'I don't understand,' he said.

'I've gone into property,' said his mother. She giggled like a naughty schoolgirl. 'Your father will be livid.'

John's jaw dropped. 'I don't understand. It's difficult enough for women to get bank accounts without their husbands knowing.'

'Not if you're called "Finley's Holdings Co",' she smiled. 'That sounds very masculine.'

'Mother...' John grinned.

'A year ago, the magazine sent a photographer round,' she went on. 'He's very good, isn't he?' She pushed some more magazines under his nose and he glanced at some of the other transformations she'd done. 'I've written a book about it,' she said. 'A sort of "how to" book. They say they'll be all the rage one day. Anyway, I came up to London today to sign a contract from a book publisher and Sebastian says…'

'Sebastian?'

'Oh didn't I tell you?' his mother teased. 'Sebastian took the pictures. I hope you'll like him, dear. He's become rather important to me.'

With that, John threw back his head and laughed. He was still laughing when Dinah came.

Grace was sitting at the table with a cup of tea and a pile of letters when Rita came in from work. It was obvious that her mother had been crying.

'What's happened?'

'Sit down, love,' said Grace. 'It's about Bonnie.'

Rita's heart sank. She lowered herself into a chair, all the while watching her mother's face. What now ... not more bad news.

'Miss Reeves's niece came round,' said Grace. 'Your sister was writing to Miss Reeves and she's found the letters.'

'That's wonderful,' gasped Rita. 'So where is she living?'

'We don't know,' said Grace fighting back the tears again. 'She used a box number.'

'But we can still write to her,' said Rita eagerly. 'She'll keep checking the box, won't she?'

Grace blew her nose. 'I suppose so.'

Rita shook her mother's arm. 'Come on, Mum. Don't give up yet. We'll find her. We'll be a family again one day.'

Grace put on a brave smile. 'There's a letter for you on the mantelpiece.'

Rita tore open the official-looking envelope eagerly. 'It's about the divorce. I have to go to court on Thursday.'

There was a sharp knock at the front door. When Rita opened it, Snowy fell in.

'My God, Grace, have you heard? The police came to the factory today looking for Norris Finley.'

Norris was beside himself with worry. When he'd got back to the flat, the concierge refused to let him in and threatened him with the police. He'd waited outside all day but neither Bonnie nor her wretched kid had turned up. He had to get that letter and destroy it.

He'd sorted everything else from the safe. He should have destroyed it all but in the end, he couldn't bring himself to do it. They were so enjoyable to look at. Shame about little Polly. She was a little peach but he dared not risk taking her to a hotel again. He'd foolishly given her a couple of pieces of his wife's jewellery so he'd created a row and she'd thrown them back into his face. He smiled to himself. Women were so predictable. He had planned to accuse Polly of theft when he grew tired of her and that would have bought her silence.

He was the first to admit he'd gone too far with the Wilcox girl. He'd been as shocked as the next man when she'd taken herself over the bloody cliff. What did she do that for? It was only a bit of fun. He never would have gone to the police about the gold watch. He was only making sure she kept mum.

He would have liked a bit more of Grace Follett but she hadn't come back to the factory after her mother died and besides, he'd picked up with Polly by then. The only thing he'd never found was that locket. Somehow or other, Grace had got it. Well good luck to her. If she did manage to open it up, it would silence her for good. Just touching that stuff was deadly.

He'd told Grace the locket was her daughter's but of course it wasn't. What would a kid like that be doing with a Nazi suicide pill on a chain? No, it belonged to Manny Hart. Manny had dropped it in the factory on the day he'd done for that boy so he'd kept it as insurance in case Manny tried to pin the blame on him for George's death. He never should have got involved with the man but loyalty to the party and the good old days had clouded his vision. They'd never expected someone like George Matthews to work out who Manny was. That's why he had to be silenced. It was pure luck that George had telephoned Norris with the revelation that he'd recognised Manny at the station. Norris had arranged to meet George at the old factory but as soon as he'd put the phone down, he had rung Manny. Manny said he'd deal with it. Norris shuddered. He'd never wanted to be a part of murder, but what could he do?

He looked at his watch again. It was almost seven. The girl wasn't coming back, was she? He jumped as a bobby on the beat tapped his near-side window. Norris wound it down.

'You seem to have been here rather a long time, sir?'

'Yes, officer,' said Norris willing his voice to sound casual. 'I'm beginning to think she's stood me up.'

'Better move along then, sir,' said the police-man touching his helmet. 'Only we've had a report that a gentleman was harassing one of the residents in this block of flats.'

'Poor woman,' Norris sympathised. 'I hope she's all right?'

'She'll be fine,' said the bobby. 'Probably gone home to Mother by now.'

Norris started the car.

Thirty-Seven

When she came out of the front door first thing in the morning, the fog was so dense Rita couldn't see the end of the street. She had been on 7 till 2s for a few days but today she was on earlies. It was 5.15 and everywhere was deserted. Her footsteps sounded muffled as she walked towards the bus depot along the sea front.

Along the High Street, Bob came out of his house and fell into step beside her.

'Nice day,' he smiled.

'Grand.'

Rita was a person of few words first thing in the morning but she and Bob had worked together for long enough for him to be used to her abrupt manner. They walked in what seemed like a companionable silence the rest of the way. She liked being with Bob. He made her feel so ... comfortable.

When they finally arrived at the depot, the few drivers, conductors and conductresses who had turned up were gathered in a huddle by the office door. Joseph Thompson, the area manager, was busy allocating the routes.

'We're still going out then?' said Bob.

'I think you should cancel,' another driver said, shaking his head. 'You can't see a thing out there.'

Joseph shook his head. 'We're supposed to provide a service to the public no matter what the weather,' he said gravely. There was some mumbling but they all knew he was right.

Rita and Bob were put onto the Horsham run. 'Take it steady,' Joseph cautioned. 'If you're late, you're late, but for God's sake get there in one piece.'

The fog hung around for most of the morning. Rita and Bob did the first run to Horsham with few passengers and managed to arrive more or less on time. It wasn't until the mid-morning return that it began to lift in places, but if the fog was easing off elsewhere, it was much worse inland. By the time they reached the outskirts of Findon, Bob had to slow the bus down to less than twenty miles an hour, even less as they headed towards the village. On this run they had quite a few passengers and everyone was good-natured even though the bus was already fifteen minutes late.

Visibility was down to three to four yards and as they turned into the high street a wall loomed out of the fog. Bob slammed on the brakes. Fortunately, all the passengers were seated but Rita was propelled at breakneck speed down the aisle.

'Are you all right, dear?' Her concerned passenger was a middle-aged woman in a thick Harris Tweed coat buttoned right up to her neck. She and her companions had been swapping horror stories about London pea soupers.

'I'm fine thanks.' Rita straightened herself up and tugged at her jacket to put it back in place. She had been tipped sideways, but fortunately the moneybag had stayed upright, which was a relief. The thought of scrabbling around on the floor for loose change wasn't very appealing. She made her way back to the back of the bus and got off.

'Everybody OK?' Bob asked as she stood outside his cab.

'Yes. You all right?'

He was busy rubbing his right hand. 'Bashed my finger on the wheel.' Bob looked around. 'I'm all over the road. Can you see me back?'

'Are we still going on?'

'I think we have to,' said Bob. 'It's further to go back than on. Just help me get straightened up.'

Rita made her way back to the platform and told the passengers what was happening. Leaning out on the pole so that Bob could see her in the mirror, she waved him on calling, 'Wowah!' when he'd finally reached the right side of the road. Bob straightened the steering wheel and they set off again.

As he pressed his foot on the accelerator to go through the village, a car careered out of the fog on the wrong side of the road. Bob swerved but, being a little uncertain of the contours of the road, his nearside wheel hit a low wall and the bus came to another abrupt halt. He heard several passengers cry out in panic and the middle-aged woman leapt up and banged long and loudly on the window of his cab.

Bob tut-tutted. Passengers were not supposed to distract the driver. Irritated, he glanced in his mirror and gasped with horror. Rita lay sprawled across the pavement, her head against a red pillarbox.

By the time Bob had leapt down from his cab and got to her, several passengers were already leaning over Rita.

'Excuse me,' said Bob pushing them out of the way. 'You all right, Rita?'

'She looks as if she's fainted,' one passenger observed.

Bob said anxiously, 'Somebody get an ambulance, will you?'

Rita could hear Bob's voice close to her ear as

she struggled to make sense of her surroundings. The back of her head was throbbing and she had a thumping headache.

'It's OK, Rita,' Bob was saying. 'Keep still. We're getting some help.'

Rita opened her eyes. Where was she? She wasn't in the bus. She was outside, on the pavement with everyone from the bus crowding around. What had happened? Panic rose in her chest. Bob was leaning over her with an anxious frown. She could feel him stroking her hair with the tips of his fingers and she relaxed.

'Are you all right, dear?' It was a woman's voice. Rita looked above Bob's head and the middle-aged passenger in the Harris Tweed coat leaned over him. 'That was a nasty knock you had.'

Rita tried to get up.

'Don't move!' Bob yelled, then seeing her eyes widen he added in a softer voice, 'You'd better stay where you are, Rita. You don't know what damage you've done.'

She shivered. Bob pulled off his jacket and put it over her.

'Well, it can't be doing her any good lying about on the wet pavement,' the Harris Tweed woman remarked. 'She'll catch her death.'

'I'm all right,' said Rita struggling into a sitting position. As well as a headache, her shoulder hurt too.

'Bring the young lady inside,' called a man's voice somewhere in the distance.

'That's Wilf Barber,' the Harris Tweed woman said. 'He runs the Black Horse.'

'I'll get you a drop of brandy.' Wilf Barber was closer now. 'Brandy's very good for a bit of a shock.'

'We've all had a bit of a shock,' said the Harris Tweed woman, 'if you're offering.'

'You're welcome to come in,' said the landlord.

The Harris Tweed woman smiled. 'Here,' she said to Rita, 'let me help you up, dear.'

'Don't worry,' said Bob. 'I'll take her.'

'No,' Rita protested feebly, but before she could stop him, he had swept her up into his arms and was carrying her towards the Black Horse.

'I've picked up all the money,' someone else said. 'I'll bring it in for you.'

The small party of passengers followed hard on Bob's heels.

Rita's head was banging like a drum and she felt a bit sick. Her heart was pounding but she couldn't make up her mind if it was as a result of her fall or the fact that she was in Bob's arms. She looked up at his face and felt her heart strangely warm.

Once inside, he laid her gently on one of the horsehair benches in the snug while the rest of the party headed for the bar.

'It's OK,' said Bob curtly to one of the passengers. 'I'll see to her now.'

'Thanks for picking up the money,' Rita whispered.

The swing door closed and they were alone. Bob took his coat and rolled it into a pillow. Lifting her head, he pushed it gently underneath.

'God, Rita, I had such a fright when I saw you on the pavement like that.'

Their eyes locked for what seemed like an eternity. Rita's heart was racing but as hard as she tried, she couldn't tear her eyes away.

'Rita,' he whispered. He bowed his head towards her. 'Oh Rite … I couldn't bear it if something happened to you.'

His first kiss was as light as a feather on her lips. Closing her eyes in a moment of pure ecstasy she told herself she was helpless to stop him but that wasn't true. She could have stopped him if she'd wanted to…

When she opened her eyes again he was still looking at her. She made no protest, no attempt to stop him, so he bowed his head once more. His kisses were full of passion and she responded. She felt like a giddy schoolgirl. She had never been kissed like this before, certainly not by Emilio. Her blood pounded in her head and her heart felt as if it would burst out of her chest. Then the judge's face swam before her eyes and Rita pushed Bob in the chest, turning her head away. 'No, Bob, no.'

He looked down at her with a look of mild surprise.

'You ... we mustn't,' she said helplessly. 'I'm still married to Emilio.'

'But I thought you said you were getting a divorce,' said Bob.

'Who told you that?' she snapped angrily. He looked away. 'It was my mother, wasn't it?'

'Sorry, Rita,' said Bob. 'It was just that when you moved back home, I thought…'

Her expression softened. 'When I'm free...' she promised.

'Oh, Rita...' he said huskily.

They heard a movement by the door and the landlord burst in with two glasses of brandy. 'Here you are, son.'

Bob stood up quickly. 'Thanks.'

'What happens now?' said Wilf. 'I mean, you can't carry on with an injured conductress.'

Bob shook himself into action. 'I'd better ring the depot. They'll send a relief bus and an inspector.'

'The coppers will be here soon,' said Wilf. 'The wife phoned up as soon as the crash happened.'

'Did you see what happened?' asked Rita.

'Some lunatic came out of the fog on the wrong side of the road,' said Bob.

'Where is he now?'

'Gone,' said Wilf, with a shrug.

'I didn't stand a chance. He was driving like a bat out of hell.'

Rita pulled herself onto her elbow and sipped some brandy. She probably shouldn't be drinking it, not with a head injury, but it was warming.

'I'd better not have a drink,' said Bob apologetically. 'It's really decent of you to offer but if my governor thinks I've been boozing on the job...'

'Never even thought of that,' said Wilf. 'Anyway, the wife is making some tea.'

No sooner had he said it than a grey-haired woman with a blanket over her shoulder came into the room carrying a tea tray. Putting the tray onto a table, she arranged the blanket over Rita. 'Now you just stay there nice and quiet until the ambulance comes.'

The Harris Tweed passenger put her head around the snug door. Her cheeks were flushed and she held a sherry glass in her hand. 'The poleesh are here,' she slurred as she left again.

'That lot must be costing you a fortune,' said Bob.

Wilf chuckled and jerked his head. 'She hasn't looked at the clock. It's already opening time and she's paying.' He turned to go. 'You'd better come with me and tell the coppers what happened.'

Bob glanced down at Rita. 'I'd rather stay here with my colleague.' He reached for her hand but Rita slid it under the blanket. She didn't dare be alone with him again.

'You go,' she said. 'I'm fine.'

He hesitated, still staring down at her. Rita closed her eyes, pretending to be sleepy. She opened them again only when she was sure he was leaving the room. Gazing longingly at his receding back, Rita sighed. Oh Bob, she thought. What a fool I've been. I never knew... I never knew.

Norris went straight to Central Station. As soon as Manny had a moment, they went into the broom cupboard together.

'If that letter falls into the wrong hands,' Norris grumbled, 'the police will be all over me like a rash. I'll be ruined.'

Manny grabbed Norris's lapels and pushed him against the wall. 'You'd better keep your mouth shut about me,' he threatened. 'If you blab about anything we've done, I'll make damned sure you hang with me.'

Thirty-Eight

Having a car in the street caused quite a stir. Grace knew something was happening when she heard the kids shouting 'Hurrah', as they ran alongside it. She glanced out of the window and was surprised to see it pull up outside her own house. A posh-looking lady climbed out of the passenger seat and headed towards the little gate. Grace wiped her hands on her apron and whipped it off. Stuffing it behind the breadbin, she looked frantically around her kitchen. It was clean and tidy but she would have made more of an effort had she known someone was coming. Who was she anyway? She seemed vaguely familiar and yet she couldn't place the face.

There was a gentle knock at the door. Grace opened it and her jaw dropped. Mrs Finley was the very last person she would have expected to come to her house, but politeness allowed Grace to step back and let her in without a word.

'Mrs Finley,' said Grace.

'Mrs Rogers,' said Mrs Finley.

'Has something awful happened?' said Grace, her thoughts immediately going to John.

'No, no, please don't concern yourself on that score, Mrs Rogers.'

There was an awkward silence then Grace said, 'Please, do sit down. What can I do for you?'

They sat opposite each other at the kitchen

table. Mrs Finley took off her gloves. 'I'm afraid this is not going to be an easy occasion for either of us, Mrs Rogers,' she said with a sigh, 'but you have been done a grave wrong and I must put it right.'

Grace looked startled. As Mrs Finley began to adjust her jacket, Grace remembered her manners. 'I'm sorry,' she said. 'Here, let me take your coat. Can I offer you some tea?'

'That would be lovely, Mrs Rogers. I have just driven down from London and I'm feeling quite parched.'

'I have some cake,' said Grace. 'Or some biscuits, although I'm afraid they're only broken ones.'

'Tea would be fine, thank you.'

Grace made the tea with a trembling hand. She'd never actually come face to face with Mrs Finley before. Twenty-five years ago, when the deed was done, it had been behind closed doors. The only glimpse she'd had of her son's new mother had been from the window of the home when he had been handed to Mrs Finley sitting on the back seat of a car. The two women had both locked eyes for a split second and then John was gone from her life.

It was only when she'd placed the cup and saucer in front of Mrs Finley that she began to talk.

'Mrs Rogers, all those years ago, did you ever actually sign an adoption paper?'

Grace shook her head. 'Please call me Grace.'

'Grace,' smiled Mrs Finley. 'My husband is very anxious to get hold of a certain letter Mr

Edward Finley wrote to you. I believe your daughter took it with her when she left home.'

Grace gasped. 'How did you know that?'

'I have been in contact with Bonnie.'

Grace clutched at her throat. 'You have? How is she? Is she well? Where did you find her?'

Mrs Finley held her hand up. 'One at a time, Grace. By the time I leave this house I promise you will know everything there is to know.'

With supreme effort Grace calmed herself and waited.

'My son is engaged to Dinah Chamberlain. As soon as your daughter realised who he was, she put two and two together and realised that he was her half brother. What she didn't know was that my husband falsified John's birth certificate. He had him registered as our natural-born son.'

'Can you do that?'

'It's a criminal offence,' said Mrs Finley, 'but nonetheless, my husband did it.' She sipped some tea. 'He's been trying to keep it under wraps ever since.'

Grace touched her lips with the tips of her fingers anxiously. Her mind was struggling to put all the pieces together.

'The wrongdoing was done on the part of my husband,' said Mrs Finley. 'Please don't concern yourself that you will be in any kind of trouble. He persuaded me that I was as involved as he was, and so all these years I have kept my silence.' She touched Grace's hand. 'My dear, I am sorry.'

Grace avoided her gaze. This was a lot to take in.

'It gets worse,' said Mrs Finley. 'Sebastian and

I have been going through my husband's papers because I want to get a divorce. We have discovered that Norris and I never formally adopted John because you had been left some money. It was only payable to you while you had the boy. Unfortunately for him, Norris has been unable to cream it off because it was tied up in such a way that the payments had to be put into an account with your name. Norris was executor of his father's will but he's never passed it on to you, has he?'

Slightly bemused, Grace shook her head.

'I thought not,' Mrs Finley continued. 'It appears that my husband was content to let it accumulate, because when John is twenty-five, any residue would pass to the Finley estate.'

'I don't want any money,' said Grace stoutly.

'What you do with the money is up to you, my dear,' said Mrs Finley. 'But the law says it's rightfully yours and it should have been given to you to help with the upkeep of your child.'

Grace offered her another cup of tea and poured it. Her mind was in a whirl. She could have kept her baby. All these years without him and it was his grandfather's wish that she should keep him.

'Now I will get to the crux of the other matter,' said Mrs Finley. 'Your daughter and John have become great friends. You may be shocked to know that Bonnie has a child, but Shirley is a delightful little thing who is coming up for two and a half now.'

Grace stared at her in shocked surprise, her hand over her mouth and her eyes glistening with tears. 'George Matthews?'

'Yes, dear,' said Mrs Finley. 'John and Dinah are to be her godparents which is so touching, don't you think?'

Grace swallowed hard. 'Was that why Bonnie went away?'

'She and George were planning a new life,' said Mrs Finley. 'When he didn't show up, Bonnie thought she had been deserted, but it appears that George met with an accident.'

'Now I have a shock for you, Mrs Finley,' said Grace quietly. 'I am convinced that George was murdered and I'm rather afraid that Mr Finley may be involved. I happen to know that right now the police are looking for him.'

There was a small silence then Mrs Finley smiled. 'Oh good.' Grace was speechless with surprise. After a second or two she took a deep breath. 'If this is the time for being honest,' she began, 'then I have something to tell you. I'm not proud of what I did, but believe me when I say I felt I had no choice.'

Mrs Finley raised a hand. 'You don't need to tell me, my dear,' she said. 'I can guess. Norris had half the women of Worthing sleeping in his bed. Frankly, so long as he stayed away from my bed, I didn't care what he did. He can only get them by coercion or blackmail, and I know from bitter experience he's very clever at that.'

Grace looked her full in the face. 'You must have suffered a great deal.'

'You too, my dear.'

'Part of me wants to make him pay for what he has done,' Grace said quietly.

'And you will, my dear. John's forged birth certificate will be a good place for the police to start and once they have my husband under the spotlight, I am sure everything else will be revealed. It only takes the removal of one to make the whole pack of cards fall.'

'You want me to expose your husband?' Grace said cautiously.

Mrs Finley smiled.

Grace couldn't resist a small smile too. 'Can I ... is it possible for me...'

'To meet John?' Mrs Finley finished the sentence for her.

Grace gave a breathy, 'Yes.'

There was another knock at the door. Grace was halfway out of her chair as Mrs Finley pulled on her gloves and said, 'That'll be Sebastian. I expect he's wondering how much longer I'll be.'

But when Grace opened the door, it wasn't Sebastian. It was Bob all out of breath from running.

'Mrs Rogers,' he blurted out. 'There's been an accident. Rita's all right but she's been taken to hospital.'

The doctor in casualty insisted that Rita stay overnight on the ward.

'You can't be too careful with a head wound,' he said as the nurse wheeled her to the ward.

If she was honest, Rita was a little bit relieved. She had a thumping headache and when the police came to take a statement, she was glad that the ward sister shooed them away. They gave her some pills and she'd slept until late afternoon.

When she got up to go to the toilet, she felt a bit stiff but apart from a bruise on the back of her head and a graze on her arm, she was none the worse for wear.

Visiting time was six to seven. As the nurse opened the swing doors to let them in, Rita settled down and closed her eyes. She wasn't badly hurt and she would be out tomorrow, so when the nurse said her mother had rung up, she'd told her to tell Grace not to come in. There would be no visitors by her bedside tonight.

She kept thinking about Bob. How could she have been so blind? She thought back to all the times he'd been there and she'd never really noticed him. Not once. Her heart fluttered whenever she thought about him now, and every time she closed her eyes, she dreamed of that kiss.

Someone touched her arm. She opened her eyes and Bob was looking down at her. Her heart lurched at the sight of him. How come she had never noticed how handsome he was before?

She pulled herself to a sitting position. 'I wasn't expecting you to come.'

'You try and keep me away,' he said taking her hand. He put an orange onto the bedside locker.

Rita smiled. Her heart was thumping now.

Bob pulled up a chair. She didn't mention that kiss, but she found herself unable to meet his eye as she thought of it. It never should have happened.

'I thought I'd killed you, Rite,' he said. 'I couldn't bear it if something happened to you. They sent me home for the rest of the day.'

'It wasn't your fault,' said Rita. 'And don't

worry. I'm fine.'

The swing door to the ward opened and her mother came in. Bob stood up and offered Grace his seat. Grace embraced her daughter and looked at her anxiously.

'I'm fine, Mum,' said Rita. 'They just wanted to keep an eye on me that's all.'

'I'll go,' said Bob.

'No, no,' said Grace. 'Don't go on my account.'

Bob went to fetch another chair from the stack at the end of the ward.

'He looks nice,' said Grace, when he was out of earshot.

'I've been an absolute idiot, Mum,' said Rita.

'You could say that,' Grace grinned. 'It took you a long time to see what everyone else has known for ages.'

'I love him,' said Rita. 'I know it's too quick, but I've never felt like this about anyone.'

Grace laughed softly. 'After what you've been through, I'm glad. You enjoy it.'

Bob came back and they told her what had happened on the bus. Eventually she asked, 'Does anyone know who was in the car?'

'One of the passengers said it was Norris Finley,' said Bob. 'Whoever it was, the police are going to get him for dangerous driving.'

Grace suppressed a smile. Oh dear, she thought. You are in trouble, Norris.

'What time will you be out tomorrow?' Grace asked.

'The doctor comes around at about ten,' said Rita. 'I should be out by lunchtime.'

'I'll borrow a car and come and collect you,'

Bob announced.

When the visiting times were over, a nurse came in with a school bell and walked down the ward clanging it loudly.

Grace stood and kissed Rita goodnight while Bob took the chairs back. 'Get well soon,' said Grace and then she left them to it.

Bob leaned over the bed and took her into his arms. As she felt Bob's strong body through her thin hospital nightie, Rita could feel her own body surging with desire. Was this what it felt like? Was this really love? Resting her head on his chest, she willed her pounding heart to slow down and savour the moment.

'Now that I've got you,' he told her, as he kissed the top of her head, 'I'll never ever let you go.'

Norris Finley had had a terrible day. He'd driven back from London like a maniac, narrowly missing a collision with a double-decker bus at Findon, and arrived back at his house to find Major Freeman on the doorstep. He'd forgotten that he'd arranged to come to the house for his answer. Norris' heart sank. He still hadn't got that bloody letter and without that, there was a very real danger that something might come out of the woodwork. He'd have to bluff his way through this.

'Come in, come in,' he'd said congenially. 'I've no idea where the wife is, but I'm sure you could do with a drink.'

'If you're offering another glass of that malt whisky,' said the major, 'I wouldn't say no.'

I bet you wouldn't, Norris thought darkly. They

went to the den and Norris was surprised to find his drawers open and some papers scattered across the desk. Somebody had been riffling about in here. He could feel himself getting angry but he didn't want to create a scene while the major was around.

'I apologise for the mess,' he said gruffly. 'I had to go up to London in a bit of a rush and I forgot to tidy up. I don't allow the wife or the maid in here.'

The major threw himself onto the chesterfield sofa. 'Lovely bit of leatherwork this.'

'I've just got it recovered,' said Norris. 'Archie Warren. He's got a place near Worthing Central. Capital man.'

The major was in no mood for chitchat. He got straight to the point. 'The Lodge meets tomorrow. Do you want me to put your name forward?'

'Absolutely,' said Norris. He hadn't meant to sound keen. It looked a bit bigheaded but he'd have to take a chance. Everything else had been taken care of. His tenants all had proper rent books now and the factory was whistle-clean.

'Good, good.' The major downed his drink in one. 'I hope you'll share some of your overseas contacts with us when you've been voted in. We all help one another in the Lodge.'

So that was it. At last Norris understood why the major was so keen to have him join. He and his cronies had obviously found out that his factory was exporting to Canada and the States and wanted a piece of the pie.

The doorbell rang.

'Must dash,' said the major. 'Got a dinner at

the golf club tonight.'

He followed Norris to the door. The maid must be out. She didn't answer it anyway. When he opened the door Norris nearly died. Two policemen, one in uniform, stood on the doorstep.

'May we come in, sir? We need to talk to you.'

Norris glanced at the major who had gone a strange colour. 'It's not convenient right now,' he said stiffly as the major pushed past him onto the driveway.

'We could do it here, or down at the station,' said the plain-clothed policeman.

'Not now!' Norris snapped.

'In that case,' the policeman began again. 'I am arresting you for questioning as accessory to the murder of George Matthews on November 12th 1947 or thereabouts.'

Norris gasped in horror. The major was climbing into his car. 'Shan't be calling again, Finley,' he snapped. 'Our business is at an end.'

Thirty-Nine

When Grace got back from the hospital, there was a soft knock on her door. A young couple stood on the step. The woman smiled. 'Hello, we meet again, Mrs Rogers.' It was Dinah Chamberlain.

'Come in, come in,' smiled Grace. 'How nice to see you again. I'll get the kettle on.'

They came in sheepishly and the young man

with her looked around.

'Sit down,' smiled Grace as she busied herself with filling the kettle. 'Make yourself at home.'

'Mrs Rogers,' said Dinah. Grace kept her back to them. She knew what was coming and yet she was totally unprepared. She was supposed to be going to the hospital to fetch Rita in the morning. She took a deep breath and made her hands into fists as she fought to keep control of her feelings.

'Mrs Rogers,' said Dinah again. 'This is John.'

Grace didn't move. Her heart was pounding. She wanted to look at him but she couldn't. She never should have let him go but at the time she was a young girl and she didn't know what to do. She should have fought for him. She should have taken him and run, and now he was all grown up and it was too late. She felt a gentle touch on her shoulder. She turned around and looked directly into his face. He was so good looking, so like his father. He had his nose and his strong jaw. Her tears blinded her and she blinked them away.

She gulped back a sob. 'You're so handsome,' she said. 'I can't believe it's you.'

'Don't cry,' he said softly. 'It's all right.'

Grace was aware that Dinah had taken over the making of the tea. She continued to look at John. 'I should have fought harder... I wanted to do what was best... Norris told me you wouldn't want for anything.'

'Shh, shh,' he said.

They sat at the table. She couldn't take her eyes from him. Her boy. Her baby, all grown up. Dinah pushed some tea in front of her but John had hold of both her hands and was looking at her. 'Bonnie has told me so much about you,' he said. 'I've got a lot of catching up to do.'

'I wouldn't want to hurt your mother,' Grace said. She let go of his hands to search for a hankie.

'You won't,' he said.

'She came here yesterday,' said Grace. 'She was wonderful.'

'My mother is an amazing woman and full of surprises.'

Dinah kissed the top of John's head. 'I'm going to leave you two to get acquainted, darling,' she said. 'I'll be back in an hour.'

Norris had woken up with a headache. His solicitor had told him to keep quiet but once the police confronted him with what Manny had been telling them, he had to make sure they had his side of the story.

'The kid recognised Manny from a photograph he'd been given at one of the camps,' he told them. 'Manny worked with Mengele.'

DS Nyman looked Norris straight in the eye. 'How come you got involved with this man?'

'Manny and I met before the war,' said Norris. 'Then after the fall of Germany they asked us to help some of the German high command to escape. We used the cold room as a hiding place until we could move them on.'

'Tell us what happened that day,' said Nyman.

'George rang me,' said Norris. 'He said he'd seen an ex-Nazi at the station and he didn't know what to do.'

'How did he know the man was a Nazi?'

'George liberated some concentration camp and one of the inmates gave him an old photograph.'

'The photograph in his case,' Nyman mused. 'Why did he tell you and not the police?'

'Because I was his boss, I suppose.'

'Go on.'

Norris put his hand on his forehead. 'As soon as he told me, I rang the station and spoke to Manny. I told him I'd arranged for George to meet me at the old factory. Manny said to keep him there. He told me there was some whisky in the first aid cupboard. He told me to give some to George, get him drunk if I could, but not to have any myself.'

'And you gave it to him.'

'I never knew what was in it,' cried Norris. 'It wasn't until Manny got there that he told me he'd laced it with cyanide.'

'So between the two of you, you got him in the cold room and locked up.'

'Yes,' said Norris.

DS Nyman leaned back in his chair. 'Funny thing is,' he began, 'Mr Hart tells me it was you who laced the whisky.'

'That's not true,' Norris wailed.

'He says he only came to the old factory to beg George not to expose him.'

'He's lying.'

Nyman went over everything again and again but Norris never once changed his story.

'You've lost everything, you know,' Nyman said eventually. 'We've just had a message from your wife. She wanted you to know she's made a statement and she's suing you for a divorce.'

Norris Finley's jaw dropped. 'Bitch. She can't do that.'

'She just has, sunshine. And it seems like she and her friend Grace Rogers can't tell us enough about what you've been up to.' He began counting them out on his fingers. 'There's the question of an assault the Christmas before last, a young girl who committed suicide, and something to do with falsifying official documents. More recently, there's a case of driving without due care and attention and leaving the scene of an accident. Oh, and then there's a question mark over Des Peterson's conviction for wife battery.' He chuckled. 'My, my, who knows what else they'll find under that particular stone?'

Norris was white. 'There's another one,' he said as Nyman called for him to be sent to his cell.

'Another what?'

'Cyanide pill. He dropped it.'

Nyman stared at him. 'Who dropped it, and where?'

Norris smiled maliciously and tapped the side of his nose. 'That's for me to know and for you to find out.'

After another hour of questioning, DS Nyman, himself exhausted, let him go back to the cells. 'Do you think he's telling the truth?' he asked his colleague as they both headed for home that night.

'Nah,' said the man. 'He's just trying to get his own back, that's all.'

'I think I might mention it to Manny in the morning,' said Nyman. 'If there's a cyanide pill running around, he'd be more likely to know where it is.'

And now that it was morning, Norris sat up and rubbed the stubble on his chin. He supposed he'd better tell them about the pill. He didn't want another death on his conscience.

The cover over the cell door window slid back noisily and a face peered at him. Norris heard the bolts sliding back and a couple of seconds later a policeman brought in some breakfast. A couple of fried eggs, hard looking, and a rasher of bacon. He slopped an enamel mug of tea onto the table in the corner.

'Tidy yourself up, Finley,' he growled. 'They'll be taking you to the magistrates' court in an hour.'

'But I'm innocent,' Norris cried helplessly.

'Save it for the judge,' said the copper. 'Whatever happened in that storeroom, you'll hang along with Hart.'

He went out, slamming the door behind him. Norris stared at the wood for a second or two, then he leapt up and letting out a tremendous roar he kicked it. This was all because of that bloody Grace Follett's daughter.

'I'll get you for this, bitch,' he yelled.

He sat back down on the bed and put his head in his hands. Presently he sat back up with a smile. Ah yes, there was still one way he could exact his revenge.

Forty

Grace thought she had never seen anything more beautiful as the train came into view. She'd told Archie what was happening on her way past the shop. He was washing the windows.

'I'm really, really pleased for you, Gracie,' he'd smiled. 'You've waited a long time. Enjoy your day.'

Rita squeezed her mother's hand tightly. She had come out of hospital the day before and after a day of complete rest at home, she was fully recovered from her ordeal. Bob was back at work, but Rita had been given the rest of the week off.

Grace had hardly slept a wink last night. Her daughter and her granddaughter were coming home. There was a new ticket collector at the barrier, Harry Dawson, Elsie's husband and the father of Mo and Bob. Grace had put in a good word for him when Manny was arrested. He smiled and clipped their platform tickets. 'Good luck, darlin',' he said.

Grace scanned the carriages for her first sight of them. The train juddered to a halt and she heard the engine letting off steam. People began to open the doors and climb out: a man in a grey suit, a woman with a shopping basket, somebody in painting overalls. Where were they? Grace turned around frantically.

At the far end of the platform she saw a man

getting out of the first-class carriage. She recognised John at once. He held his hand out and a woman took it. She climbed onto the platform and they both reached back into the carriage. When John closed the door, Grace could see that the woman was Bonnie. She was holding a little girl with golden curls.

'Bonnie!' Almost three years after her last cry, Grace shouted at the top of her voice and began running. Her comb fell out of her hair and it tumbled untidily around her shoulders but she didn't care what she looked like. Her daughter, her beloved Bonnie was home at last. Bonnie put the child down and, keeping hold of the little girl's hand, they began to run too. Within ten yards of each other, they both stopped and looked at each other. Confused, Shirley looked up at her mother.

'Is this my granny?' She was such a little sweetie Grace fell in love with her immediately.

'Yes, darling,' said Bonnie, never once taking her eyes from her mother. 'Oh Mum, I'm so glad to be back.'

Then Grace opened her arms wide and her two daughters and her grandchild came to them, then John put his all-encompassing arms around them all.

There was so much laughter in the house, Grace could hardly believe it. They had caught up with just about everything. Bonnie's plans with George for South Africa, Norris's arrest, Manny Hart turning out to be a German and an escaped Nazi to boot, Rita and her forthcoming divorce,

John and Archie Warren. By lunchtime, they'd all talked until their jaws ached and the teapot ran dry.

Shirley loved all the attention she was getting as she moved from lap to lap. The old Christmas toys were a bit tired but she found plenty in the box to keep her amused. Grace handed Bonnie the locket. 'You dropped it the day you went to the factory,' she reminded her when she saw Bonnie's puzzled expression.

Bonnie shook her head. 'That's not mine,' she said. 'The one George gave me had a horseshoe shape.'

'Then who does this belong to?' asked Grace.

Bonnie shrugged. Shirley took it from her and began to chew the heart shape.

Rita gave her mother a hug. 'One thing I don't understand, Mum,' she said quietly in her mother's ear. 'I'm not judging you but how could you bring yourself to go with Norris Finley?'

'I already told you,' said Grace, wishing she could put this shameful thing behind her once and for all.

'No,' said Rita. 'I meant the first time, when you had John.'

Grace frowned for a second and then began to laugh. 'No, no, you've got it all wrong,' she said. 'I was in love with Max Finley.'

'Max?' cried Bonnie.

'Norris isn't John's real father,' said Grace. 'His brother, Max, was killed in a car crash before we could get married.' She turned and smiled at Bonnie. 'So you see, darling, history repeats itself.'

'So Norris adopted his brother's child?' said Rita.

Grace nodded and smiled wistfully. 'Only he pretended John was his own flesh and blood.'

'Did you love Max very much, Mum?'

John had gone to the other side of the room. Grace nodded and, making sure John was out of earshot, whispered, 'I certainly did, but I think I loved your father more.'

They could hear someone outside calling her name. 'Grace, Gracie...'

'Ahhh,' Rita teased. 'It's Archie.' She opened the door and they saw Archie running up the road. 'Get the locket,' he was shouting breathlessly. 'Get the locket.'

'What locket?' said Bonnie.

'He must mean the one you gave Shirley.'

Archie arrived at the door with no breath left. He bent over and clasped his knees. 'Oh God, where is it?'

'Where's the fire more like?' Rita joked.

'Where's the locket you took from Norris?'

'It's all right,' said Grace. 'It wasn't Bonnie's after all. Shirley's playing with it.'

'My God, Grace,' shouted Archie. 'They've just rung me from the police station. It's got a bloody cyanide pill inside it!'

Everyone fell over themselves to get hold of Shirley and take the locket away from her. Bewildered she began to cry when her mother snatched her up in her arms. Bonnie pushed her finger into her reluctant child's mouth. 'Open your mouth, darling. Let Mummy see.'

'Where is it?' Grace was shouting.

Rita was on her hands and knees on the floor. 'Here it is.' She held it up but the sight of it gave nobody relief. The heart shape was wide open and there was no sign of the pill.

Forty-One

April 21st 1951 was a glorious day. After all the sadness and loss the family had suffered, the sun was shining and although there was a light breeze, already it felt as if the halcyon days of summer were on the way.

The congregation at St Matthews chatted among themselves as they waited for the bride to appear. At the front of the church, the groom fidgeted nervously. They were lucky that they'd been allowed a church wedding; Rita had been granted a decree absolute because her first marriage had never been consummated and therefore, in the eyes of the church, she had never been married in the first place.

Surprisingly, although she was angry with Emilio for using her to gain social respectability and a home in the UK, Rita bore him no real animosity. She only felt a sadness that he and Jeremy had suffered so much at the hands of society. They had nowhere to go to be together. Rita didn't like what they did but right now, they were both in prison again. They'd been caught by an off-duty policeman in the gents' toilets by the pier. Jeremy had been dismissed from the army, and Salvatore and Liliana had sold the shop and moved away without leaving a forwarding address.

The organist struck up the music and the mother of the bride looked nervously over her shoulder. The sight of her second daughter on the arm of her first-born son brought an immediate tear to her eye. John looked so handsome and Rita was a vision of loveliness in a beautiful dress they'd all clubbed together and bought from Hubbard's.

Grace remembered what a tower of strength John had been to her and to Bonnie that dreadful day when Shirley opened the locket and got the cyanide pill. They discovered later that Norris knew about it but had kept quiet in the hope that some harm might befall Grace or her family. Luckily for them, Manny had come clean to DS Nyman the day Bonnie came home.

'I hung on to it in case I got caught,' Manny told him. 'I thought I'd sooner die by my own hand than the hangman's noose.'

'What happened to it?'

'I dropped it somewhere,' said Manny.

'What did it look like?'

'Heart shaped, on a silver chain,' said Manny. 'Why, have you seen it?'

DS Nyman did some quick thinking. He already knew about the watch Norris had accused Kaye Wilcox of stealing. Could Grace or Bonnie Rogers have been blackmailed in the same way? He had risked a telephone call to Archie, and Archie remembered Grace saying she was looking for Bonnie's locket. It didn't take long to put two and two together and while Nyman got the police cars out, Archie had dropped the phone and run up the street.

They'd got Shirley to hospital in double-quick time and faced an anxious wait until Nyman's officers did a fingertip search in the room and found the pill, intact, where it had rolled under the sideboard. It had come to rest beside a newly created mouse hole. When they pulled it into the light, it had what looked like teeth marks on it. A policeman got on his bicycle and pedalled down to the police box by the station to relay a message to the hospital. When he got back to the cottage, to everyone's relief, the only casualty was a dead mouse just inside the hole.

Now Grace could see Mo Dawson, Bob's sister, followed by Bonnie as matron of honour holding hands with Shirley as a posy girl. They were all dressed in the same pretty pink taffeta bridesmaids' dresses she'd spent hours making. Grace felt her heart swell with joy. What more could a woman want?

A tear dropped off the end of her nose and Archie pushed a handkerchief in her hand. 'Thank you, Mr Warren,' she said softly.

'You're welcome, Mrs Warren,' he smiled.

The congregation rose as one to its feet and the wedding began.

Grace's mind went back to the events of the past year. Norris had been sent to prison and although he would be there for a very long time, he'd avoided the hangman's noose. Manny Hart hadn't been so lucky. Oswald had lived to see his son's murderer pay the ultimate price but Mrs

Matthews hadn't. Oswald was just across the aisle from Grace watching his little granddaughter, the light of his life, as she walked proudly beside her mother.

Before the trial began, Archie had wheeled Michael's chair back to her house and then sat her in it while he got down on one knee to propose. Grace couldn't believe it. She'd argued that she wasn't a good woman, that her reputation was in tatters, but he'd stopped her mouth with kisses.

Using the money old man Finley had left her, they'd bought a house in Findon and married in the autumn. Grace had questioned whether or not she was entitled to it because she had never actually raised John, but in the end she had been persuaded to take it. Bonnie had gone back to finish her NNEB and was now a staff nursery nurse. Mrs Finley, whose company had bought Granny Chamberlain's cottage from Dinah, was still busy buying up property in Worthing and nobody minded having her as a landlord. She asked for fair rents, everybody had a rent book and she modernised all her properties. John and Dinah were well set up for their future as well. They had married last year and Dinah was currently sitting in a position that maximised the chances of everyone seeing her gently rounded stomach. Grace was going to be a grandmother again before the year was out.

As Rita reached Bob at the front of the church, Mrs Dawson turned around and looked at Grace. Both women had been so sure Bob and Rita belonged together, they couldn't resist a mutual grin of triumph.

As they sang the first hymn, Archie whispered, 'Happy?'

Grace nodded vigorously and sang with great gusto.

The bride was making her responses now and as she did so in clear ringing tones, Grace looked up at Archie and mouthed the words they had spoken to each other just a few short months ago: *For better, for worse. For richer, for poorer. In sickness and in health...*

'Remember what you once said to me?' she smiled.

He frowned thoughtfully. 'Was it ... what's for tea?'

'No,' she said shaking his arm playfully. 'You once told me, "Better days will come."'

He nodded. 'I remember.'

'I'm glad that from now on, I'm going to be spending all of them with you,' she smiled.

A recipe from Pam, as featured in this book

Grace's Cut and Come Again Cake recipe

12oz dried fruit
4oz margarine
4oz sugar
¼ pint cold water
Simmer ingredients on the hob for 20 minutes in a saucepan.
Allow to cool, then add 8oz self-raising flour
2 eggs
Bake for 1½ hours at gas mark 2 (300°F/150°C)

Giving up Baby

Back in the late nineties, *Kilroy,* a chat show TV programme hosted by Robert Kilroy-Silk, was very popular. One episode in particular had a profound effect upon me. In it, a woman in her sixties was confessing that as a very young woman she had been forced to give up her newborn baby for adoption. It was a heart-rending story but the audience was completely unsympathetic. Young single mums with their own babies in their arms rounded on her. 'There's no way I would ever give up my baby!'

Today's society has little concept of neither the difficulties nor the pain that the previous generation experienced when it came to having illegitimate children. Our culture has evolved so far that it is no longer a 'shame' to have a child outside of marriage and government allowances mean that single mums can keep, house and feed their offspring. Up until the sixties, women who had illegitimate children were stigmatised in all sorts of ways. It takes two to make a baby but the man was seen as merely a bit of a Jack-the-lad, sowing his wild oats, while the woman was regarded as a slut and a tart. If she was unsupported by her own family, and most were, she had no choice but to go into a mother and baby home. There she was subjected to a constant pressure to give up her baby for adoption. There were no brickbats, it was subtle: 'You do want the very best for your baby, don't you? He'll have a mummy and a daddy to love him. They can give him a good education, a place of social standing, the security of a good home...' When the alternative was a one-room bedsit, no childcare, no job and no social security, it is hardly surprising that mothers gave up their children for adoption.

In the sixties and seventies, I worked in children's homes and nurseries, and saw at first hand how hard it was for a mother to make that life changing decision. In this day and age, great care is taken when placing a child that his or her 'roots' are well documented. Back then, the authorities believed that it was better to sever all knowledge of a child's background and start afresh. I was adopted myself and speaking personally I still haven't a clue about any of my father's personal details.

In my book *Better Days Will Come,* there is a mother who was locked in the cellar when her baby was taken away for adoption. That is a true story, told to me in person by a woman who has already put her experience into the public domain. Once she had dressed her little son in an outfit she had bought from Woolworth's (the last thing she ever did for him), she was taken downstairs into the laundry room where she had to stay until her boy had gone. It was done, they said, for her own good and with a misguided belief that it would stop her making a fuss. Even as she talked about it, forty years after it happened, the pain was still so raw there were tears in her eyes.

Following the 1975 amendment to the Adoption Act, many biological parents and their children have been reunited. But when this woman's son came to find her and she told him what had happened, he simply didn't believe her. He revealed the same level of incredulity as did the young women on *Kilroy*.

Many adoptions were kept within the family or done amongst friends. Apparently, I was the child of an American GI over here for the D-Day landings. My parents were not married and most likely my father died on those beaches in France. The friends of my natural mother adopted me but an added complication was the fact that my father was black. However, like Patsy in my first novel *There's Always Tomorrow,* I was lucky enough to end up in a loving family environment with my biological mother as part of the same community. Unfortunately, I never found out that she was in fact my natural mother until after her death. Nobody talked. Secrets were secrets back then, but with an older and wiser head, I don't condemn my mother for giving me up. She did the best she could and I applaud her selfless love, which let me go.

A short story from Pam Weaver

Just the Ticket

It was wonderful to be able to enjoy a day out together at the shopping centre. By end of the morning, Jim and Rita were weighed down with bags, a new sweater for Jim, a dress for Rita, some lovely cushions and a few new ornaments. It felt like Christmas all over again.

For once they didn't have to worry about what Terry Andrews was up to. Terry was their next-door neighbour, the life and soul of any party, but he was always playing pranks on them. Jim enjoyed a laugh the same as any man but Terry was becoming a real problem.

'Lighten up,' Terry laughed when Jim complained. 'Can't you take a joke?'

No one actually saw Terry throw the bucket of mud over Jim's car but they knew it was him. The galling thing was, when Jim washed it off, a small stone had scratched the bonnet. It was going to cost quite a bit to have it re-sprayed and Jim would have to dip into their holiday money.

'Whoops,' said Terry, giving Jim a hearty slap on the back, 'Sorry about that, mate. I'll buy the next round in the pub to make up for it.'

When their front gate 'walked' off its hinges,

Jim bought a new one. As soon as it was in place, he found the old gate leaning against the hedge.

'Well ... you needed another one, didn't you?' said Terry when Jim challenged him.

'It's not funny!' Jim cried.

'Keep your hair on,' said Terry. 'It was a joke.'

No matter how many times Jim told him the joke was wearing thin, Terry just couldn't stop.

The latest thing was cold calling. For the past few days Jim and Rita had been inundated with people calling with quotes for garages, or a new roof or double-glazing. It got so bad that they were too afraid to leave the house unattended. There was no telling what Terry might do next and Jim was terrified that he might come home to find a cubic metre of manure or a pallet of bricks on the driveway, so one did the shopping while the other stayed at home.

Earlier in the week, they had heard that Terry's brother Malcolm was getting married and Terry was to be the best man. Best of all, the wedding was two hundred miles away. When Saturday came, Jim and Rita heaved a sigh of relief and went for a lazy lunch in Beales, a restaurant in the shopping complex. It was wonderful.

They were just paying the bill when they bumped into Bob Clements, their other next-door neighbour. 'I suppose you heard about Malcolm's wedding?' he said sadly.

'No?' Jim frowned.

'The groom was taken ill,' said Bob. 'He'll be OK but the wedding's postponed.'

Rita went pale. Jim quickly gathered their bags. 'We'd better get back home, love,' he said.

But when they stepped out of the shopping centre their hearts sank.

'Oh no, Jim,' said Rita, tears springing into her eyes. Jim slipped his arm around her waist and gave her a comforting hug.

A traffic warden was standing next to the car, his ticket machine in his hands. He seemed a little unsure and gave Jim a quizzical look.

'Hang on, mate,' said Jim rather belligerently. 'Give an OAP a break, won't you? There's only half a wheel on that double yellow.'

The poker-faced warden leaned back and looked at the back wheel. Then he drew himself up to his full height and began writing the ticket.

Jim frowned. 'What is it with you guys?' he demanded. 'You could see me coming and yet you still write the blinking ticket!'

Rita tugged his sleeve nervously. 'Jim, don't,' she cautioned.

But her husband was unrepentant. 'If I didn't know better,' he began, 'I would say blokes like you enjoy making people miserable.'

'For goodness' sake, Jim,' Rita gasped. 'What are you saying? You'll only get his back up.'

Jim shook his head. 'Have you no compassion?'

'Just doing my job, sir,' said the warden. He gave Jim a long hard stare before carefully putting the parking ticket under the windscreen wiper and moving on.

Jim appealed to some passers-by. 'Money, money, money,' he snarled. 'That's all they're interested in.'

The traffic warden stopped and looked around again. His gaze fell on the rear nearside tyre.

'I know that needs replacing,' said Jim standing in front of it. The traffic warden got his camera out and walking round the other side of him, took a picture.

'Why don't you take one of me and the wife while you're at it?' Jim challenged.

But the warden was busy writing out another ticket.

Jim put down his shopping bags, threw his hands in the air and then put them on his head. 'If you keep on giving out tickets like that,' he cried, 'it's going to cost an arm and a flipping leg!'

Rita was shaking. She got a tissue out of her handbag and pressed it to her mouth.

A small crowd gathered.

'We haven't been outside the door for weeks,' Jim complained bitterly to them, 'and we come into town to find this! Why don't I make life easier for you, mate? You may as well report the faulty brake light too.'

The traffic warden said nothing. He was looking at his watch. The town hall clock struck two and he began to write a third ticket.

'Now what are you doing?' Jim gasped.

The warden pointed to the road sign. *Residents' parking only between 10am and 11am and 2pm and 3pm.*

'So if I hadn't stopped to talk to you,' Jim groaned, 'you would have been well on your way by now and you wouldn't be writing that ticket?'

The warden smiled and took a picture of the broken brake light.

'You should have kept your big mouth shut,' said Rita.

'I know, I know,' Jim wailed.

They looked up and saw the number four bus coming round the corner. Jim and Rita picked up their bags and hurried to the stop.

'Hey!' shouted the traffic warden. 'What about your car? I'll give you another ticket if you're still here in an hour.'

'Go ahead, mate,' said Jim, flashing his bus pass at the driver. 'It's not my car anyway. Just my little joke. And to make it easier for you, the owner's name is Andrews. Terry Andrews.'

The publishers hope that this book has given you enjoyable reading. Large Print Books are especially designed to be as easy to see and hold as possible. If you wish a complete list of our books please ask at your local library or write directly to:

Magna Large Print Books
Magna House, Long Preston,
Skipton, North Yorkshire.
BD23 4ND